From the reviews of

Inspector Hobbes and the Blood

'Andy Caplet, the Everyman protagonist of *Inspector Hobbes and the Blood* provides the sole tie to normalcy in this fast-paced, quirky crime-fantasy novel. It will leave you gasping with laughter over the domestic oddities of Hobbes' home one moment and shuddering over the wittily macabre ghouls and other supernatural denizens the next. Hobbes himself is endlessly fascinating; he steals the show with his Holmesian intellect, exaggeratedly brutish looks and boundless energy. A wonderful debut that turns its unlikely medley of genres into a thrilling, hilarious and unexpected whole.'

Cammi Motley
The Yellow-Lighted Bookshop, Tetbury and Nailsworth, Cotswolds

'I liked *Inspector Hobbes and The Blood* from the word go. It hit the road running with more double entendres than a Carry On film and developed into quite an intricate story with an interesting plot featuring the theft of various items with Romanian connections. These thefts appear to be linked but the linkage is not obvious for quite a long while, in fact not right up to the action packed climax. … This is an entertaining and amusing book which provides the reader with many an inward chuckle along the way. … I think that this is a cast of characters which will be even more appealing as the reader becomes more familiar with them.'

Brett Hassell
Amazon Top 50 UK Reviewer, Amazon Top 100 USA Reviewer, Amazon Top 10 CA Reviewer and Hall of Fame Reviewer

'Fast, funny and a little bloody. The way life is in the Cotswolds. A good read.'

PC Phillips

Cotswolds resident, A

D0731471

unhuman

I

Inspector Hobbes and the Blood

II

Inspector Hobbes and the Curse

III

Inspector Hobbes and the Gold Diggers

Inspector Hobbes
and the Blood

unhuman I

Wilkie Martin

Shortlisted for the Impress Prize for New Writers 2012

The Witcherley Book Company
United Kingdom

Published in United Kingdom
by The Witcherley Book Company

First published in paperback and ebook (Kindle)
by The Witcherley Book Company in 2013

British Library Cataloguing in Publication Data.
A catalogue record for this book is available from the British Library.

ISBN 9780957635104 (paperback)
ISBN 9780957635111 (ebook)
ISBN 9780957635166 (ebook)

LIC Library Subject Headings: Character., Cotswold Hills (England)--Fiction., Cotswold
Hills (England)--Humor., Crime fiction, Crime and the press—Fiction., Crime--Great
Britain--Fiction., Detective and mystery fiction., Detective and mystery stories, English--
Fiction., Dracula, Count (Fictitious character)--Fiction., England--Fiction., English wit and
humor--21st century., English wit and humor--England--West Country., English wit and
humor--Great Britain., Fantastic fiction., Fantasy fiction, English., FICTION / Crime.,
FICTION / Humorous., FICTION / Mystery & Detective / General., Humorous fiction.,
Humorous stories., Humorous stories, English., Journalists--England--Fiction., Mystery
and detective stories--Fiction., Police--England--Cotswold Hills--Fiction., Police--England-
-Gloucestershire--Fiction., Transylvania (Romania)--Fiction

As I paused beneath the sodium glare of a streetlight to pull a crumpled Post-it note from my jeans, for the fifth time in as many minutes I read the fateful words I'd jotted down earlier: *Meet Inspector Hobbes. 5.30 at 13 Blackdog Street.*

The ranks of smart Cotswold stone shops flanking the broad avenue known as The Shambles were funnelling wind down my neck, and rain, or maybe sleet, was spotting my sweatshirt. I shivered, wishing I'd stayed in the office long enough to pick up my cagoule, but, having missed deadline with my piece on the senior citizens' whist drive, the Editorsaurus was on the rampage and a discreet, rapid withdrawal had been the sensible option.

The church clock striking the quarter hour, I took a deep breath, and resumed my walk, knowing I couldn't afford another screw-up. With fifteen minutes to spare, though, I would at least be early, which would be no bad thing. Still, I wished I was heading almost anywhere else.

Turning right past the church tower, I entered Pound Street, where an arthritic yew tree had survived the centuries and paving slabs. A set of traffic lights shone red to dam the flow of early evening traffic, so, taking my chance, I crossed into Blackdog Street.

A shambling old man in a shabby raincoat, clutching a paper carrier bag to his chest, hobbled to the front door of a tall, drab building, struggling with his keys. Walking past, I hesitated, before turning back, smiling, helpful.

'Excuse me,' I said. 'You … umm … look like you could do with a hand.'

He glared over his shoulder. 'Are you trying to be funny?'

'No,' I said, taken aback. 'I just thought you might need a hand.'

He turned to face me, the bag slipping to the pavement with an ominous shattering of glass. Where his left forearm should have been was a hook.

'Ah … umm …' My cheeks were heating up, reddening.

'Get lost!'

'Sorry … I hadn't noticed.' I'd embarrassed myself again, and it didn't get any easier with practice. 'I just thought you might need some help with the door.'

'You're the one who needs help, mate.'

As he raised his hook and shook it, I, cowed beneath a storm of imaginative and anatomical abuse, left at an undignified pace. When certain he wasn't in pursuit, I slowed down, catching my breath, resolving, not for the first time, to get fit, to spend less time in pubs.

I ran my fingers through my damp hair in an effort to make it presentable and found myself outside a terrace of old stone houses, almost threatening, like cliffs looming over the narrow street. I counted down to number 13. Three steps led towards a black door with a brass knocker, glinting beneath the white streetlights of this ancient part of town.

I still had plenty of time, or so I reckoned, being without a watch. Mine had blown up in the microwave, slipping off when I was bunging in a frozen curry on return from the pub. The acrid, black, plasticky smoke had completely spoiled my supper, not to mention killing my microwave. A month later, I was still living off sandwiches and takeaways.

A sharp gust spattered stinging raindrops into my face, goose pimples crawled across my skin and, since it seemed foolish to hang around outside, I made a firm decision to ring the doorbell. But, striding up the steps, raising my ringing finger, I found I couldn't go through with it. Standing outside Inspector Hobbes's door was as close to him as I wanted to get.

I was scared of him, or, rather, of his reputation, yet the Editorsaurus had decreed we should meet. This, he'd stated, was neither a punishment, nor that my name had sprung to mind as a competent and reliable reporter. It was because no one else was available. Such remarks, typical of the man, made me question why I worked for him. I wouldn't have, had I believed anyone else would employ me, and had I dared hand in my notice, for the Editorsaurus was a big, scary man, yet neither as big or scary as Hobbes, if rumours were to be believed ... and I believed them.

The rain was beginning to penetrate my sweatshirt so, with a shudder and a muttered prayer to whatever gods might protect local newspaper reporters, I leaned forward and jabbed at the bell.

Before I made contact, the door swung open. Recoiling, I stumbled back down the steps as a diminutive figure smiled at me, her face, a toothless network of fine wrinkles and deep ravines, was framed by a green headscarf. Wiping her hands on a pink pinafore, patterned with red flowers, she stared at me, a pair of twinkling blue eyes behind thick spectacles.

'Hello, dear,' she said, her voice high and quavery. 'You must be Mr Donahue. Please, come in.'

'Umm ... I'm not Mr Donahue, actually ... he couldn't make it. I'm ... umm ... Andy from the *Sorenchester and District Bugle.*' Fumbling for my card, I realised I'd left it in my cagoule. She didn't seem to mind.

'In that case, come in, Andy.' She gestured me inside. 'Get a move on, I've got a stew on the hob. I wouldn't want it to spoil.'

'Oh ... right ... the hob ... which reminds me, is Inspector Hobbes in?'

As I entered, she closed the door with a crash.

'Not yet, dear but he'll be back shortly. Please take a seat.'

Sitting down on a worn, if surprisingly comfortable, red-velour sofa as the strange old woman left via a door in the corner, I surveyed my surroundings. I was in a small, plain, yet neat, sitting room, containing a pair of old oak chairs and a coffee table with a copy of *Sorenchester Life* magazine on top. An incongruous widescreen television stood in one corner and an old-fashioned standard lamp in another. The walls were papered in a faded yellow pattern, depicting various exotic plants. I experienced an odd twinge of disappointment: from the rumours, I'd expected something out of the Addams Family. Still, beneath the sweet scent of lavender and wax polish, the room held a faint, feral taint, reminiscent of the wildlife park, and which topped up my nervousness.

Allowing myself to relax into the softness, I sighed, for it had already been a difficult day. The Editorsaurus had made some caustic, not to say brutal, remarks on realising my article wasn't finished and his language had deteriorated further when I'd confessed to having not actually started it. He hadn't been impressed by my argument that no one really wanted to read about whist drives.

At least Ingrid had been a comfort, and a vision of her lovely face beneath its thicket of blondish hair proved life at the *Bugle* wasn't all bad. She had a bright, sympathetic smile, was neat and efficient, smelled of soap, and would often make time for a chat. After the Editorsaurus had, temporarily I feared, exhausted his ranting, she'd made me a mug of coffee, sharing her packet of Bourbon Creams. I never felt guilty about taking her biscuits, feeling, in fact, that I was doing her a favour: losing a little weight would not hurt her.

Picking up *Sorenchester Life*, I flicked through its heavy, glossy pages until reaching a section devoted to Colonel Squire's latest charity ball at the Manor. My suspicion that it might merely have been an excuse for a bunch of rich blokes and their toffee-nosed wives to flaunt their wealth and feel good about themselves was confirmed by the magazine's failure to mention the charity the extravaganza had supposedly been aiding. In the midst of sneering at the hypocrisy, my attention was caught by a familiar figure. Before me, in full colour, magnificent in a crisp dinner jacket, stood Editorsaurus Rex, barrel gut precariously restrained by a crimson cummerbund, an expensive-looking blonde woman leaning on the arm not occupied by holding a drink. 'Mr Rex Witcherley and wife, Narcisa, enjoy a joke', claimed the caption. I wondered whether wife, Narcisa, would be entirely happy with the photograph, which showed her baring her teeth like a wolf.

A high, quavering voice rang in my ear. 'I've got all my own teeth, you know.'

I couldn't have leaped up any faster had I sat on a pin. As I landed and turned around, the magazine fluttering to the carpet like a dying pigeon, the blood pounding through my skull, my shin bruised from a sharp encounter with the table, the old lady, standing by the sofa, gave me a gummy smile. Though I could have sworn she did not have a single tooth left in her head, I thought a positive response was appropriate.

'What?' I said. 'All your own teeth? How wonderful.'

'Isn't it?' Reaching into the pocket of her pinafore, she pulled out a jar, rattling it.

I took a step back as the horror hit. It was full of teeth. Lots of teeth. Hundreds of human teeth.

The gummy grin broadened. 'I collect them. Aren't they beautiful?'

Nodding queasily, humouring the crazy woman, I looked around for an exit.

'Of course,' she said, 'they do take such a lot of polishing but they're worth it.'

'That's excellent,' I said, with what I hoped would develop into a reassuring, calming smile. 'Everybody should have a hobby.'

She stepped towards me. 'Do you keep teeth, dear?'

'Only the ones in my mouth.' My smile grew more alarmed.

She peered up. 'Ooh yes! Aren't they beautiful? I can see you've really looked after them.'

'Umm … yes, my father's a dentist,' I said, attempting to put the coffee table between us. 'He's always been a great believer in looking after one's teeth.'

'Can I have 'em?' Her bright little eyes widening, she took another step towards me. 'When you've finished with them, of course.' She laughed.

I did too, for panic was not far off. 'Why, certainly, you can have them all, when I've done with them. Please, help yourself.'

'Ooh, you're a lovely young man. I got these beauties the other night.' Upending the jar, she poured a pile of discoloured teeth into her hand. 'Mr Binks at the pub lets me have the ones that come out on his premises. He's a very nice man. Do you know him?'

'Featherlight Binks? At the Feathers on Mosse Lane?'

'That's the one, dear. I often get teeth from the Feathers.'

I nodded, knowing the place rather too well. It was a disreputable dive full of seedy low-lifes, while Featherlight, its landlord, not at all a nice man in my opinion, was a surly brute who never showed reluctance when it came to fisticuffs. I could guess to whose head those teeth had belonged. A customer, not a regular who would have known better, had complained about the head on his beer. When Featherlight, purple-faced and twitching, had asked what was wrong with having a head on beer, the customer had retorted, not unreasonably, that everything was wrong when the head had once belonged to a mouse. I'd slipped away on hearing him demand a fresh pint in a clean glass. Featherlight doesn't like that sort of thing and the heaviness of his brow and the stormy tinge of his skin had led me to forecast imminent violence.

Cackling, the crazy woman held out the teeth, some still showing traces of blood, for inspection. I swallowed the hot taste of vomit and, on the verge of flight, glanced towards the front door.

It swung open.

A vast figure in well-polished black boots, baggy brown trousers and a flapping gabardine raincoat, stood framed in the doorway. As he pulled the door behind him, his blood-red eyes scrutinised me from beneath a tangle of dark, bristly eyebrows. 'I'm Inspector Hobbes. You must be Mr Caplet?'

His voice rumbled through my chest, as if a heavy lorry was passing. I nodded and he stepped towards me, holding out his hand, which I shook with trepidation, mine feeling tiny, soft and feeble, like a baby's, compared to his, as hard and as hairy as a coconut.

'Pleased to meet you, Inspector.'

'Likewise. How is Mr Donahue?'

'Mr Donahue? Oh … Duncan? He's fine.'

Hobbes, frowning, released my hand. 'Fine? I heard he's got two broken legs?'

'Ah … umm … yes.' The question had thrown me for a second, in a similar way that someone had thrown Duncan, the *Bugle's* crime reporter, from a speeding car, which was just my luck, for otherwise it would have been his responsibility to cover Hobbes. 'I mean apart from that, he's OK. Oh … and he broke his jaw, too, so that's all wired up.'

Hobbes raised his eyebrows, the eyeballs beneath exceedingly red. Reaching into his pocket, he pulled out a bottle of Optrex. 'Well, I hope the poor man gets better soon. It was a nasty incident but, at least, I was able to make a quick arrest since the perpetrator is an old acquaintance of mine, one Gordon Bennet, a ne'er-do-well who decided to try his hand at carjacking. The last time I had occasion to arrest him was for persistent indecent exposure. He claimed he'd considered giving up but wanted to stick it out for a little longer. I dissuaded him. Now, if you'll excuse me, I'd better go and bathe my eyes.'

'Oh, right … too many late nights?'

He grinned. 'No, too many camels. I have an allergy.' He turned to the old girl. 'Could I trouble you to make a pot of tea? I'm parched and I'm sure Mr Caplet would like a drink too.'

'Of course,' she said.

They both departed, leaving me to my thoughts. Though I had a feeling getting on his wrong side would be a foolish idea, it seemed he might not be as bad as I'd heard. Yet, on reflection, I wasn't quite sure if I'd heard much at all; I'd just seen the expressions on the faces of those who'd met him professionally. The old lady, on the other hand, scared the wits out of me.

I tried to calm down by concentrating on *Sorenchester Life*, its glossy pages, filled with nothing of consequence, having a restful effect, so I was well relaxed by the time Hobbes strolled back into the room.

'Well, Mr Caplet,' he said, 'Superintendent Cooper informs me that, due to Mr Donahue's accident, you will be my shadow for the next week.'

I nodded. 'That's right. Ed … umm … Mr Witcherley … told me to report on local policing from your perspective. He wants really in-depth stuff to enlighten and enthral our readers.'

I tried to speak with a confidence I didn't feel, yet, only that morning, I'd been complaining to Ingrid about never getting important assignments. Certainly, I'd made the odd cock-up in the past, but I felt I'd learned enough in eight years as a cub reporter to be entrusted with something meaty, though I hadn't envisaged anything quite as meaty as Hobbes.

'Enthral, eh?' he said. 'I'll see what I can do. However, you never know what will turn up and, though much of our work is routine, I ought to warn you it can occasionally be dangerous or shocking, even in such a quiet little town as this.'

I nodded, making a show of nonchalance, though his words chilled me even more than had the November air. I was not good with danger.

He sat beside me and continued. 'What's more, we don't work office hours.'

'Nor do reporters,' I said, which was true, for Phil Waring, the Editorsaurus's blue-eyed boy, was working round the clock on a story that kept him away from the office, sometimes for days at a time. More importantly, so far as I was concerned, it kept the git away from Ingrid.

'Good.' He smiled, giving me a closer view than I wanted of great, yellow fangs.

I wondered how my father would react if faced with such a mouth, and felt my left hand creeping up to protect my throat. Hobbes, not appearing to notice, sitting back with a huge sigh, closing his eyes, rested his feet on the coffee table. He'd changed his heavy boots for a huge pair of slippers: they were pale-blue with a dinky little kitten pattern. I stared, shocked.

He stretched, yawning. 'Caplet is quite an unusual name. French?'

'It was originally but, please, just call me Andy.'

'Very well, Andy. I expect you'll want to hear about what I'm working on at the moment?'

'Yes, please … umm … the Editorsaur … Mr Witcherley said you were investigating the Violin Case.'

'Correct,' said Hobbes, 'according to the *Bugle's* headline yesterday.'

'Oh, yes. Body Found in Violin Case – most amusing.' I laughed. 'It was like you'd really found a body in a violin case.'

He gave me a funny look. 'We did. Didn't you read the article?'

'No, I was too busy,' I said truthfully, for Rex had assigned me to sorting out the stationery cupboard. 'I mean it sounded like someone's body had been found in a violin case. You know, where you'd normally find a violin?'

He frowned. 'It was precisely where we did find the body.'

'Oh, I'm sorry.' I grinned, still not grasping the point. 'It must have been a very small body, or an outsize case. You're sure it wasn't a double bass case?'

'It,' said Hobbes, scowling, 'was a very small body.'

Shock hit me like a slap round the ears. A sick feeling welled up from my stomach. 'Not a child?'

He shook his head.

'Whose body?'

'That,' he said, 'is what we need to establish.'

'But if it wasn't a child … how could an adult fit into a violin case? And was it a man or a woman?'

He pulled his feet off the table, a strange, knowing expression, half a smile, appearing on his face. I gulped, my flippant mood shattered.

'It's not easy to fit even a child's body into a violin case, at least without boning it first. In fact, this body had been mutilated but there was enough left to prove it was neither a man, nor a woman.'

I shook my head in confusion. What he was saying made no sense and his casual reference to boning a child had unsettled me. 'I don't get it,' I said.

'I'm not surprised. I don't think I do. Would you like to see it?'

'The body?'

As he nodded, I flinched as if he'd threatened to nut me, an icy tingle chilling my spine. I took a deep breath to steady myself. I'd never set eyes on a real corpse, though, of course, I'd seen plenty in films and on the news when they'd never seemed real. They'd always felt too far away, always somebody else's problem, even when the stories had struck me as especially sad or horrific.

Yet, I was there to show interest. 'Yes, I'd love to see it,' I said.

Hobbes's frown made me wonder if perhaps I'd sounded over-enthusiastic.

I bit my lip. 'I mean, I'd be delighted, no ... glad ... happy ... damn it!' I was babbling, intimidated by the frown that appeared to be deepening. 'Look, I don't actually *want* to see the body but if it might help me to understand the case, I think, perhaps, I should. Where is it?'

At that moment, the clink of crockery announced that the old woman was at my side. Though the suddenness of her arrival made me gasp, I calmed down on realising she was carrying a metal tray with a vast brown teapot and essentials, including a plain, giant mug, a normal-sized mug, decorated with a picture of a cat, a silver bowl of sugar lumps and a milk jug in the shape of a cow. In addition, my greedy gaze locked onto a white plate, layered with what must have been an entire packet of Hobnobs – chocolate ones, I noticed with some approval and more drool. Their scent made me realise just how long it had been since I'd scoffed my lunchtime sandwiches.

'Thank you.' Hobbes beamed, with no trace of anger on his face.

Still, it was not a pleasant face and I doubted whether even his mother would have considered him good looking, assuming he actually had a mother. I supposed he must have, or have had. How old was he? I couldn't have said, for though his face might have been described as craggy, or possibly leathery, I couldn't detect any grey in the black bristle of his hair. The dark stubble on his chin, protruding like spines on a cactus, made me pity any poor razor having to cope with it.

'Did you two have time to introduce yourselves?' he asked, as the old woman poured the tea.

'Umm … no … not properly.'

'Right then. Andy Caplet, this is Mrs Goodfellow, my housekeeper. Mrs Goodfellow, this is Mr Caplet, whom we will call Andy. He'll be working with me for a few days.'

'Delighted,' said Mrs Goodfellow.

'So am I,' said I, keeping a wary eye on her.

Her work done, she drifted away. Hobbes leaning forward, heaping a pyramid of sugar cubes in his great paw, tipping them into the big mug, stirred the scalding liquid with his finger.

'Help yourself,' he said, helping himself to a Hobnob and sliding back into the sofa.

Without the covering of mugs, the tray revealed its decoration, a chipped portrait of Queen Victoria. Still, there's no accounting for taste and, despite everything, Mrs Goodfellow made a brilliant cup of tea. Taking a sip from the cat mug, I crammed a biscuit into my mouth. Hobbes was still nibbling his as I took another, trying to fill a chasm within and, for a few minutes, we sat without talking, just slurping and munching and I could almost have forgotten the body.

Then, thumping his mug back onto Queen Victoria's lumpy face, Hobbes arose. 'Come on, Andy. Let's take a look at it. And quickly.'

Putting my empty mug down, grabbing another biscuit, though only a couple remained, I realised I'd guzzled nearly the entire packet. Hobbes, I think, had taken only one.

'Right then,' I said, lifted by the sugar steaming through my veins. 'Where is it?'

'This way, I'll show you.'

His slippered feet scuffing the carpet, he led me through a door, down a short corridor and into the kitchen. My initial impression was of a cheerful, old-fashioned sort of room, mellowed red bricks echoing beneath my feet, the gas cooker looking like a museum piece, a deep, white enamelled sink standing beneath the window, the shelf of which supported a miniature, yet prolific, jungle of pot plants. There was no sign of Mrs Goodfellow. The odd, feral smell I'd noticed earlier seemed stronger, despite a mouth-watering savour bubbling from a stew pot on the hob.

I'd assumed the body would be kept in the morgue or a forensic laboratory or something, so it would not be a lie to say I was surprised, if not alarmed, when he opened the fridge door and reached inside. I couldn't see over his shoulder but when he turned he was carrying a metal dish covered in Clingfilm, misted by condensation. As he clunked it onto the scrubbed wooden table in the centre of the room, I leaned forward for a better look.

He peeled back the film. I gasped, horrified, for a body, naked, hairless, not even two-foot long, filled the dish. It still had four limbs, though the hands and feet had been hacked off, as had the head; I had no doubt it wasn't human. When Hobbes turned it onto its back, there was a long gash down the front where someone had eviscerated it. I turned away, both hands covering my mouth.

'Oh, my God!' I forced myself to look again. 'What is it?'

Hobbes shook his head, a strange expression in his eyes, which were no longer red. 'It looks like a gnome.'

'A gnome? That's ridiculous. There's no such thing. Is there?'

He shrugged.

The horror was growing inside. 'I don't get it. Why would anyone want to kill a gnome?'

'For illegally fishing in a garden pond? And, if you don't believe it's a gnome, what else do you think it might be?' He waved his thick, hairy finger at the abomination.

I shrugged, trembling, feeling as if I might be sick, or faint, or both, yet I couldn't help thinking what a fantastic story this would make, one that would even impress E. Rex. It could be my ticket to fame and fortune. I could become known as the reporter who uncovered the gnome.

'The trouble is,' said Hobbes, rubbing his chin thoughtfully, 'that

I can't afford to spend any time investigating. After all, has a crime actually been committed? There's no law against killing gnomes. Indeed the law does not officially recognise them.'

'There must be something you can do. Have you any idea who could have done such a terrible thing?'

'Well,' he said, slowly, eyes wide, 'I suspect it might have been the Butcher of Barnley. Last time I saw anything like this, he was the culprit for sure, though he was never charged.'

'The Butcher of Barnley?' I shuddered, horrid thoughts fluttering into my mind like bats into an attic, images of blood and guts and death flapping behind my eyes. 'And you said last time – do you mean this sort of thing has happened before?'

He nodded.

'What happened?'

'Money changed hands and the Butcher of Barnley was free to go about his bloody business.'

'And what did you do with the body? Poor little thing.'

'I did the only thing I could.' He grunted. 'What anyone would have done in the circumstances. I ate it.'

'What?'

'Stewed in cider with onions and carrots. Very tasty. Very tender. Mrs Goodfellow had some too, though only the juice. She can't chew you know.' He licked his lips.

I stared at him, disgusted, scared by the sly, crazy look in his eyes, feeling totally lost for words. I mean, what can you say to someone who has just admitted to eating stewed gnome? I became aware my mouth had fallen open.

'What's that doing out?' Mrs Goodfellow had materialised behind us. 'It's for your supper tomorrow.' She glared at Hobbes with an expression of half-amused exasperation, like a mother gives to a naughty child. 'I thought I'd stew it in cider again. I remember how much you enjoyed it last time.'

I stared at the old woman and then at Hobbes. I'd fallen among despicable people and didn't like it. I now understood why everyone spoke of him in hushed tones. I'd known he had a reputation, everyone knew it, but I'd never guessed he'd be the sort to devour a gnome. Three minutes earlier, I hadn't even realised the poor little creatures existed, except in fairy tales and suburban rockeries, yet these horrible people relished them stewed. I wanted to leave and began to feel vulnerable. Why, I wondered, had he let me eat so many of the biscuits? For what was he saving his appetite?

'The butcher said he'd send his bill next week, if it's convenient,' said Mrs Goodfellow.

'Yes, of course.' Hobbes glanced at me.

'He says he'll let me know next time he gets any in, because he knows how much you like a bit of rabbit.'

'Rabbit?' I said.

He shook silently, an expression of manic glee on his face, an explosive guffaw bursting forth, followed by a long, rumbling laugh.

'Sorry Andy,' he said after a while and started again. 'Your face, you should have seen your face! Gotcha.'

He'd gotcha'd me alright. I'm no cook, so how could I have guessed what it was? But a gnome? Feeling an utter fool, I tried to laugh it off. 'Yeah, you really had me going. I don't know what I was thinking. It's obviously a rabbit.'

'Yes,' he agreed, 'gnomes are much squatter and,' he paused, smacking his lips, 'they're not such good eating: a little on the stringy side.'

I forced a laugh through clamped teeth.

'Right,' he said, 'I'll just put it back and then I'll really tell you about the case.'

Returning to the sitting room, I slumped back with a sigh and a touch of indigestion. A few seconds later Hobbes came in, grinning as if he'd done something clever, sitting next to me with a slow laugh, patting me gently on the shoulder. It felt like it would leave a fine bruise.

'The Violin Case, as your paper calls it, has led to the apparent suicide of Mr Roman, a gentleman who lived in Fenderton. It's all quite tragic. Someone broke into his house, causing some damage. However, according to Mr Roman, the only thing stolen was his violin.'

'Was it a Stradivarius or something?'

'So far as we know, it was just an ordinary modern instrument, not a cheap one, in fact rather a good one and more than acceptable for playing in amateur orchestras. However, it was nothing out of the ordinary. Mr Roman played in the Fenderton Ensemble and normally played well, according to the other musicians, though he'd not been up to his usual standard in the day's rehearsals.'

'But surely he could buy another? Why kill himself?'

'That's what I want to know. Unfortunately, he wasn't very helpful when I spoke to him. He seemed overly distressed, even though he was insured. Anyway, a couple of days after the burglary he disappeared and a woman walking her dog found him hanging from a tree in Ride Park.'

Though sorry for Mr Roman and the dog walker, I felt it was going too far to kill oneself over a lost violin. I said as much.

Hobbes agreed. 'I suspect there was something else. Maybe he'd had something stolen he shouldn't have had in the first place: something illegal or embarrassing perhaps? Or, possibly, someone was after him.'

'An assassin? Surely not.'

He shrugged. 'Just speculation, and, though we don't get many assassins around these parts, a copper's got to keep an open mind. Anyway, the burglary was the real crime and that's what the lads are investigating. It looks fairly straightforward. Someone waited till Mr Roman drove out to rehearsal one evening, climbed over the back gate and snagged his trousers on a splinter. Forensics has a few fibres to keep 'em happy. It looked to me like our culprit wore old blue jeans, so I'm not expecting they'll learn much. Once he was in the back garden, the burglar chucked an ornamental birdbath through the window to get in.'

'Did no one hear it being smashed, or see anything?'

'No. The house is set back from the road and his neighbours are on holiday. I found quite a pile of cigarette butts and chocolate wrappers under a bush in the front, so it looks like the perpetrator watched and waited for Mr Roman to go out. He must have realised there was no one in next door and yet didn't break in there.'

'So, Mr Roman was targeted.'

'Very good, Andy.' He grinned. 'That is what I suspect, though most of the lads reckon the burglar was disturbed and ran off. They may be right but parts of the house were well-ransacked so he must have been inside for some time. Oddly, some unusual jewellery had been tipped out on the bed and left behind.'

'Unusual?'

'Yes, big and heavy. Middle-European and rather old I'd guess. Probably rather valuable, too.'

'So, he left valuable jewellery and stole an ordinary violin. It's crazy.'

'I agree. That's if he did take the violin, because, how could he have done, if Mr Roman was playing it at rehearsal?'

I raised my eyebrows in what I hoped looked like a perceptive manner.

Hobbes continued. 'I reckon the burglar found something he wanted more, something he was searching for, perhaps. Oddly, Mr Roman wouldn't say anything and I got the impression he wouldn't even have called us if he'd had his way.'

All the tea I'd drunk began to make its presence known. 'May I use your bathroom?' I asked.

He looked surprised. 'If you want. There's plenty of hot water.'

He may have been joking, I didn't think so. 'What I mean is that … umm … I need to use your … umm … toilet.'

'Well, you might have said. Upstairs and first on the left. It's in the bathroom.'

I walked up the gloomy staircase. There were four doors at the top, all closed. I entered the first, a small room containing a gleaming white bath, a large hand basin and a toilet with an overhead cistern and chain, a sort I hadn't seen since I was a boy. As I stood over it, I noticed a chipped mug with a single toothbrush, a burst tube of toothpaste, two towels with portraits of cats, soap and some rose-scented talc. Some of the stuff belonged to Mrs Goodfellow, I supposed. There was nothing unusual, except for the electric sander on the lino beneath the basin. I speculated that Hobbes used it instead of a razor. I finished, flushing the toilet, which thundered like Niagara Falls, walked out and started down the stairs.

'You forgot to wash your hands, dear.'

I spun on the spot, maintaining my balance with difficulty. Mrs Goodfellow stood on the landing, looking me right in the eye, her expression stern.

'What?'

'You didn't wash your hands.' She tapped her foot impatiently. For some reason she was wearing wellingtons. She gestured towards the bathroom and frowned.

Meek and embarrassed, I turned around, washing my hands and drying them. She'd vanished by the time I headed back down.

I got back to business. 'Who was with Mr Roman when he discovered the break-in?'

'Some of the Fenderton Ensemble: its fiddle section to be precise. They'd insisted on going back with him to practice a piece he'd had trouble with. When they got inside it was obvious a burglary had taken place and one of them called us. Mr Roman was in a terrible state, shaking and nearly hysterical when uniform got there. He was worse when I turned up. Those are the bare bones of it, except his car hasn't been found yet.'

'It's very puzzling.'

Hobbes grinned. 'Aye, lad, isn't it just? Isn't it great?'

I nodded. I wasn't sure I agreed, even though I'd just experienced a frisson of excitement, as if I was getting into some real journalism. The last 'big' reporting job Rex had assigned to me was the Moorend Pet Show. Hamsters, not the fluffy balls of fun they appear, have teeth like needles, as I'd discovered when playfully pulling the winner of the rodents' section from his cage to conduct a mock interview. The kids had loved it when I asked the beast how it felt to be a champion, holding it up to my ear as if awaiting a reply. They'd loved it even more when its jaws clamped onto my earlobe, like a bulldog onto a bull, before seizing my finger which was trying to prise it off. The *Bugle* had never even printed my article, preferring the photograph of me, cowering in a corner, the blood-slathered brute bearing down on me. Readers had apparently found it highly amusing, yet all I remembered was the pain and the humiliation. For days afterwards laughing people would point at me in the street.

'Anyway, Andy,' said Hobbes, 'that's what we'll be working on tomorrow. Now, I've my supper to eat and then I've got to see a dog about a man. I'll see you at the station, tomorrow morning at eight.'

He rose like a wardrobe and the interview, if that's what it was, terminated. I had intended to ask some penetrating questions but they would have to wait. He showed me to the door and I stepped into the street, silvery light reflecting from the damp surfaces as I walked away. All in all, the day had not gone so badly, even though I'd been shouted at, been made a fool of and had been alarmed, horrified and disgusted. Hobbes had not been as bad as I'd feared. Nonetheless, I did not fancy meeting him again next morning and, hoping it might help me sleep, decided to dose myself with a few strong drinks. Not at the Feathers, though, for Mrs Goodfellow's teeth haunted me.

I paid a visit to the Bellman's on The Shambles, a pub with little to recommend it other than being located just down the road from the *Bugle's* offices and supplying food of a sort. Despite the biscuits, I felt the urge for a slap-up meal and, popping a couple of Rennies from my pocket to ease the indigestion, I scurried out of the rain.

The tough, tasteless chop, the cold, limp, over-boiled vegetables and the lumpy mashed potato from a packet failed to meet expectations, though I had expected little. I still ate it all, because I'd paid for it, and even told the fat, gravy-stained barman it was 'very nice'.

However, the drink was good and, having knocked back several bottles of strong lager, I made my way home to Spire Street, number 2, flat 2 and passed out on the sofa, where I was afflicted by nightmares in which Mrs Goodfellow and my father argued about the most excruciating method for extracting my teeth.

2

The sofa was vibrating, a noise like thunder pounded through my head and I didn't know what the hell was happening. Only one thing was clear; I stank of stale pub. It felt like the whole world was shaking and the only explanation making any sense was that I was in the middle of an earthquake. Panic dragged me to the front door, unlocked it and wrenched it open. I ran.

After half a step, something as solid as a wall bounced me back inside.

Hobbes, standing in the doorway, his great, hairy fist raised for knocking, a scowl the size of a continent corrugating his brow, greeted me. 'Good morning, Andy. You're late.'

Swallowing a scream, I slumped back onto the sofa, my entire body shaking, struggling for breath as his laughter rumbled through me.

'Did I alarm you? I did knock.'

I kept my mouth firmly clamped, certain I would scream if I didn't, not convinced I'd be able to stop once I'd started. My head ached.

'At least you're dressed,' he observed, 'but you'd better move yourself, and quickly; villains don't catch themselves.'

Nodding, I took a deep breath, trying to calm down, waiting until I'd regained the power of speech.

'Umm … what time is it?' I asked.

'Eight-thirty. You were supposed to be at the police station by eight.'

I stood up. 'Sorry. I need the bathroom.'

I fled for sanctuary, last night's lager throbbing in my skull, bladder close to overflowing, guts ready to burst. For some time, sitting on the toilet, I held my head, biding my time, trying to round up my stampeded wits. Occasionally, I heard Hobbes snort like an impatient bull.

Finished at last, I washed my hands, splashed cold water into my eyes, brushed my teeth and gazed into the mirror. My face was pastry-white beneath ragged stubble, my eyeballs, glistening like pink mushrooms, stared back. I groaned, finding it difficult to believe I could feel even rougher than I looked. On bending to drink from the tap, my brains felt like they would explode and I had to swallow hard so as not to throw up. The water was cool and, gulping it down, I berated myself, hating that I'd drunk so much again. Only then did I remember that I should have drafted and delivered a succinct account of my meeting with Hobbes to the *Bugle*. Cringing at what the Editorsaurus would say, I hoped to redeem myself with something brilliant later.

'Hurry up.' Hobbes's voice reverberated through my soul.

Opening the bathroom door, I stepped out, attempting to smile through the nausea, intending to explain that I needed a long, hot shower and a long, slow breakfast but, before I could start, he seized my shoulder, hauling me from the flat, down the stairs and into the street. The morning sun, reflecting off the damp pavement, left me blinking and rubbing my eyes, nearly blind and helpless. As my vision adjusted, I noticed he was dragging me towards a battered, rusty Ford Fiesta by the kerb. Opening the passenger door, he pushed me into it.

'Make yourself comfy and don't forget your seatbelt,' he said, getting in the other side, grinning, his mouth a mass of yellow fangs.

Fighting the impulse to protect my throat, I nodded, trying to project an image of polite alertness and interest. The belt clicked around my belly and he started the engine with a roar. Why he roared, I'll never know and I came within a whisker of wetting myself. I felt how I imagined I'd feel if someone locked me in a cage with a tiger, except tigers are beautiful. The car screeched away and, before I could plead for release, we were speeding to work.

He was really speeding, not simply exceeding the speed limit. Gripping my seat, wrestling with the urge to bail out, I hoped that, with luck, I might end up in hospital with nice nurses to look after me and no Hobbes to worry about. Yet, as I stared at the road flying past, I knew I couldn't do it; even if I survived the leap and the inevitable splat, I'd have trouble explaining my actions. After all, he'd never done anything to threaten me and flinging oneself from a moving vehicle because of a vague feeling of horror is a sure way into the nuthouse. Instead, I shut my eyes, letting my crazy thoughts divert me from his driving and, eventually, when it looked as if I might survive, it occurred to me I had no idea where we were heading.

Opening my eyes, peering around, I saw we were out of town, passing between avenues of tall, bleak trees, somewhere, I guessed, on the Stillingham Road. 'Umm … where are we going?'

Hobbes turned to face me, the car swooping back and forth across the road like a drunken swallow, causing a van coming the other way to flash its lights. 'To where Mr Roman's body was found. It's not far. Hang on and relax.'

He chuckled and, briefly, the idea of leaping from the car regained its appeal as it crossed my mind that Duncan's so-called 'accident' might have been a cunning ploy to get out of this assignment. Making an attempt at a smile, sitting back, I closed my eyes and thought of Ingrid, who sometimes spoke to me. I couldn't understand what she saw in that smarmy Phil.

Our brakes screeched, jerking me from my reverie. We swerved, accompanied by the long braying of the horn from a big, shiny, black car, and both vehicles, pulling into a lay-by, stopped.

A furious, red-faced, young man stepped out. He looked like trouble. So did the other three, their appearances perfectly matching my definition of 'yobs', especially the one twiddling a baseball bat. As they approached, Hobbes was fiddling with a map, while I cringed into my seat, aiming for invisibility. The red-faced one rapped on the door with heavy brass rings.

Hobbes wound down the window. 'Can I help you, sir?'

'What the hell d'you think you're playing at, arsehole? You forced us off the bloody road. You need a lesson.'

'Mind your language, please, sir,' Hobbes's voice rumbled. 'I wasn't playing. It appeared to me that you weren't paying due attention to the road conditions. In fact I considered you were driving to the imperilment of the public and so I forced you here so I could tell you to drive more responsibly.'

'No one tells me nothing.' The man cracked his knuckles.

'We'll see,' said Hobbes, unbuckling his seat belt, opening the door.

I slid further down, a cold, sick feeling entering my belly.

Taking a step back, beckoning with both hands, the red-faced man laughed. 'C'mon then, granddad, if you think you're hard enough.'

Hobbes, squeezing from the car, straightened up. He was a bulky bloke, I knew, yet it was surprising how big he'd become, though it was still four against one, and one of the four was armed. Swallowing as Hobbes advanced, the red-faced man took another step backwards, looking to his mates, who showed little inclination to be heroes, except for the one with the baseball bat, who, lunging forward, yelling fiercely, took a great swing at Hobbes's head. I turned my face away, hearing a cry of pain; when I looked back, Hobbes was on his knees, the gang standing around him. Fearing it wouldn't be long before they started on me, I made up my mind to leg it. After all, what point would there be in me getting beaten up, too?

Leaping from the car, glancing over my shoulder, I stopped, for, although Hobbes was kneeling, his legs were straddling the man who'd swung the bat and who now appeared to be unconscious. He was gently slapping the man's cheek. At least, I supposed it was meant to be gently.

'Wakey, wakey,' he said.

The man groaned, and came to, the splintered stump of his baseball bat beside him.

'I'm sorry,' said Hobbes, 'I broke your stick.'

Standing up, he lifted the groggy man to his feet, holding him by the scruff of the neck, and addressed the yobs. 'Your mate needs a bit of a lie down. Now, you will all be certain to drive sensibly in future won't you?'

The man with the red face had changed, his expression of fury replaced by one of bewilderment, his complexion turned white, with a hint of muddy-green, reminiscent of some toothpaste I'd once bought in a hippy shop. He nodded.

'Promise?' said Hobbes.

'I promise.'

'Okey-dokey.' Hobbes smiling, swung the patient into the back of the big, black car. 'You may go now.'

Meekly, the men got in and drove away.

'That was fun,' said Hobbes, 'but I should get to work. Come along.'

Where we'd parked, the road cut through an expanse of desolate, grey, woodland. Hobbes, sniffing the air, strode into it with me on his tail. The season's fallen leaves were mouldering in deep drifts around our ankles, the closeness of the trees making everything gloomy and oppressive, an odour of damp decay filling my nostrils.

While he moved swiftly, quiet as a wood mouse, I stumbled over roots, banging my head on low branches. I was gasping for breath by the time the woods opened out into a clearing, in which stood a single oak tree, encircled by police tape.

Hobbes stepped over it. 'Stay where you are. This is where the body was found, hanged by the neck until dead.'

Although sweat was already trickling down my back, I shivered, as he squatted on all fours like a monstrous toad, appearing to sniff the grass. After a few seconds, he ducked back under the tape, loping into the woods, his knuckles brushing the ground. I toiled after him as well as I could, for he was following an erratic course at a deceptive pace, though, as far as I could tell, we were always heading away from the hanging tree. I blundered along behind, sweating, cursing, struggling to keep him in sight, already uncertain of finding

24

my way back to the clearing, never mind to the car, and fearing I'd be in real trouble if I lost him. My rising fears kept me lumbering forward while too many lagers, takeaways and days sat on my backside slowed me down. I puffed and gasped, the blood throbbing in my aching head.

After stumbling over a crumbling, mossy log, I leaned against a green-streaked tree trunk, catching my breath, and, by the time I was able to stand upright again, he'd gone. He'd abandoned me in the woods, in the wild, where anything might happen. My legs giving way, I knelt in the sodden leaf mould, feeling the damp and cold spreading through my jeans, longing for the familiarity of town, particularly that bit where my bed offered warmth and security. I didn't even know why we'd been running. I'd just been following because I couldn't help myself.

'Come on, Andy, keep up, lad.' He was standing over me, not even breathing heavily.

Shocked beyond speaking, filled with an adrenalin rush, I sprang back to my feet. Nodding, he set off again in the same hunched run, if just a little slower and, somehow, I did keep up for what I guessed was about twenty minutes. When he stopped and straightened up, I ran into him.

Without appearing to notice, he stepped away. Bending forward, resting my hands on my knees, dripping with sweat, throwing up water, I gulped down air, waiting for my pulse rate to drop to something feasible, and realising I wasn't as fit as I'd thought, though I'd thought I was pretty unfit.

'Found it,' said Hobbes.

Raising my head, I let my gaze follow his pointing finger towards a silver Audi, parked down a rutted track through the trees.

'That's Mr Roman's car.' He shambled towards it, rubbing his huge, hairy hands together in triumph. 'He must have parked here and wandered through the woods before hanging himself. There are no signs anyone was with him, so the suicide theory looks solid.'

He'd impressed me. I'd seen no trace of any trail.

'Right, I'll take a look.' He turned to me, efficient and commanding. 'You stay where you are, and don't touch anything.'

'OK.' Despite the nausea and headache, I was excited, seeing some real police work. Reaching into my jeans pocket for my notebook, I remembered it was still in my cagoule, still in the *Bugle's* office.

Hobbes, taking a large, red handkerchief, or possibly a small, red tea towel, from his coat, used it to open the car's door. Scanning the interior, he bent forward, and the boot opened with a click. There lay a violin case. Opening it, Hobbes revealed a violin.

'Interesting,' he said. 'Someone broke into his house, ransacked it and he claimed the only thing stolen was his violin, which was really in the boot of his car. Mr Roman was fibbing.'

'But why?' My teeth had started chattering as the heat of my exertions dissipated and cold air penetrated my clammy sweatshirt.

He shrugged. 'Who knows? Possibly he really did have something to hide.'

'It must have been something serious if it made him kill himself.'

Hobbes frowned. 'That seems likely. Maybe the burglar discovered a secret and tried to blackmail him, or perhaps the burglar took something so important he couldn't live without it.'

Pulling a mobile phone from his bulging coat pocket, he pressed a few buttons using the sharp, yellow nail on his little finger. I hadn't really noticed his fingernails before, which puzzled me, as they seemed to protrude like claws but, when he put the phone to his hairy ear, they appeared normal, if thick, horny and yellow is normal.

Having issued orders to someone, he thrust the phone back into his pocket. 'A couple of the lads will be here soon,' he said. 'Stay put while I have a poke around.'

Getting down on hands and knees, he crawled, sniffing and touching. Although fascinated, I couldn't settle, for throwing up had made me feel better, despite the chill, and my stomach, now empty, was demanding a fill.

The lads, actually a gangly constable and a fierce-looking young woman, drove down the track towards us about twenty minutes later. After briefing them, leaving them in charge, taking a glance at the sky and a sniff of the air, Hobbes led me straight back through the woods to the car.

As he squeezed inside and let me in, my stomach rumbling, I realised just how sharp hunger pangs could be, though I was glad the excitement and exertion had overwhelmed my hangover. My head felt clear, my brain ticked over sweetly: all the fresh air and exercise must have done me a deal of good. All the same, I would have preferred a couple of aspirins, several mugs of strong coffee and a relaxing morning in bed. I risked a question.

'Is there any chance of getting a bit of breakfast? I'm starving and a cup of coffee would be nice, too.'

He looked astonished. 'Have you not had breakfast? I thought you must have done, with those grease stains down your front.' He paused. 'I'll tell you what, we're heading back to the station and the canteen hasn't killed anyone recently. They'll do you some grub. I wouldn't touch the coffee but there's a kettle and stuff in my office.'

He started the engine and we sped back to Sorenchester, stopping with a squeal of brakes. Opening my eyes, I got out, wrinkling my nose on account of the stench of burned rubber, noticing the bumper touching the police station wall. He led me through a side-entrance straight to his office.

It was not the first time I'd been in a police station. I'd once become involved in an unfortunate incident at the Wildlife Park, although I have always maintained my innocence; my arrival and the hippopotamus's disappearance being entirely coincidental, but that's another story, one entirely different to what the *Bugle* published, without my contribution. Yet, Hobbes's office looked unlike anything I'd seen before, except, perhaps, when I'd watched reruns of *Dixon of Dock Green*. The furniture, not that there was much, would have been at home in a junk shop: a battered and dented mahogany desk with brass fittings, two substantial oak chairs, looking as though they might once have been upholstered, a rusting filing cabinet, with a black, Bakelite telephone on top. Cardboard boxes had been stacked in one corner and a hat stand, constructed from lustrous dark wood with bullhorns for hooks, lurked behind the door. A vast aspidistra on the window ledge, gave the room a gloomy, greenish tinge like being in the jungle. A small table with a gas ring stood in the corner opposite the entrance, supporting a dented copper kettle, a stained white teapot, a few tins and two chipped mugs. The room smelt of dust, old books and, of course, the feral scent of Hobbes. Mounds of papers littered the desk, along with a solitary picture frame. I glanced at it, expecting a photograph of … actually, I'm not sure what I'd expected: maybe his family, assuming he had one. I wouldn't have bet on a sepia photograph of Queen Victoria.

'I see you're admiring my picture of the queer old dean.' The room shook as he laughed. 'Right, d'you fancy a cup of tea?'

'Yes, please,' I said.

'Good. Make me one as well, would you?' A banana-sized finger pointed to the kettle.

'Oh, right. Of course. Umm … do you take milk or sugar?'

'Two lumps of each, please. When you're done, I'll show you to the canteen.'

The kettle, being already full, and discovering a box of matches on top of one of the tins, I lit the gas and rummaged for tea bags. There weren't any, just loose leaves in a tin caddy, for which my training as tea-boy at the *Bugle* had not prepared me. Still, I had learned of the possibility of making tea without bags; Phil had been telling Ingrid how tea tasted 'so much nicer if made properly', while I'd listened sarcastically, never thinking I might one day be grateful. When the kettle boiled, I poured a little into the pot, swirling it round to warm it and then, since there wasn't a sink, opened the window, flinging out the contents. A roar of anger followed, prompting me to slam it shut and duck out of sight. Hobbes, sitting behind his desk, writing on a form, merely snorted. I tipped three spoons of tea into the pot, inundating it with boiling water and picked up the chipped mugs.

'Careful with those,' said Hobbes, 'they're Chippendale.'

'Oh right, of course.'

I held them with exaggerated care. They showed images of Chip and Dale, the cartoon chipmunks. I grimaced, putting them down, Hobbes grinning as he returned to his paperwork. Sprawling in the spare chair, I waited while the tea mashed.

His fountain pen looked the size of a matchstick in his great paw, and he wrote slowly, his brow furrowed, the pink tip of his tongue between his lips, looking like a monstrous schoolboy, lost in a world of his own. Occasionally, he would hum a few bars of a tune I thought I nearly recognised. For those few quiet minutes he looked at peace with the world and himself and had a strange air of vulnerability. I almost felt friendly towards him.

The tea smelt fantastic as I poured it out and placed the Chip mug on the desk beside him. He was dreamily stirring it with a finger as I sat back down, taking a sip from the Dale mug, the fragrance steaming away any last vestiges of hangover. I relaxed, closing my eyes, leaning back in my chair. The office was warm, the distant hum of the world seemed far away and I felt strangely happy until, upending my mug, I got a mouthful of tealeaves. Spluttering, I spat the dregs back.

'Manners, Andy,' said Hobbes, shooting me a disapproving look, putting down his pen, picking up his mug and standing up. 'Right, give me a top-up and have one yourself if you like and I'll take you to the canteen.'

Having drained the teapot into our mugs, I followed him through the dark panelled doorway into a large, airy and untidy room where half a dozen officers and civilians were hard at work. Some looked up from their computer screens as we passed, seeming surprised to see me, one or two nodding as Hobbes acknowledged them with a gesture like a benediction. Turning into a corridor, he pushed open a double door and the rich warm scent of fried bacon overwhelmed me. I'd quite obviously not really been hungry earlier. What I'd experienced then had been a passing peckishness, but this was the real thing. Ordering an all-day breakfast, though lunchtime approached, I proceeded to stuff my face, while Hobbes sat quietly, as if in deep thought. When I'd eaten enough to allow some of my attention to wander from the plate, I noticed, with suppressed amusement, that his little finger, on raising his mug, was crooked like that of an old lady at a vicarage tea party. He left the canteen as I polished the plate clean, returning as I finished off the last slice of toast and marmalade.

'Right, Andy, I want to take a proper look at Roman's house. Let's see what we can find.' He hustled me from the canteen to the car.

Feeling fully awake and fit by then, I was really able to appreciate the journey, which only went to show the advantage of having felt like death earlier. Hobbes, I decided, knew only one way to drive: with the accelerator pressed flat against the mat. For him, speed limits were restrictions applying, and only applying, to other road users. It was the same with one-way signs and he regarded red lights as optional. As we hurtled past the speed camera on Fenderton Road, he waved his warrant card in the instant it flashed. Gripping my seat, wide-eyed, speechless, I sat, anticipating a violent end at any second. As we passed the cemetery, I tried to take my mind off the fear by imagining which plot I'd fill, assuming they didn't cremate me. Would, in fact, enough of me survive the inevitable smash to make a funeral worthwhile? My strategy was not working so well as I'd hoped and, once again, I was considering flinging myself into the road when Hobbes, with a crazed chuckle, spun the wheel to the right.

'This is it,' I said to myself, shutting my eyes as we turned in front of a council lorry, 'I'm going to die.'

I didn't and, when I looked again we'd made it into Alexander Court, a quiet side road lined with tall trees, behind which stood a scattering of large, old houses. Hobbes braked as we approached the end of the road, gravel crunched, and he skidded to a halt on the drive of a house, impressive, even by comparison to the others.

He smiled as we got out. 'Roman's empire. Nice isn't it?'

'Not bad,' I said.

From its high gables, its banks of chimneys, rising like towers, its neat rows of glittering, leaded windows, looking out over formal gardens, seemingly large enough to form a small farm, I guessed it dated from Victorian times.

'He was well off, then?'

'Rolling in it,' said Hobbes. 'At least by normal standards. He admitted, if that's the right word, that he was a wealthy man, though I gather times had been harder in the recent past. He wasn't forthcoming on the source of his wealth, though I suspect his parents left him plenty. They certainly bought this place just after the last war and he inherited it. Mr Roman lived quietly and rather well and, for the most part, without the necessity of having to work for a living. He enjoyed foreign holidays, good restaurants, Saville Row suits and those sorts of things and, until fairly recently, kept a cook, a maid and a gardener. It seems he spent his time playing the fiddle and painting.'

'A gentleman of leisure? Lucky bastard.' I grinned. 'I've always wanted to be like that.'

'May I remind you the lucky bastard hanged himself?' Hobbes's stare nearly knocked me backwards.

'Sorry,' I mumbled, 'was he … umm … a good painter?'

He shrugged. 'From what I've seen, he was a decent draughtsman with a real eye for colour, though with something of a magpie style. One work would be reminiscent of Cézanne, the next Rousseau or maybe Matisse. He even appears to have gone through a Daliesque phase. In my estimation, his paintings look good but reveal little of the artist, except to suggest he was intimately acquainted with the works of the masters. His work is more pastiche than original, if you follow me.'

Though my knowledge of art is poor, in truth almost non-existent, I nodded as Hobbes stood before me, his voice soft, his demeanour thoughtful. It was hard to believe he was the same man who'd just threatened my life with his lunatic driving.

'Come on,' he said, approaching the front door. 'Let's take a look inside. Stay behind me and don't touch anything. Right?'

I stood back, expecting him to have a key. Instead, he thumped the door once with both fists and, as it swung open with a tortured creak, I followed him inside.

Mr Roman obviously hadn't tidied up after the burglary. The finely patterned carpet, though well worn, was deep and soft, sprinkled with shards of broken china. Hobbes strode into what he called the drawing room, where the French window had been boarded up and slivers of glass glittered on the floor. Dropping to his hands and knees, he crawled about, apparently oblivious to the risk of cuts. He searched thoroughly, occasionally grunting, once or twice sounding as if he was sniffing, while picking up a number of wedge-shaped slivers of dried mud from the carpet, which, he remarked, came from the soles of a well-worn pair of boots.

I soon grew bored watching his broad backside and studied the room, which, though a mess, was a rich mess. However, something about the old ornaments and furniture, something to do with their colours and chunkiness, suggested they weren't British. Engaging my brain for a moment, I remembered Hobbes talking about the foreign-looking jewellery left behind in the burglary and Roman's parents having bought the house just after the war. Perhaps, I thought, they had been foreigners who'd arrived in Britain at the time and, perhaps, they'd done something bad, or had acquired something they shouldn't have, when Europe was in turmoil. And what if someone had tracked the hiding place down after all these years? I tried my theory out on Hobbes, who sniffed and stuck his head under a sideboard.

Crawling backwards, he squatted on his haunches, staring up at the panelled wall and down at the turquoise patterned carpet, scratching his chin with a sound like someone sawing wood. At first, I couldn't see what had interested him. Then I became aware of faint scuffs on the carpet, suggesting the sideboard had been pulled away from the wall on one side and then pushed back. As I turned my head, the light striking the wall revealed a thin vertical crack along one side of the panelling. My heart lurched with excitement.

Hobbes stood up, hauling the sideboard out the way, poking the panelling with his thumbnail until a section swung back with a ping, revealing a wall safe. It wasn't locked but it was empty. He glanced at me over his shoulder, raising his shaggy eyebrows.

Leaning forward, he sniffed and poked the combination lock with the tip of a fingernail. 'There's no sign of forced entry but the burglar's been in here alright. Hallo, what's this?'

There was a scrap of screwed up paper in an ashtray. He picked it up, spreading it out, revealing a page from a small, cheap, wired jotting pad, much like journalists used at the *Bugle*, just like I should have had with me. Someone with large, sprawling, handwriting had scrawled five numbers on it in black biro. Hobbes, after studying them for a second or two, twiddled the combination dial, using the tips of his horny nails, smiling when the lock clicked.

'What does it mean?' I asked.

'It means the burglar knew the combination to the safe, which suggests an inside job – except it wasn't, unless Mr Roman burgled his own house. Besides, whoever did it didn't have a door key.' He nodded at the boarded-up French window.

'What about the servants?'

'He'd got rid of 'em about a year ago during a temporary financial problem. Still, it might be worth having a word with them at some point. Well, well, well, there's something else here.'

Taking the paper, he turned it over, holding it up to the light, laying it down on the sideboard, pulling a pencil from his coat pocket. As he delicately rubbed the lead over the page, faint, white indentations began to stand out, slowly turning themselves into letters. Even I could tell the small, neat, carefully formed capitals were in a different hand to the one that had jotted down the numbers.

'What does it say?' I said, struggling to look over Hobbes's bulging shoulder.

He stood aside, frowning, puzzled. 'See for yourself.'

I could make out, quite clearly, that the letters formed the words, though oddly spaced, *EX WITCH IS A JOY OK.*

'What on earth does that mean?'

He shrugged. 'No idea, but it might all become clear, eventually. Then again, it mightn't. What is most interesting is that I'm certain this bit of paper wasn't here on my last visit. Anyway, I'm done in this room and at least I now know someone, other than Mr Roman, knew how to open the safe and they've been back, assuming it was the same person.'

'So will it help you solve the case?'

'It may provide a lead. Possibly more than one. I'm going to take a look in his files.'

Folding the paper carefully, shoving it into his pocket, he led me to a small study, a smart, cosy, little retreat with a green leather chair on casters behind a leather-topped desk, with a laptop computer and a modern telephone. Rows of books lined the walls, obscuring polished oak panelling. A fax-machine rested on a small table in a corner by the desk, beside a brim-full shredder; a filing cabinet locked by a steel bar occupied another corner. The carpets, as rich and luxurious as in the rest of the house, gave the impression of comfortable, modern wealth. There was no sign of the burglary.

Hobbes, muttering about not having the key, wrenched the locking bar from the filing cabinet, propping it against the wall, rummaging through the folders inside.

Taking a seat, I stared out into the back gardens, imagining them in the springtime, an explosion of colour and life, wondering what fate held for them. Few houses possessed such a space and I suspected it might all be sold off for development, which I thought a shame. Hobbes, switching on the laptop, began tapping at the keys.

'Well, well,' he said after a few minutes.

'What have you found?'

'Nothing of interest, which may be significant.'

I shrugged. Finding nothing didn't sound very significant to me. It more or less summed up my journalistic career. The *Bugle* had only ever printed my stuff when desperate for fillers, or one time, after the office party, when everyone was a little drunk, and my article sneaked in. At least my piece on the history of smoking had prompted more letters to the editor than he'd ever received before. I blamed bloody Phil, who, swaying under the influence of several crème de menthes, had told me tobacco came from potatoes and was introduced into the country by Mr Chips, who'd also invented the Raleigh bicycle. I should never have trusted the git, even though he claimed he'd been joking.

'By the way,' said Hobbes, 'when you were staring out the window, did you notice how soggy the patch of lawn by the French doors looked?'

I shook my head. 'Is that significant?'

'Probably not. Right, let's get out of here.'

We got out. The last thing he did was to pull the front door back into place, wedging it shut with a piece of wood he broke from a small occasional table.

'Fake Chippendale,' he grinned. 'It's worthless. Especially now.'

3

As we got back into the car and he started the engine, the butterflies in my stomach began fluttering. The feeling was getting too familiar.

'Where to?' I asked, expecting to be heading back into town, probably to the police station.

'To the cinema in Pigton.' He glanced at his watch. 'We'll be just in time for the late afternoon show.'

'Are you off duty?' I asked, hacked off that, if so, he was taking my presence for granted – not that I had anything planned.

'I'm never really off duty, but I find films relax the mind and allow me to think. By the way, I'm on the graveyard shift later and you're welcome to come along. I've had a tip off and it might be fun.'

The journey to Pigton proceeded without incident until, as we were hurtling down the dual carriageway, a white Mercedes van had the temerity to pass us.

'Did you see that clown speeding?' asked Hobbes, crushing the poor accelerator under his foot.

'No.' I stared ahead, helpless.

Despite the engine squealing like a soul in torment, we would never have caught up had there not been a steady line of lorries in the inside lane and had not a yellow Citroen in the outside slowed down, signalling to turn right, blocking the van's progress.

Hobbes shook his head. 'Now what's he doing?'

The van driver made an attempt to squeeze into an inadequate gap in the inside lane, 'undertaking' the Citroen. He failed and red brake lights stabbed through the gloom.

Hobbes chuckled. 'Now I've got him.'

I didn't mean to, but I whimpered as he squeezed us between two lorries, filling a gap barely big enough for a skateboard. The driver behind hooted and I turned to see him gesticulating and swearing. Hobbes acknowledged him with a cheery wave and waited his chance, managing to sneak in front of the van as it tried to accelerate, controlling its speed and position until, as soon as the inside lane was clear, he forced it to stop on the verge.

'Right,' he said, 'let's see what this clown's problem is.'

Once the immediate prospect of death had receded, I was horrified to hear him speak so disrespectfully about a member of the public, and might have said something, had he not already burst from the car and been marching towards the van. Scrambling after him, I was glad, at least, that the wrath of Hobbes would be directed at someone else. Despite the glare of the red dipping sun on the windscreen, the van driver's face was pale and I wondered how I'd look after being stopped in such a manner.

Hobbes rapped on the window, which hummed open, and leant into the van. What he said next took me completely by surprise.

'Who d'you think you are? Stirling Moss?'

A soft Irish voice replied, 'No, Inspector, it's Pete Moss – as you well know.'

'You're a clown.'

I winced.

'I am that.'

The man was wearing full clown make-up and regalia, except for the big boots, which were lying along the passenger seat, on top of a huge suitcase.

'Why are you in such a hurry?' asked Hobbes. 'Don't you know speed kills?'

I nodded vigorous agreement.

'Actually, Inspector, it's usually the abrupt cessation of speed that kills, but I take your point. I'm rushing because I'm booked to entertain some sick children at Pigton Hospital and I'm running late. I got delayed by … business and I'm not sure quite where I'm going. I'd hate to disappoint those poor kids.'

Hobbes, smiling, nodded. 'Alright, Pete. Follow me. Move yourself, Andy – and quickly.'

He hustled me back to the car and I threw myself into the passenger seat, just in time. From somewhere, he whipped out a blue-flashing light, sticking it on the roof, and speeding off, Pete Moss's van close behind. He turned on a siren and we hurtled towards the big town, ignoring traffic lights and give-way signs, forcing other vehicles out of our way. A sign flashed by saying 'Pigton 10', yet I could have sworn that within five minutes we were screeching into the hospital car park.

Hobbes opened the window, pointing to a low, modern building as the clown got out. 'The children's ward's over there. Mind how you go in future.'

'I will that,' said Pete, running towards the hospital, struggling with his case, a giant boot wedged beneath each arm.

'Nice chap,' said Hobbes, accelerating away, cutting through the traffic like a scimitar through tissue paper. 'I barely recognised him under all the makeup. I knew him when he was a lad, you know.'

'Shouldn't you turn the siren off?' I asked, embarrassed, as well as scared.

'All in good time. We've got a film to catch.'

He turned it off as we reached the cinema car park. I barely had time to get out before he'd locked up and was marching towards the foyer, pulling out his wallet and removing some cash. The wallet was small and hairy and strangely disturbing. I wished I hadn't seen it.

'Two for screen one, please, miss.' He slapped his money down in front of the cashier.

Her hands shook as she handed him the tickets.

'Let's go.'

I followed because I'd had no time to consider my options. I didn't even know what was showing. When we took our seats in the gloom, the auditorium was half-empty, which was fortunate as he overspilled his seat and I had to make myself comfortable in the next but one. Though the film was already in progress, he shuffled out for a quiet word with the projectionist and very soon it restarted. I don't remember its name: it was a Western and not the sort of thing I'd normally go for, though it passed the time enjoyably enough. Hobbes barely moved during the next hour and a half and once or twice I glanced at him as he watched the screen through narrowed eyes, apparently entranced.

He emerged from his trance only once, when a spiky-haired, baggy-shirted youth in the seat in front opened a bumper-sized packet of crisps. From deep inside Hobbes's chest emerged a rumble of disapproval. The youth, ignoring it, munching his crisps, kept scrunching the bag, until, after a few seconds, Hobbes leaned forward and tapped him a crushing blow on the shoulder.

'I am a police officer,' he whispered, his voice as soft as a hurricane, 'and I must warn you, that unless you desist from making that noise, and quickly, I will arrest you.'

The youth had guts. He rubbed his shoulder, looking back over it, barely flinching. 'On what charge?'

'Rustling,' Hobbes drawled. 'See there?' He pointed to the screen, where the broken body of Luke Kinkade dangled from the gallows. 'Some places you can still be hung for rustling and don't you forget it, boy.'

The youth had the good sense to turn away and keep quiet. Hobbes settled back with a contented sigh, watching in rapt silence until a shootout signalled the end. As we got up to leave, the youth turned, as if planning to say something. Hobbes put his head to one side, sticking out his tongue, twisting his mouth horribly, making a hanged man gesture, until the youth fled. I felt rather sorry for him but Hobbes was smiling like a cheerful wolf.

There was something of a nip in the air as we left the cinema under a sky seemingly weighed down with cloud.

'I enjoyed that,' said Hobbes, walking to the car. 'Now it's time to go home for supper. A nice dish of gnome, I expect.' He grinned evilly. 'Hop in and I'll drop you off at your flat or anywhere else you like. I expect you'll be hungry again by now.'

I nodded, the hot scent of charred steak from some nearby eatery moistening my mouth. Swallowing, I got into the car, as if hypnotised. 'Can you drop me at the Greasy Pole?'

Hobbes was easing the car through the car park as he waited his opportunity to flatten the accelerator pedal. 'The Greasy Pole! By heck, Andy, you do like flirting with danger. Have you heard what Eric does with his—? No, that's unfair, it was never proven, although you won't ever find one of our lads in there, except when we have to escort the rat catchers.'

'I ate a burger and chips there a couple of days ago,' I said.

'And you're still with us?' There was a hint of admiration in his voice. 'Isn't nature wonderful?'

As we reached the main road, the car leaped forward, weaving through the traffic like a skier down the slalom.

Clutching the seat until we were back on the dual carriageway and there seemed less immediate chance of being smashed into eternal darkness, I had a few minutes for reflection. 'Actually, could you drop me at the Cheery Chippy? I'm not sure I fancy the Greasy Pole tonight.'

When at last we stopped, I opened my eyes to find we were outside the Cheery Chippy. Something seemed odd, disorienting, until I realised he'd gone the wrong way down a one way street. I didn't know why I was surprised.

'D'you know this is a one way street?' I asked.

'Of course. I was only going one way.'

'But don't the arrows mean anything to you?'

'Arrows usually mean an attack by them pesky redskins. There ain't too many redskins in Sorenchester.'

I nodded, knowing I was wasting my time.

'Right, Andy, off you go and get your chips. I'll pick you up at your place at ten.' He drove off up the road, forcing two cars and a bus onto the pavement, and turned out of sight. I heard a screech of brakes as I stepped into the warm, greasy interior.

Carrying my haddock and chips home, I turned on the television, eating, relaxing in the pool of normality. On finishing my meal, I took a leisurely shower, changed my clothes and watched more telly, luxuriating in my vegetative state, relieved to forget all about Hobbes for a few minutes. Of course, that careless thought took me straight back to thinking about him. There was something about him I didn't understand at all, something that made me want to run and hide. In his company I felt like a nervous climber must feel on a snowfield, where any false move or noise might set off the avalanche. I'd been terrified half the day, yet I'd come to no actual harm, though I feared for the state of my nervous system. I guessed that with luck, in time, assuming I survived, I would get used to him. Oh God! I hoped I wouldn't have time to get used to him. I raised my hands. They appeared steady and for a moment I felt good about my nerves of steel, until I realised my whole body was trembling in time.

Finding my way to the bedroom, lying on the bed, burying my face in the pillow, I let loose the fear that had been growing throughout the day. It emerged as a long, long, long scream, from the soul, from the guts and most of all from the lungs. I counted myself fortunate I'd had the foresight to muffle it, just in case anyone heard and called the police, for Hobbes might have been sent round to investigate and might have been angry I'd disturbed his supper. He might … in fact, what might he do? In truth, and in his own way, he'd looked after me. He was an enigma. He was a monster. He was a policeman. He was someone I ought to be writing about.

A sharp crackle of rain on the window and the wind humming and whistling drove me to snuggle under the duvet. It sounded as if we were in for a fine storm and my tatty little flat had never felt so cosy or so safe.

Not meaning to fall asleep, I awoke to the storm rattling the windows and beating against my front door. As consciousness slowly returned I wondered how that could be, for my flat was upstairs and down a corridor. Raising my head, I glanced at the alarm clock, which showed *2200*, ten o'clock, triggering an alarm in my brain that resulted in an attempt at a vertical take-off. I'd been lying on one arm, which felt all big and clumsy and useless, as far as I could feel it at all. It tingled back to life as I ran, jerking open the front door. Hobbes was standing there, his fist again raised for knocking and, though I'd been expecting him, I gasped and cringed.

'Evening,' he said. 'Good chips?'

'Oh ... umm ... yes. Very good.'

'Excellent.' He smiled. 'D'you fancy the graveyard shift?'

Not really, I thought, the rain pounding down with renewed vigour. Nevertheless, I nodded, for the evening might lead to a fantastic article, assuming I ever got down to writing anything.

'Great, get your things and we'll be off.'

Grabbing a thick jumper, the front curry-stained, stinking a bit of sweat under the arms, yet the warmest top I'd got, and pulling it on, I looked around for my cagoule, before remembering it was still in the office. I disinterred a dusty old anorak from under the bed and, before I'd really woken up, found myself back in the car, hurtling through the darkness. After a short while we turned onto the Fenderton Road.

'Are we going to Mr Roman's house again?'

'No,' said Hobbes, sounding puzzled, 'we're on the graveyard shift.'

'Yeah, so you said, but where are we going?'

He gave me a glance and replied slowly, as if to a simpleton, 'To the graveyard.'

'Umm ... the cemetery?'

The night was very dark and very stormy.

'Precisely. We're going to be doing some surveillance.'

'In the cemetery? Why?'

'I have received information that a person, or persons well-known, might attempt a little grave robbing. We're going to watch and ensure no harm is done.'

I wished I were back in my flat.

'It might be a long night,' he said, turning onto a side road with a squeal of tyres.

After a short distance, he stopped on the kerb in a spot offering a panoramic view of the cemetery, if it hadn't been so dark, and, reaching into the back, pulled out a paper bag. 'Have a doughnut. Mrs Goodfellow made them.'

I took one, though I wasn't hungry. It was rather good and cheered me up a little. Then we sat and stared into the darkness, the windows steaming up, time crawling into the bleak, small hours. When I couldn't take any more, I flopped into the back, huddling beneath a musty old tartan blanket and dozing.

The car was buffeted by the pounding fist of a wind, howling in rage that anything dared stand in its way. Hobbes flicked on the windscreen wipers, combatting a fresh spattering of rain, sitting up abruptly as distant white headlights pierced the sodden darkness, illuminating the grinning grey headstones. When the lights turned away down Tompot Lane, he sighed, slouching back into his seat.

'It's on nights like this,' he remarked, 'that I wish I was tucked up in bed with the wife.'

'Really? I didn't think you were married?'

'I'm not but I can wish, can't I? Any doughnuts left?'

'No, sorry.' I emerged from the comforting warmth of the blanket, shivering. 'What time is it?'

'Nearly two. Looks like they're not coming. Hold on ... what's this?'

He leaned forward, peering in the mirror, and I turned to see the vague shape of a car rolling down the hill towards us, lights off, vanishing now and again in the shadows. Hobbes sank down his seat, presumably in an effort to remain inconspicuous and, despite my fatigue and the cold, I chuckled. There could never be the remotest chance of him hiding in such a small car; it would be like trying to conceal a warthog in a wheelbarrow. Yet, I had little time for amusement with the other car approaching slowly, silently, as the hairs on my scalp stiffened. I couldn't see the driver and had a sudden horror that it was a ghost car. Although I'd heard whispers of strangeness happening in the vicinity of Hobbes, I'd never expected anything like this. When it drew alongside, I nearly wet myself. It was a hearse.

My mouth, opening and shutting involuntarily, only a feeble, stuttering whimper escaping, I stared wide-eyed over the edge of the window as the driver's door opened. The shriek that had been growing inside burst from dry lips and I fell back quivering.

'Oh, do be quiet, Andy,' Hobbes growled. 'This is supposed to be covert surveillance.'

I'd read books in which a character supposedly growls but, before meeting Hobbes, I'd just taken it as a literary affectation. Dogs and lions might growl but people didn't, except for him; he could growl fiercer than any of them.

Still, it had its effect and shut me up. I'd discovered one of the advantages of working with him that I failed to appreciate for some time: no matter how scary things got, he could always be scarier.

I heard a click, the front passenger door opened, clean night air blowing away the greasy doughnut fug and the faint animal odour.

'Evening,' said Hobbes.

He'd spoken to no one. At least, to no one I could see.

'Wotcha,' said a high-pitched voice.

'What's the word on the street?'

I struggled up, staring through the open door into the black night. The driver wasn't, in fact, invisible, he was just short: very short. I'd seen him in town, now and again, mostly at the Feathers, where, bizarrely, he seemed to get on well with Featherlight, often working behind the bar.

'I can't stop, guv, but I thought you might be interested in some news. You scratch my back, y'know? Cos I'm a bit short this month.'

'Cheers, Billy,' said Hobbes, handing him a twenty pound note.

Billy grinning, screwed it up, thrusting it into his trouser pocket. 'Ta, guv. Right, the guys are gonna do it tonight, like I told you, but they're gonna do it in St Stephen's down Moorend. The rain's made it too wet to dig here and there's better drainage at St Stephens. Plus, their bike broke and it ain't so far for 'em to walk.'

'Great work.'

The dwarf nodded, returned to his hearse and drove away. It

seemed to dissolve into the night.

'Good man, that,' said Hobbes. 'He keeps his ear close to the ground.'

I nearly remarked that he kept all of himself pretty close to the ground, but something in Hobbes's expression suggested it might not go down too well. Instead, I asked a question. 'Why did he come here in a hearse?'

'Because it was too far to walk.' His reply had an unanswerable logic.

The engine bursting into life, the acceleration flinging me back into my seat, we roared through the rain to St Stephens, a Victorian churchyard on the Moorend edge of town.

'It's a thirty,' I squeaked, as Hobbes's buttress foot squashed the accelerator.

He flashed his yellow teeth in what I supposed was a grin. 'What's a thirty?'

'The speed limit.'

'Well, I never.'

'And wouldn't headlights be useful?' I asked, rechecking my seatbelt, clinging to the passenger seat in front.

'If we weren't on covert surveillance.' He was grinning like a maniac.

I groaned, shutting my eyes, holding on, cursing myself for accepting the assignment. If I'd just resigned on the spot, I'd be safe and warm back home in bed.

The car, stopping abruptly, I opened my eyes, blinked and tried again. It was just as dark as when they'd been shut.

'Where are we?' I whispered.

'Just outside St Stephens in a derelict garage. No one comes here but derelicts. You may find the aroma is rather … pungent. Now, let's move, we're supposed to be on watch. Be quiet and follow me. And quickly.'

We left the car and, he was right, it didn't half pong. Holding my breath, I followed the sound of his footsteps until we were in the open air, where a glimmer revealed the silhouette of a kneeling angel, marking the edge of the churchyard. I could just about pick out Hobbes's hunched form.

I wiped rain from my eyes. 'Shouldn't we have back-up?'

'I don't normally require it. Anyway, I have you.' I caught a vague glint of teeth.

'Mightn't it be dangerous?'

'Let's hope so.'

As he slouched forward, a huge, creeping gargoyle, I shuffled after him. I didn't want to be with him, yet daren't lose him.

Lights flashed from behind a huddle of overgrown gravestones. I froze, heart pounding, as the rumble of chanting male voices reached me, making the hairs on my neck quiver, starting a dull ache in my stomach. Hobbes had melted into the blackness. I blundered forward, close to panic, needing the reassurance of his hulking presence and, unfortunately, he wasn't present. He'd left me, lost and alone, in a churchyard at night and my head was filled with chanting that chilled even more than the icy stab of the rain.

'Turn the bleeding music off, you daft berk,' said a rough voice, like someone was gargling with hot gravel. With a click, the chanting ceased and, at the same instant, a light shone in my face.

Dazzled and disoriented, I turned to run, my heart racing like a dog's at the vets. My feet missing the ground, I dropped through blackness until something hard transformed my gasp of terror into a groan of pain, leaving me to endure a few seconds of stunned confusion.

My groping hands touched wet, muddy walls. A sharp, earthy odour filled my nostrils. I'd tumbled into an open grave. The next horror was discovering I had an audience. As the grave filled with light, voices coming from above, I rolled onto my back, blinking, temporarily blinded. After a few moments, I began to make out two faces that, if I hadn't spent the past day with Inspector Hobbes, would surely have given me an immediate cardiac arrest.

'Blimey, this one's still moving. What we gonna do with it?' The gravel voice I'd heard earlier sounded hesitant.

Another voice, softer, yet creepy, replied. 'Dunno. Maybe if we fill it in again, it won't be next time. Nuffing like this ever 'appened to me before. They've always been still ... and packed inside the box.'

'Good evening,' I said, putting my hope in politeness and affability. At least I had the satisfaction of making them jump.

'Wah!' said Gravel Voice. 'It talks.'

'Certainly, I talk. Look, I appear to have stumbled into this hole and I wonder if you could see your way to giving me a hand out?'

'Give you a 'andout?' said Creepy Voice. 'Do I look like I'm a charity? What are you? A bleeding scrounger?'

'No, sir, I mean, could you help me to get out?'

''elp you to get out?' Creepy Voice sounded shocked. 'I'm not sure that's allowed. What are you in for anyway?'

'It was an accident. I slipped and fell. I shouldn't really be here.'

'That's what they all say,' said Gravel Voice, knowingly.

'Oh,' I said as I pushed myself onto my knees, 'it's most remiss of me. You must think I'm terribly rude. I haven't introduced myself. I'm Andrew Caplet, Andy. And you are?'

'I am not,' said Creepy Voice, 'you're wrong there, mate. I'm not Andrew Caplet Andy.'

'No.' I forced a smile, struggling to my feet, for the muddy coffin top was as slippery as an ice rink. 'I meant, who are you?'

'Ghouls,' said Gravel Voice.

I held up a hand. 'Nice to meet you. Umm ... I'd appreciate a bit of help, it's getting very wet down here.'

The two faces looked at me, then at each other. They whispered a few words.

Creepy Voice nodded and spoke. 'Er, look, mate, we'd like to 'elp but we're worried that if we was to let you out, then all of them would want out and then what would we 'ave to eat?'

'Yes,' said Gravel Voice. 'And we 'ave our reputations to fink of.

We wouldn't want anyone to fink we're just a couple of ghouls who can't say no.'

'So, we're gonna 'ave to bury you again,' said Creepy Voice. 'It's for the best. I'm sure you'll understand. No 'ard feelings, eh?'

'You can't bury me again. I haven't been buried at all.'

'Then what are you doing in a grave?' Gravel Voice was mocking. 'Now, enough of your nonsense. Lie down and get buried before this 'ole fills up with water and we 'ave to bury you at sea.'

Mud began to thud around me as the ghouls set to work with shovels. No matter that I screamed for help and sobbed for mercy, they shook their heads and carried on. Black despair and terror took me, madness seemed my only escape, and I was considering taking that dark path when I heard two metallic clangs, two grunts, two soggy thuds. A massive hand engulfed mine and before I knew what had happened, I was dangling over the open grave while Hobbes inspected me for damage. He set me down on solid ground, the two ghouls stretched out at his feet.

'Thank you.' My voice quavered. 'That was horrible.'

'Was it?' He shrugged. 'Well, it's all over now, so you can help me tidy up.'

He set to work, filling in the grave, stamping down the black, oozing mud, refitting the toppled headstone. I helped as much as my trembling body would allow. One of the ghouls groaned.

'What are they?' I asked at last.

'Just a couple of local ghouls. They eat old skeletons and they're quite harmless really, providing a valuable service to the community. Otherwise, we'd be knee-deep in bones and no one would like that, except for dogs. Still, I like to make sure these lads tidy up afterwards. If they don't, folk get upset and I won't stand for bad feelings between them and the ghoul community. Not on my patch.'

'Old bones? Aren't they rather hard?'

'They grind 'em up and make a sort of ghoul hash.'

I nodded. 'Do you know their names?' I reached for my non-existent notebook, believing I'd got a major scoop on only the second night of my assignment. With luck, it would make Editorsaurus Rex forgive me.

'They don't have names like you and I, though you could call them Doug and Phil.'

'Why?'

'Well that one,' he said, pointing at Creepy Voice with an inappropriate snigger, 'dug the grave and this one,' he poked Gravel Voice with his boot, 'was going to fill it.'

I sighed. 'What are we going to do now?'

'Take them home.' Bending, he hoisted both of them over one shoulder and straightened up. 'Then I'll make my report and we can call it a night. By the way, tonight's little escapade will not be appearing in the *Bugle*. As far as that's concerned, we had a quiet night, apart from having to take a couple of drunks home. Understand?'

'But …'

'Understand?' Hobbes repeated, standing a little closer than was necessary.

'I understand.' Self-preservation had asserted itself. I wanted to ask questions, wanted to know so many things, yet I was afraid, as if I'd fallen into a nightmare. My perception of Sorenchester as a nice, cosy, little town had been blown to pieces, I'd seen things I shouldn't have, and had a terrible sickly feeling my life had changed forever.

4

My old anorak proving no match for the storm, icy water trickled down my back, making me shudder. Though the rain was as heavy as a tropical downpour, the cold and a wind, too powerful to even consider going around me, blew that idea away.

Hobbes loped to the edge of the churchyard, the limp ghouls bouncing on his shoulder. 'Follow me. We'll take care of these two and then we're done and can head back to the station.'

As I jogged after him, a worrying habit I had no intention of forming, the effort started giving me just a little wonderful warmth. Still, my feet skidded and squelched inside my shoes, while my trousers, clammy and stiff, flapped whenever they took a break from clinging to and squeezing my poor legs. I wasn't used to the kind of activity to which I'd been subjected in the last few hours and every muscle was aching. I muttered to myself about what I'd do to Editorsaurus Rex should I ever chance upon him in a darkened churchyard – not that I could imagine him ever allowing himself to fall into such an awkward or uncomfortable situation, never mind into an open grave. Besides, I wouldn't really have done anything: I wasn't like that at all, and not merely because he was bigger than me.

We passed through a covered gateway into a deserted street, where sad cars dripped into oily puddles, glinting under orange streetlights. A shredded plastic carrier bag, pale and ghostly, flapped into my face. Flinching, I beat it off, watching it skid along the gutter, twirling in eddies, vanishing as it rose over the rooftops. Crossing the street, we plunged down an alley that funnelled the wind into such a full-frontal gale I found it a struggle to get through. Hobbes, oblivious, turned left along a pot-holed back lane, ducking beneath a broken fence into the overgrown backyard of a decayed terraced house. He proceeded without problem. I, however, in following, snagged my trousers, my anorak and my skin on the sickle thorns of the brambles that infested the yard. I sucked a scratch on the back of my hand, while he opened the rotting door, lugging the two ghouls into the darkness within. A gut-turning stench billowed out and only Hobbes's urging made me enter.

'Come in,' he said, 'and mind how you come down the steps. You'd better turn on the light. You'll find the switch by your hand … left a bit … a bigger bit … and down.'

I groped and turned it on. The narrow room didn't exactly flood with light, because the grime-encrusted, bare bulb dangling above us failed to match up to the task. Nonetheless, it dribbled out sufficient illumination to show a bleak, damp cellar, the crude painting of a funeral on the far wall doing nothing to improve it. Hobbes deposited the ghouls onto two filthy beds, tucked into a corner, where they lay messily, matching everything else down there. Their's was a cheerless, comfortless home, black with mould, a sticky nastiness coating the bare brick floor. All it contained was a pair of plain stools, a grubby, slimy-looking table, apparently constructed from coffin lids, some gruesome pans and bowls, a sink I doubted had ever been washed and, bizarrely, a stuffed crocodile.

While Hobbes rinsed out a pan and filled it with water, I took a proper look at the ghouls: thin, insipid creatures, dressed in filthy overalls and muddy boots, from which fetid white toes peeped. One was bald, while the other sported a greasy comb-over plastered across his translucent scalp. Yet, it was their faces that stuck in my memory and, although I'd formed an impression when I'd been in the grave, I wasn't prepared for their full awfulness. They looked like what would happen if some ham-fisted incompetent, having carved a pair of pumpkin lanterns, had left them outside for a week or two to moulder and fall in on themselves. The only parts that appeared substantial and healthy were their small, sharp, white teeth, set in jaws a bulldog might have been proud of. Yet, no dog had ever been cursed with breath like these two.

The one with the comb-over groaned as Hobbes splashed water in its face. Eyes, as cold and dark as those of a shark, opened and it sat up, rubbing its head with its claws. Looking up at Hobbes, it laughed, its mouth open, causing me to turn my head away as the charnel stench wreaked havoc on my stomach. Tottering upstairs into the garden, I threw up and leaned against the wall. Strange noises rose from the cellar as if two people were burping while a cat and a dog fought to the death. I stayed in the clean air, glad now of the cleansing rain and wind, until Hobbes emerged, pulling the door behind him, his brow corrugated in deep thought.

'What was that horrible noise?' I asked as he led the way back.

'I expect you mean my conversation with the ghoul. I don't get a chance to practise my Ghoulish very often and I think my accent amused him. However, the young fellow did tell me something interesting. Let's get out of this storm and I'll tell you. Hurry up.'

We jogged back through the rain, Hobbes silent until we were back in the car and on the move.

'The young ghoul,' he said, 'denies opening the grave you were mucking around in.'

'They must have. Who else would have done it?'

'Ghouls may have their faults but they don't lie. I don't think they understand the concept. No, as far as I could gather, the grave you were in was one they'd emptied years ago after the bones had matured; they prefer them dry.'

I winced. 'They're horrible.'

'They're not so bad, really. Live and let live. They only eat a few old bones their owners are done with and, mostly, they tidy up afterwards. Tonight, though, they were delayed because someone else was digging in their pantry.'

'Another ghoul?' I yawned, longing to be warm and dry and asleep.

'No, not a ghoul, a man. They watched him digging, apparently rather amateurishly and the interesting thing is that he removed something from the grave before running off without bothering to refill it.'

'Well, the last part's true. I really thought I was going to die down there.'

'These things happen.' He swerved and stopped the car. 'This sort of thing shouldn't, though.'

He got out, dragged an enormous branch from the road, and slid back in. 'Someone should have been taking care of that. It was rotten and could have caused an accident to the public.'

'Yeah ... but any idea who was robbing the grave?'

The car shot forward.

He shrugged. 'I don't know. Ghouls aren't good at describing humans. He was wearing a black balaclava, though.'

'Well, that narrows it down.' My heavy irony went unremarked, so I continued. 'And what did he take?'

'Something small and shiny and, since it didn't look edible, the ghouls weren't interested. They lurked in the shadows until he'd gone before starting on the grave they wanted. Unfortunately, you blundered in and ruined their plans. They'll go hungry tonight, poor things.'

'Poor things? They're disgusting. They shouldn't be allowed amongst ordinary, decent people. Aren't there laws against grave robbing?'

'You get used to them and there are many humans who aren't pleasant: humans such as the grave robber tonight. I hope we catch him.'

'But you took the ghouls home. You didn't even arrest them.'

He laughed. 'As you should know by now, most laws in this country are specific to humans. They simply don't apply to ghouls. The law doesn't recognise them.'

'Like it doesn't recognise gnomes?'

'You're catching on.'

I nodded. Since I'd met him, reality and dreams, or nightmares, had become intertwined. 'Umm ...' I said, 'do you know whose grave it was? Might that be important?'

'Good lad.' He nodded, slapping me on the back as he swung the car round a bend. 'It belongs to a chap called Lucian Mondragon who, according to the gravestone, departed this life on the thirty-first of October 1905. I don't believe I ever met him.'

'1905? Why would anyone dig up such an old grave?'

'I wish I knew,' he said. 'Oddly, the ghouls said they smelled fresh meat. And, come to think of it, whatever you were jumping about on was still solid. What's more, it didn't sound like wood did it?'

'I don't know. Are you getting at something?'

'I suspect there's more in that grave than mud, more than there ought to be.' He pondered. 'I think I'd better take another look.'

'No, please.' I heard the panic rising in my voice. 'I'm cold, wet and tired. I can't do anymore tonight. I really can't.'

Hobbes nodded. 'I understand. Tell you what, I'll drop you back at your place. You take it easy and have a lie-in and I'll pick you up at ... let's say ten tomorrow. OK?'

'Thank you.' I nearly wept. Fatigue was overwhelming me and I hadn't expected kindness.

Hobbes chuckled. 'Hang on.'

I'd barely noticed that, up to then, he'd been driving relatively slowly, almost with due care and attention, but he made up for it and I could hardly express my relief when he stopped and I was still alive. As I got out, he accelerated away between the lines of parked cars before I could even say goodnight. Trudging upstairs to my flat, switching on the electric fire, I stripped, washed off the worst of the mud, and collapsed into bed. It had been a horrible night.

A crash burst into my dreams and I awoke with blurred mind and senses, squinting at the alarm clock; it was just gone four. Why was there an orange light glowing under the bedroom door, and why could I smell smoke?

'Fire!' I screeched, leaping up, lurching towards the bedroom door, grabbing the handle and letting go with a yelp of pain. The handle was red hot and I was in deep trouble. Up till then, I'd been acting on instinct but cold terror was growing inside, weighing down my legs and stomach. Choking fumes tormented my throat and I began to cough uncontrollably. I pulled myself to the window, struggling to open it. Everything began to happen too fast. My head was spinning and I knew I was going to die. It was ironic, I thought, falling to my knees, that I'd only just returned from the grave. The window burst inwards as I slumped onto my face to sleep.

On opening my eyes again, I appeared to be outside, in mid-air, looking onto the patio beneath my window. It got closer, yet slowly. I was dropping gently, like a leaf.

I awoke in a bed. I knew it wasn't mine because of the clean, white sheets, though I was certain I'd crawled under my own duvet, with the familiar pong of stale curry and socks. A screen surrounded me and a table stood by my bedside. I groaned and a face appeared, a young woman's face, and I remembered being too tired to put on pyjamas. As I pulled the sheets around my chin, I found I was dressed in a sort of dress.

'Good afternoon, Mr Caplet.' The face spoke, its smile pushing through the screen.

A woman's body, dressed in nurse's uniform, followed the smile. It was all very puzzling. I was, it appeared, in hospital, but how? A memory surfaced, an idea of flinging myself from a speeding car to get away from Hobbes. Yes, Hobbes! Sitting upright abruptly, I groaned.

'How are you feeling?'

'Ohhhh!'

'Are you alright?'

'Ohhhh.'

'I'll get the doctor.' The nurse hurried away as I struggled to pull my wits within touching distance.

Coughing up something disgusting and acrid, brought back a hazy memory of fire. A quick check indicated that all of me was still present, though I'd acquired a white dressing on my right hand.

A boy in a white coat approached. 'Hello, Mr Caplet, I'm Dr Finlay. No jokes please. How are you this afternoon?'

My voice came out as a croak. 'OK, but my throat and chest are sore. So's my hand.'

'A bit of smoke inhalation and a minor burn. You were lucky the policeman was passing and got you out before there was any lasting harm.'

'Policeman?'

'Yes, apparently he was going off duty when, noticing the smoke, he broke in and got you out, before alerting the other residents and calling the Fire Brigade.'

'What policeman?' I had to ask, though I was sure I already knew.

'An officer named Hobbes brought you in. You're lucky to be alive but you'll be alright. We'll keep you in for observation overnight, though I doubt there'll be any problems. You'll probably cough a bit and you might feel a bit confused during the next few hours.'

'I've been feeling a bit confused ever since I met Hobbes.'

'You know him then?' Doctor Finlay's voice registered surprise. 'He's obviously a great bloke.'

'Obviously. What about my flat?'

'I'm afraid you don't have one anymore.'

'What happened?'

'It caught fire. You must know better than I how it might have started.'

Maybe the doc was right but I didn't wish to think about it. Not then.

I spent the rest of the day in hospital. Most of the time I was sleeping or drinking pints of water to wash the smoke taint from my tubes. The rest of the time seemed to involve me tottering round, looking for the bathroom. In my more lucid moments I wondered where I might stay when it was time to leave.

In the early evening I had a visitor. It was Ingrid. She was looking very pretty and worried and joy erupted at the sight of her. She sat beside me, asked how I felt, patting my hand, making sympathetic noises, finally crushing me by saying she couldn't stay long, as Phil was taking her to the opera. What a git he was.

I barely had a chance to say anything before she rose to leave. Then, as she turned, she hesitated and handed me a carrier bag. 'Mr Witcherley asked me to give you this.'

Inside were my cagoule, and a brown envelope.

'Rex? I didn't think he'd remember me. That's nice of him.' She smiled. 'See you.'

'Goodbye, Ingrid. Thanks for coming.' I deflated as soon as she was out of sight.

A couple of minutes later, I tore open the envelope with a warm feeling of gratitude. Perhaps Rex wasn't as bad as I'd thought.

Dear Mr Capstan.

It got up my nose that he'd got my name wrong, and not for the first time.

The Sorenchester and District Bugle has been undertaking a review. As a result of this, and because of your continued failure to produce requested articles on time, I regret to inform you that your services are no longer required. Please find enclosed a cheque for one month's salary in lieu of notice. Many thanks for your contribution and get well soon.

Yours,

Rex Witcherley.

I'd never exactly been a high-flyer, yet the thud of my ego hitting rock bottom left me stunned. I had no job, no home, no girlfriend and, I realised, no clothes, apart from a short cagoule. At least things couldn't get any worse.

Rock bottom split apart and plunged me into Hell.

'Evening, Andy. How are you?' asked Hobbes cheerfully, approaching.

'Not bad,' I said. 'More like bloody awful.'

'I'm sorry to hear that. Dr Finlay informed me you were on the mend.'

I was ashamed. After all, Hobbes had saved my life, such as it was. Still, I couldn't help but feel he was partly to blame for my misfortunes and that, if I'd died, things might have been better. No matter how hard I tried to look on the bright side, I couldn't see round the dark side. 'I'm sorry,' I said, 'but the last couple of days have been a bit traumatic. I didn't have much and now I've got nothing. I've got nowhere to live, Ingrid's going to the opera with Phil and I've just been sacked.'

Hobbes shrugged. 'Don't despair,' he said. 'Adversity often brings out the best in people. You'll be alright, your friends will help out.'

That didn't improve my state of mind, merely bringing home the fact that I had no friends, not real ones, anyway. Apart from Ingrid and some blokes I sometimes talked to in the pub, there was no one to turn to.

'Anyway,' he continued, 'you'll be out of here in the morning and you'll have to stay with someone until you can sort out another place.'

I tried to think. There were my parents of course. They would take me in. She'd be delighted to have me to mother again. She meant well but it had been such a struggle to escape her stifling affections the last time my life had gone belly up. As for him? He'd love letting me know just how useless I was, pointing out every mistake I'd ever made from childhood onwards. I couldn't do it to myself; there had to be another option.

'If you're really stuck,' said Hobbes, 'I've got a spare room.'

I listened, considering the proposal, highlighting just how low I'd sunk. Those were my choices: Hobbes or my parents.

'Thank you,' I said at last. 'I am really stuck and your spare room seems my best option.' God help me, I thought.

'Great.' He grinned. 'I'll let Mrs Goodfellow know, so she can make up a bed.'

'Oh good,' I said. Incredible though it might seem, I'd forgotten her. Maybe it was self-defence, for there are only so many horrors a mind can hold. 'I've got no clothes, or money, apart from this cheque.' I read it. It was for five hundred pounds and made out to Andrew Capstan. The Editorsaurus had got my first name right.

'I'll get Mrs Goodfellow to sort you out some clothes and pick you up tomorrow.'

'Thank you.' Despite everything, I really meant it.

Then I slept.

Shortly after breakfast, a cheerful Dr Finlay told me I was fit to go, though he advised taking it easy and keeping the dressing on my hand for a day or two. I sat up in bed, wishing I didn't have to leave. It had been pleasant to lie between clean sheets and have nurses caring for me.

'Hello, dear.' Mrs Goodfellow was standing by my bed, her eyes bright as a cat's in the morning sun. My body jolted with the shock and my heart thumped like a drum roll. Somehow, I found myself standing on the floor with the bed between us.

'Did I shock you?' she beamed. 'That's a nice frock you're wearing. I didn't know you liked women's clothing or I'd have brought you some.'

'I don't normally wear this sort of stuff,' I explained. 'This is just a gown they put on me because I lost all my clothes, man clothes, in the fire.'

'Have it your own way, dear. I don't mind. The old fellow says we have to live and let live and I reckon he's right. I hope these suit you.'

Hauling a battered leather case onto the bed, she opened it, pulling out a carefully folded tweed suit in rusty-herringbone, a gleaming white shirt, a silk tie with a subtle flower pattern that matched the suit exactly, a pair of thick black socks, white cotton underwear, a pair of glossy brown brogues and a white linen handkerchief. Everything looked old-fashioned and I was more a jeans and sweater person, yet they were all I'd got and, until I could get Rex to change the name on the cheque, all I seemed likely to get. It struck me I really was penniless and destitute and reliant on Hobbes's charity.

'They look OK, thanks,' I said. 'Umm ... would you mind turning your back while I put them on?'

'Bashful are you, dear?' she twinkled but turned around and sat on the bed.

I dressed, surprised how everything fitted perfectly, though it felt stiff and heavy compared to my usual garb. I noticed the faint odours of cigar smoke and lavender and wished I could see myself.

'Very smart, dear, now, come along and I'll take you home.'

'Thank you.'

She led the way from the hospital at a surprising pace, down the hill, past the supermarket, up Goat Street, along Rampart Street, Golden Gate Lane and finally to Blackdog Street. Though, she'd swapped her wellingtons for a pair of trainers, the rest of her, apart from the absence of a pinafore, was as I remembered: a green headscarf that didn't quite match her woolly, yellow cardigan and a voluminous, brown and cream checked skirt. The sun shone on my arrival at Hobbes's.

'Here we are.' Unlocking the door to number 13, she stepped inside.

Taking a deep breath, I followed as she led me upstairs, opening the door into the end room. I was pleasantly surprised, if puzzled. It was a good size, with bare white walls, low black beams, a polished wood floor, a dressing table with a stool and a small wardrobe. What it lacked, was a bed.

'The old fellow,' she said, 'asked me to make up a bed for you. I haven't had time yet, but all the bits are in the attic.'

I offered to go up and fetch them down but she said some of the planking was rather ropey and might be dangerous.

'I'll do it, dear, and it won't take five minutes.'

She was right. It took the best part of an hour because, having hauled herself up the foldaway ladder into the attic, she discovered an extended family of mice had taken up residence, and took up the pursuit with gusto and a wooden tennis racquet. I could hear her feet thumping above, interspersed with occasional thwacks as she found a target. At any minute, I expected to see her plunge through the ceiling. Eventually, everything went quiet: too quiet. I waited a couple of minutes.

'Umm ... Mrs Goodfellow? Are you alright?' Not a sound.

Hesitating for a few more seconds, I started up the ladder. The faint light in the attic was squeezing through the bars of a tiny window, dust dancing in its beam, and I glimpsed wonderful things in the instant my head poked through the hatch. Hearing a thwack and a mad cackle, I lost my grip, stretching my length on the landing rug.

A wizened face poked through the hatch upside down. 'Got the little devil! Are you alright, dear?'

I nodded, standing up, feeling a little groggy.

'Can you catch with that bandage on?'

'Umm ... yes well, probably.'

'Good,' she said, 'catch these.'

She patted a small brown object with her racquet. It twisted through the air and, despite fumbling, I grabbed it before it hit the floor. It was a limp mouse.

'Next one.' She patted another.

In the end, I had eight little bodies in my hands. I stared at them, aghast, not knowing what to do as she slid down the ladder.

'Better hurry,' she said. 'Let's get 'em to the park before they wake up.'

They were already stirring when we got there, one taking a speculative nibble at my finger. I released them and they disappeared into a hedge and began a frantic rustling. I sucked away a bead of blood as Mrs Goodfellow took my arm.

'Come along, dear. It's time I had you in bed.'

A smart, young woman, wheeling a child in a pushchair, gave me a most peculiar look. Though I tried a tentative smile, she turned away as Mrs Goodfellow propelled me back to Blackdog Street.

Once we were inside, I watched amazed as she disappeared into the attic and emerged with bits of iron, slats of wood and a mattress, building the bed in five minutes, making it up with sheets, blankets and an eiderdown. It all looked antique, yet was clean and smelled of fresh lavender.

'There you are, dear,' she said. 'I hope you'll be comfortable. You'll find more clothes in the wardrobe. Help yourself.'

'Thank you. Umm ... whose are they?' I knew they weren't Hobbes's; I doubted whether he'd even be able to pull the trousers over his arms.

'Yours, if you want 'em.' She grinned her toothless grin. 'They belonged to my husband but he doesn't need 'em anymore.'

'You're very kind.' I assumed Mr Goodfellow had passed away.

'Kind? Not really. It's more of an advanced payment for when you let me have your teeth.'

As I smiled, I noticed the gleam in her eyes, examining my mouth like a connoisseur. I snapped the display shut.

'I can't wait to get my hands on that lot,' she said as she left the room.

I sat on the bed and tried to get my thoughts in order.

'Liver? What about liver?'

I flinched and leaped to my feet as she leaned towards me. 'You can't have my liver!'

She laughed. 'I don't want your liver, I was asking if you like to eat liver, because not everyone does, you know. I'm planning a liver and bacon casserole for supper and was wondering if you like good, old-fashioned food.'

'Oh,' I said, ashamed, 'it sounds lovely. Are you sure Hobbes ... are you sure Inspector Hobbes won't mind?'

'Mind? Of course he won't. He'll be glad of the company. He doesn't get too many visitors, more's the pity.'

'Well,' I said, because I had not yet given food a thought, 'in that case, I would be delighted.' I made an attempt at a smile.

'Ooh,' she said peering up at me, 'you do have a really lovely smile. I can hardly wait.'

I forced a laugh, which sounded rather hysterical. 'Well, let's hope it won't be for many years.'

She cackled and patted my arm. 'Lovely smile, lovely smile.' She walked away. 'Likes liver, too. Lovely boy, lovely smile.'

I sat on the bed, trembling. In happier times I would sometimes sit and think. On this occasion I just sat and stared at the wall, my mind cowering in a dark corner of my skull, refusing to come out.

I must have been there for a couple of hours when I heard the tortured whine of a car's engine, followed by the sound of brakes, and I knew Hobbes had returned. Gulping, taking a deep breath, I went downstairs.

5

'Good afternoon,' Hobbes boomed. 'Has Mrs Goodfellow made you comfortable?'

'Yes,' I said, 'very comfortable, thank you.' Truthfully, she made me feel exceedingly uncomfortable, but it would have been churlish to say so.

'Good.' He rubbed his hands together, making a sound like someone vigorously wiping their feet on a coconut doormat. 'What are you going to do with yourself for the rest of the day?'

He had me there. What was I going to do? Obviously, I needed the Editorsaurus to amend the cheque, yet I didn't feel up to confronting him just then, if ever. I supposed I ought to sign on as unemployed, except I guessed that, being a Saturday, the job centre would be shut, and, besides, I hadn't the foggiest where it was or what to do. I wondered about taking myself round town to see if there were any vacancy ads in shop windows, though I wasn't sure anyone did that sort of thing anymore.

'I don't know,' I admitted.

'In which case, how about coming with me, if you're still interested in police work now you're not working for the *Bugle*?'

I pondered for a moment. I had more than a few misgivings, but then I realised he'd shown me things that had rocked my perception of the world and, deep within, a seed of curiosity had sprouted. I was astonished to discover how much I wanted it to grow, for it might change my life, which, just then, felt like a great idea.

'I'd like that,' I said and, though a sensible part of me was screaming no, my new spirit of curiosity, proving more powerful, stifled it. 'And, if the *Bugle* doesn't want me, maybe I can go freelance.'

Hobbes, nodding approvingly, patted me on the back, knocking me to the floor, and helped me back to my feet. 'Take a seat. I've got a few things to tell you.' He indicated the sofa.

We sat side by side and he turned to me with a grin that might have revived my sensible part, had the scent of baking bread, wafting in from the kitchen, not soothed my nerves.

'I took another look into the grave the other night,' he said, 'and the box you'd been jumping around on was, in fact, a plastic wheelie bin, resting on the remains of the original coffin, which the ghouls had evidently broken into decades ago. However, the wheelie bin contained a fresh body. Well, fairly fresh.'

'Murder, then?' The thought of how close I'd been to a corpse, not to mention how close I'd been to becoming one, made me feel sick. Fighting back the feeling, I forced myself to concentrate.

'Almost certainly, though let's not be too hasty.'

'It could hardly have been suicide.'

'No, I think we can rule out suicide.' He looked thoughtful. 'That's unless he was very inventive. It seems to me that, if someone wants to hide a body, where better than in a grave? It's the last place anyone would look for one and, if it hadn't been for us keeping an eye on those ghouls, someone would probably have got away with it. It still begs the question of why anyone would dig it up again.'

'Umm ... whose body was it? You say it was a he?'

'He was an adult male and, apart from that, it's hard to tell. There was no ID or anything and his face was bashed in, so I've got our forensic lads checking dental records, DNA, prints and so on. The corpse's clothes were muddy, yet the mud wasn't the same as that in the graveyard. Plus, he was wearing wellington boots with worn soles.'

'Cheese and pickle?' said Mrs Goodfellow's shrill voice from behind.

Gasping, shocked by the suddenness of her voice and how silently she'd got there, I stared at her over my shoulder. Her head was tilted to one side, her eyes glittering like a sparrow's.

'Would you boys like a cheese and pickle sandwich? Or are you going out for your dinner?'

'A sandwich would be lovely,' said Hobbes.

'It would be very nice,' I said, voice quavering to match hers.

'I'll do it right away. I expect you'll be hungry.'

She was correct. Hospital breakfasts are inadequate, at least for me. I turned back to Hobbes, expecting her to leave.

'Tea? Or coffee?' Her voice rang in my ear.

My heart jumped and I clutched my chest, which must have looked somewhat theatrical, yet was genuine. I had a sudden panic that my much-abused ticker was going to burst from my rib cage. Unexpected noises had always alarmed me and I seemed to be getting worse at dealing with them.

'Tea, please,' said Hobbes.

'Hahaha,' said I, nodding my head, 'and the same for me.'

She smiled and I watched her walk towards the kitchen, making sure she left the sitting room. Her startling appearances were doing me no good at all.

'With all the excitement recently,' said Hobbes, 'I haven't had time to interview Mr Roman's staff, so I thought we might do that this afternoon. Unfortunately, Superintendent Cooper has suggested I should concentrate on the grave case and let sleeping Mr Roman's lie. She believes it was just a minor burglary case, that I've already proved no one else was involved in Roman's death, and that there are more important cases to attend to.' He paused, looking thoughtful. 'The trouble is, I'm intrigued, because, though it may only have been a break-in, it led to suicide; I want to know why.'

'So, what are you going to do?'

'Interview Roman's staff, as I said.'

'Won't the superintendent be angry?'

'Not if I don't tell her.' He grinned. 'And I'm not really supposed to have you working with me now you've got the push from the *Bugle*. I'm not planning on telling her about that either.'

'Will there be any danger?'

'If we're lucky.'

Nodding, I wondered again why I'd agreed to go with him. Perhaps, I was crazy. More likely, I just wasn't good at saying no.

'Tell me,' I asked, as a thought occurred, 'what, exactly, is your job?'

He looked at me, obviously puzzled. 'I'm a police officer, a detective inspector to be precise.'

'I know that but, what I mean is, don't you get assigned to things like the flying squad, or traffic, or fraud, or something? That is to say, don't you have a speciality?'

Hobbes displayed his happy wolf grin. 'You sound just like my old Super. He would demand that I stuck to his orders, even when I pointed out that policing was policing and that I would always do whatever it took. He kept insisting that I was wilfully disobeying his orders, even when I pointed out how foolish they were.'

'Did he get mad?'

'Yes,' said Hobbes, 'he got quite mad in the end, poor chap. Still it was only when he took to throwing pointy cabbages at passers-by from the station roof that they had to take him away – not that they were much danger to anyone, because he'd over-boiled them.'

'You mean he literally went mad?' The news shocked and scared me. If Hobbes had been responsible for driving a police superintendent mad, what chance did I have of keeping my sanity? Of course, I'd already agreed to stay in his house and to continue working with him when I didn't need to, so already I wasn't acting entirely rationally. Thinking about it, I had, in the last few hours, been nearly buried alive by ghouls, burned in my own bedroom, and caught handfuls of live mice patted to me by an old lady in an attic. Perhaps there was no reason to fear going mad, maybe I had already tipped over the edge. I chuckled as Hobbes continued.

'Went mad? I don't know if he actually went mad, because the lads reckoned he must already have been mad to try and tell me what to do in the first place.'

'What about your new superintendent?'

'Superintendent Cooper is a very sensible woman and only makes suggestions and I can't wilfully disobey a suggestion. Besides, I think she's mostly happy to let me police in my own way.'

'Sensible indeed.' I knew I wouldn't care, or dare, to reprimand him.

'Your dinners are on the table,' Mrs Goodfellow piped up by my right ear.

'Aghh!' Springing lightly across the room, catching my foot on the coffee table, I stumbled against the standard lamp.

Hobbes caught the lamp before it fell and guffawed, shaking his head. 'By heck, Andy,' he said, wiping his eyes, 'your comic tumbling turn ought to be shown on the telly. Funniest thing I've seen since they took the old superintendent away.'

Mrs Goodfellow beaming, nudging me in the ribs, whispered, 'I'm glad to see you getting on so well with the old fellow. I haven't heard him laugh so much for months.'

After rubbing my bruised shin, I followed the laughter into the kitchen, Mrs Goodfellow reaching up and patting my back.

Still, there were compensations to staying at Hobbes's, as I discovered on the kitchen table. The old woman had prepared a huge plateful of sandwiches and, sitting down, I grabbed one from the top, took a bite and savoured the wonderful carnival of textures and flavours filling my mouth. Now, cheese and pickle sandwiches were not something I'd normally rave about, but, the crusty bread still being warm and fragrant from the oven, the primrose-yellow butter dripping through like honey, the cheese tasting tangy and sweet, and all cut to a satisfying thickness, then it was a meal fit for a king.

Mrs Goodfellow clicked her tongue and Hobbes frowned, gesturing for me to stand. He lowered his head. 'For what we are about to receive, may the Good Lord make us truly thankful. Amen.'

'Amen,' said Mrs Goodfellow.

I felt the blood rushing to my face.

'Don't worry,' said Hobbes, sitting and helping himself to a sandwich, 'you weren't to know our customs, but you will next time. Now, tuck in.'

I tucked in. The steaming mug of tea Mrs Goodfellow poured for me was excellent, too. Hobbes was well looked after and, evidently, so would I be during my stay. I quite forgot my embarrassment and my problems at that scrubbed table. Perhaps madness had something going for it.

Eventually Hobbes finished and pushed his chair back. 'Thank you,' he told his housekeeper, 'that was most excellent.'

'Yes, indeed,' I enthused, 'it was really good.'

She grinned gummily and blushed like a schoolgirl.

'Right, then,' said Hobbes, 'to business.'

'To business!' I raised my mug in a facetious toast.

A baffled frown wrinkled his forehead.

As he got up from the table and left the house, I followed, meek as a lamb, though the butterflies were, once again, taking wing in my stomach at the prospect of more of his driving. I was, however, spared, at least temporarily, for he led me down The Shambles in a brisk five-minute walk. Despite the pale sun shining in a watery sky, a fierce north-easterly wind obliterated any warmth and I was glad of my tweed suit, which, in addition to its insulating properties, must, I felt, be giving me a most distinguished air. When a couple of women chatting outside the church smiled as we walked by, my back straightened and my chin lifted, until self-doubt launched a counter attack: they'd probably smiled because I looked so ridiculous and old-fashioned. Yet there was no time to brood for Hobbes, shoulders hunched, shambling but surprisingly fast, was getting ahead of me. I took great, long, strides to keep up, stumbling on a cracked paving stone.

A portly youth smirked. 'Enjoy your trip?'

Ignoring him, I hurried after Hobbes, who having turned onto Up Way, entered the Bear with a Sore Head. It was great to slam the door in the face of the biting wind and appreciate the log fire glowing from the far side, casting shadows against the low-beamed ceiling. Customers lounged in pairs or small groups around brass-rimmed tables, a shaven-headed barman in a gaudy silk waistcoat pulled a pint of cider for a red-faced, giggling girl, and a plump, pretty woman, probably in her late-forties, in a white apron, chatted to a tall, slim man in a smart, grey suit, who was leaning against the bar. He turned as we approached and stepped towards me, hand outstretched. It was bloody Phil.

Grinning, he shook my hand, squeezing my fingers, maintaining his grip for slightly longer than felt comfortable.

'Hiya, Andy. I hardly recognised you. Nice clothes.'

'Hello,' I said.

'I was very sorry to hear about your flat.' He smirked. 'It must have been a real bummer, and then losing your job! Rex might have been a bit kinder.'

'Thanks,' I said, hating his smug concern.

'Still, you're looking good and that suit really is something else, very much the country gent.'

I snarled internally. 'Did you enjoy the opera?' I asked, with a friendly smile.

'Not much. The tenor tended to sing flat and it turns out that poor Ingrid is allergic to lobster. We had to leave before the interval and she threw up all over me.'

'Poor girl,' I sympathised, concealing my delight.

Hobbes beckoned.

'I'm sorry,' I said. 'I've got to go. See you.'

I stepped round Phil to where Hobbes was introducing himself to the lady in the white apron.

He smiled as I approached. 'A friend of yours?' He nodded towards Phil, who was just leaving the pub.

'No,' I said, 'that was Phil. He's a git.'

The lady frowned. 'He seemed a very pleasant young man to me. He's a reporter but very polite and well-spoken, unlike that one at the pet show. My sister said she'd never heard such language, and in front of the kiddies, too, and all because a hamster nipped him.'

'Mrs Tomkins,' said Hobbes, 'may I introduce Andy Caplet, who's assisting me on this case? Andy, this is Mrs Tomkins, who used to be Mr Roman's cook. She has graciously agreed to talk to me for a few minutes. Would anyone like a drink?'

'A coffee please,' she said.

'A pint of lager.' I reckoned I could do with a drink.

'And I'll have a quart of bitter. No, better make it a lashing of ginger beer, I'll be driving soon.' Hobbes nodded at the barman and placed his order.

'How much?' he asked when the drinks were poured.

The barman shook his head. 'On the house, Inspector.'

I smiled at Mrs Tomkins who did not reciprocate; evidently she had not yet forgiven me for my remark about Phil. Hobbes, escorting her to a round table, pulling out a chair for her, sat down opposite.

After a few pleasantries, he got down to business.

'How long did you cook for Mr Roman?'

'Twelve years. It was part-time; I didn't live in like in the old days. None of us did.'

'And why did you leave?'

'Because we were no longer required. That was almost a year ago now, I suppose.'

Hobbes nodded. 'So I'd heard. Do you know why?'

'No.' She shook her head. 'At least, not for certain. I believe he might have had some money troubles. He had to sell a painting, but not one he'd done, one of the good, old ones he was fond of, one his parents had brought from wherever they came from. Did you know they weren't British? To be honest, I was glad it had gone: it gave me the creeps. It was a nasty, evil-looking king holding a dagger. I suppose it must have been worth a bob or two.'

'Though,' said Hobbes, 'not enough to enable him to keep his staff on.'

'Apparently not,' said Mrs Tomkins.

He continued. 'What did you feel about Mr Roman when he sacked you?'

Her face flushed. 'I was pretty angry. We all were, especially Jimmy, the gardener. It was all so sudden. One day we had jobs, next

71

day he called us in and gave us our marching orders and a cheque for a month's pay. Two thousand quid doesn't go far and I had a lad at college to support. Still, it all worked out pretty well in the end. I got a job here. It's close enough to walk to and the pay's better. So's the company.'

I'd been listening, nodding and sipping lager quite happily, until she mentioned her pay. Two thousand pounds a month? For a cook? For a part-time cook! I'd been getting a quarter of that at the *Bugle*. It wasn't fair. I muttered under my breath, railing against Editorsaurus Rex and his antediluvian pay scales, until Hobbes growled at me to shut up.

He turned back to Mrs Tomkins. She'd not much liked Mr Roman, who'd been brusque, though not actually rude, to her and to the other staff. She believed Anna Nicholls, the maid, and Jimmy Pinker, the gardener, had also disliked him. She had, however, loved the house and mentioned how conscientious Anna had been with her dusting and vacuuming, moving the furniture nearly every day, despite its bulk. Hobbes listened intently, occasionally scratching with a pencil in a small leather-bound notebook he'd taken from his coat pocket. She could cast no light on why Mr Roman had been burgled, or why he might have committed suicide. Neither Anna nor Jimmy had kept in touch, though she'd heard they shared a flat in Pigton. Eventually, Hobbes thanking her, drained his ginger beer, rose from the chair and led me out.

Still fuming about my wretched cheque, I came close to marching into the *Bugle's* offices to confront the Editorsaurus, but Hobbes was restless, itching to interview Anna Nicholls and Jimmy Pinker. My resolve proved as firm as wet tissue paper and I found myself walking beside him to his car.

I cursed my weakness as we set off to Pigton. Very quickly though, I was cursing his driving. What on Earth was wrong with me? I didn't need to be with him, I could have been cadging a lager off someone, somewhere with a fire and a jukebox, somewhere where I was not in constant fear.

I gritted my teeth, clinging to the seat as we hurtled into Pigton, stopping outside a damp-stained, concrete block of flats. Getting out, I followed him up the steps to the door, which, though it had once been an electronic security door, was hanging open from one twisted hinge, a stench of smoke and stale urine emerging from inside. We entered, heading towards a concrete staircase, where three boys, about fourteen years old, slouched on the tiled floor below, smoking and giggling. Hobbes approached them.

'Hullo, hullo, hullo,' he said, and I swear that's what he said, 'what's going on here then?'

One of the boys spoke from deep within a grey hood. 'We're just chilling, so don't go giving us no hassle, man.' His two companions giggled again and I caught a whiff of their smoke. It wasn't tobacco.

'It doesn't surprise me you're chilly,' said Hobbes. 'It is draughty out here and a seat on cold tiles could give you piles. Why don't you go to a nice warm café?'

'Ain't got no money, 'ave we?' The biggest of the lads, sporting a stud through his lip, his face erupting with pimples and pale whiskers, sneered.

'Tell you what,' said Hobbes, squatting down to their level, 'I'll trade you.'

His right hand flashed forward, ripping the spliffs from their mouths. He stubbed them out on the palm of his left hand, the three lads staring open-mouthed and wide eyed, and reached into his coat pocket for his horrid, hairy, little wallet, removing a ten-pound note, handing it to the smallest youth. 'There you go, boys. Remember, smoking can damage your health. And now you can have a nice warm drink in the café. Can't you?'

There was a moment's silence and all three stood up, obediently, looking completely bemused, being quite polite. The one in the hood even said, 'Thanks,' as they walked away.

'Just chilling.' Hobbes snorted and chuckled. 'Where do they pick up these expressions? In Pigton of all places?' Scrunching up the remains of the cigarettes, he took them outside and let them blow away on the wind. When he returned to the lobby, he bounded up the stairs onto the second floor. I puffed after him.

He knocked on a door. After a short pause it opened a little, restrained by a chain. A scared young woman, with short dark hair and huge blue eyes, tear-stained behind heavy glasses, peered through. On seeing Hobbes, she gasped, recoiling, trying to slam the door. He used his fingers to keep it open.

'Sorry to bother you, Miss Nichols.' He showed her his ID with his free hand. 'I'm Detective Inspector Hobbes from Sorenchester. I was wondering if I might have a word with you?'

'Oh, you're the police.' She smiled. 'Please come in.'

Unchaining the door, she let us in. She was small, dark and neat, dressed in old jeans and a faded T-shirt, her smile transforming her into something of beauty. 'I'm ever so sorry about your fingers,' she said, 'but we've had some trouble with burglars in the flats, I thought you might be them.'

'Fingers?' Hobbes looked intrigued. 'What's wrong with my fingers?'

'I trapped them in the door.'

'Think no more of it. By the way, the young fellow lurking behind me is Andy, who's assisting with my enquiries into a burglary at Mr Roman's house.'

'Mr Roman's been burgled? How dreadful. How's he taking it? Please take a seat.'

Indicating a saggy, threadbare old sofa, she seated herself in a corduroy beanbag. Everything was clean and orderly, the scent of Flash and polish trying hard to mask the stink of boiled cabbage from the tight, ugly kitchenette, yet it was a poky little flat, with threadbare carpets, mouldy walls and sparse furniture. Piled in the far corner, still in their boxes, were iPods, laptops, a plasma television and various other items I couldn't make out.

'I'm afraid to say,' said Hobbes, 'that Mr Roman took it rather badly and committed suicide.'

'How awful.' She wiped away tears. 'Poor man.'

'Hadn't you seen anything about it in the news?' I asked.

'No, I've been busy. I clean at the hospital and I'm doing all the overtime I can get. Money's been so tight since we lost our jobs at Mr Roman's.'

She noticed Hobbes's glance at the boxes.

'Jimmy picked those up. He said he'd had a bit of luck on the horses.' She turned her face away, wiping her eyes.

'Where is Jimmy?' Hobbes's voice was gentle.

'I don't know.' Her tears began to flow. 'He's gone. We'd argued about money and things and he stormed out saying someone in Sorenchester owed him and it was time he paid up. He never came back.'

'When was that?'

'Last week.' She sniffed. 'On Thursday. I don't know what to do.'

'Do you have a photo I could take?' Hobbes looked troubled.

Nodding, she pulled one from her handbag.

He studied it and grimaced. 'Thank you. I'll look into it. In the meantime, do you know any reason why Mr Roman might have been burgled or killed himself?'

'No.' She shook her head. 'He wasn't the sort who'd make enemies, though I don't think he had many friends either. Some of his stuff must have been worth a bit, but I don't believe he had much spare money.'

'Were you upset when you lost your job with him?'

She nodded.

'And Jimmy?'

She closed her eyes a moment and spoke in a quiet, controlled voice. 'Jimmy was furious and said some wild things, but he wouldn't do anything like burglary ... I don't think so ... would he?' She hesitated and even I could see the appeal for reassurance in her eyes. She must have had suspicions.

Hobbes shrugged. 'People sometimes do desperate or silly things when they need money badly.'

'You think Jimmy did it?' Her face was a mask of misery.

'I don't know,' said Hobbes. 'However, he seems to have gone missing the day Roman's place was burgled. It may just be coincidence.'

He asked me to give her some privacy, so I stood outside, while he spoke softly to her. I couldn't hear very much, yet her tears had stopped by the time he left and she gave him a grateful smile. It struck me as peculiar how she'd responded to him. Though her first reaction had been terror, as soon as he'd shown his ID it was as if all she could see was the reassuring bulk of a policeman.

It was starting to get dark when we left the flats, and the pavements were awash with people, many spilling over into the road. Most, those wearing dark blue, looked morose, but small groups sporting red and white favours were smiling and making all the noise.

Hobbes sighed. 'The football's finished already. I'd hoped to get away before the crowds. Oh, well, it can't be helped. Looks like Pigton lost again and to Hedbury Rovers, too.'

To my astonishment, he eased the car through the crowds with care and consideration. I pointed this out.

'There are far too many uncertainties to proceed any faster with safety,' he said, 'there's too much I can't predict and too many variables to consider. A member of the public might step into the road or stumble or get pushed and the public is astonishingly prone to damage if hit by a car, even a small one such as this.'

I would have liked to question him more about his philosophy on driving, because, it seemed to me that he was normally close to the edge of disaster and, in my opinion, the public, specifically myself, was astonishingly prone to damage if smashed into a tree or a wall or an oncoming vehicle at the speeds he went.

I was trying to phrase a question in such a way as not to offend him when the trouble started.

A bottle flew from the mass of Pigton supporters, glancing off the shoulder of one of the red and white Hedbury fans, shattering the plate-glass window of a shop, Sharif Electrical Supplies. The fan turned with an expression of anger and pain, hesitated, shook his head and continued walking, rubbing his shoulder. Someone in the crowd, leaning through the shattered window, grabbed a watch. Someone went for an iPod and within a few seconds it had become a free-for-all. People seized radios, food mixers, steam irons, anything. The shopkeeper, a plump, bearded guy in a white robe, ran out, waving his arms, shouting, trying to save his goods.

A fist struck the side of his head. I felt a sick sensation of utter helplessness, chilling like ice in my stomach as the shopkeeper fell, a pack forming around him. When one beer-bellied, tattooed lout raised his booted foot to deliver a kick, I couldn't watch and turned away. Though most of the onlookers looked as horrified as I was, no one was going to the poor man's aid.

'Can't you do anything?' I asked, but the car had already stopped, the door was open and Hobbes was gone. It all went quiet.

Three men were lying motionless on the pavement as he helped the shopkeeper to his feet. A phalanx of about a dozen shaven-headed thugs, muscling through the crowd, charged as Hobbes pushed the shopkeeper behind him. I'm not quite sure what happened next, since those in the rear of the charge blocked my view. There was a loud crack, as if heads had knocked together, and then most of those who'd been following were sprawling over those who'd been in front. Hobbes was standing exactly where he had been, his great teeth glinting red in a shaft of light from the setting sun that had just peeped below the evening clouds.

By the time two police vans arrived, uniformed officers bursting from them, looking mean, the trouble had ceased. All was weirdly quiet, except for the moaning of the debris piled at Hobbes's feet. The police looked at the shop front, then at the groaning heap, and then at Hobbes. I sensed indecision. They must have suspected him of being responsible, yet no one appeared willing to accost him. Their relief was evident when he flashed his ID.

'These men attacked the shop,' he said. 'It was a set-up, using the cover of the football crowds. Fortunately, I happened to be passing and prevented the situation getting too ugly, though Mr Sharif was assaulted by this gentleman.' He poked a groaning man near the bottom of the heap with his boot. 'This man broke the window.' He pointed at a body near the top. 'This one,' he hauled one from the middle, collapsing the pile into individual moaning invalids, 'tried to put the boot in.'

'These good people,' said Hobbes, pointing at a group, shamefacedly holding electrical goods, 'witnessed the attack. Didn't you, lads?'

They stared, dumbfounded and, one by one, nodded.

'I see they've picked up a few items for safekeeping with the intent of returning them to Mr Sharif. If they put them back immediately, we will say no more about it. Right?'

They returned the goods.

'Great.' Hobbes turned his bulk towards the police officers. 'I'll leave it in your hands.'

Smiling, he strode back to the car, got in and began threading it through the crowd. People, talking in small groups, pointing at us, raised their thumbs or nodded as we passed. I acknowledged their gestures, feeling the warm glow of satisfaction and reflected heroism.

All too soon, the crowds thinning and Hobbes's foot growing heavier, we were hurtling back down the dual carriageway towards Sorenchester. He was humming sonorously over the engine. It was a tune I thought I ought to recognise and I tried to decipher it, since it took my mind off the speed, though, whenever I was getting close, the car would swerve or brake and my thought process would tumble like a pile of child's bricks. I never did get it.

6

We'd parked outside the police station and were heading for the entrance when it occurred to me to ask to see what Jimmy looked like. Hobbes, stopping, fished in his coat pocket, pulling out the photograph and holding it under a light. Jimmy, more than a little pie-eyed to judge by his expression and the number of empty glasses heaped around him, was smiling. I'd guess he was about thirty, small, with dark, slicked-back hair, an undergrowth of stubble sprouting from chin and cheeks. He was in a black shirt and jacket and, since the flash had turned his eyes red and his skin deathly pale, looked extraordinarily sinister.

'I wouldn't want to meet him on a dark night,' I said, sniggering, unthinking.

'I suspect you already have,' said Hobbes.

Realisation hit me like a punch to the stomach. 'It was Jimmy in the bin?'

He nodded. 'I fear so, though I won't know for certain until the forensic lads report. Of course, his face had been bashed in, but the bits left looked like bits on the photograph, though not necessarily in the same place.'

'Poor Anna,' I said, feeling sorry for the little woman. 'Who could have done it?'

He shrugged. 'I don't know yet, but I agree, Miss Nicholls will be distraught. Still, in my opinion, she could do far better than Jimmy Pinker.'

'Umm ... d'you think Jimmy is connected with the burglary?'

'I'll be surprised if there isn't a connection, but shouldn't we go to my office? Or do you prefer standing out here?'

The wind, whistling around my ears, left them feeling as though they'd been boxed.

I shivered. 'Let's go in. I'm getting cold.'

'Not as cold as Jimmy.' Putting the photograph back in his

pocket, he turned towards his office, sniffing the air. 'I wouldn't be at all surprised if there was a frost tonight.'

All I could smell was car fumes, burnt rubber and, blown in from afar, a subtle hint of chips. I followed him inside, making tea, while he, slouching at his desk, wrote laboriously on a sheet of paper. I supposed it was a report, although I wasn't sure he actually reported to anyone.

It gave me time to sit and think about the case. If Jimmy had been the burglar, then who'd killed him? Perhaps, whoever it was had wanted to get their hands on his swag, if he'd actually stolen anything that was. But why? And who had buried the body? And why in that particular grave? What really puzzled me was why whoever had done it had then returned and dug it up again. The whole affair was grotesque, yet it felt right that Hobbes was investigating. I just wondered what my role was.

Though no answers came, more questions did. Was the body, in fact, that of the burglar and, if so, had Mr Roman been responsible? It might explain why Hobbes had found him so distracted, why he'd made up such a bizarre story and killed himself. Still, I found it incredible that a respectable man would murder and dispose of the body in such a crazy manner. Why would he? And, of course, it couldn't possibly have been Roman who'd dug it up again, because he was dead by then. So, perhaps Roman hadn't killed Jimmy at all and we were looking for someone else. I concluded that I didn't know what the hell was going on and that merely thinking about it would give me a headache.

Hobbes, still engrossed in his paperwork, I placed a mug of tea beside him, looking around for distraction. There was a pile of books on the rug by my chair and, sitting back down, I selected a leather-bound, musty volume from the top of the pile and flicked through. It was filled with pages of old-fashioned handwriting, a mess of loops and blots and the occasional smudge, and appeared to be a record of old Sorenchester crimes. Heinous offences they'd been too, judging by the first item to catch my attention, one about a certain Thomas

'Porky' Parker who'd been arrested on suspicion of pig stealing. Though the pig had never been recovered, a substantial quantity of sausage had been returned to its rightful owner. I chuckled, looking at the following page, where Mistress Katherine Boot, having been discovered intoxicated in the parish church, tried to put the blame on her next door neighbour, Gramma Black, claiming she'd cursed her.

As I bent to replace the book, a scrap of yellowed paper, a cutting from the *Bugle*, fluttered to the floor. Picking it up, I noticed it was from August 1912 and about an aerobatic display in the church grounds. Though marvelling at the blurry photograph of the aeroplane, a flimsy structure of wood, canvas and wire, with an astonishing curved propeller, it was the women's enormous hats and the men's vast whiskers that struck me as most remarkable.

Or so I thought, until, when about to return the cutting, I noticed the police constable holding back the crowd. The unfortunate fellow was almost a dead ringer for Hobbes, though not quite so bulky, and with his face partly concealed behind a dark, drooping moustache. Finishing my tea, I speculated whether he might have been an ancestor. Hobbes laid down his pen and sat back.

'Was your grandfather a policeman as well?' I asked.

He looked up with a small frown. 'As well as what?'

I held out the cutting. 'This policeman looks a bit like you and I was just wondering if he was a relation?'

'No.' He pushed aside his papers and leaned back in his chair with a strange grin. 'He's no relation. I never knew my grandparents, or my parents for that matter; I was adopted.'

'I'm sorry.'

'Don't be. My adoptive parents were kind and looked after me as if I was really their own. They forced me onto the straight and narrow and held me there long enough that I wanted to stay. They were good people and it's a shame there aren't a few more like Uncle Jack and Auntie Elsie.'

'I sometimes wish I'd been adopted,' I said. '"They fuck you up, your mum and dad," to quote Jim Betjeman … or was it L S Eliot?'

'Larkin, I think you'll find.' He shook his head, sighing. 'It's always easy to blame others, particularly parents, for one's own shortcomings. I have observed that bringing up a child is never easy and that the majority of parents and adoptive parents do their best, most of the time. People just find it difficult to take responsibility for themselves and their own mistakes.'

'Do you ever make mistakes?' I was astonished to hear him speak in such a way.

'Of course, though not so many as I used to. For instance, in my younger days I would sometimes miss mealtimes when on a case. I don't do that anymore, unless it's an emergency, which is why we are leaving now.'

'Are we leaving?'

He was on his feet, nodding. 'Put the cutting away, it's time to go home. Mrs Goodfellow will have our suppers ready.'

I did as instructed, happy at the prospect of being fed, for I'd had a growing feeling of hunger, and followed him into the night air. A few shreds of cloud, clinging to the face of the half-moon, were torn away as I looked up, and were lost in the darkness. Despite the town's brightness, stars glittered in the open sky and I blessed the thick tweed suit, shrugging into it as the rising wind chucked leaves and grit into my face.

I expected we'd drive but Hobbes wanted, he said, 'a brisk walk to blow away the cobwebs and stir the juices before supper'. Turning up my collar, taking an almost wistful glance at the car and its promise of shelter, I followed down an alley into The Shambles, where a handful of Saturday night revellers were braving the chill in their search for fun and alcohol. Pub windows glowed with welcome. Passing whiffs of cooking piqued the appetite.

'Are you originally from Sorenchester?' I asked, struggling to keep up.

'No. We had to move around a lot when I was young. They were troubled times. I first remember living near the Blacker Mountains on the Welsh borders. Afterwards we lived near Hedbury in a cottage in the woods until there was some trouble and we had to move to London, where Auntie Elsie worked in a hat shop and Uncle Jack became a docker. I went to school there until there was some trouble and we left for Wales. I used to love the mountains and the green valleys and the singing. After the trouble in Tenby, we lived in a caravan, touring round the shows and carnivals. Later, Uncle Jack worked at a factory in Pigton, where we lived until there was some trouble, and moved here when I was eleven. There was never much trouble here, so we stayed.'

'Trouble seemed to follow you around.'

He chuckled. 'So they told me. I regret being the cause of much of it, in the days when I was young and wild.'

We crossed The Shambles opposite the church, from where we could hear a choir practising. Hobbes, dawdling outside the great studded doors, closed his eyes, evidently enjoying the sound. Being no fan of choirs, preferring a good stonking beat in my music and lots of volume, I was glad when the song ended and we could get on. I shivered, hoping there might be an overcoat hanging in the wardrobe.

'I know you were adopted,' I said, as we turned up Pound Street past the old yew tree, 'but did you ever try to trace your real parents?'

Hobbes shook his head. 'Uncle Jack said they were killed.'

'An accident?'

'No.'

'What? D'you mean someone killed them?'

'That's enough. They died. Uncle Jack and Aunt Elsie looked after me.'

'But—'

'Enough.' He scowled and I shut up.

Though curious to know more about him, and pleasantly surprised at his brief openness, I knew he'd closed up again, and feared my probing had touched a sore spot. I consoled myself that there would be plenty of time for further investigations for, though my remark about going freelance had been no more than bravado, the thought had been growing. I really could write something about Hobbes, something to amaze the people in Sorenchester and, maybe, those as far away as Pigton, or even further, would find him fascinating. I could make a name for myself with a racy article in the national press. Or why not a series of articles? Or a book? Hobbes could be my ticket to fame and fortune. I'd have a flat in London, probably a penthouse, a mansion in the country, a villa in Spain and there'd be girls and parties and designer suits. Editorsaurus Rex would grovel to get my reports and he'd be sorry he sacked me. Plus, I'd be able to sneer at my father's pathetic little dental practice from a safe distance. I felt I was scaling new heights.

Arrival at 13 Blackdog Street brought me down to earth. My penthouse and all the rest were way over the horizon. For now, I'd have to make do with Hobbes's spare room, Mrs Goodfellow, suppers in the kitchen and Mr Goodfellow's old suits. I hoped it would be worth it.

The door opening, an enticing savoury aroma welcomed us and my mouth was awash by the time Hobbes shut the door on the cruel night. As we took our places at the kitchen table, I restrained myself until he'd said grace and then got stuck into the casserole, as if I hadn't eaten all day. Mrs Goodfellow, opening a bottle of red wine, left us to it. When I'd slowed down a little, had enjoyed a sip of the smooth, fruity wine and the kitchen's warmth had soaked into my core, my optimism began to rise, for Hobbes wasn't so bad when you got to know him and Mrs Goodfellow was just a harmless old biddy who fed me and brought me drinks.

So, she wanted my teeth? Well, she could want. I intended hanging on to them as long as I could. I was attached to them and they were deeply attached to me, apart from one in front that was a little wobbly since I'd fallen down the cellar at the Feathers. Featherlight Binks, who'd been changing a barrel, had broken my fall. A moment later he'd broken my lip and loosened the tooth with an uppercut. I always knew where I stood with Featherlight, or on this occasion, where I lay. He had a regrettable tendency to lash out without thinking. He did most things without thinking.

'Excuse me,' I said, on finishing eating, 'what do you make of Featherlight Binks at the Feathers?'

'He is a thoughtless, charmless, soap-less, hopeless lout, who runs a squalid drinking hole and can't even keep his beer well. He should not be allowed to meet the public and has been arrested more than anyone else in town.'

'Ah,' I said, 'though I've heard he has a bad side, too.'

'That is his bad side.' Hobbes frowned. He must have noticed my grin because he nodded. 'I see, that was a joke. In fact, he's not all bad: he just reacts like an animal. To give him his due, he doesn't have an ounce of real malice in his entire corpulent frame. Yet, he can be dangerous, especially when he's full of drink, which is most of the time.'

He pondered a moment. 'There is some good in him. In a way, he's like a child and genuinely dislikes hurting people, though he doesn't often remember until after he's clobbered them. A couple of years ago he was the one who told me Billy Shawcroft had gone missing.'

'The dwarf in the hearse?' The memory of the silent, sinister shape rolling towards us was imprinted on my mind.

Hobbes nodded. 'Once again, Featherlight had been brought into the station for assaulting a customer. This one had complained about his jacket potato having skin on it.'

'Jacket potatoes should have skin on them. Isn't that the point?'

'But not cat skin. The customer put two and two together and made certain allegations about the spicy meat stew that Featherlight took rather badly, being proud of having once served as an Army cook. To cut a long story short, he rammed the customer's head into the stew pot.'

'Was he hurt?'

'The customer? No, not much. It wasn't very hot, though the pot became well and truly stuck and he had to go to hospital to have it removed. When they got it off, they found a little collar and bell at the bottom.'

'No!' I said, horrified. 'I once had his spicy meat stew.'

'The worst part,' Hobbes continued, 'was that the customer worked for the Food Standards Agency and happened to be a keen supporter of the RSPCA and Featherlight ended up in court again. However, he was only prosecuted for serving unfit food, as there'd been no animal cruelty. A dustbin lorry had run over the cat and Featherlight was just being thrifty. He claimed he'd eaten far worse in the Army and didn't see what all the fuss was about.'

I grimaced, wishing I'd had the sense to keep away. 'But what had happened to Billy?'

'I was coming to that,' said Hobbes. 'Billy's a regular at the Feathers, often helping out behind the bar, but hadn't been seen for a couple of days. Featherlight grew concerned. At his trial, he claimed to have been too distracted by worry to buy meat and had been forced to use the cat. The point is, he informed me about Billy's disappearance and, thanks to his information, I was able to trace the poor little chap. He'd been kidnapped and was being held in a cage. I got him out and closed the case.'

'Who kidnapped him?' I didn't remember hearing anything about it.

'A kidnapper, who would have become a murderer had I not got there when I did. If it hadn't been for Featherlight, I doubt there'd have been a happy ending.'

'So, umm … who kidnapped him? And why?'

'That's all I'm prepared to say. Ask Billy if you want more of the story. It was a good thing for me that I rescued him because he's since proved a most valuable ally. When you're in a tight spot, Billy's the sort of man you want with you, because there's so little of him. Mind you, he can put away a surprising amount of beer, which reminds me, if you fancy a drink later tonight, I haven't looked in on Featherlight for a while.'

'Sounds good to me.'

'In the meantime, let's go through to the sitting room. The lass will bring us tea and she says she's got me a bone to pick.' As he drained his glass, a drop of blood-red wine ran down his chin.

I took my place on the sofa, wondering why sheets of newspaper had been spread in the corner of the normally immaculate room.

I glanced at Hobbes, who, all of a sudden, seemed twitchy and tense.

Mrs Goodfellow came in, carrying a huge bone in both hands. Raising it above her head, she tossed it towards the newspapers.

Hobbes growled like a dog. The sofa jolted backwards.

I jerked my head to see what he was up to. He was a blur on the edge of vision. My eyes focussed just in time to see him roll with the bone into the corner. He'd caught it in mid-air. In his jaws.

Slavering, he crouched over the bone on all fours and the crunching began. His teeth, tearing off great lumps of bloody, raw meat, he swallowed without chewing. The feral smell grew stronger, wilder and more predatory. His eyes flashed red and his upper lip pulled up in a snarl, like a hyena's. I couldn't stop myself from hugging my knees. A strange whimpering filled the room, as if a frightened animal had come in, and it was a few seconds before I realised I was responsible. Though within a minute or two he'd stripped the bone of meat, he continued gnawing until he'd cracked it open and could slurp the oozing marrow.

'Cup of tea, dear?' She was back.

My normal, civilised inhibitions taking fright, I cried out in horror. What had I let myself in for? Why had I ever considered that staying in this madhouse would be a doddle? I must have been mad. What the Hell was happening?

Mrs Goodfellow, placing a steaming mug at my side, glanced at me, then at Hobbes, and shrugged. 'Don't you go letting the old fellow worry you. It's just his way. He'll not hurt you … probably.' She patted my shoulder.

I nodded feebly, understanding how a lamb must feel inside the lion's den. Yet lambs don't drink tea. That's what an Englishman does in a crisis. Reaching out with unsteady hands, picking up the mug, I took a sip and turned to thank her but she'd already gone. The tea was hot and sweet, ideal for cases of shock. The old girl knew what she was doing. I tried and failed to ignore the crunching and sucking from the corner. I drank and concentrated on not spilling any, though my whole body was quivering. In times of stress, say the experts, our physiology prepares us for fight or flight. Mine didn't. I couldn't force any bits to move at all. I couldn't even look away. It made no sense whatsoever.

Aeons passed. At some point Mrs Goodfellow materialised and refilled my mug. I didn't jump and hardly even noticed, though conditioned reflexes kept me sipping. By then, my vision was narrowing and I felt as if I was cowering, trembling and sweating, in a long, narrow tunnel, with Hobbes at its mouth, shattering raw, white bone with his teeth. From behind, unseen demons urged me to retreat into the blackness and hide forever. Then, I could no longer see him and the dread grew that he was creeping up, preparing to spring. My breathing grew rapid and shallow and the blood pounded in my head like tom-toms. Darkness folded around and embraced me.

'Are you alright, Andy?'

I recognised the rumbling voice.

'Wake up.'

I opened my eyes to see Hobbes frowning down at me, his eyes dark, his teeth concealed behind bulldog lips. I gasped and flinched and found I was still on the sofa. My mug was empty.

'Are you alright?' he repeated.

I decided his frown was one of concern and nodded, while striving to rediscover my power of speech. The room was bright and warm. There were no tunnels or demons, just a heap of torn and scrunched newspaper in the corner. Something small, warm and soft patted the back of my hand and Mrs Goodfellow gave me a gummy smile.

'Good lad,' she said. 'All this excitement's been too much for you. You just sit a while and you'll feel better.'

'Thank you.' I shut my eyes. The animal odour faded.

I did begin to feel better. I don't know how long it took, yet when I opened my eyes again the newspapers had been removed and Hobbes was sitting beside me, engrossed in *The Times*.

'What happened?' I asked.

'You had a turn. Don't you remember?'

'Yes, of course. What I mean is, what happened to you? I mean the bone and … and everything?'

He shrugged. 'I just enjoy a bit of a chew sometimes. It's good for the teeth and exercise for the jaws. It stops me getting a double chin.' He peered at my face and grinned. 'Maybe you should give it a try.'

'But, you went strange.'

'Sorry. There's a lot of stress in police work and we all have our little methods for coping with it. It's best to let loose the beast within on a bone rather than on a member of the public.'

'That's true,' I said, imagining horrible things.

He smiled. 'You've had a tricky few days too, and dealt with it by having a funny turn. Each to his own. By heck, though, you had me worried when your eyes turned in on themselves.'

'I had you worried? Good.' I tried to appear nonchalant, though I was still trembling. In all honesty, I'd never been so terrified in my life for, though the ghouls had been horrible, they'd been strangers and I'd thought I was getting to know Hobbes.

He smiled, putting down his paper. 'These crosswords are getting too easy. I remember when one might take me as much as fifteen minutes. Now, how about that drink?'

I don't remember much about walking to the Feathers, except feeling cold and detached. Hobbes talked about aubergines, and I think I nodded a few times. Now and again I wanted to cry. It was a relief when he opened the door and ushered me into the warm, smelly fug. Featherlight lounged behind the bar, flouting the law by smoking a stinking pipe, while taking great swigs from a pewter tankard and snubbing any customers demanding drinks. Nonetheless, pints of beer kept appearing on the counter and cash disappeared behind it, though no one appeared to be serving. Featherlight, ignoring me, glowered at Hobbes.

'What are you here for? I've done nothing.'

'Nothing?' said Hobbes. 'I'm not sure about that. Didn't you knock out a customer's teeth on Wednesday?'

Featherlight scowled. 'That's a lie. I did no such thing – it was on Tuesday and it wasn't all of them. I didn't hear the customer complain.'

'He was unconscious.'

'He was out of order, whinging about a dead mouse in his beer when it was only a bit of one.'

Hobbes raised his eyebrows. 'Well, fair enough, but this is just a social visit.'

Featherlight, grunting, concentrated on his beer, several of his bellies resting on the counter. At least he'd changed his vest since the last time I'd been in, though it didn't smell as if he'd washed it and a dark patch down the front looked rather like blood.

'What are you gawping at?' he glared. 'D'you fancy a knuckle sandwich?'

'We've already eaten, thank you,' said Hobbes, 'but a couple of beers would go down well. We'll have two pints of this.' He tapped a handle.

'No, I'd rather have a lager.'

'… and a pint of lager for Andy.'

'Coming right up, Mr Hobbes,' said a piping voice with no body.

I leaned over the bar to find Billy Shawcroft grinning up at me. 'Hello, ice cream man.' He turned on the lager tap and simultaneously pulled Hobbes's pints.

'I'm not an ice cream man,' I said, puzzled. 'I'm a journalist … or was.'

Billy chuckled. 'No, I mean 'I scream, man'. You were screaming your head off in Mr Hobbes's car the other night.'

'Oh!' I blushed. 'I suppose I might have cried out when I saw you roll up and couldn't see anyone driving. I was tired and it was a dark and stormy night and it just got to me. It was nothing.'

'Well, you gave me a laugh anyway.' Smiling, he pushed a glass of lager towards me. 'There you go.' Turning away, he topped off Hobbes's glasses and lifted them onto the counter.

'Cheers Billy.' Hobbes handed over some cash.

'Very kind of you, Mr Hobbes,' said Billy, putting a little of it into the till and the rest, including at least one twenty pound note, into his pocket.

Sitting down at a greasy table by the bar, Hobbes drained one of his glasses in a single slow movement. Joining him, I was about to make a comment when he raised his hand to shut me up. He appeared to be listening, though I could hear nothing other than the usual bar noises. Looking around the shabby pub, filled with its usual mix of lowlifes, students and weirdoes, I doubted that Featherlight had ever decorated the place, apart from periodically replacing the dartboard in the corner. The pub was impregnated with decades of smoke, spilt beer, sweat and Featherlight's cooking, the furniture was chipped, dented and stained, the floor covered in a grey-brown growth that might once have been carpet. It was a gruesome place with a foul-tempered landlord, yet retaining a loyal clientele. I wondered whether they went there through choice, or bravado, or simply because nowhere else would have them.

Hobbes, still listening, I spotted a knothole in the side of the bar near to his ear and surmised Billy was on the other side. Hobbes's gaze flicked round the room before settling on one of the group playing darts, a medium-sized man in his mid-thirties with short hair, long sideburns and tinted spectacles. Despite the cold outside, he was wearing a flowery blue Hawaiian shirt, showing off a chunky gold chain around his neck and the matching Rolex on his wrist. I'd seen him around town, I was nearly certain, but couldn't quite remember when.

As Hobbes stood up and ambled towards him, the man's eyes

widened, he turned and ran. Although, he was at least six strides nearer to the door than Hobbes and wearing expensive-looking trainers, Hobbes came within a shoelace of grabbing him. The man slammed the door behind him.

'I only wanted to play darts with him,' said Hobbes.

Featherlight scowled. 'Don't you go scaring away my customers.'

'I'll see if he wants to come back.' Hobbes opened the door, stepping into the night. Throwing back the dregs of my lager, I followed.

He was thundering up Vermin Street, hot in pursuit of the man in the shirt. I jogged after them, the lager sloshing uncomfortably round in my stomach, noticing that, despite the man's head start, Hobbes was gaining on him fast. I puffed along as well as I could but there was no way I could keep up. I'm sure I'd have fallen behind at the best of times and, with the earlier horror, a full meal and the lager, not to mention my heavy tweed suit, I had no chance at all. Turning sharp left into Rampart Street, the fugitive barged through a group of young ladies waiting at the Pelican crossing, knocking two to the ground. Hobbes stopped to help them, letting me catch up.

'Are you alright?' he asked.

'Just out of breath,' I gasped, leaning against a shop's wall.

'I wasn't talking to you.' He stepped into the road, halting the traffic to allow one of the girls to retrieve the scattered contents of her handbag.

A car driver, held up for a few seconds, honked his horn repeatedly, leaning out the window, shouting abuse. Hobbes waited, smiling, as the girl picked up her belongings. Then, having escorted her back to the pavement, he sauntered towards Mr Impatience, drawing himself up to his full height. The man cringed, his face turning as pale as the moon as Hobbes bent and looked in at his window. I couldn't make out what he said. I did, however, hear the driver yelp, 'Have mercy.'

Hobbes nodded and let him drive off. 'A little courtesy goes a long way,' he remarked and, having assured himself of the girls' well-being, saluted and loped off along Rampart Street. The fugitive was long out of sight. I offered a sickly smile to the ladies, who seemed more stunned by Hobbes's intervention than by the collision, and toiled behind him as he sped up Hedbury Road. It wasn't long before I gave up; all the exercise was killing me and I had to rest, bending forward with my hands on my knees, gasping, contemplating the cracks in the pavement and wondering whether I should throw up. By the time I felt better, Hobbes had vanished. Though I began walking towards where I'd last seen him, it wasn't long before I realised it was pointless. I rested on the wall by the Records Office.

Then I spotted the guy we'd been chasing. He'd doubled back and was sneaking into the town centre. He crossed the road and into the Records Office car park, ignoring me completely.

A wild thought entered my head; I could arrest him. I'd heard of a citizen's arrest, though I wasn't really sure what one was. Nor had I any clue why we'd been pursuing him, yet Hobbes was a policeman and, therefore, must have had a reason, probably a good one. The man's shirt was drenched with sweat despite the first crystalline hints of frost and he looked exhausted. I stepped towards him at the same moment he glanced over his shoulder. His eyes bulging behind his tinted lenses, he gasped and ran before I could lay hands on him. Hobbes was still on his trail. I started after the man as he fled downhill through the car park, by the side of the wall, and out the far gate. Hobbes passed me, his stride long and loping and, despite his heavy boots, almost silent. He didn't appear to be breathing hard, though his coat flapped around him like an enormous bat's wings. As he disappeared through the gate, I realised they were getting away from me again and reckoned I might save a few seconds by going straight over the wall. Taking a running jump, I scrambled up and over.

'Look before you leap' is a wise maxim, though I doubt whoever coined the phrase knew anything of supermarket trolleys. I didn't hit the ground running as I'd expected, I hit a supermarket trolley, sprawling. The lazy individual who'd abandoned it there instead of returning it to the trolley park probably never thought of the danger, that someone might drop into it, that the impetus of that someone's landing would set the trolley rolling downhill. Despite frantic struggles, I was stuck on my back in the wire shell, legs in the air, helpless as an overturned tortoise as the speed inexorably picked up. Typically, I'd fallen into that rare breed of supermarket trolley that runs freely, and my teeth rattled with every crack in the pavement. There was an instant when I experienced the sensation of flying, followed by a bone-jarring smack as the trolley left the kerb and landed in the road. Raising my head, peering between my knees, I could see the cars hurtling along Beechcroft Road directly ahead. I gulped and my struggles grew frantic though no more productive. I shouted for help.

It was no use. The front wheels hitting a pothole, the trolley tipped over, flinging me in front of a speeding van. Too dazed to move, all I could do was close my eyes and prepare to be smashed into oblivion. I heard the screeching of brakes before something seized my legs.

I found myself flat on my back on the pavement, winded and shocked, smelling hot metal and burnt rubber.

Hobbes squatting next to me, grinned. 'By heck, Andy, you do lead an exciting life. Are you alright?'

I nodded as well as I could and sat up, rubbing bruises and grazes. The van driver and crowd of concerned onlookers began dispersing when they saw I was still alive.

'Did you catch him?'

'No,' said Hobbes. 'I thought I'd be able to talk to him any time, whereas I only had one opportunity to save you.'

'Thanks.' I really was grateful because, for the third time in as many days, I'd been sure I was going to die. 'And … umm … sorry about the one that got away.'

'Don't mention it.'

The pavement was seeping coldness into my bones and I was glad when Hobbes helped me to my feet, though I needed his support for a while. As I was counting my injuries, bloody Phil drove past in a new blue Audi and stared. What a day I was having! Still, enough was enough. 'I want to go home now.' My words came out perilously close to being a sob.

'OK,' said Hobbes. 'I'll come back with you.'

Strangely, I was pleased, although only an hour or two earlier he'd been crunching bone like a wild animal. I was happy I was going to sleep under his roof and that Mrs Goodfellow would be after my teeth. He led me back, humming to himself.

'What's the tune?'

'Ribena Wild.'

'I don't think I know it.'

'You must do,' he said. 'It was playing on Pete Moss's car stereo. You know, Ribena wild rover for many a year?'

I grimaced and was relieved to get back to 13 Blackdog Street. I went straight to my room, dressing in thick, stripy pyjamas and, despite the horrors of the day and the not-so-distant thump of music, quickly fell into a deep sleep.

7

Coming awake to the faint tang of smoke triggered a memory of fear. I jerked upright with a racing heart, yet there was no fire, just a lingering hint of cigars, noticeable over the scent of lavender. Though my eyes were open, I could see nothing apart from a feeble glimmer of street lighting through heavy curtains. The lack of curry and sock pong made me realise I was not in my own room, or even in my own flat. The time, I guessed, was somewhere in the aptly-named wee hours, and I desperately needed to relieve myself, but, apart from the fact of being in a bed, I had no point of reference. It took a couple of minutes of disorientation to work out I was in Hobbes's spare bedroom, and that my room had burned, along with my socks.

My drowsy brain failing to remember where the door was, I was forced to fumble and grope around the walls until locating it allowed me to lurch towards the bathroom, getting there in the nick of time. Afterwards, I washed my hands, in case Mrs Goodfellow was lurking, although the faint, ladylike snores from her room were reassuring. On the way back, and considerably more at ease, I noticed Hobbes's door was open. Greatly daring, I peeped inside. The curtains had not been drawn and light from Blackdog Street showed he wasn't there. I was blurry with fatigue, a biting draught from his open window making me shiver, so I groped my way back to bed, instantly dropping back into sleep. At some point, I was vaguely aware of a clunk, as if a window was closing, and it was light when I woke again.

Yawning and stretching was good, despite a superficial tenderness from a hundred bruises and scrapes. My burned hand didn't feel too bad beneath its dressing, just a little stiff and tight. I hadn't slept so well for ages and was able to take pleasure in the ache of muscles, muscles that had barely been active during most of the previous decade. My stomach being empty, I lay a while, relishing the anticipation of what Mrs Goodfellow would prepare for breakfast. There was sufficient light for me to notice that yesterday's underwear and shirt, carelessly tossed into the corner, had vanished and miraculously been replaced with clean, pressed garments, lying neatly folded on the dressing table, alongside a fluffy white towel. I got up and went to the bathroom.

Both Hobbes's and Mrs Goodfellow's doors were shut and the house had an odd stillness, suggesting I was alone. After washing, returning to my room and dressing, I went downstairs, to find that the kitchen, apart from a mouth-watering aroma of roasting beef, was empty. A note lay in the middle of the table. It had been written on pink paper with a fountain pen and the writing was infested with loops and the occasional blot.

Dear Andy,

I trust you slept well. The lass and I have gone to the Remembrance service and didn't want to disturb you. We will be back around noon. Please help yourself to breakfast – there's bacon and eggs in the pantry and a loaf in the bread bin. I recommend the marmalade. The lass makes it herself out of oranges.

Hobbes.

PS. There was a break-in at the museum last·night.

I shrugged away a sense of disappointment. There was nothing for it but to look after myself. I've never been a dab hand at cooking and reckoned marmalade sandwiches would do me well enough. A pat of primrose-yellow butter lay in a white china dish on the table, alongside a pot with a hand-written label declaring its contents as marmalade. Filling the kettle, setting it on the hob and lighting the gas, I located the bread in a cream-coloured, enamel bread bin with a wooden lid. On opening it, I hit a snag: the bread was all in one lump - and I'd usually known it to come in slices. A childhood memory surfaced from when I was staying at Granny Caplet's while mother was in hospital having my baby sister, who died. Granny was using a big, shiny knife with a serrated edge to cut a Hovis loaf. A similar knife lay on a gleaming, wooden breadboard next to the marmalade.

Sawing energetically produced two slices or, more accurately, wedges of the fragrant, crusty, brown bread, which I buttered and marmaladed while waiting for the kettle to boil. As soon as it did, I made tea, taking the loose leaves in my stride. Then, satisfied with my achievements, sitting down at the table, I tucked in. Hobbes had been right to claim the marmalade was excellent. It held just a hint of whisky smokiness, lending a satisfying warmth and depth to the citrus tang and sweetness.

I drank a mug of tea, cut another hunk of bread and remembered the last breakfast in my flat: left-over chop suey, still in its foil box. Washing down the congealed mess with the warm, flat, dregs of a can of Special Brew, I was blissfully unaware of the cigarette butt until it caught in my throat. As smoking is a vice I've never indulged in, and I was pretty sure I'd been alone when I got home from Aye Ching's takeaway, it was a mystery. I never did get to the bottom of it, unlike the bottom of the can. At least, I couldn't imagine anything quite so horrible happening in Mrs Goodfellow's kitchen.

Smoke seemed to be on my mind a lot and it was almost as if I could smell it again. Actually, I could. The kettle was glowing red, its wooden handle carbonising. I'd forgotten to turn off the gas, though in my defence, I was more used to electric kettles. Jumping up, I grabbed the smoking handle, releasing it with a yelp, lucky my hand was still partially protected by its dressing. A souvenir of Margate tea towel was hanging on a rail by the sink and, grabbing it, wrapping it around the handle, I hurled the incandescent kettle into the sink and turned on the tap.

My cheerful waking mood dissipated, unlike the cloud of steam that arose around me with a hiss. I flapped the tea towel to clear the air, bewildered why it was making things worse, nearly setting the curtains alight before realising it was on fire. It, too, ended up in the sink. I opened the back door and, when the smoke and steam finally cleared, grew even more miserable on seeing the red, plastic washing-up bowl with a perfectly circular hole right through it. I spent the next half-hour with the bread knife, cursing and muttering as I chipped and peeled congealed lumps of red plastic from the sink and from the bottom of the kettle.

I could just imagine Phil's smug grin should he ever find out about my misfortunes, which reminded me of seeing him in his new car the previous evening. He hadn't been alone: someone had been in the passenger seat, someone with a ratty face and tinted glasses. It had been the man we were chasing and I felt guilty about not mentioning it to Hobbes, though I had been a little distracted at the time.

'I said get yourself some breakfast, not set fire to the kitchen.' Hobbes was standing framed in the kitchen doorway. He was wearing a smart, if old-fashioned, suit with a dark-blue pinstripe and a poppy in the buttonhole, his cheeks were shaved smooth and his hair was plastered flat.

I gasped and the knife clattered into the sink. 'I'm sorry,' I said, 'I … umm … had an accident.'

'Just the one?' He looked around, frowning. 'Tell me.'

As I did, he roared with laughter. I had to repeat my tale of woe for Mrs Goodfellow. Doubling the audience doubled the mirth.

Hobbes wiped his eyes, shaking his head. 'By heck, Andy, if laughter's the best medicine, you should be available on prescription. Aye well, there's no real harm done. I'd better go and change into my work things.' He went up to his room.

Mrs Goodfellow winked as she headed towards the stove, pulling on her pinafore. 'Well done, dear, you've snapped the old fellow out of it. He usually becomes quite morose on Remembrance Sunday.'

'Oh,' I said. 'Is that today? I … umm … used to keep an old poppy in my flat, one I'd found. It saved me having to buy new ones.'

Mrs Goodfellow was bending down to open the oven with her back to me and I still felt the reflected force of her frown.

'I was joking,' I said, though I had actually neglected to buy one. 'Why does it make him morose?'

'It brings back memories.' She basted the joint, poking it with a fork. 'He remembers too many faces from the past. Old comrades, old enemies, old times.'

'Was he in the forces?'

Shutting the oven, she straightened up and faced me. 'He was a soldier, a decorated war hero, though he doesn't talk about it much. Now, I've got the vegetables and Yorkshire puds to see to.'

Hobbes a war hero? There was more to him than I'd supposed. His heavy footsteps clumped down the stairs and he reappeared in everyday apparel before I could ask any more.

'Let's leave the lass to get on with dinner,' he said, 'and I'll tell you what's happened at the museum.'

'Oh, yes. The break-in.' Following him through to the sitting room, I made myself comfortable on the sofa.

Hobbes rested his boots on the coffee table. 'Since it's just round the corner, I took a quick look while you were still snoring. It's rather a peculiar case. Someone dug a hole through the wall to get in.'

'It sounds like hard work. Why not just break a window or force a door?'

'The windows and doors have alarms fitted. Whoever got in must have known – though any visitor might have noticed.'

'Do you know who did it? Surely they've got CCTV?'

'They do, but only on what are regarded as valuable exhibits. None of them was taken, so nothing was recorded.'

'It sounds like something was taken.'

'Correct,' said Hobbes. 'The only item that appears to be missing is a bronze bracelet from the store, an interesting piece, according to Mr Biggs, the curator, though of no great value, worth a few hundred pounds at most.'

'Someone put in a lot of effort to steal a piece of no great worth. Why?'

He shrugged. 'I don't know yet. Mr Biggs says the bracelet is probably fifteenth century and of central European origin. The museum only received it a few weeks ago and he hadn't got round to classifying it. It's in the shape of a sleeping dragon, with its tail coiled around its neck. Unusual.'

'Whoever went to so much bother to nick it must be a nutter,' I said, scratching my head. 'One thing, though – wouldn't he have made a lot of noise digging through a wall? Did no one hear anything?'

Hobbes shook his head. 'Not so far as we know. There was a private party at the Blackdog Café last night and they were playing loud music.'

'Yeah,' I said, 'I heard. It had stopped when I went to the bathroom.'

'When was that?'

'I don't know. The middle of the night? It was dark and you weren't in your room.'

'I was out looking for the gentleman in the flowery shirt.'

'Did you find him?'

'Not yet.'

'Why were you after him?'

Hobbes grinned. 'I'd received information that he'd suddenly come into money and wanted to ask him about it.'

'Did Billy tell you? Is that why you paid him?'

Hobbes nodded. 'Billy is a valuable ally in the fight against crime, and the man we were after, he's called Tony Derrick, has never done an honest day's work in his life, yet has suddenly acquired a wallet full of cash.'

'Tony Derrick, eh? It sounds like you know him.'

'Yes, he's lived around here for most of his life and was involved in Billy's kidnapping, which is why Billy has issues with him, and why Tony wasn't pleased to see me again.'

I was indignant. 'You said the kidnapping nearly became a murder. If the bastard tried to kill Billy, how come he's not in prison?'

'Tony wasn't going to kill him. He might be a loathsome, sneaking rotter, but he's not a killer, just an opportunist. If he sees a chance, he'll steal. Billy was blind drunk and Tony robbed him. That would normally have been as far as it went had someone not made it clear that she was willing to pay good money for someone like Billy.'

'He sold him? That's outrageous, yet who would want to buy him? And why?'

'Dinner's ready.' Mrs Goodfellow was just behind my right ear.

I leaped up, twisting in mid-air, landing and facing her, wishing she'd stop doing it.

'You're keen, dear, I can see you're hungry.' She turned to Hobbes. 'Did you see how fast the young fellow was?'

Hobbes chuckled as he stood up. 'He's fast enough on his feet where vittles are concerned, yet maybe not so nippy when chasing villains, eh, Andy?'

I made a weak attempt at a laugh while he told her about my misadventure with the supermarket trolley. Her reedy cackle joined his deep guffaws. Entering the kitchen, I was feeling more than usually ridiculous. But no one would laugh when my book came out. I would edit out the unflattering parts, make myself the hero. I would be cool, debonair, successful and people would respect me.

Still, I forgave their laughter when Mrs Goodfellow served lunch, a sirloin of beef, cooked to a succulent, tender perfection, fiery horse-radish to die for (or of, perhaps, if you were reckless with your helpings), crispy roast-potatoes and parsnips, and the most gorgeous, lightest, tastiest Yorkshire puddings in the whole world. Her gravy was the most delicious ever made, without even a hint of Bisto, and even the cabbage tasted special. She was an expert and I'd never before been presented with such a meal. For afters, she served the best rice pudding in the universe, one for which you would not blame little green men from Mars for invading merely in order to sample a spoonful. Nothing was quirky or exotic, everything was just superb and my palate, more used to dodgy pub grub and takeaways, went into overload. I couldn't talk, even if I'd wanted to, while the meal lasted, lost in my own little ecstasy. Only when I'd finished did I realise she was no longer with us, and that I'd never yet seen her eat anything. I sat back in my chair with a feeling of enormous well-being.

'Coffee?' She'd done it again.

'Yes, please,' said Hobbes. 'Thank you for dinner, lass.'

I nodded, too shocked to speak. She smiled, bustling around, as Hobbes took me back to the sitting room and resumed talking, as if there'd been no interruption.

'Strange individuals find their way to Sorenchester,' he said.

I looked at him and agreed.

'And strange events happen. Billy was caught up in one with a very weird individual until I put a stop to it. A clue pointed to Tony's involvement and, after I'd nabbed him, he made some amends by providing vital information. After I'd persuaded him, of course. I can be very persuasive.'

'Umm … why didn't he go to prison? And who was the weird individual? And—'

'One at a time, Andy,' said Hobbes with a smile. 'Firstly, Tony did not go to prison because he was never charged. Any evidence was burned in the rescue. However, shortly after our little chat, Tony enrolled in a monastery. I hoped he'd go straight but it was a forlorn hope; Tony will always be what he is. It's not all his fault, he had a difficult childhood, but he's always been one to make the worst of things. At least in the monastery he was delivered from temptation for a short time. I didn't know he'd come back, though Billy says he reappeared about a month ago. He was broke then.'

'Tony broke, you could say,' I smirked.

Hobbes nodded. 'Yet, in the last few days, he's been flashing handfuls of cash around and I don't believe he's got himself a proper job.'

'I'm sure I've seen him around town before,' I said slowly. 'I thought so in the pub and I'm surer now. What's more I think I saw him again last night.'

Hobbes shrugged. 'Of course you did. We were chasing him.'

'Yeah, I know. It was when I was lying on the pavement.' I paused. I'd be dropping Phil in it, right up to his silk-collared neck. Could I do such a thing to a former colleague? Of course I could. 'One of the cars that went by,' I said, 'belonged to Phil from the *Bugle* and I'm pretty certain Tony was in the passenger seat.'

'Really?' Hobbes raised his eyebrows. 'Then I'd better have a word with this Phil some time. Do you know his surname and where he lives?'

He nearly had me there. I'd grown so accustomed to thinking of him as 'Bloody Phil' or 'Phil the Git' that it took me a few moments to remember. 'It's Waring. I don't know his address, though they'll have it at the *Bugle*.'

'Thanks. Your information might prove useful.'

Gotcha you smug git! I thought. Maybe Ingrid would now see him for what he was. I just hoped I'd be there when Hobbes had his word with him. It might be entertaining.

'Here are your coffees,' said Mrs Goodfellow in my ear. She placed the tray on the table before us.

Hobbes laughed and took a great slurp from his mug. I poured a drop of milk into mine, took a sip and gasped.

He poured himself a second mug from the huge cafetiere. 'Mind, it's hot.'

It certainly was; the tip of my tongue was par-boiled and tender and it was a few minutes before I risked another sip, by which time he was well down his third mug. When mine was cool enough to enjoy without agony, he was becoming twitchy and tense. Though I had a few moments of horror in case he was going to do the bone thing again, all he wanted was to get out and take another look at the museum. Having nothing better to do, I drained my mug and went with him.

The biting wind of the previous day had lost its teeth and grown gentle under a pale sun. It only took us five minutes to walk down Blackdog Street, turn right up Ride Street, past the Blackdog Café, and reach the museum, which was just opening its iron gates for the afternoon. A small group of visitors started moving inside and we joined them, passing beneath a genuine Roman arch into the foyer. I expected Hobbes to push past the tourists, yet he seemed content to wait his turn. When he showed his ID, the woman behind the desk nodded and waved him through with a smile. All she could see was the reassuring presence of a policeman. And me. All I warranted was a suspicious glance.

'It's alright,' Hobbes explained. 'He's with me.'

She smiled at him and let me in. I admit to feeling disgruntled. Surely, in my tweed suit and tie, I looked most respectable? More respectable than he did in his flappy old gabardine coat.

'C'mon Andy,' he beckoned. 'This way.'

We walked through a hall filled with Roman antiquities and, though I'm not much of a history student, I wished I could have stayed for a proper look. For some reason, I'd never visited before, which, seeing all the wonderful things on display, struck me as foolish. A bit of history would undoubtedly have been healthier than spending so long in pubs, especially in the Feathers. The thought of the cat in the stew pot turned my stomach. What had ever possessed me to eat there? I knew what Featherlight was like.

Hobbes, pushing open a door marked 'private', loped down a short corridor into a storeroom, filled from floor to ceiling with loaded shelves and boxes, apart from the space by the window, where a worried little man sat at a desk, leafing through papers.

He looked up, forcing a smile. 'Good afternoon, Inspector. Any developments?'

'Not yet, sir.'

Hobbes introduced me to the curator, Mr Biggs. An ironic name

I thought, shaking his podgy hand, for Mr Biggs was small. Everything about him was small, except for spectacles that made his pale blue eyes goggle like a goldfish's. He must have been getting on for two feet taller than Billy Shawcroft, yet Billy was larger than life and seemed to occupy more than his own small volume. The curator, by contrast, looked like he'd collapsed into himself and his thin, white hair was dishevelled.

'A terrible thing, Inspector,' he said. 'No one's ever broken into my museum before. Dreadful times we live in.'

'Indeed, sir.' Hobbes nodded. 'However, don't despair. We may be able to trace the thief and recover the item.'

Mr Biggs snorted, shaking his head.

'Now,' said Hobbes, 'I need to look into the hole.'

He walked along an aisle, lined on both sides with plain cardboard boxes that, no doubt, concealed a host of wonders. A cold draught blew around my ankles, a mess of rubble littered the beige carpet. There was, as he'd said, a hole in the wall.

'Stand back and don't touch anything,' he commanded.

I nodded, already used to the routine. Squatting on his haunches, he began moving slowly and deliberately forward over the rubble towards the wall, shifting his feet so as to leave no marks. On reaching the wall, he crouched and poked his head into the hole. He began humming his 'Ribena Wild' song again.

'I went to an ale house I used to frequent,' he murmured, reaching out for something. When he straightened up he held a sticky-looking, grey-brown tuft of fibre between his nails. He sniffed it, his nose wrinkling.

'What is it?'

'Fluff from a carpet, a pub carpet and I'd stake my reputation it's from the Feathers.'

'Do you think Featherlight robbed the place?'

'I doubt it,' said Hobbes, pointing at the hole, 'and there's no chance he could squeeze through that.'

'Billy could.'

He shook his head. 'Billy has his faults but he's one hundred per cent honest, except, possibly, when he plays cards. Not that I've ever caught him out.' He paused, 'No, I suspect someone else who's been at the Feathers.'

'Tony Derrick then?'

He shrugged. 'Could be. He's skinny enough to squeeze through. Unfortunately, uniform tramped around in here before I got a proper look. Those lads have big feet, though they do their best.' He stopped and thought for a moment. 'The only thing is, it doesn't feel right. Tony's a nasty little sneak thief, an opportunist, and this took time, planning and knowledge. I can't see him doing this. Unless ...'

'Unless what?'

'Unless, he's working for someone again.' His forehead furrowed in thought and he muttered something under his breath. I didn't catch it all and had to try filling in the gaps. I think he said, though I couldn't swear to it, 'You'd have thought he'd have had enough after the old witch.'

'Excuse me?'

'Just thinking out loud,' said Hobbes. 'No, I'm sure, if Tony Derrick was involved, he didn't plan it. Someone else did.'

A happy thought came into my mind. 'Phil?'

'Possibly.' He grinned. 'Unfortunately, apart from being in a car with Tony, there's no evidence against him. I will talk to him, though he's not high on my suspect list. Just because you don't like him, Andy, it doesn't mean he's a criminal.'

'Oh,' I said, surprised by his perspicacity, 'I suppose that might be true. He is a git, though!'

'Mrs Tomkins didn't think so and Ingrid likes him.'

I glowered. 'Only because he's a smooth-talking, flash git.'

'And you're jealous?' He raised his eyebrows.

'Of course not.' Though part of me I tried to ignore agreed Hobbes had a point, I wouldn't admit it. 'There's nothing to be jealous of.'

His eyebrows twitched, making me think of a pair of bristly

caterpillars wrestling. 'So you don't mind him going out with Ingrid?'

'No. Well, yes, I do. Umm … it's up to her.'

He walked back to the desk. 'From where was the bracelet taken, sir?'

'I'll show you.' Mr Biggs stood up. With his fluffy white hair, it was like watching a tuft of thistledown wafting in a breeze. He was obviously still in some distress and drifted up and down the aisle until he found the right box. He tapped it with a brittle finger. 'From here, Inspector.'

Hobbes leaned forward, sniffing the outside of the box, a box identical to the hundreds of others in the storeroom.

'Were any of the others touched?' he asked.

Mr Biggs shook his head. 'No. At least, it doesn't appear so.'

'So, what drew your attention to this one?'

Mr Biggs looked puzzled. 'What do you mean? The bracelet was missing that's all.'

Hobbes, frowning, glanced along the rows of boxes. 'How did you know something was taken from this particular one? Did you check all of them?'

It sounded like a good point to me.

Mr Biggs's face, which had been as pale and lumpy as uncooked pastry, reddened. 'What are you trying to say? Are you accusing me of something?'

'No,' said Hobbes mildly. 'Is there something I should be accusing you of? I was merely trying to establish a fact. How did you know something had been taken from this particular box?'

'This is outrageous.' Mr Biggs was getting himself into a strop. His little feet stamping on the ground, he puffed out his chest like a robin. 'I shall have a strong word with your superiors, Inspector. I don't expect to be treated like a criminal in my own museum. Now get out!'

Hobbes scowled, leaning ever so slightly towards him, looming like an elephant's foot over an anthill. 'I am investigating a crime.

Please answer my questions, sir.'

Mr Biggs's bluster collapsed. 'Don't hurt me!'

'I never intend to hurt anyone.' Hobbes's smile held all the friendliness of a hyena.

Though he hadn't done or said anything threatening, I felt the intimidation like an approaching storm at sea. Mr Biggs's eyes goggled behind his spectacles, his jaw moved up and down wordlessly and he staggered as if he'd been punched.

Hobbes helped him to his chair. 'Now, sir,' he asked, his voice gentle, 'how did you know something had been taken from this box?'

'I didn't know.' Biggs's voice grew shrill. 'I just suspected something when I saw the hole.' His breathing had become heavy and runnels of sweat streaked his face.

'What did you suspect?'

'That the bracelet had gone. It's an unusual piece. I don't mean the workmanship or the materials. They are not exceptional. It's the design.'

'Go on,' said Hobbes.

'The ... er ... Order of St George used the symbol of a dragon with the tail coiled round its neck in the fifteenth century. It is rare to come across them nowadays: unique, I believe, in Sorenchester. Though they have little intrinsic value, they are worth a great deal to collectors interested in the Order.'

'What is the Order of St George?' I asked, too intrigued to keep shtum.

'All in good time, Andy,' said Hobbes, raising his hand. He turned to Mr Biggs, 'How did you know it had gone missing, sir?'

'I saw the hole and guessed it had been stolen.'

Hobbes persisted. 'Why?'

'I don't know. It was a guess.'

Hobbes stared at Biggs who squirmed and twisted like a worm caught in the mid-day sun. 'What made you think the thief would bypass all the other boxes and go straight for this one?'

It was obvious even to me that Biggs was hiding something, yet the man looked so deflated and shrivelled I couldn't help feeling sorry for him. He was gulping like a fish, his face pale again, with an unhealthy sheen like on a lump of putty and the thought occurred that he was going to pass out, just as he passed out. His eyes rolling, his mouth dropping open, he clattered from his chair with all the elegance of a sack of potatoes.

'Oops,' said Hobbes. 'I didn't think I was pressing him too hard.' He knelt, loosening the man's collar, checking his pulse. 'Still alive at any rate, though I'd better phone for an ambulance.'

He did so and prowled round the storeroom for a few minutes until the paramedics turned up. They bustled in, performing some quick tests on the patient, and wheeled him away. They obviously knew Hobbes of old and gave no indication of surprise to see him beside an unconscious witness.

Hobbes grinned. 'Well, that's mucked things up. Still, it wasn't my fault. I suppose he just fainted. It's a shame, because he knows a lot more than he wants to tell.'

I nodded, shaken by the little man's collapse. I'd never seen anyone go down in such a way before, yet Hobbes was right, he hadn't touched or threatened him. Not exactly.

'Have you ever heard of the Order of St George?' I asked, since it meant nothing to me.

'No more than Biggs told us.' He shrugged. 'Still, it might be worth finding out whether anyone does collect that sort of stuff around here. I rather formed the opinion that someone does.'

I agreed. 'It was as if he expected someone to steal it.'

'Right, and yet he didn't try to stop it, though I think he was upset it had gone.'

'He looked frightened to me,' I said, 'even before you interrogated him.'

'It was hardly an interrogation, but it's an interesting observation. Frightened, you think? I wonder why? Anyway, we'd better go.'

We left the storeroom, passing some of the museum staff who'd gathered to watch their curator being removed. Some angry comments were directed at Hobbes but I don't think he heard them. It was a relief to get outside into the fresh, cool air. Still, the day was proving more exciting than the previous Sunday afternoon, when I'd had my lunch in the Bellman's, drunk too much, returned to my flat and fallen asleep on the carpet in front of my telly. My ex-telly, I reminded myself, on my ex-carpet in my ex-flat.

Hobbes, staring at the railings around the museum, began crawling slowly along the pavement. I watched, fascinated, once again reminded of an enormous bloated toad, though toads don't sniff.

'Aha.' He stopped, squatting before a section of railings.

'What is it?'

He pointed. 'Look, the paint's chipped near the base and there's no sign of rust, so it must be recent – and look up there. Can you see the smudges? That must be where the thief climbed over to get access to the wall. Hallo, hallo, hallo, what have we here then?' Reaching round the back of the railings, he held up a pair of latex gloves between dagger-like fingernails. 'He was careful not to leave any prints anyway. Still, though this isn't a busy road at night, there would have been a risk of being seen, unless there was a lookout.' He sniffed at the gloves and wrinkled his nose. 'Too much powder in these.'

'Phil and Tony Derrick?' I said, more as an accusation than a suggestion.

'Perhaps,' he said, 'but don't jump the gun. It may not have anything to do with either of them. Coincidences can happen.'

'Now what?' I asked. 'Do we go and find Phil?'

'Later. First, I'd rather have another chat with Mr Biggs, when he's in a more cooperative frame of mind.'

'You mean a conscious one?'

He grinned. 'That would, of course, be an advantage. Until then, there's one or two things I must do back home and I ought to go and make some notes back at the station. What do you want to do?'

'Actually, I think I might go and have a look at my flat. What's left of it.'

'Fine,' said Hobbes. 'I'll see you at suppertime. At six o'clock.'

We parted and I walked through town to the remains of my former home. From a distance – and from the right angle – the block looked the same as always. Then the outside of my flat came into view, the walls stained with great, heavy swathes of smoke, as if some careless painter had used a huge, broad brush to streak black paint. Every window was shattered and the roof had partly collapsed. The whole block had been boarded up and tape was stretched across the front door, warning that the structure was unstable. I realised I had not been the only victim: all the other flats had been evacuated, too. I had a sickening suspicion that I'd started it, certain I'd left the electric fire on when I'd crashed out, remembering being careless when discarding my clothes. As I gazed up at the ruined first floor window, I realised just how lucky I'd been that Hobbes was passing, because I doubted anyone else could have done what he'd done. In fact, if he hadn't actually done it, I wouldn't have believed anyone, least of all a big bloke like him, could have scaled the wall and carried me down. There really was something strange about him.

During the following hour or so I mooched about, staring at the block, kicking up leaves in the overgrown communal garden, thinking about Hobbes, while trying to remain inconspicuous in case any of my fellow former residents showed up. Though I didn't know any of them, except to nod to on the steps, I had a feeling they might not be happy to see me.

8

Dusk descended, dragging the temperature down with it, making my breath steam and curl. I shivered, thrusting my hands into my pockets, trying to turn my mind to Ingrid, as my feet turned homewards. Home? I was already thinking of Hobbes's place as home. I put it down to shock.

Ingrid was the only thing I missed from the office, apart from the pay, which reminded me of the urgent need to see Editorsaurus Rex and force him to change my cheque. Then I could give him a piece of my mind, if I dared, though it would have to be a small piece: the way things had been going I couldn't afford to lose much more.

I was fond of Ingrid's soft brown eyes and friendly smile. I liked to think of her hair as blonde, though I suspected an impartial observer might callously describe it as mousy. Again, some might have considered her a little short for symmetry; I suspected my impartial observer might even consider her dumpy, the boorish lout. 'You, sir, are no gentleman,' I would tell the swine before thrashing him within an inch of his life. My problem was that, since I no longer worked for the *Bugle*, I wouldn't be able to impress her with my ardour and prove I was 'arder than Phil. I was worried he'd be able to have his wicked way without me to protect her.

I wondered about her motives for going out with him. Sure, my impartial observer might consider him good-looking – and he did keep himself fit and dressed well and had nice manners and a smart new car – but the impartial observer was a fool, as he'd shown with his views on Ingrid. He didn't recognise Phil was a git. He was always smiling, feigning friendliness, ready to help anyone. He'd be the first to dig his wallet from his trendy trouser pocket and buy a round at the Bellman's, or to contribute to a birthday present, or to make a donation to charity. I despised him and every little thing he did to show-off to Ingrid.

And now he'd started taking her to the opera. Well, at least she'd had enough taste to throw up on him, if not enough to avoid lobster. That, at least, gave me a reason to cheer up.

A treacherous part of my mind interrupted the mental rant with a suggestion that, maybe, she would have gone out with me had I ever taken the trouble to ask her and that, maybe, I should have bought her a birthday present, or, at least, a card. I laughed it out of sight. Why should I have to act flash like Phil? I reckoned she only liked him because he was nice to her and bought her presents and took her to the opera. I was who I was and she ought to appreciate it. The treacherous part rallied and whispered that I'd never even hinted that I liked her, and asked why she should have gone out with me if I'd never asked her. I squashed the notions with ease; we were living in the twenty-first century and a woman could ask a bloke out perfectly easily. No, though she might be gorgeous, in her dumpy, mousy way, the girl had no taste in men and I sometimes wondered if she was right for me.

It came as something of a surprise to find my feet had carried me into Blackdog Street, for I'd hardly been aware of walking with all the turmoil in my mind. It was satisfying to know that Hobbes planned having a word with Phil and that, with luck, I'd be present to see him squirm. With more luck, he'd collapse like old Biggs or, even better, Hobbes might tear out his throat. I chuckled, wondering whether I might be able to give a little shove, something to ensure Phil dropped right in the shit. Then I'd have a free run at Ingrid, because there was no way a girl as pure and intelligent as her would associate with a criminal. My treacherous part made a final effort. What made me think she was pure? A bastard like Phil would, surely, have got into her pants at the first opportunity and, therefore, deserved everything he'd got coming.

Reaching number 13, I raised my fist to knock.

'Hello, dear,' said Mrs Goodfellow's voice.

My stomach contracting, I spun around, unable to see her anywhere, yet sure I'd heard her. I couldn't have imagined it.

'You'll be wanting to come in I expect.'

She couldn't have become invisible. I looked behind me, along the street and even up the side of the house, as if she might be hanging there like a monkey.

'Down here, dear.'

A wizened face, pale in the streetlights, winked up at me from behind the bars covering the cellar.

She grinned. 'Just seeing to the mushrooms. I'll be up in a minute.'

'Oh, good,' I gasped. 'Mushrooms. Very nice. I'm sorry, I didn't see you there.'

She chuckled. 'I expect you thought I was invisible, or hanging around like a monkey?'

'No, of course not,' I lied, laughing, but she'd gone. I stared into the black hole by my feet.

'Come in, dear.'

I hadn't heard her approaching the front door and my jump wouldn't have disgraced the Olympics. I forced a smile, stepping into the warmth.

She pushed the door to. 'The old fellow's not home yet, but he's normally back in time for his supper. By the way, dear, he asked me to give you this.'

Reaching into the pocket of her pinafore, pulling out a key, she handed it to me. 'He said it was best if you had your own, so you aren't locked out if no one's home. He said to treat the house like your own.'

'Thanks,' I said, touched that he trusted me.

'Mind you, he also said how you wasn't to go burning the house down, like your last place.' She chuckled.

I grimaced.

'Would you like a cup of tea, while you're waiting?'

'No thanks. I didn't know you'd got a cellar.'

'Oh yes. All the houses down the street had cellars, though most have been turned into basements or filled in. The old fellow sometimes likes the peace of being underground and it's where he keeps his wines and where I grow my mushrooms and force my rhubarb.'

I wondered what on earth she was forcing it to do. There had been, I remembered, a frisson when venturing into Granny Caplet's cellar, all dark and mysterious, when I was very small. 'Can I see the cellar?'

'Of course, dear.' Taking me into the kitchen, she opened what I'd assumed was a cupboard door. 'Down there. Will you be wanting the light on? The old fellow fitted an electric one.'

'Oh no,' I said, intending humorous sarcasm, 'I'd much rather flounder around in the dark.'

'Suit yourself,' she said. 'Just beware the pit of doom. They do say it's bottomless.'

'What?'

'Oh sorry, dear. Did I say the pit of doom? I meant to say mind your head. The ceiling's a little low in parts.'

Smiling, she flicked a light switch and let me descend the creaky, narrow, wooden staircase. It was cool down there, yet dryer than I'd expected, with a pleasant, earthy odour and just a hint of damp, coming from trays of compost in a corner, some covered in mushrooms as big as cauliflowers. Beneath the grille, next to where I'd seen Mrs Goodfellow, was a pile of coal and against the near wall stood a great rack loaded with bottles. Unable to see any rhubarb, I guessed the old girl must have forced it into hiding. I'd been down there some minutes before it struck me just how cavernous it was. It appeared far wider than the house.

I was considering returning upstairs when I noticed what appeared to be another door, partially concealed by coal. It puzzled me because, if it actually was a door, then it led in the direction of the road.

Hobbes's voice rumbled from above. 'Who's that down there?'

'It's me, Andy.' I peered up through the grille at his face, cratered like the moon.

'Oh dear,' he sighed. 'I thought the lass had given up on locking men in the cellar. She hasn't done it for ages. I'll come and let you out.'

'It's alright. I asked to come down.'

'Really?' His face ascended as he straightened up. I heard the front door open and shut and his heavy footfall as I headed back to the stairs. She had locked me in.

He released me, rolling his eyes skywards. 'Sorry. She's got a thing about locking men in the cellar. I wouldn't worry about it though. I'm sure she means well.'

'But why?'

'I think it's because her father went away when she was a little girl and she reasoned that if he'd been locked in the cellar he wouldn't have been able to go. She only does it to men she likes. It's a compliment really.'

'Not the sort of compliment I like,' I said, though in all honesty it was about the only one I'd ever received from a woman, except from mother. 'Is she safe?'

'Oh, I shouldn't think so.' He grinned. 'She's only human after all. Are they ever safe?'

I shrugged. 'Dunno. Has she ever locked you in?'

'Oh yes,' he said airily, 'she used to do it all the time but I kept escaping and, since I always came back, I think she decided I was here to stay.'

'Well, it is your house.'

'True,' said Hobbes, 'and it's her home. Yours, too, as long as you want it.'

Again, I was touched. 'Thank you,' I said, though I still planned to write the book and was glad of any scraps of information about him and his crazed household. 'Umm ... I noticed a door in the cellar.'

'Well of course you did.' He frowned. 'Which is how you were able to enter and exit.'

'No. Another door.'

'Are you sure?' Without apparently doing anything, he seemed suddenly threatening.

'Yes,' I said, though his reply and manner had confused me and made me unsure. 'I've just seen it.'

'I don't think you should have just seen it.' He leaned towards me a fraction, the animal scent strengthening. 'It would be far better if you hadn't just seen it. If I were you, I'd forget about it. That door is not for you. Not yet. Maybe never.'

He patted me on the shoulder. It felt like being cudgelled.

'Now, come along, Andy.' He spoke slowly and emphatically. 'There is no other door in the cellar and you didn't see one because there was nothing to see. Do you understand?'

I knew how Biggs had felt. I was trembling all over, my knees knocking together, yet I managed to nod.

He smiled. 'Good man.'

The animal odour dissipating, my knees settled back into their accustomed supporting roles.

'Supper'll be ready soon. In the meantime, why not take a seat and take the weight off your mind.' Propelling me into the sitting room, he sat me on the sofa.

'Thank you,' I said, as he left and bounded upstairs. Though I tried to stop thinking about the door, I couldn't understand why he'd reacted in such a way. A horrible thought made me clutch at the lapel of my tweed jacket. What had happened to its original owner, Mr Goodfellow? Was he locked behind the door, walled up, never to escape? Or maybe his mortal remains were hidden there … or was there something worse? I sat in an ecstasy of doubt and fear until supper was ready when Hobbes reappeared, guided me into the kitchen and said Grace.

I wouldn't have said I was hungry until I saw what lay on the table. It was what is sometimes referred to as a spread. There was a plate of sandwiches, generously cut from Mrs Goodfellow's still-warm crusty bread and packed with ham and mustard or cheese and pickle. Then there was egg and cress, cucumber and salmon, paté, cheeses, cold tongue and homemade pickles. To follow, she produced a cream trifle, drowning in sherry, a coffee cake smelling as fragrant as if the coffee had been freshly ground and was as light as air, a luscious dark fruit cake and a bowl of tinned pears. The latter surprised me, yet turned out to be Hobbes's favourite. I made myself at home. So what if I spent half my time in a state of fear and horror? I could at least eat well. And, by golly, I did eat well.

Afterwards, I sat back in my chair, hands folded across a distended stomach and belched happily.

'Manners, Andy. Manners.' Hobbes wagged a finger at me. He looked almost friendly, yet a glint in his eyes reminded me of Granny's cat. That evil orange beast used to slink towards me, exuding bonhomie, purring, begging to be stroked. As soon as I touched him, he'd roll onto his back in ecstasy, dig his claws into my hand and bite my thumb. He'd got me every time, and I was determined to stay on my guard with Hobbes. Though I'd once overheard a drunk in the Feathers state that Hobbes's bark was worse than his bite, I'd bet Hobbes had never bitten him, and my fear of being bitten was not the least of my worries about him. Even so, I was managing to live in his house, was fit and well, and gathering material for a book that could be the making of me, though a doubt had begun to take root; would anyone believe it?

I'd fully expected Hobbes to want to talk about the break-in after tea but, to my surprise, Mrs Goodfellow, bringing out a Scrabble board, invited me to join them in a game. I agreed. I was, after all, a journalist, one who'd increased his word power with *Reader's Digest* often enough. Though my confidence was high, humiliation was on its way as they thrashed me using words I'd never heard. Early on I challenged Hobbes over 'quitch', which he claimed was a type of grass, giving him a triple word score, and demanded a dictionary. He proved to be correct and, furthermore had just ruined my next move; all I could do was add an 's' to the word 'rat'. 'Rats.' At least it summed up my feelings. When Mrs Goodfellow followed my brilliant addition of 'san' to a 'g' to get 'sang' by expanding it to 'sanguineous' I knew I was in trouble. We played four games over

119

the evening, Hobbes and Mrs Goodfellow winning two each, while I came a poor third every time. And that was to flatter myself, for in the final game, my total score was less than either of them achieved in a single move and, even worse, I was convinced they were trying to let me do well, giving me plenty of opportunities that I didn't, or couldn't, take.

'Bad luck, Andy.' Hobbes sounded sympathetic. 'Sometimes the letters run against you. Anyway, we're older than you and have had longer to pick up vocabulary.'

I nodded. 'Well done both of you.' At least I could play at being a good loser. I went up to bed shortly afterwards with a mug of cocoa.

'Make sure you clean your teeth when you've finished.' Mrs Goodfellow looked stern. 'We wouldn't want them rotting away would we?'

'No, we wouldn't.' I made a special trip to the bathroom just to make sure she didn't have an excuse for leaping out on me. Then I slept until late on Monday morning.

Once again, fresh clothes had been left on the dressing table. I supposed I ought to thank the old girl for that and for the meals, and for making my bed, too. When I was enjoying a leisurely bath, I noticed the sander still tucked under the sink and I wondered what Hobbes used it for. I wondered what was behind the door in the cellar. I wondered what was up in the loft. I wondered if I'd been born under a wondering star.

Though I'd only glimpsed inside the loft, I'd had an eyeful of colours and pictures. There was much to look into in this house, yet, now he'd entrusted me with a key, I had access all the time.

So did Mrs Goodfellow. The bathroom door swung open. 'No need to get up, dear.' She beamed her toothless smile, flicking a duster around.

I dropped back into the water, covering myself with my hands, squirming. 'Do you mind?'

'Of course not, dear.' She fixed her bright little eyes on me and chuckled. 'And don't mind me either. I'll only be a few minutes.'

'Couldn't you dust later? It's rather embarrassing.'

She tittered. 'From what I've seen, there's no reason for you to be embarrassed, dear. Now, Mr Goodfellow, he might have been embarrassed.'

'Mrs Goodfellow, please!'

'Oh alright, dear. Don't get into a state. I'll go and dust the old fellow's room. He's out already, you know.' She sat on the corner of the bath. 'Do you know, someone broke into the church last night? He's gone to investigate and he's upset. He doesn't like crimes on his patch and there have been a few recently. Now, the other year, there was a spate of car break-ins and—'

'Mrs Goodfellow,' I squeaked, 'please!'

'Oh, sorry, dear, I'm going.' She left me, closing the door behind her; her grin was the last thing to vanish, like she was a toothless, wrinkled, Cheshire cat.

Washing in haste, getting out the bath, I dried myself and scurried to my room where I tried to dress while leaning against the door. I could hear her flapping round in the bathroom as I went downstairs. At least I thought I'd heard her, for when I walked into the kitchen, she was stirring a copper pot.

'All dressed and safe from prying eyes, eh?'

I nodded, forcing a laugh to show how nonchalant I felt.

'Lovely teeth,' she cackled. 'Now would you like to get them stuck into something?'

'Like what?' I asked, nervously.

'Like bacon and eggs with mushrooms. It's what the old fellow had.'

'Mmm, it sounds lovely,' I said. I was wrong. It was better than that; it was divine. The scent of the frying mushrooms started me drooling and, when the bacon and eggs had been added, I feared my mouth would spill over. It tasted even better than it smelled and then I stuffed myself with toast and her superb marmalade, all washed down with fresh orange juice and as much tea as I could fit in. A little embarrassment seemed a small payment for such a breakfast.

'The old fellow asked what you were going to do today,' said Mrs Goodfellow when, having finished eating, my mouth became available for talking. 'He says he'll be down the church for a while if you want to meet him there. Mind you, he said it a while back when you were sleeping like a puppy. Then he said he'd have to go to Pigton, so, if he wasn't at the church, he'd be somewhere else and you were to do what you wanted to do. He reckoned you had to go to the *Bugle* sometime to get a name changed on a cheque, so he wouldn't be worried if you didn't show up. And he asked, if you were in the *Bugle's* office, if you'd find out where someone called Philip Waring lives. And—'

'Say no more,' I said, desperately trying to hold back the torrent of words. 'I'd better go.'

Standing up, I nodded and walked away, stepping out into the street, shutting the front door behind me, jumping down the steps. A flurry of sleet spattered the icy pavement at my feet and the cold wind had returned. Despite shivering, I was too proud to go back and pick up the old overcoat I'd found in the wardrobe. Since I had to pass the church on the way to the *Bugle*, it struck me as a good idea to look in. Hobbes might still be there and, even if he'd already gone, someone should be able to tell me what had happened. And if no one could then, maybe, I'd pick up sufficient divine inspiration to deal with Editorsaurus Rex. I'd bet bloody Phil, the editor's blue-eyed boy, never had problems like mine. Bastards the both of them. Still, I might be able to find Phil's address and then I'd do my best to ensure he had a really hard time at Hobbes's hands and, with luck, at his feet too.

Cold thoughts almost took my mind off the cold wind and, besides, it was only a short walk to the church. I was still glad to rush inside, pushing through a party of tourists, grateful for shelter. I can't claim I knew the church all that well, as I'd only been in once before, during a sudden downpour when returning from the pub. The dark, sombre atmosphere combined with the massive, mediaeval architecture and ancient treasures had impressed me then and still did.

A guy in a dog collar minced by. 'Excuse me, Vicar,' I said, 'has Inspector Hobbes left already?'

'Indeed he has,' he replied in a voice often described as fruity.

'Oh well. I'd hoped to catch him. I hear there was a break-in last night?'

'I'm afraid so.'

'Was anything taken, Vicar?'

He nodded.

'What?'

'Who wants to know?'

'I do. My name's Andy Caplet and I've been helping the Inspector for the last few days.'

'You don't look like a policeman and, I'm not the vicar, by the way, I'm the curate. The name's Kevin Godley; just call me Kev.'

I shook the hand he held out. It was cold, limp and flabby like a dead man's and gripped for rather longer than I liked. I jerked my arm away.

'I'm not a policeman. I'm just hanging out with Hobbes.'

'Oh, I see. A camp follower.'

I wasn't too chuffed with the stress he put on the word 'camp'.

I asked again. 'Can you tell me what was taken?'

'I can. Some lost sheep has swiped our Roman cup.'

'A Roman cup? Was it valuable?'

He nodded. 'I should think so. It was made of gold.'

'Wasn't it protected?'

'Yes, of course. It was displayed in a safe built into the wall, with a bullet-proof glass front until someone got it out last night.'

'How?'

He shrugged. 'They ignored the glass and cut through the mortar. Your Inspector mentioned an angle grinder but I don't really know what that is.'

'I think it's a tool.' I scratched my head. 'What's this cup look like

123

anyway?'

Kev nodded towards a desk by the main door, where there were piles of books and pamphlets for sale. 'There's a photo in one of those pamphlets. Now, if you'll excuse me, I really must go, I've got a service to arrange.'

'It's OK,' I said. 'For Vespers?' I felt rather proud at my display of ecclesiastical knowledge.

'No.' Kev grinned. 'I meant a service for my motorbike and it's a Honda, not a Vespa. I can't abide those scooters with their piddly little motors. No, give me seven-fifty CCs throbbing between my thighs and I'm a happy curate. See you, Andy.' He patted my shoulder and walked away.

He disappeared behind a screen and I turned towards the desk, flicking through a pamphlet until coming across a photograph of the Roman cup, a large, heavy-looking goblet, plain, apart from a few foreign words in the form of a cross on the base. The pamphlet cost 50p and I was, literally, penniless but, as the severe, blue-rinsed woman in charge was occupied with a visitor, I folded the pamphlet, slipping it surreptitiously into my trouser pocket.

'That's fifty pee, sir.' The severe woman glared at me, her angry eyes glittering through horn-rimmed glasses.

'What is?' It was a feeble bluff but I'd never stolen anything before and I could feel the adrenalin coursing through my veins.

'The pamphlet in your pocket. Please pay for it or put it back. If not, I'll call the police.'

Panicking, I ran for it and, once I'd started, I couldn't stop. It was a stupid thing to do and I wouldn't dream of doing anything like it again and I would have paid if I could have and, anyway, the pamphlet was overpriced. In truth, I had no excuse – and I didn't even manage to keep it. It must have fallen from my pocket when, barging through a group of pensioners by the front door, I stumbled up the steps, before fleeing down The Shambles, weaving through the hordes of shoppers. Then, stunned by my own folly, heart pounding, I ducked down an alley, scrambling over a tall wooden fence, cowering in the backyard of a house. Out of sight, I got my breath back and listened for any sign of pursuit. I was just beginning to believe I'd got away with it when someone let the dog out.

It was a big animal, with rough, black hair and gleaming white fangs, and a deep prejudice against trespassers in tweed and I amazed myself at how fast I could move with a beast with the bulk and temperament of an angry bear snapping at my vitals. I jumped up, straddling the top of the fence, pulling up my leg before the brute could take a chunk out of it. The creature howled its disappointment and I thought I was safe. However, the fence was obviously in league with him. With a crack and a lurch, it buckled and collapsed beneath me. For a moment dog and I stared at each other. Then it gave a deep, resounding woof and I took to my heels with a yelp of terror.

I put it down to the beneficial effects of all my recent exercise that I made it from the alley before he caught me and brought me down at the feet of the gangly policeman. The severe woman was with him.

She pointed at me. 'That's him, officer, he's the one. Arrest him.'

The policeman, grabbing the dog's collar, pulled him off, handing him to his owner who had just emerged from the house, his fat red face quivering with rage.

'That's him.' He pointed at me. 'Arrest him for breaking my fence and cruelty to animals.'

'But …' I said. It was too late.

My hands were suddenly and surprisingly restrained by handcuffs and I was being led through the streets by the policeman, escorted by an angry woman, a furious man and a frustrated dog. People enjoy a good spectacle and I soon became the centre of a crowd, as wild and inaccurate rumours flew around. My sole consolation was that the excited dog, deprived of my blood, turned on his master, sinking his teeth into a fatted calf. The fat man, bleeding, roared and smacked the dog round its ears, while the woman denounced me as Sorenchester's answer to the Antichrist.

'What *have* you been doing, Andy?' asked a soft, familiar voice.

125

I turned and smiled weakly. 'Oh hi, Ingrid.' I made an attempt at nonchalance. 'It's just a misunderstanding. I'm sure it'll be sorted out soon.'

'He robbed the church!' the severe woman shouted.

'He smashed my fence down and he's been tormenting my dog. Aghh!' The angry man grew angrier as the dog nipped his other calf. 'Get off you brute.' He aimed a kick, losing the crowd's sympathy.

The woman was screaming, 'Search his pockets! Search his pockets!' at the policeman, who looked stunned by the whole procedure.

'All in good time, madam,' he said. 'At the station.'

'Don't you "madam" me. If you won't search him, I will.'

She pounced on me, and the dog, recognising a fresh target, pounced on her, growling like an over-revved scooter.

The crowd was taking sides. A spotty youth cheered on the dog and the angry man floored him with a punch. The youth's friend knocked the angry man onto his back and then it was mayhem. Quite a few joined in and even the dog had his day, snarling and snapping at random. Ingrid was swept away in a torrent of retreating townsfolk. The policeman gasped, 'Christ!' as the angry man, having staggered back to his feet, was hurled through the plate glass window of a dress shop. Fists and feet flew and a thrown bottle knocked the policeman cold. By then I was in a state of pure terror, my heart pounding, my mouth dry, doing whatever I could to protect myself, which was not easy in handcuffs. I don't know what came over me but, noticing the policeman was in real danger of being trampled, I somehow hoisted his limp body over my shoulder and staggered through the affray, taking several hits as I did so.

A voice boomed, echoing off the buildings as if a cannon had been fired. 'Stop this at once.'

The crowd went quiet. The dog fled. I looked up with my left eye, the right one, having taken a punch, had closed as tight as a clam. It was Hobbes, standing before us, hands thrust in the pockets of his coat, a scowl sculpting his face into that of a gargoyle.

'This is the police. I order you to disperse immediately or there will be trouble.'

'There's only one of him. Get him!' A big man in a red sweater incited the mob from the back. At least, he started at the back but the general retreat was so fast, he quickly found himself alone at the front.

He stared at Hobbes, quivering. He looked at the crowd.

'You were saying?' said Hobbes, conversationally.

The idiot was brave, I'll give him that. Brave, if not bright. Screaming incomprehensibly, putting his head down, he charged. Hobbes stood, watching. What happened next was a surprise. I expected Hobbes to hit him, yet all he did was shift his weight and pivot like a bullfighter as the idiot hurtled past, head-butting a lamppost, flopping back into his arms.

'This young fellow's going to have a headache,' said Hobbes, examining a gaping, oozing wound on the man's forehead and lying him down on the kerb. He gave a wolfish grin. 'Still, I doubt he had much brain to damage. Are you alright, Andy?'

I nodded and sank to the pavement with the policeman still over my shoulder, groaning as I helped him down.

'It was brave, rescuing Constable Poll like that,' said Hobbes. 'He might have been badly hurt if you hadn't. How are you doing, Bean?'

PC Poll's eyes opened. 'Could be better, sir.'

By then more police officers were appearing and the crowd had dispersed, except for a few onlookers gawping from a distance. Several dismembered bodies lay scattered in the road. I gasped; I hadn't realised things had got so bad. Hobbes picked up one, twisting its head round. 'Gottla geer,' he said like a bad ventriloquist, 'gottla geer.'

I stared, horrified. It took several long dark moments before I worked out that the bodies were mannequins from the dress shop. When the relief hit me, I must have fainted.

9

The world looked strange. My knees were pressed into my armpits, my knuckles scraped against a tatty rug and a great weight was forcing my head down. I could see my feet and the bottom drawer of a rusty filing cabinet upside down between the legs of a chair. As I groaned, the weight lifted, a hairy hand took me by the shoulder, easing me upright and, though I'd seen some strange things when waking, Hobbes's leathery face peering into mine was the most unnerving. Yet, I was sitting in his office, the handcuffs were off, and he was looking at me with an expression wavering between concern and amusement.

'How are you feeling?' he asked.

'Not too bad. What happened?' I was determined to act cool, despite not understanding what I was doing there.

'You fainted. Now put this on your eye and cover it up. It looks like a baboon's backside.'

He handed me an ice pack and I applied it with another groan.

'That's some shiner you've got.' He grinned. 'We had a doc take a look at it and it's only bruised. By heck though, you do have an eye for trouble.'

'It wasn't my fault.'

'No. Not entirely. I had the story from young Poll before they carted him off to the hospital. He's got a touch of concussion and it might have been a lot worse if you hadn't got him out when you did. Mind you,' he said and chuckled, 'it might have been a lot better if you hadn't got him into it in the first place.'

'I didn't mean to. I didn't want to be arrested. Will I be charged?'

'Of course not. I can't have it said that I harbour criminals under my own roof. I gave the gentleman twenty pounds towards fixing his fence and we agreed he won't be taking the matter any further. In addition, your pockets being empty, there was no evidence of theft and, besides, the lady is currently undergoing treatment for shock and dog bites and is unwilling to talk.'

'What about the dog?'

'I had a word with the man about his dog, just before the ambulance came for the worst casualties.' Hobbes's grin grew broader. 'We agreed he should never have been keeping a dog that is so evidently a danger to himself and the public.'

'What's going to happen to it? It's mad and vicious and should be put down.'

'So the man said,' said Hobbes, 'but I pleaded for a reprieve.'

'What? Why? It's dangerous.'

'Probably, which is why I'm going to look after him. His name's Dregs, according to his former master.'

I groaned, not being keen on dogs since one ate my football when I was six. I've always blamed it for my failure to shine as a sportsman. At least, I've blamed it when not blaming my father. 'Where is he now?' I looked suspiciously round the office.

'They patched him up, though he wasn't much hurt and he's taking Mrs Goodfellow to the shops. They're going to pick up some dog biscuits. He says he's a bit fussy and won't touch the cheapuns, so they're off to the posh shop.'

'He told you that did he?'

'Yes.'

'So you've talked to him?' Now, it seemed Hobbes was speaking with animals. I wasn't as surprised as I would have been when I'd first met him.

'He says I'm welcome to take his basket and any leftover food and reckons his wife will be glad to see the back of him.'

'His wife? He can't have a wife. It's impossible.'

'I admit it's unlikely,' said Hobbes, 'though I understand the dog was what made him so angry, and the fact that his wife hated it didn't help his temper.'

'Oh. I understand now. I thought you'd been talking to the ...' I let the sentence fade away as the colour rose to my cheeks.

He laughed. 'Maybe that knock on your head is more serious

than it seems.'

'Sorry. I got a bit confused.'

'As if I'd have a conversation with the dog.' He chuckled. 'I wouldn't do such a thing – not till we've been properly introduced.'

He guffawed and I responded with a feeble twitch of the lips.

'Anyway,' he said, changing the subject, 'did you get the editor to rewrite your cheque, or were you too busy fomenting civil unrest?'

'No, not yet.' I felt a sinking sensation in the stomach. I didn't fancy confronting Editorsaurus Rex just then, with an ice pack pressed to my throbbing eye, with torn knees on my trousers and blood splashed over my shirt – at least it wasn't mine.

'Right then,' said Hobbes. 'If you're feeling better, there's no time like the present. Come on.'

I followed him of course. By then I didn't even think about it, though I'd have much preferred to curl up quietly somewhere in the dark. I struggled to keep up, while attempting a cool and heroic demeanour for the shoppers. He burst through the doors of the *Bugle* building, bounding upstairs to the main office.

'Can I help you?' asked a male voice on my ice-packed side.

'I doubt it,' said Hobbes, marching straight towards Rex's door.

'You can't go in. He's busy,' said the voice. I didn't recognise it. Rex hadn't wasted any time in replacing me.

Hobbes opened the door and walked in, with me bobbing in after him, shrugging apologetically. Rex rose from behind his desk as if someone had cut loose a hot-air balloon.

'What do you mean by this interruption?' His stare fixed on me. 'It's Capstan, isn't it? Didn't I sack you? What are you doing here?'

'Sit,' said Hobbes. 'We'll not take long. I am Inspector Hobbes, of the Sorenchester Police.'

Rex, deflating, slumped into his chair. A skinny woman sitting opposite him turned to stare at us and I recognised her from *Sorenchester Life*: she was Mrs Witcherley. Her face, beneath a trowel-full of makeup, looked young and soft, her blonde hair shone with youthful lustre, yet her neck, though concealed under strings of lustrous pearls, suggested she was approaching sixty. She sat, legs crossed, cigarette in hand, pungent fumes coiling from between her glossy red lips. Apart from the smoker's pout, she showed no expression.

'Firstly,' Hobbes continued, 'Mr Caplet requires you to amend a cheque. Andy?' His hand propelled me towards the desk.

'Sorry to disturb you, sir.' I felt very much the humble supplicant. 'Umm … you appear to have written the wrong name on my severance cheque.'

'So what do you expect me to do about it?'

'Umm … change it, please.'

'You're damn lucky I gave you a cheque at all.' Rex scowled. 'You misled me about your interests and abilities, you consistently failed to file reports on time, if at all, and you were a constant drain on the resources of this newspaper. Now, run along.'

Hobbes leaned over the desk. 'It would be advisable to pay him, sir.' Without apparently doing anything, he reeked of menace.

Rex, jerking back into his chair as if he'd been punched, nodded. 'Only joking, Capstan. I will, of course, write you another immediately. What name should I put on it?'

'Andrew Caplet,' said Hobbes. 'And, if I were you, I would amend the figure, too, just in case anyone happened to let slip what a deplorable and possibly illegal wage you've been paying him.'

Rex, nodding again, pulled a chequebook from his desk, popping the top off his fountain pen, writing on a cheque, blotting it carefully, tearing it off and handing it to me.

'Thank you, sir,' I said as I glanced at it. It was for two thousand pounds. 'Thank you very much.' Folding it, I put it in my inside pocket.

'Good,' said Hobbes. 'Now I'd like to have a word about a member of your staff.'

'Oh yes?' said Rex. 'By the way, may I introduce Mrs Witcherley, my wife.' He gestured towards the woman who, nodding, exhaled an acrid cloud.

'Delighted to meet you, Mrs Witcherley,' said Hobbes, taking her hand, raising it to his lips. For a moment I thought he was going to bite her and, from the way her eyes widened, I suspected the same thought had crossed her mind, yet her lips unpuckered into a smile.

'Delighted, Inspector,' she murmured.

'Mrs Witcherley and I have no secrets,' Rex said. 'Please feel free to ask anything.'

'Andy, you'd better step outside.' Hobbes strode across the carpet and opened Rex's door. 'I'll see you at home for lunch.'

Raising a hand in an ignored gesture of farewell, I cringed back into the main office. All eyes were looking at me, except for Basil Dean's strange one that always did its own thing.

Ingrid bustled towards me. 'Hi, Andy. What's happened to Phil?'

'Eh?' I asked, coherently, taken aback.

'Phil. What's happened to him?'

'Something's happened to him?'

'What?'

'I … umm … don't know.'

Oh,' she said, 'I thought you'd come here because of him.'

I was confused. 'Has something happened to Phil?'

'We don't know, which is why I'm asking you. I assumed the Inspector had come to investigate.'

'Investigate what?' I was enormously miffed to find her concerned about Phil when I was so obviously battered and bruised and she'd last seen me handcuffed in the middle of a riot.

There were tears in her eyes. 'He hasn't turned up for work today, and he's not at home.'

'Bloody Phil,' I muttered.

She stared at me as if I'd just booted a puppy.

'I meant, bloody hell, Phil's missing.' I said, trying to inject the authentic note of concern for the git.

She was crying, looking worried. 'No one knows what's happened to him. I went round to his house when he didn't ring in. His milk's still outside, he didn't respond when I knocked and he's not answering his mobile.'

'Oh,' I said, 'I wouldn't worry. He's probably working on a story and if he is missing, Hobbes'll find him, or someone will – like with the body last week.'

She didn't appear to find my words very comforting. 'You think he might be dead?' She sobbed, her pudgy little hands covering her mouth. 'Poor Phil.'

'Oh no,' I said, attempting reassurance, 'I'm sure he's not dead. Not yet. Well, probably not anyway. Look, I'm sure there's a perfectly reasonable explanation. He'll turn up, just you wait and see.'

He probably would turn up, I thought, though I wished he wouldn't. Yet, I smiled, Hobbes would still want a word with him when he reappeared.

'I suppose you're right.' She sniffed and moved slightly closer.

I raised my arm on impulse, with the idea of wrapping it around her shoulders, to comfort her, yet I couldn't see past her swollen red eyes and the little bead of mucus glistening at the corner of her nose. I recoiled, my arm dropping to my side.

'Sorry,' I said, 'but I've got to go.' It occurred to me that this was a good time to start undermining Phil. 'I'm sure Hobbes will find him. He probably guessed Hobbes wants to see him, to grill him about a serious crime, and has done a runner.'

'Is he in trouble?' asked Ingrid. 'I don't believe it.'

'You'd better believe it,' I said, raising my voice so everyone could hear. 'I'm afraid Phil is wanted for questioning about some pretty heavy stuff and could go down for a long time. He's been linked to some despicable characters involved in theft and kidnapping and now he's disappeared. Well, it doesn't prove anything, but it makes you think.'

On that climactic note I left, well satisfied with the shocked look on Ingrid's face and the interest I'd stirred up in the others. Phil would have a job explaining his way out of it. I gloated as I strolled along The Shambles back to Blackdog Street. I heard footsteps running as I reached the church.

The dog brushed past me, with Mrs Goodfellow clinging to his lead like a water-skier behind a speedboat, except water-skiers aren't known to carry big red shopping bags.

'Alright, dear? What have you been doing to yourself?'

'I, umm …' I said, and she was gone.

I heard a cry of 'Whoa!' as they flashed past the front door, heading down Ride Street in the direction of the park, making me wonder what I would do for lunch.

I needn't have worried. They'd reappeared by the time I got home, the dog trotting obediently to heel, tail wagging, tongue lolling, the epitome of friendliness. They pushed by when I opened the door. As I followed them into the kitchen, she put down a bowl of water, which he lapped up noisily, before sprawling under the table.

Mrs Goodfellow attended to lunch, which had been slowly cooking in the oven and filling the house with enticing smells. It was just a cottage pie, though not like the soggy, tasteless travesties in the Bellman's. This was a pie of delights, as I discovered on Hobbes's return. As usual, we ate in silence, which felt right, because Mrs Goodfellow's meals were deserving of reverence. Still, it bothered me that she never took food with us.

Hobbes and I finished, sitting back with a pair of contented sighs, rising from the table, taking our positions in the sitting room as normal, except that Dregs padded in after us, sitting with his head on Hobbes's knees and his big, heavy, hairy backside crushing my left foot. When Hobbes rested his hand on the dog's head it was barely noticeable among the mass of wiry hairs. Though I tried shuffling my foot, the blasted mutt seemed to like it and began wriggling in ecstasy, contriving to pin both my feet down, as well as wedging my knees against the sofa.

Mrs Goodfellow cackled as she carried in the tea tray. For probably the first time since I'd been there, I didn't jump; I couldn't.

'He seems to like you, dear.'

Hobbes smiled. 'I'm glad you two are getting on so well, Andy.'

I grimaced, which was all I could do by then as the bloody thing had managed to wriggle up my legs and was lying across me. The more I tried, the less I could move and soon, the brute's weight, being concentrated on my chest, it became increasingly difficult to breathe. In fact, I saw clearly that I was going to expire beneath him and couldn't even find enough breath to complain. What a way to go, I would have laughed if I could. The colours in the room were fading to a dull grey and I was looking at the world through a rapidly narrowing tunnel. I could see brightness at the end and seemed to be rushing towards it. My consciousness flew up, fluttering round the light shade like a large moth and I watched with moth's eyes and purely academic interest as Hobbes pushed the dog from my body. It did look battered, with the huge bruise around its right eye already showing more shades of colour than a sunset. Battered and blue. I remembered a lecture on first aid. Blue indicated cyanosis, which is what happens to a body when it's been deprived of oxygen for too long. I wondered why Hobbes was lifting me in such a way.

I came to, dangling upside down, my ankles squeezed in his left hand, my buttocks stinging, squirming, squawking like a chicken when I saw his right hand lifted to deliver another blow. I cried like a baby when it landed.

'Told you it'd work,' said Mrs Goodfellow. 'It always got 'em breathing when I was a midwife. You can put him down now. He's alright. His face is going red.'

I found myself swinging like a pendulum, the arcs growing wider until I was fully upright when he released his grip. I experienced a brief moment of weightlessness, as if becoming a moth again, before, catching my shoulders, he dropped me onto the sofa. Then the blasted dog leaped up, licking my face, making me wish I couldn't breathe again. It came as a great relief when Mrs Goodfellow dragged him off and led him to the kitchen.

'Sorry about that,' said Hobbes. 'I thought you were playing until you turned blue. It was quite unusual; your lips matched your eyes.

You don't see that every day.'

I shook my head and groaned.

'Glad you're better. You should be more careful, though. Dogs can be dangerous. Right then, I was going to tell you about the theft from the church. The first one that is, not the one by the despicable pamphlet pilferer.'

I laughed bitterly. I was not having a good day. The church clock struck two – two o'clock in the afternoon and I'd already been pursued by a dog, handcuffed by a policeman, reviled by a mob, been in a riot and been unconscious twice.

'Someone, as you know, broke into the wall safe and pinched the Roman cup. As far as I can make out, the person, or persons, did not break into the church, so, unless they had a key, which is unlikely, it's probable they attended the service on Sunday evening and hid until everything was quiet. Then they must have broken into the safe and slipped out when the warden opened the doors this morning.'

'Aha! That bloody Phil's gone missing. He must have done it.'

'I think we do need to find him,' said Hobbes, 'because he may know something of significance. It's probably more than coincidence that he went missing right after the robbery.'

'Let's hunt him down like the dog he is.' I felt the thrill of the chase rising within.

'Calm down, Andy, I didn't say he did it. There are some interesting aspects to this theft. Firstly, look at these.' Delving into his jacket pocket, he pulled out a sealed plastic bag, containing cigarette butts and chocolate wrappers.

'Interesting? Why?'

'I found them in a pew.'

'Well? So what? Doesn't it just mean someone's been smoking and eating in church?'

'It does, yet the pews are always swept after the service. Therefore, someone must have left them there after the sweeping and the church was closed to the public immediately afterwards.'

'Then,' I said, 'the burglar left them there. All it means is that he

136

smokes and eats chocolate.' I realised Phil didn't smoke. 'Phil eats chocolate.'

'So do I,' said Hobbes, 'and I'm not going to arrest every chocolate-eating smoker in Sorenchester and district. There's another interesting little fact. D'you remember the break in at Mr Roman's house?'

'Of course.'

'Well, don't you remember what I found under the tree to suggest the burglar had been watching the house?'

I thought a moment, creasing my forehead in concentration. 'Yeah. I remember: cigarette butts and chocolate wrappers.'

'Correct, and they were the same brand of cigarettes and the same wrappers as in the church. What's more, the cigarette butts are from a brand I'm not familiar with. They've mostly been smoked well down but there's a bit of writing on one of them. See here? It says "pati".'

'So it's likely the same person did both crimes.'

'So I suspect. I wonder why they wanted the Roman cup, though? What's so special about it? There are plenty of other, much more valuable, treasures in there that weren't stolen, just like at the museum. In both cases someone knew just what they were looking for and where to find it and everything else was apparently untouched.'

I nodded. 'So you think the same burglar has done Mr Roman's house, the museum and the church? All within a week. That's three crimes linked.'

'Four,' said Hobbes. 'The death of Jimmy the gardener is another obvious link, though I don't yet know why. If only Roman had told us what really happened.'

'And Phil has done a runner.' I thought I should remind him.

'He's certainly gone missing, which brings me to another coincidence. Mr Biggs from the museum discharged himself from the hospital last evening, against medical advice, and he, too, has vanished. I visited his flat this morning. He'd taken clothes as well as his passport.'

'He must have been in league with Phil.'

'Now, now, Andy.' Hobbes frowned. 'Still, I ought to have a look at Mr Waring's house and see if I can discover a reason for his disappearance. I'd be glad of your company if you want to come.'

'I'd love to.' I was convinced, or nearly convinced, that Phil had done it and dearly wanted to be there when justice caught up with him. With any luck, he was the one who'd killed Jimmy; a conviction for murder would keep him away from Ingrid for life. Even so, deep down, a persistent suspicion lurked that maybe I was only trying to convince Hobbes of Phil's guilt, because, if he believed it, then I, too, could legitimately believe it. A nasty, nagging question popped up from the uncharted depths of my mind and wouldn't go away; was I, in some way, jealous of Phil with his looks and charm and talent and easy, courteous way with women? I had to keep reminding myself that he was a smarmy git who deserved everything coming to him and that I deserved so much more, which Hobbes would help me to achieve.

'C'mon, Andy. There's no time for daydreaming, there are crimes to be solved. Mr Witcherley gave me Mr Waring's address. It's number two, Aristotle Drive.'

'Where's that?'

'Part of the new estate on the edge of town, out Sorington way.'

I nodded. 'Oh yeah, I know. They're rather smart.' Typical, I thought that Phil would live there. I remembered my late-lamented, grotty, little flat. Life wasn't fair but I wasn't jealous: I just don't like flash gits.

'We'd better take the car,' said Hobbes.

'Oh, great,' I muttered, my stomach churning, my pulse starting to race in emulation of his driving.

'You'd better change your suit first.' He glanced at my knees. 'You're a mess.'

Going up to my room, opening the wardrobe, I picked one of the half dozen suits hanging there at random. It was dark grey, fitting like it was bespoke. It gave me the shivers that someone else's clothes could be such an amazing fit. I'd always worn off-the-peg stuff and it had never been entirely satisfactory. 'It fits where it touches,' as Granny Caplet used to remark.

When I went down, Hobbes was standing by the door, the car keys dangling from his monstrous hand like an earring on a wild boar. 'Hurry up. I haven't got all day.'

I scurried to the car after him and climbed in. 'It's a one-way street,' I moaned as we set off.

Hobbes turned, grinning. 'And?'

I shut my eyes. 'I know, I know. You're only going one way.'

He laughed like a maniac.

'And the speed limit's thirty miles per hour.' I had to say it, though I recognised the futility.

'Don't worry,' he said over the screech of tyres and the blaring of a horn, 'we won't be driving anywhere near thirty miles in the next hour, so there's no chance of exceeding the speed limit.'

'Oh, that's alright, then,' I said, my sarcasm unremarked and wasted. I wondered if he really believed what he'd said.

When I opened my eyes, we were hurtling towards a crossroads – and we were on the minor road. Whimpering, I tried to close my eyes again, finding all my muscles had taken fright and refused to comply. As we crossed the dotted line, a blue car sped towards us from one direction, a white van approaching from the other. Though I don't know how, we avoided them both by the thickness of a layer of paint, zipping up the road ahead, leaping the traffic-calming bumps with the exuberance of a spring lamb and landing with a sickening thud. I know it was sickening because it made me sick. I only just managed to wind down the window in time. Mrs Goodfellow's cottage pie decorated the side of the car like lumpy go-faster stripes.

'Are you alright?' Hobbes asked.

'Never felt better in my entire life,' I said, my groan becoming a retch, ending as a hysterical laugh. I flopped back in the seat. He was staring at me, with a puzzled expression.

'Everything's just wonderful,' I giggled. 'Live fast. Die young. Leave a beautiful corpse. Or one smashed into a million bloody quivering fragments. Oh, yes, everything in the garden's roses.'

Hobbes was still frowning as we took the next speed bump. I guessed we were doing seventy. We'd have been faster if the wheels had stayed in contact with the road for longer.

'Yeehah!' I screamed.

Without looking away from me, Hobbes spun the wheel, skidded into Cranberry Lane and braked rapidly and smoothly. Only my seat belt prevented a close encounter of the painful kind with the windscreen. I stopped my crazed giggling, watching a small, dishevelled, black cat flee across the road in front of us, pursued by a fat ginger tom. At least we hadn't killed them and the thought calmed me until his foot stamped on the accelerator and the car leaped forward. Just to think, a couple of days earlier I'd believed I'd been getting used to his driving. No way. It's just that nerves can only take so much before exhaustion leads to acquiescence.

'I can go faster if you like.' At least he was looking the way we were going.

'No. Please.' I gulped. 'How did you do that?'

'Do what?'

'Stop before those cats ran out! You weren't even looking, for God's sake.'

'Language, Andy. I stopped the usual way, by pressing on the brake pedal and I don't need to look to find it, it's always in the same place.'

'Umm … why did you stop?'

'Because I didn't want to run over the animals.' He looked puzzled.

'What I mean is, how did you know they were there?'

'Oh, I see. Well, you learn to anticipate such things when you've been driving as long as I have.'

I thought, just for a moment, before he turned away, I could detect a hint of embarrassment in his expression. As he tugged the wheel, the car danced into Aristotle Drive. Phil's driveway was the first on the right, which meant we had to cross the road. Hobbes could have waited until the post-office van had passed but, no, he turned in front of it, the brakes screeching as we came to a standstill.

'Here we are,' he said. 'Not too bad a journey, eh?'

My head shook. I wasn't disagreeing, it was just that every part of me was shaking. Taking several long, deep breaths to calm myself, I staggered from the car, making sure not to look at my mess down the side, still queasy.

Phil's house looked as smart as all the others along the road. There was a small garden in the front and the brown, brittle leaves of the neatly trimmed beech hedge rattled in the breeze. The grass had grown long and straggly. Phil was evidently not a conscientious gardener, at least not in November. Two milk bottles stood, pale and neglected, by the doorstep.

'How do we get in? Have you got a key? Or one of those big metal rams they use on the telly?'

'Usually,' said Hobbes, 'I ring the doorbell first.'

He raised his hand, his fingernail appearing to slide forward like the point on a biro, and pressed the button. The bell rang somewhere inside. We waited in silence.

'Then, I usually knock.'

He raised his hand again, forming a mighty fist and knocked. The door shuddered, flying open, revealing a hall painted in magnolia, carpeted in beige, with a wooden door on the left side, a glass door leading into the kitchen at the far end and a staircase on the right. As we stepped inside, it was quiet: as quiet as the grave and nearly as cold. Everything was very neat and clean, smelling of bleach and detergent, without even a hint of socks. Hobbes opened the door on the left and I glanced into the lounge, disgusted by the enormous television, the hi-fi, the black leather suite and the deep, cream carpet.

'Stay there.' He prowled through the lounge, disappearing

through an archway at the far end, reappearing a few moments later through the kitchen door.

'No one in there,' he said, 'though there's a defrosted single-portion lasagne on top of the oven. Let's take a look upstairs.'

He led the way. A fish tank stood on a windowsill halfway up and its inhabitants danced and fluttered as we approached.

'They're hungry.' He sprinkled the water with flakes from a tub by the side. As the fish gorged amid an ecstasy of splashing and popping, he nodded, carrying on to the landing.

Five closed doors stood before us. Opening them one by one, he revealed first a bathroom and then four other rooms, one, stinking of cologne, with an en-suite bathroom, obviously Phil's bedroom. I sniffed in disapproval. The double bed with its black satin sheets had not been made and raised the question of why he needed a double bed. If he'd laid a finger on Ingrid … never mind his finger, if he'd laid anything on her, there was going to be trouble. Hobbes moved on, barely glancing into the sparsely furnished spare room and a box-room filled with sports gear and heavily loaded bookcases.

He headed straight into the last room, done out as an office, starting the computer in the corner, leafing through a diary while it warmed up, or whatever computers do. I'd never quite come to terms with them. I wasn't technophobic or anything, but machines just hated me. One computer had lost an article I'd struggled with for over two hours. I still maintain it wasn't my fault, it was just that the can of lager had got all shaken up as I ran from the Old Folks' Origami Extravaganza to file my report before deadline and it could have happened to anyone. Rex didn't see it like that, of course. After a long and vicious rant he'd assigned Phil to be my mentor. I couldn't believe it, for I'd been working for the *Bugle* far longer than he, and the worst part was when the bastard agreed. Rex loved Phil, just because he got reports in the paper every day. Luck always seemed to be on his side.

While Hobbes was hunched over the computer, jabbing away at the keys, I stood looking out the window, watching the expectant birds hopping around on the empty bird table in the back garden. A fluffy grey cat, springing from a shrub, completely missed them all as they scattered into the bushes.

Phil's business cards were stacked on the windowsill. Typical, I thought, for him to have business cards. For what reason? He didn't need that sort of thing to prove what a pretentious bastard he was. As I sneered, a thought occurred. They might have a use, one he would never have thought of. Hobbes, appearing engrossed by something on screen, I slipped a few into my pocket.

'That's interesting,' said Hobbes.

I started guiltily but he was still looking at the screen.

'It appears Mr Waring was researching an article on Mr Roman's death and had linked it to the body in the graveyard, too.'

'Oh?' I said. 'He was probably trying to give himself an alibi.'

'Enough, Andy,' Hobbes growled.

I flinched.

'There's no evidence that Philip Waring has committed any crime and it appears more likely he has been a victim of one. Investigative journalism can be dangerous, you know.'

Of course I knew. I had, after all, been mauled by a hamster in the course of my work. Besides, I was working with Hobbes. How much more dangerous could it get?

He looked at the diary again. 'Last night he was going to meet someone called "T".'

'"T" for Tony?'

'Possibly,' he mused. 'However, there may be other possibilities. Mr Waring obviously expected to return, otherwise he wouldn't have defrosted the lasagne. There's no evidence of a struggle or of anyone else being here in the last few days, so he left of his own accord. I think we ought to catch up with Tony Derrick and see if he is the contact.'

'So how are we going to find him?'

'With patience and skill,' he grinned. 'I called in on Billy earlier. Tony wasn't in last night and no one had heard from him. Mind you, Tony's not the sort to have friends and most of his acquaintances are not the sort to talk.'

'He was in Phil's car on Saturday night and Phil is always pretending to be friendly.'

'Pretending?' He grimaced. 'Everyone else I've spoken to remarked on his friendliness.'

'That's cos he's a phoney.'

'Well, someone is,' said Hobbes with a scowl. 'It hardly matters anyway. He's a member of the public and I suspect he's in trouble. Therefore, it's my job to get him out of trouble.'

Affronted by Hobbes's implication that I might be the phoney, I made up my mind to show him evidence proving how much of a git Phil was, even if I had to make it myself. All of a sudden in a sulky mood, I followed him around the house, barely noticing what he was up to, silently sneering at Phil's taste in everything, especially his cabinet filled with sporting trophies. The guy was unbelievable, even owning Wagner CDs and no one has that sort of crap, except to impress the feeble minded. Well, it didn't work on me. And then there was his book collection. Why have all those volumes on Roman Sorenchester? As for his spice rack and everything else in the sodding house, I found it all too much.

I was happy to leave. The whole house reeked of his achievements. I wasn't jealous; I was just glad he was out of the picture.

10

Still in a deep sulk when we got back into the car, not inclined to pay attention to anything, I was barely aware of Hobbes's mobile chirruping and him answering.

Turning towards me, putting the phone back in his pocket, sticking the key in the ignition, he said, 'There's been a robbery with violence.'

'Oh.'

'I don't like such crimes on my patch. They make me angry and that is a bad thing … for someone.'

'Oh.'

'Don't you want to hear about it?' He sounded puzzled. 'I thought you'd be interested.'

With a huge effort, I forced myself to be fair. 'Sorry,' I said, 'I'm just upset about Phil.' I was being truthful, in a way.

'I understand,' he said. 'It's a bad feeling when a comrade goes missing, though, for some reason, I'd formed an opinion that you didn't like him. I believe everyone deals with bad news in their own way.'

I nodded. Again, I felt I might not be entirely in the right. Ignoring the feeling, I asked about the robbery.

'I'll tell you on the way over.' He started the car's engine with a throbbing series of revs and in moments we were hurtling along the road. I didn't know where, because with Hobbes behind the wheel, ignorance was, if not blissful, less terrifying.

'It happened this morning,' he said, 'just out of town on the Green Way.'

'The Green Way? Isn't that an old Roman road?'

'So it's said. Why?'

'Oh, I don't know. It's just with the Roman Cup going missing and the bracelet – wasn't that something to do with the Order of St George? – and wasn't St George a Roman?'

'I am aware,' said Hobbes, 'that St George is venerated by Eastern European churches, who believe he was a tribune in the Roman army. If I remember rightly, the despotic Emperor Diocletian had him beheaded.'

'So he was a Roman.' I enjoyed the brief elation of triumph.

'If the old tales are true.' He shrugged. 'What are you getting at?'

'Well, everything seems to have a Roman connection: Roman cups, Roman saints, Roman roads.'

'Not to forget the unfortunate Mr Roman,' said Hobbes with a grin.

'Yes, well. Though it does make you think, doesn't it?'

'It does. And I expect you're going to tell me all about Mr Waring's collection of books on Roman Sorenchester.'

'Does he have one?' I asked, innocently. 'Well, how strange, he never told me he was interested in antiquities. I wonder where he got them from.'

'He is a Friend of Sorenchester Museum and many of the books are on loan from there.'

'Then he'd have known all about the museum and he'd be likely to know what was in the store.'

'Quite possibly and I'm sure it will be extremely useful to have a word with him. However, it's really not difficult to make all sorts of dubious Roman connections round here. After all, they founded the town. And there are three hundred and twenty-seven Friends of the Museum. I checked because, you're absolutely right, the burglars knew exactly what they were looking for and where to find it.'

'OK,' I said, 'I was only saying. It just hit me, that's all. Now, what happened this morning?'

The car's engine roared. Now and again car horns blared, sometimes coinciding with wild and erratic movements. I, however, saw no evil, though it is amazingly difficult to keep your eyes closed when peril is all around.

'What I know,' said Hobbes, 'is that a robbery occurred at a house used by a Mr Arthur Barrington-Oddy – and I have no evidence to suggest he's a Roman. Apparently, when Mr Barrington-Oddy opened his front door to answer the doorbell, two masked men were standing there ...'

'Two men? How very interesting.'

'...and, before he had a chance to defend himself, they overpowered him, rendering him unconscious by means of a noxious substance that caused minor burns to the skin around his mouth and nose.'

'What would do that?'

'Chloroform sounds most plausible at this stage. Mr Barrington-Oddy woke some time later feeling giddy and ill but managed to reach a telephone and call for help. He is now recuperating in hospital.'

'So, what was stolen?'

'He doesn't know, because he's only renting the house. However, he could tell a display cabinet had been broken into.'

'So, whose house is it?'

He laughed. 'Give us a break, Andy, I was only on the phone a minute, not long enough to ascertain all the facts. Anyway, if detecting was that easy then anyone could do it.'

'Even me, you mean?'

'Well perhaps not everyone. Now, hold tight!'

The car, lurching and banking, gravel scrunching, we stopped with a skid and I opened my eyes. We'd stopped within an inch of a police car, from which a pale-faced, grey-haired constable was emerging.

'Here we are.' Stopping the engine, Hobbes opened the door.

Undoing my seat belt with shaky hands, I got out onto a gravelled drive. A turreted old house stood in front of us, lurking in the shadows of a large, tree-infested garden that I suspected would look right impressive in the summer, though it was desolate in grey November. A gleaming plaque on the studded door, above a polished brass knocker in the shape of a bear's head, indicated the house was called Brancastle.

The constable saluted. 'Good afternoon, sir.'

'Afternoon, George,' Hobbes nodded. 'What's going on here then?'

'A forced entry, sir, and a robbery. Mr Barrington-Oddy has already been released from hospital and is returning by taxi. He may be able to answer some of your questions.'

'Good,' said Hobbes. 'In the meantime, I'd better take a look around. Andy, would you stay here with PC Wilkes?'

'Yeah, OK.'

Hobbes squatted down, crawling over the gravel towards the front door, PC Wilkes and I, standing by the police car, watching until he disappeared inside the house.

'Weird,' said Wilkes. 'Was he sniffing then?'

'Umm … it sounded like it.'

'I don't know what it is but something about him gives me the creeps.'

'I know what you mean,' I said.

'Yeah.' Wilkes grimaced. 'I know he's a copper, and a good one, and there's less crime on his patch than most others and a better clean up rate, but there's something unnatural about him. No … not unnatural; if anything he's too natural. Unhuman, is that the right word?'

'Inhuman?' I suggested.

Wilkes pondered. 'Maybe not – inhuman sounds like he's cruel or something and he isn't. Well, not really.'

I agreed. 'I see what you're getting at.' I thought for a moment about all his oddities. 'Unhuman sums him up rather well.'

'Still,' said Wilkes, 'he's a feature of Sorenchester Police. All the regional coppers know him by reputation at least. I guess he must be about due for retirement. Mind you, that's what I thought when I transferred here, nearly twenty years ago. What's your connection with him?'

'I'm staying with him temporarily, because my flat burned down last week. By the way, my name's Andy. Andy Caplet.'

'George Wilkes.' He nodded, his broad, slow face brightening with a smile of recognition. 'You're the journalist aren't you? The bloke from the *Bugle*? I've heard about you. What on earth did you do to get saddled with the Inspector?'

'I don't know.' I frowned. 'I've left the *Bugle* now. I'm freelance.'

'Yeah, I heard you'd got the boot. And aren't you the guy that got his ear chomped at the pet show?'

I acknowledged the fact.

He laughed. 'I can still remember your photo in the paper: what an expression! Yeah, that's it, you're doing it again.' He continued to laugh, leaning against the police car, until a taxi turned into the drive, scattering gravel. Then wiping his eyes, grinning, he stood upright, patted me on the back and stepped towards the taxi.

Rage and fury built within me and, though I wanted to say something fine and biting, a retort to cut him down to size, I couldn't think of anything. 'Hah!' I said, frustrated, turning away, wishing I had something to kick. Anything.

Then I had a brilliant idea. Walking towards the door of the house, my hand casually thrust into my jacket pocket, climbing up the steps, I peeked into the entrance hall, seeing no sign of Hobbes. Casually, removing my hand from the pocket, letting one of Phil's cards flutter to the dark, parquet floor, I used my foot to push it partly under the rug.

It was a lovely rug with a startling pattern of flowers, trees and birds woven amid brilliant colours and I guessed it was very old. My parents' friends, the Moffatts, used to have one a bit like it, which they'd picked up in Turkey, having beaten a desperate peasant down to a ludicrously low price. I'd heard them boast about it many times, yet this was far finer than theirs.

I heard a clatter from within. 'Mr Barrington-Oddy's returned,' I shouted.

'Thanks.' Hobbes's voice replied from behind a tall, dark dresser, glittering with expensive looking knick-knacks. 'I'll just be a minute.'

I went back down the steps, strolling towards the cars, my heart thumping, knowing I'd dropped Phil right in it, convinced Hobbes would now see him for what he was. Yet, I already felt guilty, and might have turned back and retrieved the card had Hobbes not appeared in the doorway, flattening my good intentions under his heavy boots. I'd really done it, for good or ill; I half hoped he wouldn't notice it.

Wilkes was assisting Mr Barrington-Oddy from the taxi as Hobbes came alongside and introduced himself. Barrington-Oddy shook his hand without even flinching, obviously a man with great stiffness in his upper lip. He was very tall, very thin and very grey, wore a heavy, dark suit with a waistcoat and regimental tie and I wasn't at all surprised to learn he was a retired barrister, though barristers are rarely portrayed with angry-looking blisters around their mouths and noses.

When Hobbes introduced me, I didn't warrant a handshake, just a curt nod.

Barrington-Oddy, possessing a clipped, posh voice, the sort rarely heard except in parody, addressed Hobbes. 'I trust you will brook no delay in apprehending the miscreants. In the meantime, shall we go inside? I find the clammy chill this time of year to be exceedingly bad for my constitution.'

Hobbes and I followed him inside, Wilkes taking up his position by the car. He grinned sarcastically, while I smirked, glad he was being left outside in the cold. As Hobbes shut the front door behind us, I was astonished how gloomy it became.

'Take a seat,' said Barrington-Oddy, entering a room, turning on the lights.

It was, I guessed, a drawing room, impressive in an oppressive way. Everything looked heavy and fussy. Dark panelling lined the walls, on which hung dark portraits of stern, humourless individuals in rich, dark clothing. An old black clock, intricately carved with grotesque demon shapes ticked on the mantelpiece, looking both fascinating and repulsive. The only thing in the room I could admire without condition was the carpet, similar to the rug in the entrance hall, though even richer and heavier. A sad fire glowed in the grate and I was grateful when Barrington-Oddy stirred it with a poker and placed a couple of chunky logs on top; the place certainly needed some heat. Shivering, I almost envied Wilkes who was, no doubt, lounging comfortably in his police car. I sat next to Hobbes on a solid, leather-backed chair in front of a solid, leather-covered table. Nothing in the room looked even vaguely Roman, with the exception of Barrington-Oddy's nose.

'I apologise. My man, Errol, would normally have attended to the fire but he's been called away on urgent family business.' Barrington-Oddy, straightening up, shut the drawing room door and relaxed into a deep, dark armchair.

I wished I'd positioned myself a little closer to the heat as I had to keep clamping my jaws together to stop my teeth rattling. Hobbes never appeared to notice the cold.

'Right, Inspector,' Barrington-Oddy began, his tone suggesting he was in charge, 'I suppose I ought to inform you of what happened. I might as well, as I'm sure I've already told most of your colleagues.'

'If you would be so good, sir,' said Hobbes.

'Let me begin. I intend residing in Sorenchester until the New Year while researching a book concerning the influence of Roman law on aspects of modern English jurisprudence.'

Jumping at the mention of Roman law, I glanced significantly at Hobbes, who ignored me.

'I chose this place,' Barrington-Oddy continued, 'because the local museum has a number of fascinating artefacts and documents that are proving exceedingly valuable.'

The museum connection had reappeared and I wasted another significant glance on Hobbes. Somehow, I felt as if I was trying to build a jigsaw puzzle from a handful of pieces and no idea of the overall picture. Yet, everything had to fit together.

'I was transcribing some notes I'd made last week and was indexing the details when the doorbell rang,' said Barrington-Oddy. 'I waited, expecting Errol to answer and when it rang again I recalled he was absent. I was somewhat annoyed as I dislike being interrupted when at work, yet I thought I ought to go. I rather wish I hadn't.'

'I'm not surprised, sir,' Hobbes said, 'you've had a most unpleasant experience.'

'Most unpleasant indeed. When I opened the door, two masked figures were standing there and before I could react they sprang on me. A pad impregnated, so I am informed, with chloroform was clamped over my face, the world began spinning and that is all I can remember until I awoke in the entrance hall. As soon as I felt able, I contacted the police and made a quick surveillance of the house. I am not aware of anything being taken. However, that cabinet,' he pointed towards a mahogany and glass monstrosity in the corner, 'has been broken into. As far as I can tell, nothing else was touched. The two men had gone.'

'Thank you, sir,' Hobbes said gravely. 'A most succinct account. Now, sir, could you describe your attackers?'

'Well,' said Barrington-Oddy with a frown, 'I didn't have long enough to form anything other than the slightest impression of them. As I said, they wore masks, or rather, one wore something like a balaclava with eyeholes and the other had a brown scarf around his face and a trilby hat pulled down low. I can't recall anything further.'

'Any idea of their sizes or ages?' Hobbes asked.

'Sorry, not much. Though I believe neither was as tall as I, the taller of the two, the one wearing the scarf, appeared somewhat skinny. That's really your lot, except, yes, there was a faint smell like flowers before they got the pad over my nose. They took me entirely by surprise, I regret to say.'

'Any idea how long you were unconscious, sir?'

'No, though it can't have been long because I'd just prepared a pot of coffee and it was still warm when I came back in here. I took a sip because of an unpleasant taste in my mouth, which felt as dry as water biscuits.'

'Do you have any idea what was taken, sir?'

'Not really. There are a number of antiques in the cabinet but I'm not so familiar with them that I can identify what has been removed, though there may be a space where there wasn't one before. Errol could probably tell you, because he dusted in here. Unfortunately he's in Jamaica.'

'What about the house's owner?'

'She would probably know,' said Barrington-Oddy. 'Unfortunately, she's in Switzerland, I believe.'

'That is unfortunate,' said Hobbes. 'Do you happen to know how I can contact her? And what her name might be?'

'It's Mrs Jane Ilionescu. I don't know the woman – I'm renting through an agent. The number's on this.' Mr Barrington-Oddy reached into a drawer and handed a card to Hobbes.

All through the interview I'd kept quiet but I ventured a question. 'Is the owner a foreigner then? I mean with a surname like that?'

'I believe she is English,' said Barrington-Oddy. 'She married a foreign gentleman, now unfortunately deceased. If you require any further information, I would advise contacting the agent.'

'Thank you, sir.' Hobbes nodded, rising to his feet. 'Now, would you mind if I take a closer look at the cabinet?'

'Please do,' said Barrington-Oddy. 'My daily routine has been entirely disrupted already. If you have any questions, please feel free to ask. I doubt, though, that I will be of much help. I am not, I regret, an observant man. I focus only on what is important to my work.'

'Very good, sir,' Hobbes said, approaching the display cabinet as if stalking a deer. He squatted onto his haunches, creeping forward, examining the carpet, sniffing the air and apparently listening.

I sat still, glad the fire had begun to compete with the damp chill. Brancastle was a grand old house in its way, yet I hated it and couldn't blame Mrs Whatsaname for going away. Mr Barrington-Oddy, lighting a pipe, sank back into his armchair, eyes closed, hands folded over his stomach, almost as if he'd fallen asleep. A heavy cloud billowed about him, curling tendrils reaching out into the room.

Hobbes, unfolding into his usual hunched stance as he reached the cabinet, opened its door, peering at the damaged lock. 'This was forced using a knife with a broad blade. I can't see any sign of fingerprints. Your man Errol obviously dusts well and the burglars wore gloves, which isn't surprising, as it's winter. Hallo, hallo, hallo. What's this?'

Frowning with concentration, leaning forward, he plucked at the cabinet, close to where the knife had been forced in. I was astonished how delicate and precise he could be, although, when he raised his fingers to the light, I could see nothing.

'What is it?'

'Some fibres were caught where the wood's splintered. I'll bet they came off a glove. A black one: woollen.' Dropping them into a polythene bag, he sniffed. 'Hmm. There's a faint hint of flowers.'

I couldn't smell anything other than Barrington-Oddy's suffocating pipe smoke that, having formed a dense layer at head height, was stinging my eyes and making my nose run.

'Two people,' said Hobbes, staring at the carpet, 'one tall, wearing shoes with a smooth sole and a bit of a heel. He was light of build, soft treading, and wore black woollen gloves smelling of flowers, a scarf and a trilby. The other one was of medium build, wearing new trainers and a balaclava with eyeholes. Well, if I see anyone fitting those descriptions, I'll be sure to arrest them.'

The doorbell rang. Barrington-Oddy's eyes opened, holding a momentary look of concern, unsurprising in the circumstances. 'I wonder who it could be.'

'Could you get it, Andy?' asked Hobbes.

PC Wilkes stood at the door. 'Sir!' he called across the hall. 'I've been ordered back to the station and thought I'd better tell you. Hallo.' He glanced down by his feet. 'What's this?' Stooping, he picked up Phil's card.

I'd nearly forgotten about it. A sudden cold feeling gripped my stomach and again, for a moment, I wished I hadn't done it.

'What is it, George?' Hobbes walked towards us.

'A business card, sir. The name on it is Philip Waring of the *Sorenchester and District Bugle*. Isn't he the journalist who's gone missing? I wonder what he was doing here.'

'I've never heard of the chap,' said Barrington-Oddy, from the drawing room.

Hobbes took the card with a glance that made my stomach leap in terror. Had my little ploy backfired?

'Perhaps,' said PC Wilkes, 'it was dropped during the struggle with Mr Barrington-Oddy. Perhaps this Waring was one of the men who did it.'

'Precisely what I was thinking, constable,' said Barrington-Oddy, approaching, looking at the card in Hobbes's hand. 'It's screwed up and grubby: hardly what a chap would leave if he desired an appointment.'

Saying nothing, my pulse racing, my breath coming in rapid gasps, I turned away so it wouldn't be obvious, trying to feel triumphant that my scheme was working. I'd dropped Phil right into the shit and Ingrid would be mine. Yet, somehow, I felt no pleasure. Now I'd really got him, confusion overwhelmed me and, though part of me was cheering, another part cowered in fear of discovery. I made a decision to dispose of his other cards as soon as possible.

In addition, my conscience was insisting that I stop right there, confessing my little ruse before any harm came of it. Yet, if I did, I'd be a laughing stock to the police, Hobbes would be furious and I wondered whether I might even have committed a crime. Besides, I daren't let Barrington-Oddy know; there'd always been something about a barrister's eyes that gave me the creeps.

'Very interesting,' said Hobbes. 'Well spotted, Wilkes. Now you'd better be getting back to the station.' He turned towards Barrington-Oddy. 'We'll be on the lookout for Philip Waring. There is a good chance he can help us with this investigation. And I'll be in contact with the house agent to find out what's been taken. Good afternoon, sir.'

He shook Mr Barrington-Oddy's hand and we left him framed in the doorway of a house that might have featured in a gothic horror film. I was glad to be out of it, glad to leave his fierce barrister's eyes behind. Wilkes, saluting, slipped into his car and headed back to Sorenchester. I expected we'd follow him back to the station. Instead, on leaving the gardens, we turned left.

'Where are we going?'

'To have a word with the next door neighbour. The evidence suddenly seems to be pointing at Philip Waring, doesn't it?'

'Apparently,' I said, 'though I don't think we should jump to conclusions.'

'Oh,' said Hobbes quietly, 'I never do that. However, I thought you'd be overjoyed your suspicions appear to be well-founded.'

I nodded, feeling sick – and not from his driving. We'd only gone a couple of hundred yards when he turned left down a narrow, rutted lane, pulling up next to an angular stone building a few bumpy moments later.

'This,' he said, 'is the Olde Toll House. Of course, it was never really a tollhouse. It's a deliberate misspelling, because people were alarmed by its original name.'

'Why? What's was it called before?'

'The Olde Troll House. We're going to have a quick word with the Olde Troll himself. His name's Leroy but he likes to be called Rocky.'

'We're going to see a troll?'

'Not just any old troll.' He grinned. 'Rocky is a friend of mine, so be careful what you say; he's a little sensitive about his appearance.'

I didn't know what to think. Life had not prepared me for meeting trolls. Still, come to think of it, life hadn't prepared me for meeting ghouls either and I'd got away with it: just about, anyway.

'This way.' Hobbes, springing from the car, beckoned me through the deepening gloom. I followed, my breath curling like dragon smoke in the clammy air as he headed towards an open porch, where a king-sized pair of green wellingtons stood beside a heavy walking stick. Though the bright red door was closed, someone had pinned a note to it, saying, 'I'm in.' A great chain hung from the ceiling. Hobbes pulled it and a low chime I could feel through my feet bonged through the structure. There were a few seconds of vibration and then silence. The door opened.

'It's a bit late for trick or treating,' said a guttural voice. A face, pale and round as the full moon before age had cratered its surface appeared, smiling, from the blackness within. ''ello, 'obbes. 'ow the devil are you old boy?'

'Pretty well, Rocky.' Hobbes shook his hand. 'This is Andy who's helping me with some cases.'

'Delighted to meet you, laddie,' Rocky beamed. 'Now come on into the parlour. I've just made a pot of tea.'

We followed him into a small room, where a cheerful fire made the shadows dance. It felt so much cosier than Barrington-Oddy's dank study.

'Please make yourselves comfortable,' said Rocky, 'and I'll get some light.' Poking a taper into the fire, he lit an oil lamp, placing it on a low sideboard.

Only then did I get a proper sight of him and gasped, because he looked so normal. That is, he would have passed for a rather chubby, human male, six foot tall, broad, bald, clean shaven, wearing well-worn khaki corduroy trousers, a checked shirt and a blue cardigan with a hole in the left elbow. I guessed he was in his mid-sixties.

'I'll fetch the tea,' he said, leaving the parlour through a door opposite to where we'd entered.

'He doesn't look like a troll,' I whispered.

'Shhh,' said Hobbes. 'As I said, he's sensitive about his appearance. Please don't bring it up again.'

I shut up, wondering whether Hobbes was having another joke at my expense, like with the so-called gnome, yet, when Rocky returned with the tea tray, there was something odd about him, though it was difficult to say quite what. His movements weren't right, his arms and legs not bending quite as they should have, while his shovel hands were huge, even bigger than Hobbes's great paws, though hairless and pale. When he handed me a mug of tea I discovered they were as smooth as marble. And, despite the roaring fire in the grate, as cold as marble, too.

'There are biscuits if you want some. I've got a tin of them 'obnobs, or there's crumpets for toasting, if you'd prefer.'

'Just a cup of tea,' said Hobbes. 'Oh, go on then, let's have a crumpet.'

Rocky returned to the kitchen, coming back carrying another tray with a full butter-dish, a smoke-blackened toasting fork and a plate of crumpets. A delicious, warm aroma filled the little room as he toasted them at the fire, while Hobbes informed him about the recent crimes, culminating in the attack on Barrington-Oddy.

'D'you know Mr Barrington-Oddy?' Hobbes asked.

Rocky shook his head. 'I've seen 'im out in 'is car once or twice but 'aven't spoken to 'im. 'e keeps 'is self to 'is self.'

'What about the owner?'

Rocky buttered a crumpet, passing it to me on a plate before answering. 'I don't know the missus too well. She's much younger than 'e was and I reckon she only married the old boy for 'is money. Mind you, 'e 'ad a lot and no one to share it with. I know 'e thought 'e'd made a good bargain and, to be fair, she stuck to it and made 'is last years 'appy ones. I knew the old man well enough. 'e came 'ere after the last war, did old Nenea. Poor as a church mouse 'e was then, though 'e 'ad a way with business and was pretty well set up in the end. 'e never married 'till 'is declining years.'

'D'you know where he came from?' Hobbes asked.

'Nenea? Yes of course. Now where was it? 'e used to call it the old country. It was where Dracula came from, though 'e said 'e wasn't from that part. Romania, that's it.'

'Interesting,' said Hobbes. 'Now, have you seen any suspicious strangers around these parts in the last day or two?'

Rocky handed him a crumpet.

I'd already sunk my teeth into mine. It was warm, the butter dripping from it like honey from a honeycomb. Hobbes took a bite.

'Excellent,' he pronounced.

'Strangers?' Rocky scratched his head with a sound like two pebbles rubbing together. 'Well, there was a car as went speeding off down the lane this morning. Blue it was. One of them German ones. An Audi. Old Fred in the village, 'is son used to 'ave one like it. Nice car. It 'ad two folks in it and they was goin' real fast so as I couldn't recognise 'em and I 'adn't seen the car round 'ere before.'

My mouth dropped open. Phil's car was a blue Audi. Maybe the seed of guilt that had sprouted in my conscience would shrivel and die. Maybe, I'd been right all along and my prejudice against him didn't necessarily mean he wasn't a genuine villain. It was only then that I finally acknowledged to myself that I had been prejudiced. It was because he was slim, because he was better educated, better spoken and, I winced, a better journalist than I would ever be. It was no wonder Ingrid preferred him. I began to wallow in self-pity.

Hobbes, having finished his crumpet, was talking. 'That's most helpful. You see an individual I wish to interview owns a blue Audi. I don't suppose you were able to get its number?'

'Sorry, old boy, it was all covered in muck: too thick to see through. Fancy another crumpet?'

'Though it's tempting, we'd better not.' Hobbes smiled. 'I've got to think of my figure and Mrs Goodfellow doesn't like it if I ruin my appetite by eating between meals.'

''ow is the young lass?' asked Rocky. ''as she got over losing that daft 'usband of 'ers?'

'She's doing well,' Hobbes said, 'and rather enjoying having a young man around the house. Mind, she's only locked him in the cellar the once. So far.'

I smiled, stupidly pleased to be described as a young man. No one had called me that for a decade. I confess a little anxiety was there, too. How many more times was I likely to be locked down there?

'Still,' Hobbes continued, 'she hasn't actually got over losing Mr Goodfellow; she can't because she hasn't really lost him. She knows exactly where he is and can't be bothered to fetch him back. She reckons he's happy where he is and she's happy he's not getting under her feet.'

'Glad to 'ear it.' Rocky laughed, reminiscently. 'I remember the first time you brought 'er round 'ere. A skinny little lass, cooing over 'er rag dolly. We 'ad crumpets then an' all. They grow up so fast.'

'Indeed they do.' Hobbes chuckled. 'You must come round to supper sometime. I'm sure she'd be delighted.'

Rocky smiled. 'That'd be nice, old boy. I 'aven't been gettin' around so much recently, cos me old joints are turning to chalk but I'd like to see the lass again.'

I gawped in astonishment and confusion. Not for the first time since I'd met Hobbes, I didn't get it. I mean, how old was this Rocky? And why did both he and Hobbes refer to Mrs Goodfellow as 'the lass'? And as for Mr Goodfellow, what on God's good earth had happened to him? I'd assumed he was dead and had accepted his old suits without too much thought, except for a vague feeling of spookiness.

It struck me how peculiar it was to feel so comfortable, so at home, in Rocky's parlour. He was a bloody troll, for Christ's sake and trolls, at least in all the stories I could remember, were bad things, savage, wild creatures who killed people and threatened to gobble up Billy Goatgruff, or whatever his name was. Yet, this one was giving me tea and crumpets in a cosy parlour while chatting with an old friend. It was all far too difficult to comprehend. Still, it says something about the change in me that, despite appearances, I had no doubt Rocky wasn't human and, what's more, was sanguine about it. What a difference a few days with Hobbes had made to my life! There was so much more going on than I'd ever imagined. Mind you, I never entirely discounted the likelihood that I'd gone quietly insane. And, if I had, so what? Things were still looking up.

Hobbes and Rocky plunged into a deep conversation about the old days and though I started to listen, the warmth and the crumpets conspired to make me drowsy. I remained vaguely aware of the trickle of melted butter down my chin and the rise and fall of their talk. I think they were discussing a mutual friend, who'd gone down with the Titanic and turned up in Bournemouth but it's possible I was dreaming.

I awoke to total confusion and the chimes of Big Ben, apparently coming from the clock on the mantelpiece.

'Six o'clock already,' said Hobbes. 'Time we were getting back for our suppers. Time for Andy to wake up.'

Hobbes got to his feet, shaking Rocky's hand. I followed his lead. It was like shaking hands with a statue, except there was flexibility and a pulse, and I was grateful for his gentleness, my bandaged hand still being a little sore.

'Thank you for your hospitality,' Hobbes said and I nodded my agreement. Stepping outside, we made our farewells, got into the car and sped home.

'A nice man ... umm ... chap, Rocky,' I said, as we narrowly avoided a wall.

'Indeed. He's the white sheep of his family; some of the others aren't quite so civilised but the Olde Troll's always been a good friend.'

Hobbes swerved to avoid a tractor and began humming 'Dooby Dun' under his breath. Though I thought I almost recognised the tune, I couldn't quite get it.

'What's the song?'

'Dooby Dun,' he replied, 'by Gill Butt and Sully Van.'

'Strange. I thought I knew it. How's it go?'

'When constabulary duties dooby dun, dooby dun,' he sang in a surprisingly mellow, if noisy, baritone.

I joined in. 'A policeman's lot is not an happy one.'

'All wrong of course,' he said. 'It's fun being a policeman.'

Looking at his manic grin as he hurtled past the red light at the end of the Green Way, I could believe it.

11

We made a brief stop at the police station and, since he said he'd only be a short while, I decided to wait in the car. After a couple of minutes, PC Wilkes walked past, grinning and waving, while I pretended to be engrossed in a map book.

A few moments later, Hobbes returned. 'We might as well leave the car here. There's plenty of time for a brisk walk home before supper and I haven't had my exercise today. Come along, and quickly.'

Understanding how a fat, lazy cat must feel when plucked from its cosy doze by the fire and turfed out into the night, I got out with as much enthusiasm as I could muster, which wasn't much, although the relief of not having to endure his driving again was some comfort.

'PC Poll's much better,' said Hobbes as we set off for Blackdog Street. 'He suffered a very minor concussion and is resting at home now.'

Though I'm sure he wasn't trying, his stride was just long enough to compel me to scurry in an undignified fashion to keep up. 'Good,' I said, two steps behind.

'Actually, they're all out of hospital and there's a nice little article about the riot in the *Bugle* – George Wilkes showed me – and there's a fine photograph of you. Here, take a look.' Rummaging in his coat pocket, pulling out the evening paper, he handed it to me.

A fine photograph? I could see why Wilkes had grinned. Cringing, open-mouthed, handcuffed, gormless, I dominated the front page, Constable Poll's long arm feeling my collar, an angry woman waving a bony finger under my nose. My expression was similar to the one I'd displayed when the bloodthirsty hamster had savaged my ear. I gritted my teeth, thinking what a proud man my father would be if he ever saw it. Still, I didn't look as agonised as Dreg's former master, who was brandishing a bit of fence while the dog ripped his trouser leg.

A teenaged-boy, all zits, lank hair and dandruff, glanced at me in passing. He nudged his mate and his mate nudged another mate who was holding the *Bugle*. They all sniggered.

'There's still no sign of Mr Waring, or of Mr Biggs from the museum,' said Hobbes, seemingly oblivious to my embarrassment.

'Oh, isn't there?' Trying to play it cool, I caught my foot on a cracked paving slab and stumbled. As the sniggers ripened into jeers and laughter, I was glad I was making someone happy. Actually, I wasn't. I'd have much preferred to make them very miserable with my boot. However, I kept running after Hobbes, trying to pretend I never noticed lower forms of life. 'Dignity is the ticket to success,' my father used to say, though I never believed there was much dignity poking around in people's mouths.

'The forensic lads got back about the body,' Hobbes continued, 'and made a positive DNA match with Jimmy Pinker, so there's no doubt he was the victim. He'd been killed by a single thrust of an extremely sharp blade into his heart. There's no sign of the weapon yet. What's more, whoever messed up his face did it with a shovel after he was dead.

'They also tested the mud on his wellingtons; it was probably from Mr Roman's garden, and the dried stuff I found in the house fits the tread, plus there were fibres from the carpet, proving Jimmy was at Mr Roman's shortly before he was killed, so it is likely he was the one that broke in. However, as he wasn't a smoker, the cigarette butts in the bush suggest an accomplice, unless by coincidence another individual hid there at roughly the same time.'

'Oh, right.' I tried to throw my mind back to the body in the grave case. All the break-ins and the attack on Mr Barrington-Oddy had almost driven it from my mind and I was surprised Hobbes was still interested. 'Poor Anna,' I said, remembering her big eyes and smile.

Hobbes nodded. 'I'd already warned her to expect the worst. She took it as badly as you might expect. She's a soft-hearted young lady and I've arranged for a friend to stay with her; she'll need one. If there's one thing I don't like about policing, it's telling bad news to people. Still, she deserves much better than poor Jimmy and maybe she'll be luckier next time around.'

I was touched by his thoughtfulness; sometimes he appeared almost human. With that, a thought, germinating in a dark corner of my brain, sprouted making me gasp and my head spin as I struggled to comprehend what it meant. PC Wilkes had suggested Hobbes was unhuman. Hell's Bells! Though, almost from the start I'd realised he was different, it had never crossed my mind that he might really not be a human being. After all, being human was the least anyone might expect from a policeman.

I doubt the possibility would ever have crossed my mind had I not already met the ghouls and Rocky, the Olde Troll, who looked like a man. Shaking my head, I tried to dismiss the idea, yet, in a crazy way, it made sense. It was more than possible Hobbes wasn't human. Yet, if not, what was he? And how would I be able to find out? Suddenly, I was trembling: not with fear but with a strange excitement.

Hobbes's great hand patted me gently on the shoulder and I stumbled. 'Chin up, Andy. It's difficult being around murder cases when you're not used to them – it's bad enough when you are used to them. I'm sure Anna will come through this ordeal and we will catch the culprit.'

I nodded, my thought processes temporarily scrambled. 'Good,' I said, flattered by the 'we', until I realised he meant 'we, the police'.

'Evening all,' said a slurred voice from ankle level.

Billy Shawcroft sprawled on his back in the doorway of the teashop, a blissful smile splitting his face.

'Hello, Billy. Are you drunk?' asked Hobbes.

'Yes,' said Billy, 'and in the morning I shall be hung-over. Featherlight's got some cheap new beer called "Draclea's Bite". It's strong shtuff, though it tashtes of oven cleaner and nobody will buy it. He shays I can 'ave it.' He shivered.

'Very good.' Hobbes, bending, lifted Billy to his feet. 'Now, mind how you go and be careful where you go to sleep. It's cold at night.'

'Tha's alright.' Billy smiled. 'I'm gonna work now. It's warm enough in the Feathersh.' A frown congealed his face. 'I got shomething to tell you.' There was a pause and an hiccup. 'Tony Derrick was in town today. Thish afternoon. He was driving a big blue car along The Shambles. I thought I should tell you.'

'What sort of car?' asked Hobbes.

'I told you, a big blue one. I dunno the make. Bye Bye.'

He began his journey to the Feathers, taking the long route, via both sides of the road, once colliding with a lamppost, and apologising profusely for his 'clumsinesh.'

'He likes a drink rather too much,' said Hobbes, unnecessarily. 'Still, he's a good man. We now have further evidence of Tony Derrick's involvement in the attack on Mr Barrington-Oddy. Now hurry up, or we'll be late and I'm getting hungry.'

As he increased the length of his stride, I alternated between a jog and a scurry to keep up. We passed the front of the church where Kev, leather clad and helmeted was revving up an enormous motorbike. With a cheery thumbs up, he roared off down the road.

Hobbes chuckled. 'There goes our curate. He used to be known as Kev the rev in the old days, when he was in a biker gang and a bit of a bad lad. It was just foolish pranks for the most part and nothing malicious, though I had to have a stern word with him in the end. Shortly afterwards, he found religion and now he's Kev the reverend. He still likes his bike though.'

I was panting by then. 'I met him this morning. He's the one who pointed me to the pamphlets about the Roman Cup.'

Hobbes turned to nod. 'Yes, he'd need to. He's only been back in town a few weeks and is still learning. If you really want to learn about the church's history you should have a word with Augustus Godley, his great grandfather. He was church warden for many years and what he doesn't know about the old place isn't worth knowing.'

We turned into Blackdog Street as the rain, which had been

threatening violence for hours, began its attack. Apart from a glance at the frowning sky, Hobbes didn't appear concerned but I scuttled for the front door of number 13, the key already in my hand. Heavy drops were already spattering the pavement as, opening the door, I dived for cover. There was a deep, booming woof, as if from an aggressive tuba, a pair of big black paws thudded into my chest, knocking me back through the door, down the steps, onto the pavement at Hobbes's feet.

He laughed. 'Beware of the dog! He's a bundle of fun isn't he?'

Pinned to the ground, on my back like a defeated wrestler, stunned and winded, I tried to work out if Hobbes's last remark had been directed at me or the dog, who had begun worrying my tie, though the tie wasn't half as worried as I was, even though he didn't hurt me.

'Drop him,' said Hobbes, 'and get inside out the rain.'

Dregs, tail wagging like he'd just done something clever, bounded up the steps with Hobbes, leaving me to stare into the night sky, rain water pooling in my eye sockets.

A middle-aged couple passed by on the other side, tutting in disapproval. The woman had a penetrating whisper. 'That one's started early. Disgusting! Someone really ought to do something about people like him.'

'I haven't been drinking. I've been steamrollered by a huge, hairy, horrible animal. I need help.' That's what I wanted to say but the only sound I could force out was a piteous little whine.

'Are you going to lie out there all night?' asked Hobbes, looking down from the doorway. 'You'll get wet and miss your supper.'

Struggling to my feet, I stumbled up the steps, the bloody dog cocking an evil eye at me as I entered the sitting room. Hobbes patted its head and it followed him into the kitchen, while I dripped upstairs to change my wet clothes, to wash away the street. In my bedroom, I unwrapped the soiled bandage from my hand, pleased the skin beneath was pink and shiny and, though it felt stiff, it appeared to be healing well. I removed my jacket, all grimy and soggy, stinking of wet sheep and, more worryingly, urine, and dropped my trousers. They were round my ankles, I was bending to remove them, when the door opened, striking me firmly on the backside.

Mrs Goodfellow entered with the trousers I'd ruined in the morning hanging from her skinny arm. 'They're all cleaned and repaired. Have you lost something?'

'Only my dignity, though there wasn't much to worry about.' I tried to cover myself and look cool. It wasn't easy.

She smiled, not at all embarrassed. 'You'd better give me those dirty trousers, dear.' Folding the clean ones, placing them neatly on the dressing table, she picked up my muddied jacket. 'Cor, you are a mucky lad. It's a good job the old fellow knows a good tailor and dry-cleaner.'

Resistance was obviously useless, so, giving up, I handed over my trousers.

'Ooh, you've got legs like pipe cleaners, dear. They're all thin and white and fluffy.'

I said nothing; nothing in life had prepared me for a comment like that. However, my legs blushed. I'd never suspected they were so bashful.

'They've gone all pink like Dregs's tongue.' She laughed. 'Now, get dressed, there's chicken curry for supper.'

All the meals she'd made so far had scaled previously unimaginable heights of excellence, yet, as a long-time addict, I needed the occasional curry fix and it might have become a serious matter of concern if she hadn't cooked one just in time. I could have kissed her had my legs not objected, refusing to take a step until she'd left the room. Then, dressing quickly, I bounded downstairs, only just avoiding Dregs who'd fallen asleep halfway.

The curry, after the inevitable delay for grace, was a truly sensational meld of mysterious spices, flavours and piquancy that nearly made me cry in ecstasy. I like to think she'd surpassed herself, though I thought the same at every meal. Hobbes, too, seemed in dreamy mood as, finishing his last chapatti, he sat back with a sigh. Someday, I thought, I would have to leave, find a place of my own, eat normally. The thought was hard to bear and I felt tears starting in my eyes.

Hobbes grinned. 'Curry too hot?'

'No,' I defended it, 'it's wonderful but I fear it's too good for this world.'

'If you like this, then you should try her vindaloo. That'll bring more than a tear to your eyes.'

I expected we'd adjourn to the sitting room as usual. Instead, Hobbes, picking up the dishes, carried them to the sink.

'The lass has her Kung Fu class on Monday nights,' he said, 'so I do a bit of washing up.'

'She does Kung Fu?' My voice soared incredulously. 'I'm surprised they let anyone her age learn a martial art. Isn't it dangerous?'

'You don't understand,' said Hobbes, 'she's the teacher and an honorary Master of the Secret Arts. She combines her class with sex education as a sort of spin-off. It was all the printer's fault; he made a mistake and some folk turned up hoping to learn the marital arts. She didn't like to disappoint them.'

I was so flabbergasted I volunteered to do the washing up myself and Hobbes, to his credit, did not stand in my way, taking himself and Dregs off for a walk. The bowl I'd melted had been replaced and I washed the dishes with a virtuous feeling. Afterwards, I dried and put everything away methodically, some of it, I flattered myself, in the right place.

Hobbes had not returned when I'd finished and I guessed Mrs Goodfellow would be busy for some time. Finding myself at a loose end, alone in the kitchen, my mind kept returning to the cellar below, the darkness beckoning me to adventure, to discover what might be hidden behind the nearly secret door below. Yet, I couldn't do it. When it came to the crunch, I was too chicken to venture down there, especially at night. I tried to convince myself I was worried that the light would shine through the grille, revealing my actions to Hobbes when he returned. In reality, I was just scared.

A happier idea struck: I'd glimpsed intriguing things in the attic, which wasn't nearly so scary. Besides, apart from Mrs Goodfellow's warning about the planks, there seemed to be no reason why I shouldn't go up there. Tearing myself away from the cellar door, I climbed upstairs.

As I pulled a cord, the ladder slid down towards me, clicking into place. I started up the rungs, breathing hard, as if doing something wrong, though no one had told me not to. When my head and shoulders poked through into the blackness, air, as cold as if blown from mountain peaks, cascading down, made me shiver. I groped for the switch, the light clicked on and I was staring into the gaping maw of a huge bear.

'Jesus Christ!' I gasped and damn near fell down the ladder. The bear was stuffed of course, its moth-eaten carcass lashed to a timber frame. Trying to control my rushing heart, I climbed up and examined a tarnished disc on its cracked, leather collar. 'Cuddles', it read and, on the reverse, 'Please return to Hobbes, 13 Blackdog Street'. Nerves made me giggle like a schoolgirl.

The place was infested with junk. I could see neatly stacked brass bedsteads, what appeared to be a penny-farthing that had come off second best in a brawl with a steamroller, boxes, crates and racks of canvasses. A threadbare cloak lay across a stack of old records and I wrapped it around myself to keep out the chill, before sitting down on an old trunk, wondering whether any other bits of elephant were concealed up there.

I eased one of the canvasses from its rack. It was a painting of a hilly landscape with an old man repairing a dry stone wall, a small town nestling in the background. Though I'm not an art buff, I found the colours, the contrasts, the vibrancy of the scene quite disturbing. It was almost photographic in its detail but there was more; the scene appeared real, yet more vivid than life and, gazing into the picture, I had an impression almost of flying above the landscape, like a kestrel, soaring and hovering on a whim, while my eyes picked out the tiniest details. The church tower seemed familiar and I realised the town was Sorenchester, though not as I knew it, as it had once been. I fancied I could make out Blackdog Street and even the number 13 on the door, such was the artist's skill. Wondering who'd painted it and why it had been confined to the attic, I looked for a signature.

In the bottom right-hand corner, a mess of loops and blots, it said W.M. Hobbes. I whistled, trying to make myself believe it had been painted by one of Hobbes's relations. I might have succeeded had he not told me he'd been adopted. Still in denial, I reasoned that he'd probably purchased the painting because of the coincidence of names and, yet, something about it made me suspect he was the artist. I realised then that I didn't actually know his first name – I assumed he had one – or his second name, assuming W.M. Hobbes really was him. To me, he was just Hobbes, or possibly Inspector Hobbes, or even, if Mrs G was correct, the old fellow. There was, to use Wilkes's word again, something unhuman about the painting, something suggestive of wildness, as if the artist related more to the natural world than to the world of the town, or even to the man working on the wall. Though they were there, and skilfully depicted, the grass, the trees, the sky and even the rocks felt more important.

Putting it back, I selected another. Again it was by W.M. Hobbes, this one showing a moonlit night in town. The details were every bit as vivid as the first, though the colours were muted and, again, it was disturbing, for there was too much in the picture, almost as if the artist had been using a night-vision scope. I shivered as my glance strayed to the shadows, for there was a suggestion of danger, of unseen beings lurking, waiting for the moon to be shrouded by the threatening clouds. It was eerie and yet compelling, exciting even.

I couldn't tell how old the paintings were, though they gave an impression of antiquity, which made me curious about Hobbes's age. I'd have guessed he was in his mid-fifties, yet Wilkes had mentioned how he'd looked about ready for retirement twenty years earlier. Recalling the newspaper cutting in Hobbes's office, I realised, assuming the policeman in the picture wasn't his ancestor, or an unfortunate look-alike, but Hobbes himself, that it would make him well over a hundred years old. I tried reasoning, to convince myself it was impossible, that his weirdness was messing up my head, and that there was no way he could be so ancient and still working. Surely, I thought, the police had to retire at a certain age, and definitely before they were one hundred. I decided he couldn't really be unhuman: it would be too stupid. I just wished I believed it.

The next painting was of Rocky wearing a military uniform, looking as if he was off to fight the Great War. Impossible, I told myself. Stop imagining things, he's not a troll, he's just a man in fancy dress.

It was then I heard an altercation in the street outside, the sound filtered into the attic. A man shouted, 'Get your dog off my bloody leg!'

Hobbes's voice came next. 'Your leg's not bloody yet. However, it might be if you don't pick it up.'

'You can't make me.'

'Can't I? My dog doesn't like litter louts, so pick up that cigarette packet or you'll discover there can be painful side effects to smoking.'

I heard a cry but that was all because, for some reason, I felt uncomfortable at the thought of Hobbes knowing I'd been in the attic. Sliding the portrait back into the rack, squeezing past the junk, I slid down the ladder and shut the hatch. As casually as could be, I strolled downstairs and towards the sitting room. All had gone quiet in the street and a key turned in the lock. The front door opened, there was an enormous woof and, as the bloody dog leaped at me, I sidestepped, dodging behind the table. The next few seconds featured a chase round and around the sofa to the accompaniment of a wailing moan, sounding as if it might be coming out of my mouth. I was vaguely aware of words in it. 'Get off! Get off! Get off! Get off!' In addition, there was, I regret, a selection of choicest swear words to fill any gaps.

'Get down,' said Hobbes.

I dropped to all fours. The dog came down on me, wagging his tail as if we'd been enjoying a great game.

Hobbes looked thoughtful. 'He does seem to like you. However, you shouldn't encourage him. Now leave him alone.'

I thought he was talking to me first and the dog second but I may have been wrong. Dregs and I parted with a relieved snivel from me and a sad whine from him. I stood up.

'Go to the kitchen,' said Hobbes.

I turned towards the door.

'Not you, Andy. Yes you, Dregs. Sit down. Not you, Dregs. Yes you, Andy.'

I sat as the dog left the sitting room with a mournful tail.

Hobbes subsided onto the sofa beside me. 'Were you looking for something?'

'When?' I replied, puzzled.

'Two minutes ago, when you were in the attic.'

'I wasn't in the attic,' I began, until I caught the look in his eye. 'Oh, you mean just then? No, I wasn't looking for anything as such. I just wondered what was up there. I hope you don't mind?'

'Oh no, not at all. Only I'm replacing some of the flooring up there. It's why I've got the sander in the bathroom, for when I have the time.'

I felt ashamed I'd suspected him of using it for shaving, though I still couldn't believe any normal razor could cope with bristles as thick as cactus spines. 'Umm … how did you know I'd been up there?'

He grinned. 'I'm a detective. Your skin is paler than normal, suggesting you've been somewhere cold, there's a speck of sawdust on your right shoe, hinting that you've been where someone has been woodworking and, what clinches it for me, you are wearing an old cloak from the attic.'

I slapped my forehead. I'd forgotten all about it. Taking it off, I draped it over the coffee table.

'Besides, I saw the light shining from the attic window.'

He'd got me bang to rights, whatever that meant and I thought I'd better explain. 'I was curious what was up there and I … umm … put the cloak on because of the cold.'

He nodded.

'There were some paintings, next to the bear,' I said. 'They were rather good. Did you do them?'

I was astonished to see his face turn pink. Surely he wasn't embarrassed? Not Hobbes, the man with the thickest skin in Sorenchester?

He avoided my stare. 'I dabble. It's merely a foolish hobby. By the way, did you like my bear? His name's Cuddles.'

'He frightened the life out of me, when I turned the light on and all I could see was his whopping great mouth.'

Hobbes chuckled. 'Cuddles was a fine bear; he used to have your room once, many years ago, after he'd retired from the circus.'

'A bear?' I gasped. 'Living here? What about the neighbours?'

'Oh,' he said, with a reminiscent smile, 'they weren't happy. They objected most strongly, so I told them he was my pal and that he was staying. They came to accept him in time.'

'But what about the smell?'

He shrugged. 'Cuddles got used to it. They're tolerant creatures, bears and well-behaved, except where salmon are concerned. He did invade the fishmongers once or twice, though I always paid for what he ate and, in time, he became quite friendly with the fishmonger, even having his photograph used in the advertisement, "He can't bear to miss his weekly fish, can you?"'

I laughed. Not that I really believed him.

'He left his mark on Sorenchester,' he said. 'You know the Bear with a Sore Head pub?'

'Yeah, of course.'

'Well, in the old days it was called the Ram but they renamed it in his honour. He often used to drink there.'

'The bear used to drink there?' I was fascinated.

'I'm afraid so. Alcohol was his weakness. I mean, many of us enjoy a beer or two but Cuddles couldn't hold his drink, which was something to do with having claws and no opposable thumbs. He had to sup from a bucket with a tap on it and they used to hang it by the dartboard, just above the number eight. He'd swig it all down, getting very drunk: hence the expression "to drink one over the eight". Incidentally, it was also the origin of pail ale. In the end, though, the drink caused his downfall.'

'Why, what happened?' I sat as still as a child who has been entranced by a fabulous tale.

Hobbes, shaking his head, sighed. 'It was very sad. One evening he fancied a drink and went down to the Ram, as it was then, and ordered a beer.'

'How?' I asked. 'Could he talk?'

'Don't be silly, he was a bear and bears can't talk, so he used sign language.'

'Ah,' I said, 'that explains it.' Actually, it didn't, though I failed to spot the flaw until afterwards.

'It,' he continued, 'was tragic. The Ram having quite run out of best bitter, they had to serve him a bucketful of worst bitter and Cuddles wasn't happy.'

'I bet he wasn't. There's nothing worse than bad beer.'

'Precisely,' said Hobbes, 'it was appalling.'

'The beer?'

'Yes. Well, to continue, though the story's harrowing, they hung his bucket up.'

'Over the eight?'

'Over the eight. By chance, there was a big grudge darts match underway. Poor Cuddles supped his beer, which was so horrific that he turned away in disgust. Unfortunately, he turned towards the dartboard and a dart aimed at the bull's-eye struck his nose.'

'Oh no.'

'Oh yes.' He nodded. 'It was awful. He staggered away, roaring in pain, and collapsed in the skittle alley, where a speeding ball struck him on the head. Hence, the pub was renamed the "Bear with a Sore Head".'

'What happened to him?' I asked, agog.

'He died,' said Hobbes, sorrowfully, 'three years later. A salmon stuck in his throat and he choked.'

'He choked to death?'

'No, it was worse than that. You see, when the fishmonger began hitting him on the back, trying to remove the blockage, poor Cuddles thought he was being assaulted and ran straight out in the road, where he was struck by a bus.'

'Oh no,' I said. 'How awful.'

'I told you so.' Hobbes's eyes filled with tears.

'And that's what killed him?'

'Not exactly. Yet, we are approaching the really dreadful bit. The bus knocked him into a music shop, where his muzzle became entangled in an antique stringed instrument that suffocated him. And so my sad tale ends, with a bear-faced lyre.'

'Wow,' I said. 'Who'd have thought it?'

'There you go. I told you it was tragic.' He sniffed back tears that, if I hadn't seen the sorrow in his face, I might have thought sounded like a snigger.

In my defence, having pondered the story for a while, I became less than convinced of its veracity. Later, I asked Mrs Goodfellow, who said the old fellow had found the bear in a skip and brought it home – but she wouldn't have it in the sitting room because its stuffing was coming out.

The rest of the evening passed quietly. Hobbes turned on the television and watched a documentary about 'The Secret Life of Aubergines', which he appeared to find gripping. Not many people know the aubergine is related to Deadly Nightshade and is not technically a vegetable but a fruit. Spread the word.

Mrs Goodfellow returned from her class and, after setting my heart pounding with her abrupt appearance, soothed it with a large mug of cocoa. Afterwards, I brushed my teeth and went to bed and, though it was barely ten o'clock, I dropped asleep in seconds. I had survived a very full day.

Something, either a sound or a feeling, woke me. I lay, listening to the silence, trying to get back to sleep. Unfortunately, my bladder had reached the awkward stage and I dithered, unsure whether to get up and empty it or to try ignoring it until daylight. When the church clock bonged only twice, morning seemed uncomfortably distant, so I got up, groping my way to the bathroom. On the way back, still drowsy, barely aware of anything, cold air blew across my bare feet.

Hobbes's door was open and in the faint light from the street, I could make out the curtains flapping. A dark figure, cloaked like Dracula, lurked in the corner by the wardrobe.

'Who's there?' The words trembled from my shivering jaw and received no reply. I tried again. 'What are you doing here?' This time, though my voice sounded firmer, more manly even, there was still no response, apart from a swaying of the cloak. Nor was there any sound from Hobbes.

A sudden horror struck that the shadowy figure might be an assassin. Fear kicked in for Hobbes, as well as for myself, yet there was also an overwhelming anger. With a yell, I dived headlong at the intruder. There was a stunning crash and pain and fairy lights danced behind my eyes before everything went black and I was struggling against an overwhelming, smothering force. Something sharp jabbing my neck, I gasped in pain and horror. Had that been the vampire's bite? Would my existence continue as some sort of half-life, one of the undead? The fight left me, my body going limp. So, to my confusion, did my assailant's.

Standing up, holding my neck, there was just enough light to see that I'd attacked the cloak I'd taken from the attic and which Hobbes must have hung on a sharp wire coat hanger from his wardrobe door. It was no wonder my head hurt and I didn't half feel a twerp, but at least I hadn't disturbed Hobbes; he wasn't in.

I walked towards the window, taking deep breaths of the clean, night air, shivering, picking up the cloak, wrapping it around me and peering out over the street. The rain had passed and everything was grey and damp. The half-moon, partly hidden by wisps of dark cloud, lit up a shadowy figure clambering up the roof on the house opposite. The way the thing moved reminded me of an orang-utan, except its hairy back was black.

Despite the cloak, I felt goose pimples erupting as the creature moved from the shadow of the chimney onto the ridge. The shock was palpable when I saw it was wearing stripy pyjama bottoms. It stood, raising its head, apparently looking for something, or sniffing, and crept along the ridge. It turned towards me and for an instant I could see its face. It was Hobbes.

The bedroom lights coming on, I spun around with a gasp as a foot hurtled towards my head. The lights went out.

12

My eyes felt as if they'd been gummed shut, while my waking mind echoed with confusion and fear. The side of my face was sore and my brain sort of connected the fact with a hazy recollection of a bad dream that made no sense. Getting out of bed, I prised open my eyelids, peering at the mirror, shocked to discover I'd become the proud owner of another black eye, a close match for the first one.

I had a vague image of a foot powering towards my head and my mind was awash with even vaguer fragments of images.

I was trying to rearrange them into coherent pictures when the bedroom door opened and Mrs Goodfellow peeped in.

'Did you sleep well, dear?'

'I'm not sure,' I said. 'I got up in the night and things went a bit strange.'

'I expect they did,' she said, 'though I'm sorry I kicked you. I heard a noise and saw a figure dressed in a black cloak and I thought to myself, there's one of them ninjas, and I reckoned I'd see if they was as good as in the movies. I was a little disappointed; you didn't put up much of a fight, dear.'

'I'm … umm … sorry.' So, it had been her foot. I hung my battered head. What else could I do when I'd been beaten up by a skinny old woman?

'Never mind,' she said. 'Though, why were you lurking in the old fellow's room dressed in a cloak?'

I told her the truth because I couldn't think of a more plausible explanation.

She laughed. Then she laughed a whole lot more. 'So, you nutted the wardrobe, thinking it was Count Dracula? You are a one, dear.' She grinned all the time she wasn't laughing and I attempted to show that I, too, was amused. Becoming suddenly serious, she said, 'It was a brave thing to do, if you really thought the old fellow was in trouble. It's not everyone who'd put themselves on the line for him.'

The vision of Hobbes crawling on the rooftops exploded into my brain, taking my breath away. I had to sit down on the bed, never again doubting that he wasn't human, except when doubting my own sanity.

'I saw him out on the roof over there. He was wearing stripy pyjama bottoms.'

'Of course, he'd hardly go out in his bare skin would he? There are laws against that sort of thing. Anyway, it's time for breakfast; he's having a bit of a lie-in. He usually does after a night on the tiles.'

'What was he doing out there?'

'How should I know? He's still asleep.'

'Does he go out on the tiles often?'

'Only when he wants to, or has to. Now get dressed. I'll make you a nice breakfast and then I'll see if I can find something to put on your eyes.'

'A bit of raw steak?'

'I was thinking more of bacon and eggs,' she said. 'I don't think we've got any steak, though the old fellow likes one for his breakfast, sometimes. Mind you, sometimes he prefers Sugar Puffs. I could nip into the butcher's? I was going out later, anyway.'

'Stop,' I said, 'I don't want raw steak for breakfast. I was asking if you were going to put it on my eyes.'

'I could if you really wanted, though it wouldn't do you much good. It might amuse Dregs, though. No, dear, I was thinking of my special tincture that I prepare from herbs and stuff: it's very good. Now, hurry up.' She turned and left the room.

I scratched my head, still the stranger in this bizarre world. Nevertheless, breakfast was breakfast, so having a wash, getting dressed, I went downstairs. Despite the ache of my swollen face, the fry-up was just what I needed, leaving me deeply indebted to the pig who'd laid down his life so I could enjoy the best bacon ever. I hoped he'd thought it was worth the sacrifice. I knew I did.

I finished off with toast and marmalade and, while I was wolfing down the last fragments, Mrs Goodfellow rummaged in a drawer.

Pulling out a small, glass bottle and uncorking it, she shook a couple of drops of pungent, green sludge onto a wad of cotton wool and handed it to me.

'Go to the sitting room, dear, and press this gently against your eyes and they'll soon be as right as reindeer. You'd best keep the bottle; you're a little accident prone.'

Dregs was occupying the sofa and, when I tried to persuade him to move over, he went limp and immovable, growling, baring his teeth, something he'd never have dared had Hobbes or the old girl been there. I gave up, sitting down on one of the hard oak chairs, holding the pad against my face. Hell, it stung! I gasped and nearly threw it down in disgust yet, as I persevered, it began to soothe and relax the skin. It was good stuff, if a little on the stinky side of ripe, and I never did discover what she put in it. All she'd say was that it was based on a recipe her Kung Fu master had taught her and that she could tell me the ingredients but then she'd have to kill me. I didn't press.

For an hour or more I sat still, the pad to my face, peeping out just once to see Mrs Goodfellow climbing upstairs with an armful of neatly pressed sheets. Shortly afterwards, hearing Hobbes's roar, I gathered he didn't appreciate his bedding being changed when still in occupancy. For some reason, Dregs held me responsible for the altercation. He emitted a deep woof and an angry growl and I uncovered my eyes to see the horrible creature leaping from the sofa, approaching, bristling and stiff-legged. His teeth looked awfully big, his snarl reminiscent of Hobbes, who sounded as if he was coming off second best in the struggle for mastery of the bed. Dregs looked ready to spring and, in desperation, I thrust the pad towards his nose. Taking one sniff, he sneezed and fled, yelping, tail squeezed between his legs as a thump from above, suggested a heavy body had rolled out of bed.

A few moments later, Hobbes slouched downstairs in his stripy pyjamas and slippers and, nodding to acknowledge me, disappeared into the kitchen. By then I reckoned I'd had enough of the stinking tincture. Standing up, walking to the stairs, intending to dispose of the cotton wool and to wash my face, I glanced into the kitchen where Hobbes, frowning and growling, his face dark and bristly, was hunched at the table over an enormous bowl of Sugar Puffs. Dregs, slumped in the corner, whimpered when he saw me. I climbed the stairs with some satisfaction.

Heading to the bathroom, I examined my face in the mirror, amazed at what a remarkable a job the gunge had done, delighted the soreness and swelling had all but vanished. What remained was a slight, barely noticeable, greenish discoloration beneath my eyes and I wasn't sure if it was a residual effect of the tincture or the remains of bruises. If the old girl had ever marketed the stuff, she'd have made a fortune.

Sometime later, when the Sugar Puffs and several mugs of tea had raised his spirits and he was washed and dressed, Hobbes called me down to the sitting room. Dregs was there too, but maintained a respectful distance from me, which felt like a victory.

A strange light was glinting in Hobbes's eyes. 'Would you like to see an arrest?'

'I'd love to,' I said, 'unless it's me getting arrested.'

He smiled. 'No, you're safe enough for now. I'm going to nab Tony Derrick.'

'Good,' I said. 'Umm … where is he?'

'He's squatting in a house over on the Elms Estate.'

The clock on the mantelpiece showed ten-thirty. 'Don't you normally make dawn raids?' I asked.

'As far as a sluggard like Tony Derrick is concerned, any time before lunchtime is as good as dawn.'

'Great. When are we off?'

'Now,' said Hobbes, 'so get your jacket on.'

'Right … umm … how did you find him?'

He shrugged, 'I did a bit of overtime last night and picked up his trail near the Feathers. I found this in the alley.' He reached into his pocket and pulled out a crumpled cigarette packet. 'What d'you make of it?'

'It's an old cigarette packet,' I said, puzzled as to why he'd been collecting junk.

'Is that all?'

The way he was looking suggested I should be seeing much more.

'Well, yes.'

'What about the label? Doesn't it suggest anything to you?'

It read 'Carpati', with some foreign words underneath 'They're foreign cigarettes?' I said.

'Very true, but is that all?' He raised incredulous eyebrows.

'Yes.'

'Alright.' He shook his head. 'Now look again.' He held the packet with his thumb over the first three letters.

'Aha,' I said, as the penny dropped. 'Pati – the same as on the cigarette butt you picked up at the museum.'

'Correct.' He grinned.

'So the burglar smokes foreign cigarettes?'

'Carpati cigarettes from Romania to be precise. Now shift yourself – we've got to walk to the station for the car.'

I was soon in the street, jogging at Hobbes's side, not really understanding what was going on, except with an idea that, as Mr Barrington-Oddy's house had been filled with Romanian stuff, then, perhaps, my Roman connection should have been a Romanian one. There was, though, something more important.

'Do you think Phil might be with Tony Derrick?' I asked, panting.

'Not as far as I could tell,' said Hobbes. 'Let's see.'

He strode ahead, not talking again until we were in the car, speeding towards Tony Derrick's squat. With my eyes firmly closed, I tried to distract myself by fretting about what would happen if Phil was there.

'Right,' said Hobbes, after a few minutes. 'Here we are.'

The car jerking to a standstill, I opened my eyes. We were parked outside a small house on an estate, one that appeared to have been

182

built in the 1960s and neglected ever since. Though a few cars rusted on nearby drives or by the kerb, no people were about. A cat, curled up on an old mattress in the cracked concrete and weed garden, opened suspicious eyes, fleeing when Hobbes emerged. As I got out, my foot scrunching on a litter of old lager cans in the gutter, noticing a lack of police vehicles, I felt suddenly vulnerable.

'Umm … don't you have any back-up?'

He grinned horribly. 'Of course I do, I've got you. What more could I possibly want?'

'Me? What can I do?'

'You can watch.'

'Mightn't it be dangerous?'

Hobbes clapped his hands together like an excited child. 'For somebody. Stay behind me and let's nab him.'

As he strode towards the front door, I expected he'd knock it open like at Phil's but, instead, after standing quietly for a moment, as if listening, he raised a cudgel fist and knocked hard, though not so hard as to damage anything.

'Open up, it's the police!' he bellowed, turning round, loping past me in his usual hunched fashion.

For a moment I thought he was playing the old kids' trick of ringing the bell and running away. Instead, he ran towards the back of the house down a scruffy alley. I trotted after him, scrambling past the battered sofa partly blocking the way, hearing a door open at the back and the sound of running feet. It wasn't Hobbes's, because he was nearly silent, despite his great, heavy boots. As I reached the end of the alley, a gate in a rotting fence flew open and Tony Derrick, vivid in a pink Hawaiian shirt, rushed out. He turned towards me, pausing, a smile creeping over his face as he removed his glasses and tucked them into his shirt pocket. Lowering his head, he charged.

At least that's what he'd planned, because he'd failed to spot what had come to a halt on the other side of the gate. He only managed two steps before Hobbes landed on him. The impact was not like being hit by a ton of bricks, for Hobbes was more solid than that; it must have been more like being flattened by a paving slab and, although he was undoubtedly a nasty, sneaky, horrible villain with a bad taste in shirts, Tony had my sympathy.

Hobbes stood up, holding him by the collar as if he were a bundle of rags. 'Were you planning on going somewhere?'

Tony groaned.

'Anthony Stephen Derrick,' said Hobbes, 'consider that you have just had your collar felt. You've been nabbed in other words. You are currently incapable of saying anything, though, when you are able to speak again, you may come to harm if you do not mention, when questioned, something which I later find to be of relevance. Anything you do say may be given in evidence. Anything you do say that subsequently proves incorrect may result in … unpleasantness.'

He lifted Tony a little higher so he could look into his face. 'D'you understand?' Still keeping a firm grip on him, he used a massive finger to make the lolling head nod. 'Good.'

Though I was certain he hadn't used the correct form of words for cautioning a suspect under arrest, Tony didn't complain.

'Now let's take a look inside your house,' said Hobbes, heaving him across his shoulder and letting him dangle.

Tony looked as if he was still wondering what had hit him as I followed them through the concrete backyard, a mess of sickly grass with stinking rubbish, spewing from tattered black bin bags. The house was hardly any better, though the stench of rot was partially concealed under cigarette smoke and stale beer. Cans and bottles littered the floor, along with takeaway cartons and pizza boxes. I'd had my eyes tight shut on the way to this hovel – I felt justified in calling it that, because it was far worse than my flat had ever been – and now I wished I could close my nostrils. I did what I could by pinching them and breathing through my mouth.

Hobbes was wearing Tony round his neck like a loud scarf – loud in both appearance and moaning, since he'd come to and was demanding to be put down.

'Language, Tony, please,' said Hobbes after one exceptionally foul-mouthed outburst.

We conducted a short tour of the downstairs with Tony yelling and cursing and occasionally wriggling, until, banging his head on a doorframe, he hung limp again.

'Oops,' said Hobbes, carrying him upstairs.

It wasn't quite so disgusting up there, if you could ignore the bathroom, which I couldn't and, though I'd never been the world's tidiest or most hygienic man, it sickened me that anyone would choose to live in such squalor. There were three bedrooms, two of them empty apart from beer cans, the third containing a mattress, a stained sleeping bag, a lop-sided pile of dog-eared porn mags and screwed up tissues scattered over the bare boards.

'Well, there's no sign of Mr Waring,' said Hobbes, bounding downstairs, three at a time, Tony bouncing on his shoulders, 'and there's nothing to make me believe he's ever been here. Now, let's see what this rogue has in his pockets.'

Turning Tony upside down, holding his ankles, he bounced him gently on a manky rug, bits and pieces dropping like apples in a storm. There wasn't much, a few coins, his glasses, a penknife, a fat nylon wallet, some keys, a lighter, a very upsetting handkerchief and a half-empty packet of cigarettes. Hobbes grunted, tossing Tony onto a burst beanbag, and picking through the spoils. The cigarette packet said Carpati, two of the keys were obviously for the front and back doors, another appeared to be for a heavy padlock and the final one, attached to a plastic key fob was a car key. The wallet when he opened it made me gasp as if entering Ali Baba's cave; it was stuffed with bank notes.

'That must be a thousand pounds!' I said, hoping it was finder's keepers and that I'd be in for a cut.

'More than that,' said Hobbes, flicking a callused thumb over the top, 'I'd say about four thousand, three hundred and fifteen pounds.' Tony wasn't doing so badly.

Looking through the rest of the wallet, he found nothing except for a plastic card, which he held out between his fingernails, letting me see. 'Hallo, hallo, hallo,' he said, 'what d'you make of this?'

'Umm … it's a credit card,' I said. 'Oh, I see! It's Phil's. I knew he was involved, I just knew it.' A surge of relief rushing though me washed away some of the guilt about the dropped business card, for this, surely, was genuine evidence that Phil was connected to the thefts. My suspicions, based only on prejudice and dislike, appeared to have been vindicated.

'However, I don't think he was involved, at least, not in the way you mean,' said Hobbes. 'I can't see him having business with a wretch like Tony, apart from as a source of information for a story. In my experience, people don't normally give their credit cards away: someone usually takes them, by fraud or force.' He dropped the wallet into a polythene bag, which disappeared into his pocket.

Tony groaned.

'He's coming round,' I said. 'Shouldn't you cuff him?'

'No, that would be police brutality, something that is frowned on these days, although, when I joined the force, the odd cuff round the ear was permitted, if not encouraged. I never favoured it myself but some of the lads used to like it.'

'No, I didn't mean that. What I meant was, shouldn't you handcuff him so he can't get away?'

'Oh, I see. No, I don't like to do that. It's undignified and I mostly find suspects are willing to come quietly.'

Another groan emerged.

'You'll come quietly, won't you, Tony?'

Raising his head, staring at Hobbes through bleary, blue eyes, he nodded, saying, 'Yeah, I suppose I will. I don't have much choice, do I?'

'Of course you do,' said Hobbes with a smile. 'You have many choices. You could come quietly, in which case it's traditional for you to say, "it's a fair cop, Guv'nor". Or you could fight and scream, which is resisting arrest, in which case I am required to restrain you, with the minimum of force necessary. Or you could try to run away and then I'm obliged to pursue you, stop you and restrain you, with the minimum of force. The end result is much the same.'

'I'll come quietly … it's a fair cop, Guv'nor.'

He didn't appear to be very happy, yet I think he made the right choice.

'Good lad,' said Hobbes, his face a mass of happy teeth. 'Now would you like to answer a few questions here? Or would you rather answer them in the nice, comfortable police station? You see? More choices.'

Tony frowned in dazed confusion. 'Uh, the station.'

'The station what?'

'The station, please?' Tony's lip curled into what was probably meant as an ingratiating smile.

'That's better,' said Hobbes cheerfully, 'good manners don't hurt do they? Oh, and before we go, do you happen to know the whereabouts of Mr Philip Waring?'

Tony shook his head. 'I ain't seen the git since Saturday.'

I warmed to him, snivelling, dirty thief though he was, for he'd at least got Phil pegged right. Still, I did experience another twinge of guilt and regret.

'Let's be having you, then.'

Hobbes, pulling Tony upright, took us outside, leading him, meek as a beaten puppy, from the house, locking the back door behind us. I was expecting Hobbes to head back to the car but he went the other way, along a cracked, concrete path to a square surrounded by garages. After scanning the flaking, wooden doors, he settled on one and strode towards it, pulling the padlock key from his pocket, opening the door with a flourish like a stage magician, revealing Phil's Audi, encrusted with mud, squeezed into the garage, as tight as a piston in a cylinder.

'We'll take this,' said Hobbes. 'It's evidence. Besides, it's much bigger than mine and we'll all be more comfortable.'

'You can't take it, it's mine,' Tony whined.

'I can if I want to.' Hobbes smiled. 'Besides, I'm not convinced it's yours at all. Doesn't it belong to Mr Waring?'

'He gave it to me.'

Hobbes raised an eyebrow. 'Did he really? Like he gave you his credit card? He's a very generous man, this Mr Waring. He must be a great friend of yours.'

'Yes.'

'And yet you still called him a git?' Hobbes shook his head. 'You know something my lad? You don't deserve such a friend. Now stand back and I'll drive it out … a little further back would be better.'

Somehow, flattening his bulk against the garage wall, he squeezed into the car. A few seconds and a puff of grey smoke later, the Audi lurched forth, like a greyhound from the trap, and came to a halt. Hobbes, getting out, examined it, while Tony slouched beside me, looking as if someone had just made off with his wallet. I wondered how often it had been the other way round.

I suffered a moment of heart-stopping horror when Hobbes, opening the boot, tugged aside a frayed green tarpaulin. I don't know why, but I half expected to see Phil's bloated corpse beneath; it was only a collection of power tools. Without being aware, I'd been holding my breath, which escaped in one long, relieved stream. There wasn't much else in the car besides an empty Carpati cigarette packet and a fragment of a chocolate wrapper under the passenger seat. Phil liked things neat.

'All aboard,' said Hobbes. 'Next stop's the cop shop.'

As I got in the front seat, Tony shuffled into the back, like a condemned man.

'Seat belt, Tony,' said Hobbes. 'I wouldn't want any harm to come to you.'

The car sprang forward again and, as I closed my eyes, I heard a whimper as if from a scared baby. Tony would have to come to terms with Hobbes's driving in his own way. The ride seeming smoother than normal, I considered opening my eyes until Hobbes spoke.

'One hundred and forty. That's quite fast, eh, Tony?'

He did not reply.

Not surprisingly, we made the five miles back to the police station in three minutes, which I supposed meant we'd slowed down at times. The car pulled up abruptly and with barely a screech.

'The brakes aren't bad either,' said Hobbes, as I opened my eyes.

He had to lift the pale-faced, trembling Tony from the back seat and carry him into the police station. On reaching the interview room, he plopped him onto a chair with a soft thud, watching as he slithered to the floor like a sack-full of quivering jelly. My legs, though shaking, still held me up and I looked down on the sad mess with a heady feeling of superiority.

'It's a bit nippy in here,' I shivered.

'Would you like a cup of tea?' asked Hobbes.

'I'd love one,' I said.

'Great,' he smiled. 'So would I and you'd better make one for our guest as well. He looks like he could do with one. Make it a sweet one; he's looking somewhat stressed.'

Having descended from superior being to tea-boy in less than fifteen seconds, I muttered under my breath as I headed for Hobbes's office to perform my menial task, though I perked up on realising I'd been presented with an opportunity. While the kettle got hot, I rummaged through some of his things, although I felt guilty, almost as if I was committing burglary. At first, I didn't find a great deal of interest, since nearly everything was locked away, apart from the piles of old reports and other such stuff on the floor. Yet, taking another look at the newspaper cutting, I was staggered how much the moustached, uniformed policeman looked like a younger version of Hobbes.

Then, not expecting much, I tugged at the drawer in his desk, a spine-tingling thrill of naughtiness running through me as it opened. I found more or less what I expected in a desk drawer: a variety of junk, some stationery, pencil stubs, a chipped twelve-inch wooden ruler and a battered tobacco tin. However, the contents of the tin were interesting. On top lay a handful of bent, flattened and distorted bits of metal, looking very much like damaged bullets. Underneath, was a faded, purple ribbon attached to a dull, black cross, bearing the legend 'For Valour', beneath images of a crown and a lion. It took a few moments for the meaning to sink in: it was a Victoria Cross, Britain's highest military decoration. Stunned, I remembered Mrs Goodfellow telling me that he'd been decorated, and I didn't feel the need to turn it over to know whose name was engraved on the back.

Yet, I was puzzled why he kept such a glorious award in a tin at the back of a drawer filled with rubbish. If I'd ever won something like that, if I'd ever won anything at all, I'd have it displayed where it might impress people. My father proudly showed off his dental certificates, yet I'd never even passed my cycling proficiency test.

At least, I didn't think so, because when the badges were handed out I was in hospital with a broken collarbone and cracked pelvis after having failed to notice the road works in time, crashing through a wooden barrier and plummeting down a hole. Though it had hurt like hell, I didn't cry when they pulled me out, or laid me in the ambulance, or during treatment. It wasn't until I lay in the hospital bed, plastered and helpless, that the tears overwhelmed me. My parents had been visiting and I'd wet the bed, because I didn't know how to get to the toilet and couldn't speak over mother's crying and father's sarcasm.

Footsteps approaching, I crammed everything back, scuttling towards the kettle, which had started to boil. I was pouring it out when Hobbes entered, giving me a quizzical look.

'Alright, Andy?'

'Umm ... yeah. Why d'you ask?'

'Because you're pouring boiling water into the tea caddy. Never mind, I expect a good strong cup of tea will do us all a power of good.'

'Oh, bugger, I'm sorry!'

I poured the run off into the teapot, trying to retrieve the situation while he rummaged behind the filing cabinet, pulling out a side-handled baton.

'I always enjoy using this,' he said, whacking it into the palm of his left hand.

'You can't,' I cried, appalled. Although I didn't think much of Tony Derrick, I was damn sure Hobbes shouldn't use a baton on him.

'Why not? It does the job and it's quicker than getting someone in.'

'No, it's wrong.'

'Of course it isn't. And even if it was, who's to know?'

'I'd know,' I said. 'I really don't think you should do it.'

'OK,' he shrugged. 'You can do it.'

'Me?'

'Why not?' He grinned. 'It makes a smashing noise, you'll enjoy it.'

'No.' He was going to overstep the mark and my hands trembled because I was going to stop him. 'I absolutely refuse to do anything of the sort.' My sentiments were strong, though my voice was a squeak.

'Well, in that case, shut up and let me get on with it. Just bring the tea in, if you can salvage any, and I'll get to work.'

Managing to squeeze something vaguely tea-like from the brown sludge I'd created, I filled three mugs and carried them through, unsure what else to do.

Hobbes held the door of the interview room to let me in. I put the tray close to Tony, who sat slouched at the desk and, who, to judge by his grimace, was not impressed by my efforts. His eyes widened when Hobbes stepped inside, twiddling the baton between his fingers as though it weighed no more than a chopstick.

'Right, this won't take long,' said Hobbes, eyeing the baton, swinging it round in a circle above Tony's head. 'These things are ever so good. We got 'em for testing but weren't allowed to keep 'em, apart from this one that accidently fell behind my cabinet. Right, a couple of good, sharp whacks should get things going. It usually does.'

I felt a numbing chill along my spine. Though it was cold in there, I don't think that was the reason. Tony shivered, looking like he was going to cry and I gulped, stepping towards him, certain that any protection I might offer would be about as much use as a soggy cardboard shield against a battle-axe, yet determined to do something.

The baton, whooshing through the air, rapped hard against the radiator. Tony, jumping from his seat, slumped to the floor with a low groan, nearly matching the gurgles of the heating pipes.

'What's up with him?' asked Hobbes, looking surprised. 'He was the one moaning about the chill in here. A good whack usually shifts the air-lock in these old pipes.'

I sagged back into a chair, shaking my head. It would have been far too difficult to explain. At least, I think it would have been. I wondered how Hobbes managed to live among ordinary people, although no one else appeared to doubt his humanity. Even PC Wilkes, who had sussed his 'unhumanity', hadn't taken the next step to enlightenment. I pondered the question of whether Hobbes knew the truth about himself. He'd told me he'd been adopted; if he'd been raised as a human, perhaps he regarded himself as one of us.

'Daydreaming again, Andy?' He ran his hand along the radiator. 'Ah, good, can you feel the heat, Tony?' He turned, lifting the whining figure back into his seat.

I emerged from my deep thoughts with a jerk.

'I've done nothing,' Tony shouted. 'I want a lawyer and I want to make a phone call.'

'And I want a decent cup of tea,' said Hobbes. 'Sadly, we can't always get what we want. So shut up, have a drink and then we'll enjoy a pleasant chat. Won't we?'

'I've done nothing.'

Hobbes, sitting across the desk from him, took a sip of tea and grimaced, his eyes widening. Standing up, clutching his throat, he dropped to the ground and lay still.

'You've done him in,' Tony jumped up, pointing a shaking finger at me. 'You've poisoned him.' He flung away his mug, slopping tea across the floor.

I sat as if I'd been nailed to the chair, unable to speak, unable to do anything other than stare at the inert body, sprawled like a clubbed elephant seal. What had I done? I knew I wasn't much cop at making tea, yet …

Hobbes sat up with an evil grin. 'Andy, I've had better bilge water than this. It's worse than the stuff from the canteen, which is saying a lot.'

'I thought you were dead.' A muscle in my cheek twitched.

'No thanks to your tea that I'm not. I'll get George Wilkes to make some; he's not bad.' Rising with a smirk, he called for Wilkes. Tony was shaking like he'd just emerged from an icy pond and had forgotten his towel.

Hobbes sat down and smiled at him. 'It's time we had a good chat.'

13

'Right then,' said Hobbes, sitting back in the chair, clasping his great hands behind his head. 'Let's treat this as a friendly little chat between old friends who happened to bump into each other.' Frowning at the quivering wretch, he leaned across the table. 'I take it, that you have no objection to a chat between old friends.'

Tony shook his head, a portrait of misery.

Hobbes grinned. 'Good. Are you sitting comfortably? Then I'll begin. What have you been doing with yourself since the little misunderstanding over Billy Shawcroft? I heard you'd gone into a monastery.'

Tony nodded. 'I did, only I didn't stay long. I couldn't be doing with all the praying and getting up early, though I kinda liked wearing those robe thingies.'

'Cassocks?' I suggested.

'No, it's true.' He gave me an angry glare. 'But the thing is, I thought a monastery'd be more fun. I'd heard they, like, brewed beer and stuff but my lot didn't. They dug gardens and kept bees and went to church, every day – several sodding times! We didn't even get Sundays off. I mean to say, it's a bit bloody over the top, isn't it?'

Hobbes nodded, rocking back in his chair, which, teetering on two legs, emitted alarming creaks.

'They wouldn't even let me eat chocolate, so after about six weeks, I gave them the shove.'

'That's funny,' said Hobbes, 'I was informed that they asked you to leave following some inappropriate remarks to a nun.'

Tony flinched. 'That's not true. Well, it is sort of true, though it wasn't my fault, was it? I thought nuns would be a bit like the girls in "Naughty Naturist Nuns". Have you seen it?'

Hobbes shook his head.

'Ah, you should,' said Tony and sighed. 'Bloody good it is. But they're nothing like that. All I did was tell one of them about it and, next thing I knew, the chief monk was calling me in for a bollocking. Afterwards, we agreed I wasn't quite ready for monastic life. Do you know, monks aren't supposed to think carnal thoughts? Not even about nuns. So I left.'

'Incredible,' said Hobbes. 'Do go on.'

'Then I did some stuff. This and that, you know. I worked as a barman, worked in a shop and worked my way back here.'

'And who are you working for now?' asked Hobbes, as PC Wilkes entered, bearing three steaming mugs of tea.

He placed them on the table, departing with a grin, which I ignored.

'No one,' said Tony. His hand shook as he reached for a mug and spilt a few drops. Taking a sip, he pulled a face and put the mug down.

'And yet you had thousands of pounds in your wallet,' Hobbes pointed out, 'how come?'

Tony took another slurp of tea. 'I've got generous friends.'

'Like Philip Waring?'

'Yeah, he's a good mate. Very generous.'

'How long have you known him?'

'Years and years.'

Hobbes, taking a gulp from his mug, turning towards me, grimaced. 'Nearly as bad as yours,' he said, turning back towards Tony, with what I guess he believed was a friendly smile. 'Years and years? Really? I find that an intriguing remark. You know, of course, that Mr Waring only came to live in Sorenchester a year ago? But I suppose you must have met him somewhere else?'

'Uh, yeah.' Tony nodded, slouching. 'That's right.'

'Where did you meet him?'

'It was so long ago, I can't quite remember.'

'Try.'

I had an inkling Tony wasn't being completely honest.

'Uh … I'm thinking.'

His eyes widened as Hobbes stared at him with a deepening

frown that threatened to rival the Grand Canyon.

'Do go on.' Hobbes growled softly, like a lion on the hunt. 'Where did you first meet your most generous friend, Mr Waring? I'd love to know.'

'Uh … Blackpool.' Tony was no longer slouching but leaning back as far as he could.

'Blackpool?' Hobbes sounded almost amused, though his brows were still furrowed.

'Yeah.' Tony clutched at straws. 'Blackpool. I was working on the … uh … donkeys and we got chatting and he invited me for a beer. Yeah, that's how it was.'

'What did you chat about?'

'Uh … this and that.' He nodded, as if reassuring himself of the facts. 'Deckchairs … candyfloss … seaweed. Those sorts of things I expect.'

Hobbes snorted. 'Of course, that makes it all clear. Just one thing, when, exactly, was this?'

'Uh … twenty years ago.' Tony, scratching his head theatrically, screwed up his weasely face. 'More or less.'

'So you really have known him a long time,' said Hobbes. 'He must have been really generous taking you for a beer, so soon after meeting you. It sounds like you two hit it off. Good for you.' He paused, looking thoughtful. 'Though, I suppose you actually bought the beers?'

Tony looked confused. 'Why me? He was flush. As I remember, he'd just had a win on the geegees and insisted on getting the beers in.'

'A win on the geegees? How amazing,' said Hobbes. 'What a lucky lad – winning on the geegees and then meeting you. Incredible, some might say, as he must have been about ten years old at the time. I know modern kids grow up fast but it's not really likely is it?'

'I don't know. Maybe I got my sums wrong.'

'By a decade?' Hobbes raised his eyebrows. 'D'you know what

I think?'

'No.'

'I think, you're not telling me the truth.' His eyebrows puckered into a savage scowl. 'I would advise you to be honest. You know I like honest people.'

He sprang with such predatory intent that it made me gasp. Tony, jerking backwards, would have fallen had Hobbes not grabbed his shirtfront. The frightened man clutched at Hobbes's hand as he was dragged upright, dangling, his trainers barely scuffing the lino, his watery eyes bulging like a rabbit's with myxomatosis as Hobbes, grinning, pulled him closer, his teeth looking as sharp as steak knives. Tony whimpered, hanging limp like a rag doll.

'You nearly hurt yourself,' said Hobbes. 'It's lucky I caught you. I knew a fellow once who broke his spine falling off a chair and never walked again. Still, such is life. Accidents can happen at any time. Now, are you ready to tell me the truth about Philip Waring?'

Hobbes, setting Tony's feet back onto the floor, held him up by the head. Though the room had begun to warm up, I shivered again, because of a horrible vision of the ratty skull, cracking like a new-laid egg, spilling its contents over the floor. I could only imagine what was passing through Tony's mind – and hope it wasn't Hobbes's fingers.

'Alright,' Tony squeaked as if the words were being squeezed from him. 'I'll tell you what I can.'

Hobbes shoved him back into the chair. There were dents in his forehead, the size and colour of plums.

'That's better,' said Hobbes, quietly resuming his seat, pulling a tattered notebook and a pencil stub from his pocket. 'Now, when did you really meet him?'

Tony swallowed. 'Uh … about two weeks ago.'

'Go on,' said Hobbes.

'It was like this. I was back in town and had got myself the squat but I was broke and on the lookout for some fast cash. Anyway, I'd got just enough for a pint in the Feathers, so I was supping it, keeping my ears open, thinking what to do, when this posh ponce walks in, taking off his jacket, hanging it over a stool and ordering a single malt.'

A slight smirk flickered across Tony's face. 'Featherlight slipped him a malt vinegar and it didn't half make his eyes water. Anyway, when he was spluttering, I sort of noticed his wallet was still on the bar. Taking my chance, I grabbed it and ran. I thought I'd got away but he collared me in the car park.'

Tony took a sip from his mug. Hobbes sat quietly, occasionally scratching in his notebook. I relaxed and the room grew warm and stuffy.

Tony continued. 'I reckoned I was in for it, cos he was a fit bugger. He'd either give me a bloody good shoeing or turn me over to you bastards, or both. He didn't, though. He took his wallet back, said he was a reporter and offered me twenty quid for my story, cos he was writing a piece about crime in the town. Well, I was hardly going to turn down twenty quid, was I?'

'I noticed,' said Hobbes, 'that you said he *was* a fit bugger. Why?'

'Well he was a fit bugger.' Tony looked puzzled for a moment. A look of shock erupted across his pasty face. 'Hey! I don't like what you're getting at. I've done nothing to him. I'm not a killer. You know I'm not.'

Hobbes snarled. 'I don't know any such thing. Billy would have been dead if I hadn't turned up in time – and it was you who'd put him in harm's way.'

'I never knew what she was up to. I swear I didn't – and I did help you find him, which was why you let me off. All I knew was that the old witch was willing to pay good money for him, cos he's so bloody small. She said a kid would've been better, though she didn't want no kids, cos of all the fuss when one goes missing.'

'You didn't care what was going to happen to him,' said Hobbes. 'You sold him and forgot about him.'

'I never hurt him.'

'Did you hurt Philip Waring?' He leaned towards Tony like a

198

tiger preparing to pounce on a tethered lamb.

'No, not me.' Tony's face was as white as a sheep.

'So who did?' asked Hobbes quietly, sitting back.

'No one.' Tony looked more disconcerted by Hobbes's sudden quietness than by his aggression.

'So,' said Hobbes and smiled, though his unblinking gaze was merciless, 'where is he?'

'Don't ask me.'

'I am asking you. Where is he? What's happened to him?'

'I don't know. Honest.' Tony's face had taken on a greenish hue and he looked as if he might be sick.

I wouldn't have blamed him; I was shaking and sweating, even though it wasn't me on the heavy, knobbly end of Hobbes's cudgel stare.

'You can do better than that.' Hobbes was as unblinking as a cobra.

'I can't.' Tony shook his head as if he hoped his neck would break. 'She told me …' His eyes were wild and scared. 'I can't say.'

'Tell me who *she* is? Does *she* know where Mr Waring is?'

The room became very quiet. I was holding my breath and you might have heard the proverbial pin drop if it hadn't been for the slither of Tony falling from his chair and the dull, soggy thump as his body hit the floor. He lay still.

'He's scared of someone,' said Hobbes.

I nodded. He wasn't the only one.

Hobbes stood up, poking the inert body once or twice without response, waving a sharp-nailed finger close to Tony's throat. 'His heart's beating and he's still breathing. He's just fainted I expect. Such a pity. I was enjoying our little chat.'

'Who do you think he could mean by *she*?' I asked.

He paused thoughtfully. 'I don't know. Last time there was a *she* in his life, apart from those unfortunate nuns, it was the wicked old witch who wanted Billy's blood. We believe she died in the inferno when I was getting Billy out, although there was no trace of her afterwards.'

'What did she want his blood for?' I asked, appalled.

'We never found out for sure, though Billy reckoned he'd heard her muttering about a blood-bath.'

'A blood-bath?'

Hobbes nodded. 'She had some crazy notion it would make her young again. I've never heard of it working, though, and it's more orthodox to use a child's blood. I'm pretty certain it wouldn't have worked using dwarf blood.'

My mind struggled to compute the data. 'When you said "the wicked old witch", I thought you just meant a nasty woman. Are you telling me she was a real witch?'

'No, I'm not telling you. I've already told you.'

'So, let's get this straight. There are witches in Sorenchester?'

'Not anymore,' he said, 'unless she resurrected herself.'

'This is too much. Witches aren't real ... are they?'

'Oh, they're real enough, they are just rare – they should be treated as an endangered species, the genuine wicked ones that is, not the harmless ladies and gentlemen who enjoy prancing around in their birthday suits; there's a few of them still around and you should see Hedbury Common at mid-summer. It's an eye opener and no mistake.'

I shook my head, struggling to make sense of the world. It was no use.

Hobbes stood with one foot on Tony's chest, like a big-game hunter with a trophy. 'I can't believe,' he said, 'that the old witch is behind this. I know we found no trace of her body, but the fire was intense. Foolishly, she'd built her house from gingerbread. It defies all logic and it's incredibly inflammable when mixed with brandy. It's a wonder she obtained planning permission.'

I thought I detected a twinkle in his eye. Perhaps he was winding me up, or perhaps not. I was becoming more and more inclined to believe the previously unbelievable. Maybe I was gullible, yet I had seen and heard things I would have considered incredible before meeting him. I realised, of course, that he made jokes at my expense but I think, in part, he was using them to prepare me for the weirdness of the world he inhabited. There were strange parallel lives being lived all around us, if only we knew where and how to look. Yet, humans have proved themselves adept at ignoring whatever does not fit with their simplistic views of the way things ought to be. Or rather, humans have proved *ourselves* adept at ignoring whatever does not fit with *our* simplistic views. Hobbes was getting to me; I hoped unhumanity wasn't catching.

'Right,' said Hobbes. 'I suppose, we'd better drop Tony off in a cell until he feels better.' Slinging the limp body over his shoulder, turning towards the door, he strolled to the cells.

The desk sergeant glanced up as we approached. 'Morning, sir. Another one fainted? Drop him in number two and I'll keep an eye on him.'

'Thanks, Bert,' said Hobbes. 'Right, Andy, since we won't get any more out of him for a while, I propose having a word with Augustus Godley.'

'Who's Augustus Godley?' My mind was blank.

'Do keep up. He's the old churchwarden. He lives only a couple of minutes away.'

'Oh, yes, I remember. The one who knows everything about the church. Umm … will he know anything about Phil?'

Hobbes shrugged. 'I doubt it. However, he does make a really good cup of tea and he's generous with the biscuits. Now walk this way.' He turned towards the door.

If I'd tried to walk that way I'd have done myself a mischief, so I contented myself with my usual scurry, interspersed with bursts of jogging. Leaving the station, turning through an alley into the bottom of Vermin Street, we crossed into Moorend Road, where a row of impossibly cute alms-houses stood. Hobbes held open the gate, ushering me onto the garden path of the first house. Four steps took us to the diminutive stone porch, blotched and camouflaged with decades of lichen and moss. Hobbes rang the bell and we waited. And waited. He rang again.

'There's no one in,' I said after about a minute.

'He's coming. Just be patient.'

He was right. A few seconds later I could hear a shuffling sound and the door creaked open.

'Hello?' A face, crinkled as a pickled chestnut and a similar colour, surrounded by a fuzz of white whiskers and eyebrows, poked out. 'Hello?' he said again, peering at us through alert blue eyes. 'Why, it's PC Hobbes.' He grinned, revealing a mouth as free of teeth as his skin was free of smoothness. Every line on his face was wrinkled, every fold was furrowed. 'I should say Inspector Hobbes. Come in, my dear fellow, and bring the boy with you.'

I glanced over my shoulder before realising he meant me. Hobbes introduced us and I trundled after them down a gloomy stone-paved corridor that was even gloomier when I'd pulled the door behind us. Though the house smelled musty and dusty, Augustus was smartly dressed in a black suit, as if he was off to a funeral. After a minute or two, and all of ten steps, he led us into a small room in which a coal fire glowed like a small volcano. A blue budgie in a cage by the window greeted us with a chirrup as the old man waved us towards a couple of faded velvet armchairs.

'I was just going to make a cup of tea,' said Augustus. 'Would you care to join me?

'Yes please,' said Hobbes, while I nodded hopefully.

As the old man shuffled off to the kitchen, I wondered how long he'd take, realising how parched I'd become. I'd hardly drunk anything at the station; my concoction had been too disgusting and I'd been too enthralled and terrified by Hobbes's friendly little chat to take more than a sip of PC Wilkes's version.

In the meantime, I relaxed, enjoying the fire and glancing round the little room. It held three armchairs, a battered old dining table with matching chairs and a small bureau covered in loose papers. To the right of the fireplace, a bookcase sagged beneath yellowing old books that I suspected were the source of the mustiness. On a shelf to the left stood a small television set that looked prehistoric and which was so encrusted in dust I doubted it would show a picture should it ever be turned on. Further to the left, a window looked out over a tiny lawn, glowing green as northern seas in the sun, which was just peeking out from beneath blanket cloud. There was a clattering from the kitchen, followed by the cheery whistle of a boiling kettle and the budgie's impression of it.

'Should I go and help?' I asked Hobbes, who was sitting with eyes closed, and breathing as deeply as if he'd fallen sleep.

'Eh? What? Oh no. He likes to look after himself. He'll be alright. You'll have to be patient. He doesn't need any help, providing he's allowed to go at his own pace.'

'He looks as old as Methuselah,' I whispered.

'He's not even close. He won't be a hundred until next August.'

'Have you known him long?'

'Since boyhood.'

The kitchen door opening, Augustus shuffled in, shaking a tray piled with tea things, plates and a heap of biscuits. When I made a move to offer assistance, Hobbes raised a finger and an eyebrow and I sat back, twitching and fretting, desperate to hurry him up. Still, it was worth the wait for the tea tasted nearly as delicious and fragrant as Mrs Goodfellow's and there were heaps of biscuits to dunk and suck.

The old man, sat next to Hobbes, and they chatted briefly about the weather and aubergines. Then he fixed Hobbes with a steady gaze. 'Now,' he said, 'you always come here for a reason. What do you want to know?'

'Could you tell us about the Roman Cup at the church?'

Augustus frowned. 'The Roman Cup? Ah yes, I remember, I hear it has been stolen. Such a pity. It was a fine bit of work.'

'Do you know anything about it?' Hobbes took a sip of tea.

'Not much, I'm afraid,' said Augustus, stroking his whiskers between thumb and forefinger of his knobbly hand. 'It is, of course, not a Roman relic.'

Hobbes glanced at me.

'It's only been in the church for a few years. It was a gift in, let me think, 1953, I believe.'

'A gift to the church?' Hobbes raised his eyebrows.

'Yes, yes. It was the year the young queen got crowned. That's why I got that.' He pointed a bulbous finger at the television. 'There hasn't been much worth watching since. Now then, if I remember right, and I usually do, the cup was given by a young couple. Foreigners they were, but very pleasant and most respectable. They wanted to make a gesture of thanks to the good folk of Sorenchester who'd looked after them when they first arrived here. Just after the war, it would have been.'

Hobbes took out his notebook. 'Would you remember the name of the couple?'

'Of course I would. I may be old but I'm not yet in my dotage, I'll have you know.'

'Sorry. What was their name?'

Augustus chuckled. 'Do you really mean to say you don't know? I thought you were trying to trick me and you call yourself a detective? Dear oh dear. Mr and Mrs Roman donated it, so we called it the "Roman Cup". I'd have thought that might have been a clue.'

'It might have been,' said Hobbes, looking comically crestfallen, 'if we'd known it wasn't a cup made by the Romans.'

'Well, you know now,' said Augustus laughing into his tea. 'Just wait till I tell the boys about this.'

'Do you know where the Romans came from? The couple I mean not the empire builders,' asked Hobbes, not appearing at all put out by his mistake.

'They were from Romania.'

I gasped. 'Romania.'

'The boy can speak then?' Augustus smiled. 'Yes, they were Romanians, on the run first from the Nazis and then from the Communists. I used to see them at the church for many years. They had a young lad, too. I wonder what happened to them?'

'They've all passed away,' said Hobbes.

'I'm not surprised,' said Augustus, nodding. 'Some reckoned it was a communion chalice that had once belonged to a king and there was some doubt as to whether the Romans really owned it, yet, since no one else claimed it and they weren't trying to profit from it, the church accepted it in the spirit in which it was offered. It became quite an attraction, you know. However, I'm afraid that is really as much as I know about the cup, except that they'd brought it with them and it was very old.'

'Well thank you,' said Hobbes. 'That was most illuminating.'

'Would you like more tea?'

'No, thank you, I'm afraid there's important work to be done and we'd better be going.'

'So soon?' asked Augustus. 'Ah well, I was only going to ask how your painting was getting on. Do you still do it?'

To my surprise, Hobbes blushed. 'No, well, not often anyway.'

'A pity. You were showing promise. Still, maybe you can take it up again when you retire.'

'Maybe. We really must go.'

We said our goodbyes and left.

'What the hell's going on?' I asked as we stepped into Moorend Road.

'I don't know yet, though I've got a hunch it's something rather unusual. I was slow not picking up the link between Mr Roman and the cup but I still can't work out what it means. With luck we'll get more information from Tony. He's hard work, though. It's just a good job he's such a bad liar. A little more pressure might squeeze something useful from him.'

'So, what about Phil?' We crossed back into Vermin Street towards the shops and the police station.

Hobbes was walking at my pace, hunched up as though under a heavy load. I had never seen him look so worried before. 'Mr Waring?' he said, 'I'm beginning to fear the worst.'

'Do you think he's dead then?' An icy coldness seemed to have invaded my blood.

'I said, I feared the worst. You've seen enough to know death is not the worst that can happen.'

My blood would have run cold if it hadn't already been frozen. I was frightened for Phil, thoroughly ashamed of my silly, spiteful trick, wishing I could have taken the card back. If I'd had the courage, I would have told Hobbes.

A woman's voice called, 'Andy! Mr Hobbes!'

Ingrid had just stepped out of Boots. She wore a long, dark coat and a beige woolly hat that emphasised her pallor. She looked tired.

'Hello,' I said, trying to sound cheerful.

Hobbes stopped, saluting as she approached. 'Good day, Miss Jones.'

'Have you discovered anything about Phil?' she asked. 'I'm dreadfully worried.'

'We've found his car,' said Hobbes, 'and the person who took it will be answering a few questions shortly. I'm afraid I have no other news, although there is some evidence to link Mr Waring to a serious criminal offence yesterday.'

'Phil?' Frowning, she shook her head. 'There's no way he'd be involved in crime. He's not the sort. Maybe he was on a story?'

Hobbes nodded. 'That is likely, though we found an item of his at the crime scene.'

'I don't believe it.'

'I'm not sure I do either, miss. I smell a rat!'

A woman screamed; another joined her. Hobbes was right, a rat the size of a terrier was sauntering down the middle of the road, as if it owned the county. Certainly, no one seemed willing to block its path or to offer any sort of challenge.

Not until there was an explosive woof and a flurry of head shaking that ended with Dregs strolling towards us, tail wagging ecstatically, rat dangling limply. I don't know how he'd got out but he was evidently trying to ingratiate himself now I had the power of Mrs Goodfellow's tincture, and dropped the corpse onto my foot.

206

Hobbes chuckled. 'Sorry, Miss, I'd better be getting back to the station and look after the dog. He shouldn't be out on his own. Clear it up, Andy.' He pointed to the rat, turning away, continuing with his hunched walk. Dregs, to my relief, followed him.

I was left with Ingrid and a dead rat. Somehow, she never saw me at my best. I shrugged, smiling, trying to make light of the situation. 'I seem to have got ratted. I'd better get rid of it.' Fortunately, the large bin standing down the alley next to Boots looked suitable for a last resting-place. Bending, shuddering, I picked the rat up by the tip of its tail, praying it was really dead. I'd had enough pain from a hamster a tenth its size to feel completely at ease, though Dregs had broken its neck for sure. I held it at arm's length with an attempt at nonchalance.

'You horrible man,' said a woman, driving her words home with solid whacks from her rolled umbrella, 'murdering God's creatures without a second thought.'

I turned towards her.

It was the blue-rinsed woman from the church. 'You again,' she said, 'I might have known.'

With solid blows raining down on my head and shoulders, I raised my arm to protect myself. The rat's tail slipping through my fingers, it flew through the air, striking the woman full in the face. Screaming, she backed off. People had stopped in the street to watch the fun, yet now, somehow, their amusement evaporating, they saw me as the aggressor. Fingers pointed, hard words were flung as, forgetting Ingrid, I fled.

14

Cries of 'police', 'stop that man', 'knock him down', and 'three for a pound', pursued me as I plunged into the alley. I'd only gone a couple of steps before I was in an arm-lock, my face pressed against the wall. The mossy brickwork was damp against my cheek, while its odour, a medley of stale urine, vomit and chips, made me feel ill.

'Well done, constable,' said a pompous male voice. 'I witnessed the incident. He assaulted the lady with a dead rat. She was forced to beat him off with her umbrella.'

'No,' said a shrill female voice, 'I saw it all. He was torturing a poor dumb animal and, when the lady tried to stop him, he threw it in her face.'

'That's not what happened at all,' said Ingrid. 'A dog killed the rat and Andy was trying to dispose of the body when the woman attacked him, without provocation. He was only trying to protect himself.'

I nodded. Good old Ingrid, she'd get me out of the mess.

'Be quiet.' The police officer bellowed. It was Wilkes. It had to be Wilkes.

The crowd around the alley's entrance shut up.

Wilkes, turning me round to face him, winked and murmured, 'Nice to see you again. What is it with you and rodents?' He glanced at the crowd, raising his voice. 'There's nothing to see here. If anyone has anything to say, follow me to the station and say it.'

Placing a heavy hand on my shoulder, he frogmarched me to the station, only a couple of minutes away. I only managed one glance back as he thrust me through the station doorway, relieved that only Ingrid had followed. I hoped it was a sign that I was starting to make progress with her, though my thoughts were mostly concentrated on what Wilkes would do. I needn't have worried. Releasing me, he smiled and patted my back as we moved inside.

'Sorry about that, mate. I saw it all, so don't worry. The show of authority was to appease the mob – it usually works better than reasoning. Now, mind how you go.' He stepped back into the street.

I smiled at Ingrid, embarrassed as usual. 'I'm glad that's over.'

She seemed genuinely concerned. 'Are you alright? It was lucky the policeman saw what happened.'

'I'm fine and George Wilkes,' I said, nonchalantly, 'is a good man.' Maybe, I thought, he wasn't so bad.

Ingrid smiled. 'Great … but I was going to ask you to let me know when you find anything out about Phil.'

Though I heard what she said, a thought gripped me. Perhaps Wilkes had only laughed at me when we first met because I was so funny. For the first time, I managed to see the hamster incident from another's viewpoint, seeing that it had been amusing, or would have been if it had happened to someone else. And the riot I'd accidentally sparked, maybe that had a funny side, too. Recalling the pained expression on my face in the newspaper, a snigger sneaked out and then laughter engulfed me.

Ingrid's pretty face contorted in outrage and, for some stupid reason, that boosted the hilarity. Leaning on the counter, I tried to stop myself collapsing into a giggling heap. I was a joke and life was a joke and she couldn't see it.

'What's wrong with you?' Her voice veered towards fury. 'How can you laugh when poor Phil's in trouble? It's not funny. You disgust me. At least the Inspector's taking it seriously and he doesn't even know him. Goodbye!'

Opening the door, she stamped away, leaving me helpless, half-blind with tears, struggling for breath, with no chance of explaining myself. Then, at last, a wave of despair broke over me, submerging the hysterics. If I'd been alone, I might have cried. The sergeant sat watching, as if he saw the same sort of thing every day.

I pulled myself upright, taking a deep breath, smoothing my emotions into a superficial calm. Remorse about Phil's card was gnawing at my conscience and it was getting harder to keep it caged at the back of my mind.

'Are you alright now, sir?' asked the desk sergeant, 'because the Inspector would like a word with you. He'll be in his office.'

'I'm OK,' I said.

Trying to stroll casually through the police station, I stubbed my foot on the carpet and stumbled. Ignoring the smirks, I carried on until, reaching Hobbes's door, I jerked it open before stepping briskly inside. At least, I envisaged it that way. In reality the door opened inwards and I nearly tore my shoulder from its socket as my head banged against wood. Hearing a snigger, embarrassment heated my face.

'Come in,' said Hobbes.

He looked up from behind his desk, a sheet of paper in his hand. 'Oh, it's you. There was no need to knock.' He peered at me. 'Are you feeling alright? Your face is extraordinarily red.'

'I'm fine. It's just a little warm in here.'

A smile flickered. 'Sit,' he said. 'I've just received this.' He waved the paper at me. 'The house agent faxed the inventory through for Brancastle.'

I made myself comfortable. 'Oh yes? What was stolen then?'

'It's long and detailed though, so far as I can tell, only one item is missing.'

'That's what old Barrington-Oddy thought.'

Hobbes nodded. 'Apparently he is more observant than he claims. It looks like the only thing stolen was a ring.'

'A ring? Is that all? There were all sorts of valuable things in the house.'

'Indeed,' he said. 'It is suggestive.'

'So, what's so special about a ring?' I attempted humour. 'Is it a ring of power, forged by the evil Lord Sauron to control mortal men, doomed to die?'

He looked puzzled. 'No. At least I don't think so. Why do you mention Sauron?'

'Sorry. He's just a character in a film about rings.'

'I know. You need to learn to separate fact from fiction, or you'll go the same way as PC Norman, who used to work with me until he started insisting he was communicating with goblins. It was ridiculous yet, as he was still capable of doing his job reasonably well, I kept him on until the day the goblins told him to take his clothes off and direct the traffic onto the golf course.'

'What happened to him?'

Hobbes sighed. 'We found him standing stark naked in the middle of the ring road, waving his truncheon and screaming, "No man is an island." When I asked, "What about the Isle of Man?" he went to pieces and we had to scoop him up and take him away for his own safety. The superintendent put the whole incident down to a PC gone mad.'

'What,' I asked, 'has that to do with the ring?'

'About as much as your remark about Lord Sauron. Now listen, Rocky was correct to say a Romanian gentleman owned the house and, according to the inventory, the missing ring is Romanian, too. It is very old, made of gold and in the form of a dragon with ruby eyes.'

'A dragon? Like the bracelet? So, it's something to do with the Order of St George?'

'It sounds plausible. I'll get one of the lads to call the agent to see if there's any more information.'

'I bet it is,' I said. 'I bet this case is all to do with Romania and the Order of St George.'

Hobbes shrugged. 'We'll see. We have Mr Roman's suicide following the break-in at his house. Jimmy, the gardener, the probable culprit, was stabbed to death, buried and dug up so something could be removed from his grave. Afterwards came the break-in at the museum to steal a bracelet. Then the Roman cup was taken and now this ring has been stolen.'

Seeing that he was thinking aloud, I kept quiet.

He scratched his ear. 'What puzzles me is how Mr Waring fits into all this and where he's got to. The discarded cigarette butts suggest Tony Derrick was involved with, at least, the break-ins at Mr

Roman's, the church and at the museum. Plus, he knows Mr Waring, whose business card was discovered at Brancastle.'

I nodded, shifting uncomfortably. In my heart, I'd already accepted that Phil wasn't a criminal, that I'd just resented him because he was the better man and, though deep down I still held a grudge, my malice didn't go so far as to wish him real harm. I hoped he was still alive. 'D'you really think Phil's involved?'

Hobbes's expression was thoughtful. 'Let's just say there are no indications that he is, except for circumstantial evidence. There is, of course, the business card that would seem to place him at one of the incidents.' He paused, staring hard at me. 'I can't work that one out.'

This was it. I gulped. 'I think I can.'

'Go on, then.' Leaning forward, he rested his head on one hairy paw.

I couldn't look him in the eye and, my lungs seemingly too tight to breathe, it was an age before I forced a faint voice. 'It's ... umm ... my fault.'

'Yours, Andy? I am surprised.'

'Yes. Oh God, I don't know how to say this.'

'Take your time.'

'OK. I'd better just spit it out. It's no use putting it off any longer. It's my fault.'

'So you said.'

I thought I could detect the beginnings of a growl.

'Oh God.' I stared at my hands. They were shaking and fluttering in time with the butterflies in my stomach.

'OK. I'd better just get it off my chest. It's my fault.'

'I'm sure it is,' said Hobbes and I was sure the growl was present.

'I ... umm ... really don't know how to say this.'

'I know I said take your time but I didn't mean take all day. Out with it. And quickly.'

'Right ... umm ... you know Phil's business card? The one Wilkes found under the mat?'

'Yes.'

212

'Right. OK. Oh God. Umm ... well, it was like this. I put it there.'

'You, Andy? Why?'

What else could I do except tell the truth?

'Because I ... umm ... because I was jealous, I suppose. Phil is everything I'm not. He's like what I want to be, yet I can't be like him and, because I can't, I came to detest him, to hate his success, to hate that people liked him. And then there was Ingrid.'

'Do go on,' said Hobbes, and I felt sure I detected rising anger in his voice.

Still unable to look at him, I took another deep, gulping breath. 'When we were round at Phil's place and you were looking at his computer, I picked up a couple of his cards. The thing is, I'd kind of convinced myself he was a villain and thought that if I put his card at the scene then you'd see him in the same light. I'm sorry.'

'Sorry?' roared Hobbes, his voice rumbling like a volcano, 'I should think you are sorry. It was a despicable act.'

Flinching, nodding agreement, I lifted my head, still unable to raise my eyes above his chest, bracing myself for when he blew his top. 'I really am sorry. I was sorry from the moment Wilkes found it and I keep wishing I hadn't done it. If there's anything I can do to help make amends?'

And then he exploded.

I cringed, sweating, caught between running for my life and curling up and taking his wrath. Yet, when I finally dared to look up, he was laughing. Tears poured down the furrows in his face as he rocked back and forth in his chair.

'By heck, Andy!' He guffawed. 'Promise me you'll never be a criminal. You'd make things far too easy for us. We do like some sort of challenge, you know?'

'Umm ... I don't understand.'

He wiped his eyes. 'Did you honestly believe I'd fallen for your silly trick? I am a detective you know. I should feel insulted; I might have been if you weren't so funny.'

Stunned, shocked, confused, humiliated, relieved and indignant in quick succession, I finally settled on being relieved, with a seasoning of confusion. It seemed he did not intend tearing me limb from limb. 'But how?'

'How? Well, firstly, I observed you removing the cards from the box.'

I didn't see how he could have done, unless he'd got eyes in the back of his head, which he hadn't. I didn't think so, anyway.

'Secondly, the card was not under the mat when I entered Brancastle and only appeared after you came looking for me. Thirdly, Mrs Goodfellow found several other cards in your jacket pocket when she took it away for cleaning. Fourthly, you had not exactly hidden your feelings towards Mr Waring and, fifthly, I've heard you muttering under your breath more than once that you wished you'd never hidden "the bloody card." Excuse my language.'

'So you knew it was me all the time? Why didn't you say anything?'

'Because it amused me and gave you the chance to make good.' He chuckled. 'The lass and I had a talk about it and decided you weren't a bad lad really. Still, I'm glad you've owned up at last. She'll be pleased when I tell her.'

'Not as pleased as I am,' I said, dizzy with relief. 'It's been horrible, especially when Phil went missing. It's true I wanted him out the way, though not like this, and, anyway, I don't think Ingrid likes me very much.'

'That's a shame. However, you can't make people like you,' he said, 'and sometimes the more you try the less they do. It's the way things are. You have to be yourself and be hopeful.'

I nodded, looking into his corrugated mess of a face, wondering how it felt to be Hobbes, feeling an overwhelming sense of loneliness. Who, I thought, could befriend him? I supposed Mrs Goodfellow, the olde troll, Augustus and maybe Billy Shawcroft might, but they were all outsiders and oddities. Everyone else just seemed to regard him either with respect as a copper who got the job done, or as a figure of fear. Surfing a wave of sympathy and well-being, I reminded myself that, in his own grotesque way, he'd shown me nothing but kindness, except for when he'd shown me terror and horror. Still, with the chains of my guilt released, the world felt a lighter, more hopeful place.

'I still don't really understand what's going on,' I said.

'D'you mean with life, the universe and everything? Or with these crimes?'

'The crimes.'

'So you understand life, the universe and everything?' He grinned. 'You're a genius on the quiet then?'

'No, I didn't mean that. I mean I'm often confused and I'm specifically confused about all these robberies. As far as I can see, there's some Romanian thing connecting them all, yet it doesn't explain why anyone would want the things they took.'

'You're right,' he said. 'I have a bad feeling, though. I fear trouble is afoot and I'm rarely wrong. Anyway, first things first; I ought to see how Tony's getting on and have another word with him.'

We headed for cell number 2. When the sergeant opened it, there was a woof and a black, hairy creature bounded out, bouncing around us.

'I put Dregs with him so he wouldn't feel lonely,' said Hobbes.

I was shocked. 'Couldn't he have hurt him?'

'Most unlikely. He's a big dog and can look after himself.'

'I meant the other way round.'

'I never thought of that,' he said, chewing his lip, peering into the cell and patting the dog's head. 'However, Tony appears to be in one piece.'

He stepped into the cell. 'How are you feeling? A little better? Good. It's not pleasant to faint. So I've been told.'

Tony was sitting on the bench, his back against the wall, his knees drawn up to his chest. When Dregs squeezed past me and bounded in, he squealed, 'Keep it away.'

Hobbes grabbed Dregs's collar. 'Sit,' he said.

The dog sat, wagging his tail, staring at Tony who cringed further up the wall.

'Now then, Tony, are you ready to continue our friendly little chat? Or would you like a bit of dinner? I am obliged to warn you that the stew from our canteen might be construed as cruel and unusual punishment, yet some of the lads seem to thrive on it. At least, they go back for more.'

'I am hungry,' said Tony, adding pathetically, 'I never had no breakfast.'

'No problem,' said Hobbes. 'I'll ask the sergeant to arrange something. We'll continue our talk later, eh? It's a shame I'm not going to let you out because my housekeeper's made chicken soup for lunch. At least I think so, because I heard her plucking the chicken this morning. Would you like Dregs to stay with you? No? Suit yourself. He probably should go home anyway.'

Hobbes turned away, Dregs walking to heel like the hero of an obedience school, as the sergeant locked the door.

'See he gets some grub,' said Hobbes and turned to me. 'We'll leave him to stew and get our dinners.'

The thin November sun radiated genuine warmth, though a chill wind dominated the shadows as we proceeded along The Shambles towards the church, the clock striking one as we waited to cross the road into Blackdog Street. I was far away, thinking of chicken soup, when a woman in a black Volvo drove past, her dull eyes staring at me from a dead head. I shivered, yet, it must have been some sort of illusion, for the driver turned her head and drove away.

'Did you see that?' I asked, as the traffic lights changed and allowed us to cross.

'What?'

'I don't really know.'

'Then, nor do I,' said Hobbes with a frown.

I shrugged, yet something still troubled me, as if she ought to have been familiar.

Lunch was nearly ready when we got in. Hobbes messed about in the back garden with Dregs, while I flopped down on the sofa, flicking through *Sorenchester Life*, stopping when I reached the photo of Editorsaurus Rex. 'Mr Rex Witcherley and wife, Narcisa, enjoy a joke,' I read and slapped the open magazine down on the table, afraid I'd been the joke. Everyone else apparently found me a source of amusement, yet, I had to admit, in my heart of hearts, that I doubted Rex would ever have given me so much thought. I'd just been an employee, a useless oaf he'd finally got rid of. Perhaps I was laughable as a journalist, a complete fool. Still, at least now I'd confessed my appalling trick, I could be an honest fool and, maybe, I could even help to put things right.

I tried to think deeply about the cases and see what I could make of them. The only connection seemed to be something to do with Romania – and Phil didn't fit, unless he was Romanian and I had no reason to suspect so.

'It's on the table!' A shrill voice rang in my ear.

I gasped, collapsing into the sofa. I had not yet developed immunity to Mrs Goodfellow's sudden appearances.

'Thank you,' I said, rising on shaking legs, sure that one day I'd suffer heart failure. At least, it would stop people laughing at me.

As I joined Hobbes in the kitchen, it occurred to me that, if I expired, I wouldn't be able to enjoy Mrs Goodfellow's cooking any more. Her chicken soup was to die for, or, more rationally, a great reason to live. As usual, she disappeared when we were eating. Unusually, I could hear her rummaging round in the cellar.

'She's searching for her roots,' said Hobbes, dunking a chunk of crusty bread into his soup and slurping with massive enjoyment.

I nodded, trying to make sense of his enigmatic statement, speculating whether it might have something to do with whatever lay behind the mysterious door. However, when she emerged after a few minutes with a basket of turnips and parsnips, I understood. Yet, the door still irked me. What did it conceal and would I ever get the chance to find out? Should I even try when it might be dangerous? Whatever the answers, there were other more important puzzles to solve first, not to mention concentrating on maximising my enjoyment of the soup.

We'd finished and were sitting on the sofa drinking tea, when a yawn erupted from deep within. A disturbed night, an exciting morning and a belly tight with chicken soup combined to induce an overwhelming fatigue and that first yawn was like the pattering of small pebbles that presage a landslide. Within moments I was engulfed and yawning uncontrollably.

'Ooh.' Mrs Goodfellow's voice seemed to reach me from a distance. 'Hasn't he got lovely teeth? And so many of 'em.'

I made a feeble attempt to clamp my mouth shut and vaguely noticed Hobbes carrying me upstairs over his shoulder. That was all until I woke up, the gloom and stillness suggesting dusk. I lay in bed in my pyjamas with no memory of changing; I'd bet Mrs Goodfellow had looked after me.

I shrugged; she'd seen more of me than any woman since I was eight. Still half asleep, I winced as an old memory forced itself to the forefront of my thoughts. Though Father didn't believe in wasting good money on holidays, the doctor had insisted that Mother needed a break, because of what had happened to my sister. So, Mother, Father and I went to Tenby. We were sitting on the beach in late September and I decided I wanted a swim, though the sea was foaming as a teasing wind goaded it to a fury. While changing, goose pimples modestly concealed behind the soft folds of a towel, having just reached the awkward point, having stepped out of my pants, I was bending to pick up my new, stripy swimming trunks when a vindictive gust tore along the beach, whipping up the sand into a stinging cloud. Turning my face away, seeing my trunks taxiing for take-off, I tried to pin them down with my foot, but only stepped on the edge of the towel, tugging it from my hand. My despairing lunge for the trunks failing, they accelerated, skimming the sand and flying. A moment later, my towel, too, took flight like a fluffy seagull, its edge slapping my cheek in farewell. I stood, exposed and humiliated, convinced the eyes of the entire world were pointed at me. All my clothes were blowing away as well.

'Don't just stand there, boy,' said Father, 'go and fetch them.'

Though I tried to argue, he wouldn't listen. He sent me running along the beach, trying to retrieve my clothes, my towel and my dignity, while the bullying wind kept tossing everything just out of my reach and the tourists pointed and laughed. It had been so long ago and yet it still made me cringe.

Still, it was all in the past, irrelevant to my current life and, cramming the thoughts back into a dark recess, I indulged my body with a long stretch. Clean sheets were still a novelty and the faint fragrance of lavender was relaxing. I thought I should get up. I'd obviously missed the afternoon and wondered what we might be getting for supper.

Apart from a faint murmur of traffic rising from the street outside, the house lay in silence. Barefoot, I padded across to the window, poking my head between the curtains, looking out on the twilit town where the streetlights had just flickered into life, a handful of huddled people hurrying beneath their glow. A glimmer off the window of a parked car suggested there might already be a hint of frost. A movement from the roof opposite made me jump and my thoughts flew towards Hobbes, though it was only a ragged flock of starlings practising touch and go before roosting.

Somehow, Hobbes had tracked down Tony Derrick; somehow his bizarre crawling around on rooftops had contributed. I supposed he might have spotted Tony during his nocturnal excursion and followed him, or possibly he'd picked up his scent – I could hardly fail to have noticed that he appeared to use his nose rather like a dog – and, perhaps, an unhuman possessed other senses, ones I couldn't even imagine. Yet I knew speculation would not get me anywhere.

I guessed he'd been interviewing Tony Derrick as I slept, which was good, for the atmosphere in the interview room had grown too heavy for comfort. It was also a disappointment, since I'd have liked to see how he prised further information from the human rat. I hoped he'd found Phil, alive and well, even if it meant I'd lose any chance of hitting it off with Ingrid. Sighing, I drew the curtains and dressed, not bothering to turn on the light. Muzzy-headed and heavy after my nap, I thought a cup of tea might perk me up. There were no lights on and no sound of movement as I picked my way downstairs, though something delicious was cooking in the kitchen.

I put the kettle on, trying to avoid looking at the cellar door, for one day, I feared curiosity would drive me down there. A click suggested the front door had opened, the kitchen door, pushed to, flew open and I was engulfed in dog. Though Dregs had apparently decided I was one of the pack, a friend, and showed delight at seeing me, his enthusiasm seemed almost as bad as his earlier aggression. He was exuding tail-wagging bonhomie and an overpowering doggy odour as he alternately thrust his head into my groin or leaped at my face to favour me with a good licking. Behind the disgust, I almost felt pleased.

'Get down, you daft brute,' I said, patting his head, making an effort to keep it where it could do least harm.

'Hello, dear.' Mrs Goodfellow materialised at my side.

As I flinched, the dog took the opportunity for one last lick.

She smiled. 'Did you sleep well? You've got to be careful not to overdo things. There's not many can keep up with the old fellow.'

'Yes, I think I needed it. Now I need a cup of tea.'

'I'll make it,' she said. 'I don't want you setting fire to anything.'

Afterwards, filled with tea, I felt better until she sidled up.

'Would you give me a hand, dear?'

'No.' I recoiled. 'You've got enough. You can have my teeth when I've finished with them but not my hands.'

She hooted with laughter, her gummy mouth beaming hilarity. 'No, dear. Could you give me a hand to wash Dregs? He stinks and I don't want a dirty dog in my nice, clean house.'

'Oh. I see what you mean … umm … do you think it's wise? He's a big dog.'

'That's why I need help. I'll hold him down and you can wash him. I've got some special dog shampoo.'

I didn't really have a choice. 'OK.'

'Right, let's get him up to the bathroom. I'll carry him and you can open the doors. Alright?'

Dregs was sniffing the flip-top bin in the corner when she bent and took him by surprise. He yelped and kicked as her scrawny arms seized him, sweeping him off his feet. Big, frightened eyes looked to me for sympathy, as I led the way upstairs.

I shrugged. 'Sorry mate, but she's right, you do stink.'

Part of me thought I ought to be carrying him, yet the old girl was already jogging upstairs as fast as I could go. At the top, I flung open the bathroom door and, as I shut it behind us, the prisoner, recognising his cruel fate, howled.

After I'd filled the bath with lukewarm water, Mrs Goodfellow dunked him like a biscuit, amid a frenzy of splashing and kicking until the futility of resistance struck him, making him stand stock still, a picture of abject misery. Lathering his rough coat with dog shampoo, I rubbed it in. Now and again, his memory failing, he restarted the struggle, yet he stood no chance and, in a strange way, it made me feel better that I'd been knocked out by her; I, too, had stood no chance.

Eventually, as she lifted the defeated creature from the water, I helped towel him down. When freed from her iron grip, he still retained sufficient sogginess to drench us as he shook his coat, shedding all gloom and resentment in that glorious act of sweet revenge, scampering round the bathroom, rubbing himself on every surface, playful as a puppy, until Mrs Goodfellow, opening the door, released him into the community. He threw himself downstairs while we did our best to dry ourselves and clean up.

'The old fellow will be back for his supper soon,' she said, scrubbing away a muddy patch.

'Good,' I said, 'what is it?'

She smiled. 'I like to see a young man with a healthy appetite. It's steak and kidney pudding, one of his favourites. I hope you like it?'

'I don't know. I've had steak and kidney pie and that was alright.'

'The old fellow likes the pudding best – it was his first decent meal after getting out of hospital in the war.'

'Was he wounded?'

'He was shot as full of holes as a colander.'

'Where was he shot?'

'In the Arras area. They thought he'd die until one of his mates patched him up and held him together.'

I was shocked, finding it difficult to imagine him ever being hurt, for he exuded such an air of invulnerability that it didn't seem right that he could bleed like anyone else. Yet, I'd recognised the sensitivity in his paintings and seen occasional compassion in his actions. Perhaps, he wasn't so very different.

Arras? I groped in the haze of memory; surely it had been a battle in the First World War? Hobbes was amazing.

'I'm glad he pulled through,' I said.

Mrs Goodfellow beamed. 'So am I dear, otherwise neither of us would be here.'

I couldn't disagree. He'd saved my skin three times already. 'Has he ever rescued you?' I asked.

She nodded, giving the bath a final wipe and standing up. 'It was during the Blitz. Our house got bombed and my family was killed. All I remember is a horrible noise and the ceiling falling down. I was buried and it felt like I lay in the dark forever. Then everything lifted and the big policeman was kind. That was the old fellow.'

It was another shock, for, although I'd worked out that Hobbes was ridiculously old, I'd assumed she was as well, because she looked ancient. The idea of her being so much younger flabbergasted me.

'I'm sorry about your family,' I said, 'but he's good at saving people isn't he?

'Yes, and it didn't stop there, because he looked after me right up to my marriage.'

I would have liked to ask her about that, specifically what had happened to Mr Goodfellow and why I'd acquired his clothes but the chimes of the church clock, striking six, put an end to our chat.

'I'd better get back down to the kitchen. I don't like to keep him waiting.'

He didn't turn up. About quarter to seven, she fed me, saying it was a pity to let good food spoil when I was so obviously starving yet, despite the steak and kidney pudding tasting truly, fantastically delicious, I didn't really enjoy it, because she never went away and kept looking at the clock and checking the oven.

He still hadn't appeared by the time I'd finished.

'I hope he's alright,' she said. 'He's not normally late for his supper and if he is, he lets me know.'

'I expect he's just busy and has lost track of time. He'll be back soon, I'm sure.'

He wasn't. She tried his mobile without reply. I phoned the station, learning that he hadn't been seen since mid-afternoon when he'd released Tony Derrick. By half-past eight, Mrs Goodfellow looked frantic. Dregs, on the other hand, had fallen asleep in a corner and snored, as if his inner pig was trying to emerge.

At last I made a decision. The snoring had started to bug me and I couldn't stand any more of Mrs Goodfellow sitting down, standing up, looking at the clock and going to peer out the front door. Her nervousness was infectious. 'I'll go and see if he left a note at the station, and I might have a word with Billy Shawcroft. Hobbes says he knows what's going down.'

Mrs Goodfellow looked grateful and I felt relieved to be out of the house, though I was glad of the long overcoat I'd found. Turning up the collar, an icy wind slapping my ears, I wished I had a hat. Actually, Mrs Goodfellow had dug out a rather fine trilby, which I'd been too embarrassed to wear in public, even if I'd thought it made me look rather cool when posing before the mirror. Returning briefly, jamming the hat onto my head, thrusting my hands into my pockets, I strode towards the police station, my breath curling like smoke. Catching a glimpse of myself in a shop window, I thought I looked a bit like Sam Spade or some other hero of film noir. Even though I laughed at myself, some of the image and attitude stuck.

Though the streets were quiet, I couldn't ignore an impression that dark things lurked in the shadows. It was fanciful, maybe, but I was beginning to see Sorenchester differently, to see the world differently. There were more things in heaven and earth than I'd dreamt of before Hobbes. I hoped he was alright.

15

A verbal altercation was taking place by the desk when I reached the police station. Though keeping my distance, I gathered it had kicked off after a van was pulled over for speeding. The cops, looking in the back, finding it loaded with suspected contraband, had arrested the driver, who was insisting loudly and coherently that it wasn't contraband at all but props for his clown act. The Irish accent being familiar, I swiftly recognised it as belonging to Pete Moss.

No one having eyes for me, I slipped past.

The rest of the station was deserted, the big office standing in darkness. Without an audience, I opened Hobbes's door with no problem and turned on the light. His room appeared the same as always and I began to suspect I was on a fool's errand. Still, I decided, I might as well have a bit of a nose around, though I felt reluctant to rummage too deeply, in case he returned. A mess of papers littered the desktop and I was about to push them aside when I noticed the doodle. Actually, it was far better than a mere doodle, more like a portrait in ink, unmistakably the face of Narcisa Witcherley, which puzzled me. Why her? I wondered. It occurred to me, thinking back to his rather gallant manner on meeting her in Rex's office, that he might have the hots for her, for she did possess a certain feminine charm, though she'd not impressed me, being too stretched, too plastered with make-up, and being a smoker of unusually noxious cigarettes. There was another sketch of her with Tony Derrick of all people, and I wished I had Hobbes's ability for, although the portraits were accurate, Tony's held a hint of weasel, while Narcisa's suggested arrogance and coldness.

Yet it made no sense to have wasted his time drawing when he was working on a case. Maybe, he'd done it subconsciously, as I'm prone to do, though my doodles look like doodles.

I uncovered another sketch showing two men standing together, one wearing a long coat, a trilby hat pulled low and a scarf wrapped around his face, the other sporting a short jacket and a balaclava to conceal the bits of his face not obscured by sunglasses. The significance was clear; they were the villains who'd attacked Mr Barrington-Oddy.

On pushing the drawings aside, I noticed the fax from the house agent, confirming the ring was fifteenth-century Romanian, yet disputing that it had anything to do with the Order of St George. It was, in fact, a relic of a different order, the Order of the Dragon and, according to the agent, a rare and valuable object. However, Mrs Iliescu, loathing it and needing the money, had offered it for sale. The fax incorporated a copy of her advert, including historical details about Sigismund, the Holy Roman Emperor establishing the Order of the Dragon in 1408 and having the dragon ring fashioned for one of his vassals, a chap with the unfortunate name of Vlad, in about AD 1430. I felt a wavelet of satisfaction that I hadn't been entirely wrong about the Roman connection after all.

Skipping the baffling details about the Troy weight in gold and the quality of the rubies, I found a photograph of the ring, an exquisite object, shaped like a winged dragon, its tail coiled around its neck, resembling the bracelet. Despite the fax being rather blurred, I could understand Mrs Iliescu's point of view, because there was something loathsome about it, despite the quality of the craftsmanship. Yet, she obviously had great faith in its value, for its price was fifty thousand pounds – a hell of a lot of money for such a small item.

I speculated that the bracelet, though only of bronze, might be worth a similar amount to, say, a collector. Few have such money available and anyone really desiring it, my putative collector for instance, might resort to stealing as the better option. I was impressed by my insight: I was starting to think like a detective. Hobbes was starting to rub off on me.

Yet all my brilliant reasoning had got me no closer to finding him. Deciding I might as well head to the Feathers and ask Billy, I was on the point of leaving when I noticed a copy of *Sorenchester Life* beside the desk, open on the picture of Editorsaurus Rex and wife. Bafflingly, Hobbes had underlined some of the letters in the caption, presumably, I thought, subconsciously, for they made no sense to me.

Still, it refuelled my speculation that he'd developed some sort of crush on Narcisa and led to a sort of reluctant curiosity about the sort of sex life he enjoyed, if he enjoyed one at all. Maybe, if there were any females of his kind he could, though I felt almost certain any human female would be repulsed by his looks, if not by his Hobbesishness. Not that I was in any position for smugness, since my last hint of an amorous encounter had been when Dregs had become affectionate. I left the police station deep in thought.

It was a quiet night at the Feathers. That is, no one was actually fighting. Featherlight Binks was in an unusually convivial mood, acknowledging my arrival with a grunt that I took as a welcome. On reaching the bar, Billy Shawcroft approached, his pale face evidence of yesterday's drinking binge.

'Evening,' I said. 'Can I have a nice pint of lager?'

'Of course you can, mate,' said Billy and, under his breath, 'though it's not so nice in this dump.'

'Thanks,' I said. 'Did you enjoy your free beer last night?'

He shuddered. 'Enjoy is not the word. I must have been mad. That Romanian stuff's corrosive.'

'Romanian?' Everything was Romanian.

'Yes, Romanian,' Billy whispered, one eye watching Binks, pouring my pint. '"Dracula's Bite" they call it and, though it's got a nice label, it's bloody awful and I've still got a man-sized hangover. If you think I look bad, you should see it from my side.'

Smiling, speculating about whether a dwarf-sized hangover should be a hangunder, I reached into my pocket, completely forgetting I was broke. Embarrassed, I admitted my predicament, 'Umm … I'm really sorry but I'm right out of cash.'

'Forget it. It's on me,' said Billy. 'I'm glad to do a favour for a friend of Hobbes. I'm indebted to the old devil.'

'Thanks, you're very kind.'

'You might not think so after you've tasted it.' He frowned. 'I feel like death.'

'I'm sorry to hear it, but you'll live.'

He groaned. 'Will I? Please say I won't. It's bloody well-named that Dracula's Bite; it makes you feel undead and you just long for a stake and I don't mean the sort you have with chips.'

'Why did Featherlight buy such bad beer?'

'It was cheap. Some Irish guy turns up from time to time selling dodgy cigarettes and last time he'd got some crates of beer. The boss bought 'em, thinking he was being shrewd but the stuff's terrible, even by our standards.'

'Would that be Pete Moss?' I asked, leaning on the bar so I could hear Billy more easily.

'Yeah, that's him. The boss is gonna punch his lights out next time he turns up, which is why he's so cheerful tonight.'

'He might have a bit of a wait,' I said. 'Pete was at the police station. He's been nicked for smuggling.'

'Lucky bastard,' said Billy, grinning. Then, clutching his head, he moaned. 'Oh God, I shouldn't move my face in the state I'm in.'

'You'll be OK,' I reassured him and took a slurp of lager, which wiped the smile off my face. Standing upright, I peeled my sleeves off the bar. 'By the way, have you seen anything of Hobbes today?'

'No. Why?'

'Well,' I said, 'he didn't turn up for his supper and didn't phone to say he'd be late. His housekeeper says it's not normal and she's worried.'

'He can look after himself. He'll turn up.'

'You're probably right. Except … umm … he was last seen with Tony Derrick.'

Billy, grimacing, held his head again. 'Well in that case, I hope Hobbes gives the bastard a right good walloping. Tell you what, I'll keep my eyes open and my ear to the ground and let you know if anything turns up, OK?'

He turned to serve an impatient customer.

I finished my drink, apart from the mysterious selection of brown lumps at the bottom. 'Goodnight,' I said, walking towards the door.

Featherlight responded by merrily chucking a soggy rag at me. When I saw what came out as it splattered against the wall, I was mightily relieved he'd missed. Slithering down the wall like a giant slug, it flopped onto a chair, just as the bloke Billy had served sat on it. I closed the door behind me, stepping into the frosty street, as a bellow of rage rang out and Featherlight answered with a roar. Normal service had resumed and I wondered whether Mrs Goodfellow would shortly be adding to her collection.

As I hurried away, the lager sloshing in my stomach, my foot struck an empty bottle on the kerb, which, rolling into the gutter, shattered. Stopping to kick the broken glass down a nearby drain where it wouldn't be of danger, I noticed the label.

'Dracula's Bite Romanian Export Beer', it said in blood-red gothic letters. Stepping into the road, I picked it up, examining it beneath a streetlight. Billy had been right to claim the label, showing a white-walled, red-turreted castle on a hill surrounded by trees, was picturesque. 'Castle Bran, legendary Carpathian home of Count Dracula', I read. I don't mind admitting it worried me. What worried me more was the roar of the swerving motorbike.

As I flung myself back onto the pavement, the bike screeched to a stop. A menacing, helmeted figure in black leathers stepped off, coming towards me, removing his heavy gauntlets. I thought I was in for it.

'It's Andy isn't it? Are you alright?' asked the figure, removing his helmet, revealing himself as Kev the Rev.

'Oh,' I said, relieved, 'umm … yes I'm alright. I'm sorry if I got in your way.'

'You didn't really. I was just passing and, seeing you looked kind of lost, I thought I'd better stop and see if I could help.'

'It's good of you.'

'Well I am a reverend, I'm meant to be good, though it's not always easy. Anyway, to coin a phrase, why the long face?'

'It's not me, I'm alright. I'm worried about Inspector Hobbes.'

'I'm not surprised,' said Kev, 'he's a very worrying bloke. What's he done to you?'

'Nothing.'

'Nothing yet you mean. I remember him putting the fear of God into me when I started getting into trouble, which is why I ended up doing what I do.'

I understood what he meant. Hobbes had the power to terrify with a glance, a word or an action, though it was not only Mrs Goodfellow who was worried about him. I had to admit it; so was I.

'No, he's gone missing and I'm looking for him.'

'Fuckrying out loud. How can he go missing? He's about as inconspicuous as a tiara on a turtle. Have you asked anyone?'

'Yeah, he was last seen leaving the station with a guy called Tony Derrick who's a right little weasel.'

'Now, now,' said Kev, 'we are all God's children. Mind you, I know what you mean. I've known Tony since I was a boy and he really is a nasty little shit. They say he had it tough; his mum left when he was a nipper and his dad was a violent alcoholic swine, but, may God forgive me, every time I meet him, I struggle against an urge to throttle the bugger. Tell you what, though, if you like, I know where he's been living, I'll give you a lift there, and you can ask him. I've got a spare lid in the box.'

'Thank you,' I said.

'You can hold onto me if you like.'

A couple of minutes later I was sitting on the back of his bike, my trilby replaced by a smelly helmet, thinking that Hobbes's driving hadn't been so bad after all. It wasn't that Kev did anything unusual for a motorcyclist, it was just that I'd never been on a bike before and was wishing I'd never been on one at all. Clinging to the back stanchion, refusing to put my arms around Kev, I hoped I'd live long enough to die of the frostbite I was convinced was eating my extremities. Yet, in a few minutes, we were safely outside Tony's.

The street was still deserted except for the cat on the mattress and there was no sign of anyone being home. Getting off the bike, approaching the front door, I knocked. Total silence. Total darkness. I returned to Kev.

'No luck?'

I shook my head. 'Umm … you don't happen to know anything about Romania, do you?'

He frowned. 'That's an odd question. Why do you want to know?'

I didn't tell him everything, though I did mention that Hobbes had been, or, I hoped, still was, working on a case involving Romania. And I did tell him about Dracula's Bite beer and Pete Moss.

'I know Pete,' said Kev, 'he's a rogue, though one with a good heart.'

'He was arrested tonight,' I said, 'for smuggling.'

'It's not the first time.' Kev's breath curled in the breeze and his mouth curled into a smile. 'He once had the brilliant notion of smuggling fake Viagra into the country. He stuffed the pills into condoms and swallowed them. The trouble was, one burst and, well, he rather stood out when he tried to get through Customs. He was so obviously a hardened criminal.'

'Leave it out. I'm not in the mood.'

'Which is precisely what his girlfriend told him when he got home.'

'Shut up.'

'Sorry,' Kev shrugged, 'I was only trying to cheer you up. Tell you what, I'll give you a lift home. I wouldn't worry about Hobbes, he can handle himself, which is, incidentally, what Pete had to do. Sorry. No, I bet he's back home right now. Jump on.'

Dropping me outside the front door of Blackdog Street, he drove away with a cheery wave. I went inside, to be greeted by Dregs as a long-lost friend. A glance at Mrs Goodfellow's face sufficed to tell me Hobbes hadn't returned. Sitting together on the sofa, we talked occasionally, flicking between television channels, starting at every sound from outside. Despite my afternoon nap, I was still whacked and went up to bed before midnight. She said she'd wait up a little longer.

As I lay in bed, dozing, I couldn't stop myself listening for the front door opening. Sleep kept its distance, my mind ticking over, trying to make sense of everything and I was still awake when the church clock struck one and the old girl came upstairs. I awoke with daylight filtering into the room through inadequately closed curtains. Swirling inside my head were dream images as substantial as mist and, like early morning mist, they soon evaporated, leaving only a residue of unease.

The clock said it was nine-thirty. I got up, opening the curtains, sitting back on the bed, yawning and stretching. Hearing movement from Hobbes's room, I leaped back to my feet, with a punch of the air and a suppressed cheer. It would have been far too embarrassing to let him know I'd been worried, so I pulled myself together and strolled out, as if on my way to the bathroom, intending to look in and say Good Morning, before finding out where he'd been and what he'd been doing.

His door, standing ajar, I poked my head inside. Hobbes wasn't there but Dregs was, walking round and round, sniffing and whimpering like a lost puppy. He was delighted to see me and even more delighted to smell me. Secretly gratified, I tried to push the beast down and keep his cold nose from my groin. I succeeded, though his long wet tongue curled across my face in a sneak attack.

'Get down,' I said and he sat, looking up as if expecting me to do something. I wasn't used to dogs and my first experiences with him had been unpleasant, yet, now I felt safe, there was something reassuring about his presence. 'So Hobbes isn't back?'

Dregs's ears perked up and he began sniffing round the room again.

'He must be somewhere,' I said. 'A bloke like him can't just vanish.' The dog tilted his head to one side as I explained. 'He's too big to hide, though I still don't know how to find him.'

Dregs wagged his tail, sniffing the carpet and giving me an idea. Dogs, I knew, could follow trails, so maybe Dregs could find Hobbes. But first I needed breakfast.

When washed and dressed I went downstairs. Mrs Goodfellow being out, I was forced to make my own tea and toast, managing the feat without any involuntary arson, eating and drinking in silence, vaguely aware of Dregs padding about above. My mind was apparently in neutral, yet something must have been going on behind the scenes because, to my surprise, I experienced a moment of inspiration. It felt almost as if someone had flicked a switch in my brain, turning on a floodlight, letting me realise what a spluttering, smoky, little candle normally illuminated my thoughts. Hurrying to the sitting room, I searched for *Sorenchester Life*, needing to see the photo of the Editorsaurus and wife. The magazine had gone; Mrs Goodfellow must have thrown it away.

A minute or two later, and to my surprise, I was running down Blackdog Street heading for the police station, barely noticing the icy air whipping my face, the slippery pavements still white with frost and the grey, frigid sky. I was gasping and sweaty when I arrived but I'd run all the way and felt mightily impressed with myself.

'Has Hobbes been in?'

The desk sergeant shook his head. 'Not yet. Can I help you, sir?'

'No, not really. I need something from his office.'

'Sorry, sir, I can't allow you in, if you're not with the Inspector. I'm afraid it's no entry.'

'It's important.' I raised my voice. 'Very important.'

'Sorry, sir, and I'd be obliged if you'd stop shouting and go about your business.'

'But it is my business! He's gone missing and there's something in his office I think might be a clue.'

'The Inspector can look after himself. He probably has good reasons for being absent and if he really has gone missing then it's police business.'

Though I argued, the sergeant was immovable. 'It's only a magazine I want.' When I tried to push past, he moved surprisingly quickly, holding me in an arm lock.

'Please leave, sir,' he said, still polite, though the pressure on my arm hinted it could become extremely painful.

Leaving, muttering furiously, yet afraid of getting myself banged up in a cell, I stamped up and down outside, fuming and fretting, unsure what to do next. Someone walked out and stood in my way.

A soft Irish accent addressed me. 'Are you alright, there?'

I stopped and Pete Moss, clown, entertainer and smuggler grinned at me.

'Yes,' I said. 'Or rather, no… umm … maybe.'

'It's best to cover all your options,' said Pete with a nod. 'Don't I know you? Yeah, weren't you with Hobbes the other day? You're not a copper, right?'

'That's right. I'm Andy.'

Reaching for my hand, shaking it, he said, 'Hobbes is a decent fellow, for a copper. He's pretty straight, even if he always makes me feel like a naughty schoolboy before the headmaster, though I've never seen a headmaster as ugly as he is. Jaysus! He gave me a turn the night I was discovered at the theatre.'

'Were you auditioning?'

'Not exactly. He discovered me backstage when I was … acquiring some bits for my act. I thought I was for the high jump and ran for it, fancying myself as an athlete in those days. Once, I even entered the London marathon.'

I was impressed. 'How did you do?'

'I walked it.'

'You won?'

He laughed. 'No. I really did walk most of it.'

'Is that a joke?'

'Actually, no.' He shrugged. 'I did try, only I hadn't run in my shoes enough and got blisters, hence, my abysmal performance. Even so, I was well fit when Hobbes came after me and, seeing the size of him, I reckoned I'd get away easily but – Jaysus! – he's bloody fast, like an avalanche.'

'What happened?' I was fascinated despite the urgency and the frost nipping my ears.

'He collared me pretty damn quick and I thought he'd run me in but he didn't. He made me put all the stuff back, gave me a good talking to and then, I don't know why, he took me shopping and paid for the stuff I needed from his own wallet.'

'Amazing,' I said because there were no words to do justice to my thoughts.

'I reckoned I was for it again when he pulled me over the other week,' said Pete, 'yet he got me to the gig on time. Sadly, I reckon I'm really in trouble after this latest incident. They caught me red-handed with contraband cigarettes and bloody awful beer.'

'Carpati cigarettes and Dracula's Bite beer?'

He nodded. 'Correct. The fags aren't so bad if you like that sort of thing but the beer is ...' He tailed off. 'Well, let's just say it's not Guinness.'

'So I've heard, from someone who got drunk on it.'

He looked shocked. 'Someone got drunk on it? Jaysus! Is he alright? He must be made of sterner stuff than me. I can only manage to force down a few sips, to impress customers with its hoppy, fruity characteristics.'

'Billy said it tasted of oven cleaner.'

'He's the little fellow at the Feathers?'

I nodded.

Pete shrugged. 'I've heard tell he'll drink anything. I wouldn't put it past him to have tried oven cleaner.' He grimaced. 'How is Hobbes?'

'He's gone missing. I'm worried.'

'Don't be, he can look after himself if anyone can.'

I shook my head and told of my concerns. I probably said more than I should have, though I had the feeling I could trust Pete.

His blue eyes looked grave. 'I wish I could help but I've got to make a few arrangements before my case comes up. Look, I don't know if it's of any use, I've only sold a few of those Carpati cigarettes round here recently. Most were to Featherlight or to a lady who was arranging a party. She was a skinny old biddy. I can't remember her name, though she drives a black Volvo. I only met her because she was with a ratty-looking fellow I'd bumped into at the Feathers. He told her my fags were OK and she bought a load of boxes. It was a nice profit and all tax-free, so I wasn't going to complain.'

Pete, I decided, though a nice enough guy for a criminal, didn't half go on when I wanted to hurry. Besides, I was getting cold. 'Sorry,' I said, 'I've got to go. Thanks for your information.' I didn't think it would be much use.

I hurried to a newsagent on the lower part of The Shambles, spending a frustrating ten minutes looking through the magazine racks for *Sorenchester Life*.

The girl manicuring her nails behind the till acknowledged my existence when I'd got to the muttering stage. 'Can I help you?'

'I'm looking for *Sorenchester Life*.'

'Is there life in Sorenchester?' She smirked.

'I mean the magazine *Sorenchester Life*.' I almost growled. Hobbes was definitely catching.

'You're standing right in front of it. On the third shelf.'

I'd been looking straight at it, only not at the issue I wanted. 'I was looking for last month's. Have you got it?'

'We did have. Last month.'

'Do you know where I could get it?'

'Haven't a clue.'

'Thanks, you've been a great help.'

I stomped out the shop as the girl went back to her nails. For want of anything better to do, feeling helpless, I started walking back towards Blackdog Street, looking around, hoping to spot Hobbes. I was out of luck. However, I did spot a plaque for a dental surgery and, on impulse, stepped inside. The waiting room was nearly full. Although it smelled of fear and sounded of drills, I ignored everything, except for the table upon which teetered a tower of dog-eared magazines. I found the right issue of *Sorenchester Life* near the top, flicking through until I came to the picture of the Editorsaurus and Narcisa.

As I stared at the caption, *Mr Rex Witcherley and wife, Narcisa, enjoy a joke,* I tried to remember which letters Hobbes had underlined, with an idea that something was starting to make sense at last. I thought back to Hobbes highlighting the faint impressions on the scrap of paper he'd found at Mr Roman's, the few letters standing out forming the enigmatic message, *EX WITCH IS A JOY OK* and read the caption again to make sure. *Mr Rex Witcherley and wife, Narcisa, enjoy a joke.*

An ashen-faced man spoke to the pretty young receptionist. 'I've got to make an appointment for root canal surgery.'

'Brilliant! That's fantastic!' I cried.

Shocked faces stared at me.

'Sorry.' Replacing the magazine, I hurried away, glad to escape; dentists reminded me of my father and made me edgy. Nonetheless, I was almost dancing on reaching the street, where a few dusty snowflakes were swirling. I had solved a clue and the fact that Hobbes had done it first hardly detracted from the satisfaction.

I could have cheered until I realised I still didn't understand anything. All I knew was that someone had written out the caption from the magazine, leaving an impression on the paper, which had then been used for writing down the combination of Mr Roman's safe. So what?

My sense of satisfaction having died by the time I reached the church, I sneaked inside, hoping for divine inspiration. I really wanted to be up and searching for Hobbes but I'd got nothing to go on except for the one clue, assuming it was a clue, and my hare-brained notion of Dregs as a tracker-dog.

The blue-haired lady at the book counter was belittling a confused Japanese couple, and didn't notice me creep into a pew where I sat, head bowed. Somehow, it felt even colder in the church than outside and I wished I'd taken the time to put on my overcoat.

All I had to work on was my clue and Hobbes's sudden obsession with Narcisa. It was time for deep thinking. So, someone had written the caption on the note pad and someone with different handwriting had scrawled the combination for the safe on the sheet below. But why would anyone copy such a caption? It wasn't interesting, just a few bland words in a dull magazine. I couldn't imagine anyone doing it.

Then it struck me and it was obvious. The reporter who'd covered the ball would have made notes, as most reporters didn't forget their notebooks, and I remembered thinking at the time that the paper had been torn from a small, cheap, wired jotting pad, much like we used at the *Bugle*.

Feeling like a bloodhound finally picking up the trail, I understood why they bayed, and might have yelled in triumph had I not been in church. Clenching my fists and shaking them at the ceiling was as far as I let myself go. I was convinced a reporter had jotted down the caption in the notebook and that whoever had written the combination to Mr Roman's safe on the following leaf had access to the notebook. Therefore, it was probable the reporter had been involved with the break-in at Mr Roman's!

A mischievous part of my brain reminded me that Phil was a reporter. However, I knew his writing and was pretty sure he was in the clear. Therefore, I needed to discover who had actually written the article. I ground my teeth because I hadn't thought to look before.

I'd have to return to the dentist's. 'Damn.' My mutter came out louder than anticipated.

'I'll trouble you to watch your language in the House of the Lord, young man.'

Glancing up to apologise, I met the glare of the blue-haired woman.

'You,' she said with a look of contempt, 'I might have known. I'm going to call the police.'

'Oh no you're not,' I said, suppressing my instinct to flee, standing up, looking her right in the eye, 'I'm leaving now on important police business. Do not interfere.' It must have been the way I said it, for she was speechless as I strode from the church.

Heading back to the dentist's, I picked up *Sorenchester Life*.

'Are you here for an appointment?' asked the receptionist.

'No, I've come for this.' I said, holding up the magazine. 'I need to borrow it. I'll bring it back.'

Hurrying into the street before she could protest, I turned to the article, which was only accredited to NW. Looking in the index, I discovered that Witcherley Publications, Editor R. Witcherley, Contributing Editor N. Witcherley, owned the magazine and, since none of the other contributors had the initials NW, concluded that Narcisa was the author. I couldn't help noticing the names of other *Bugle* journalists, including Phil Waring and even Ingrid on the list of writers. I'd never realised there was a connection between the *Bugle* and *Sorenchester Life*, much less been invited to write for it, and resentment began to bubble until I forced myself to simmer down and consider.

'OK,' I said, thinking out loud, 'she wrote it and then what? Did she give the notebook to someone else?'

'I'm sorry, I don't know,' said a little old guy in a flat cap and muffler, scuttling away, as if I was the loony that sits next to you on the bus.

A bizarre thought sprouted. Perhaps Editorsaurus Rex was behind the crimes. He would certainly have access to Narcisa's notebook and could easily have hired someone to carry out the dirty deeds. It was possible, of course, that Narcisa was, herself, the master criminal, though I didn't think she looked the type. Still, I could think of no sensible reasons why either of them would have done it. Why would they need to steal? I knew they were wealthy enough to own a holiday home abroad.

I decided to approach the Editorsaurus. My next stop would be the *Bugle's* offices.

16

I'd always suffered with butterflies in my stomach when entering Editorsaurus Rex's presence. On the whole, this had been because I was trying to work out what I'd done wrong. This time, I was pretty much going to accuse him or his wife of stealing, or worse, and it felt like I'd got a flock of vultures flapping around inside. Nevertheless, despite a brief, panicky dither on the stairs, I was determined to give it my best shot.

Taking a deep breath, I strode into the main office, looking like I meant business. Ingrid turned away as I headed for Rex's den, which hurt more than my fist when I thumped on his door in the style of Hobbes. There was no reply. I hesitated, caught between knocking again and barging straight in.

'He's not in.'

Though she was still talking to me, there was no smile, just polite indifference.

'Rex is away. Duncan's in charge.'

I grimaced. So, Duncan was back already; he had stitched me up with Hobbes.

'But I need to talk to Rex … umm … or Mrs Witcherley,' I said. 'It's important.'

'Then you're out of luck. They're away together.'

My plan had fallen at the first hurdle. 'I don't suppose you know where?'

She shrugged. 'Romania, I suppose.'

'Romania? Why Romania?' It seemed I couldn't get away from the place.

'It's where she comes from, or at least, her family did. They've got a holiday home in the mountains out there. Now, excuse me, I've work to do.' Spinning back to her computer, she stabbed at the keys.

I slouched away, no longer the hound hot on the trail, more like a whipped puppy. Leaving the building, I stopped, uncertain what to do, the fires of enthusiasm having been all but extinguished, shivering as the wind flung hard, stinging nodules of snow into my face. For want of a better idea, I headed back to Blackdog Street where, with luck I'd hear some good news and, if not, at least I'd get a cup of tea.

I opened the door of number 13, bracing myself when I saw Dregs lying there, watching and waiting, but he greeted me with a single wag of his tail, a mournful look in his eyes, almost as if it was bath time again. Mrs Goodfellow was stirring a pot on the stove when I entered the kitchen and, whatever it was smelt delicious, though I was never destined to taste it. She'd been shopping and piles of groceries were heaped on nearly every surface.

'Any news?' I asked, though her expression had already told me.

She shook her head. 'I'm cooking his favourites for when he comes back. What about you, dear? Have you found out anything?' Her voice shook, as if she'd been crying, though there were no tears.

'Not much.' I sat at the table in front of a huge, bloody leg of lamb in a dish. 'I think my editor and his wife might know something, only they've gone to Romania.'

She sighed. 'Have they, dear? Well, I expect you'd like a cup of tea and a bit of dinner?'

Glancing at the clock, I nodded. It was nearly one.

Though the cup of tea was up to standard, the bread in the cheese and pickle sandwiches was, perhaps, a little dry. This wasn't a complaint, merely an indication of her state of mind. I covered up my disappointment, eating to fill the emptiness.

I was still at the table, comfortably full and warm, when, my brain, unfreezing, started working. If Hobbes had been onto something, perhaps that had led to his disappearance. Perhaps he, too, had uncovered the link between Romania and the Witcherleys, who, of course, employed Phil, who had some connection to Tony Derrick. It struck me then that Hobbes's sketches might have been more than idle doodles. The fact of his having drawn Tony and Narcisa together, and then sketching Barrington-Oddy's attackers, sparked a possibility. I'd just assumed both assailants were men, but could one have been a woman? The taller, skinny one, whose face had been hidden by a scarf and a hat might have been. Another idea nudged into my head: Hobbes had discovered fibres with the faint scent of flowers. Could that have been Narcisa's perfume?

Then, of course, Pete Moss had sold some of his foul Carpati cigarettes to a woman who was organising a party, and had mentioned that she'd been with a ratty bloke. It had to be Narcisa and Tony. Probably, anyway. I'd even heard her party at the Blackdog Café and was willing to bet all the thumping music was to cover the break-in at the museum. By then, I'd nearly convinced myself the Witcherleys were up to their necks in crime, with Tony as their accomplice. A deluge of congratulation and excitement bursting over me, left me gasping with self-admiration, thinking I was really getting the hang of the detective game.

Unfortunately, I couldn't see how my brilliance would help, especially now the Witcherleys were in Romania and Phil and Hobbes were still missing. I discounted the idea that Hobbes had gone after them – he wouldn't without telling Mrs Goodfellow. It was then I realised his car had vanished as well. We'd left it outside Tony's squalid squat and it hadn't been there when I'd gone back with Kev. Nor had it been at the police station. Had he retrieved it and then gone missing? Or had Tony stolen it? Or was there another explanation? Detecting wasn't so easy after all.

Dregs padded in, sitting gloomily on my foot, sighing, and I wondered whether my initial idea had merit.

I jumped up. 'Where's his lead? I'm going to see if he can find Hobbes.'

'Are you, dear?' The old girl was attacking a vegetable with a cleaver. 'It's on the hook by the back door. I hope you find him, because he'll be hungry and I ought to tell you, dear, he can get rather wild when he's hungry. You'd best take the leg of lamb. I'll wrap it for you.'

'But it's not cook—' I began. 'Oh, yeah. Right.'

Wrapping the bloody leg in a tea towel, she dropped it into a carrier bag. Though Dregs watched, he'd been fed and was far too interested in the prospect of a walk to spare a thought for raw meat. Besides, he preferred his meals nicely cooked. Mindful of the cold, I donned my overcoat and trilby, and clipped him to the chunky length of chain and led him out.

'Take care, dear,' she said as I shut the door, 'and good luck.'

'Right then, Dregs,' I said. 'Find Hobbes. Got it? Find Hobbes.'

He looked at me and then bounded down the road with a woof. I struggled to hold him back, pleased how well my experiment was working, until he came to an abrupt halt by the nearest lamppost and gave vent to pent-up emotions, letting off steam in the cold air. I'd not taken into account that he'd been inside all morning. At last he finished and, after a rapturous bout of sniffing, set off with an excited woof.

Though I'd got him on a short chain and was hauling back with all my strength, I struggled to keep up, my strides growing longer and longer, sure that, sooner or later, I'd crash to the pavement, yet, amazingly, keeping going. My hat blew off as we turned into Pound Street; I never saw it again. On reaching the main Fenderton Road, Dregs had enough sense to keep away from the traffic because, so far as I could see, the only way I could even slow him was by flinging myself to the ground and acting as an anchor.

The overcoat had been a mistake, for sweat was already trickling down my chest, sticking the shirt to my back. I glimpsed my reflection in a car's tinted window; my face was puffed out, as red as a robin's chest, my hair was sticking up in damp clumps. When I managed to unbutton the coat, it flapped like heavy wings. I wasn't used to such exercise, and the cheese sandwiches were making sure I couldn't forget them.

I kept going, though my head, in contrast to my leaden body, felt light and I wondered when my lungs would give up the struggle. It was, surely, a race between them and my heart as to which exploded first. I think the speed camera on the outskirts of Fenderton flashed as we went by, although it might just have been the lights in my head. My tongue lolled like the dog's, though he was in his element, running with boundless enjoyment, apparently oblivious to the dying man he was dragging behind.

When he made a sharp turn to the right, darting across the road, I didn't. Inertia, plus both feet happening to be off the ground, meant I carried straight on until the chain, jerking in my hand as it twisted round a pole, snapped tight. The next thing I remember, I was sprawling on my side on the pavement, gasping for breath like a landed fish, panicking that my lungs had collapsed under the impact. Cars and lorries thundered past. No one stopped to help.

Though I guess I was just winded, it was ages before I could breathe normally, sit up and audit my other injuries. My wrist was raw and tender where the lead had chafed, my shoulder felt as if it had been wrenched from its socket, the side of my face was bruised and bleeding, my hip was throbbing and sore, blood was pounding through my head, and I hoped the stickiness inside my clothes was only sweat. Nothing seemed too serious but the experience gave me an insight into how Tony must have felt when Hobbes tackled him. Using the pole as support, I climbed back to my feet. A sign on top thanked me for driving safely.

I brushed myself down as well as I could, while my pulse and breathing dropped to sustainable levels. The clip on the chain had snapped off and there was no sign of Dregs, which was good, because I'd half-expected to see him flattened in the middle of the busy road. I was furious, coming close to abandoning him, going home, licking my wounds. Yet, worst luck, I recognised my responsibility for the daft brute. Groaning and swearing, picking up the bag of lamb from the gutter, I hobbled across the road into a quiet, tree-lined cul-de-sac that looked familiar. It was Alexander Court, where Mr Roman had lived.

'Dregs!' I yelled and no dog appeared. 'Where are you?'

The net curtains of number 2 opened and a tubby grey-haired

woman stared out. I could feel her suspicion burning into me.

'Here boy!' I held up the lead, making a pantomime of searching before turning towards her with a smile and a shrug. Though the curtains closed, I could feel eyes watching as I walked away.

I'd been impressed by Roman's house, yet it was rather small compared to one or two of the others. Most were set well back from the road as if they had something to hide and I caught myself staring at one that lurked behind a high yew hedge. With its Cotswold stone walls and chimneys like turrets, it might have passed as a small castle. Its front lawn, as smooth and neat as a bowling green, was edged with exotic shrubs and naked flowerbeds. A brushed gravel drive led towards a double garage, outside of which stood a Volvo, as glossy and black as a raven.

Carrying on up the road, I called again for the dog, as memory dropped a reminder into my consciousness; a black Volvo – I couldn't help thinking it ought to ring a bell.

Bong! Pete Moss had said the thin woman who'd bought his cigarettes drove a black Volvo. Coincidence? Maybe.

Bong! A second bell rang. A black Volvo had passed us yesterday, a thin woman with eyes like death staring out at me. An image formed in my mind, slowly twisting into shape. It could easily have been Narcisa, camouflaged by lack of makeup. I was almost sure.

Which meant she hadn't been in Romania then and, perhaps, still wasn't. To my surprise, I had a hunch. Perhaps, I'd just seen the same car and therefore, perhaps, it was parked on the Witcherleys' drive.

Needing to know, I turned back. A quick ring on the doorbell would show whether my guess was correct and, if not, which seemed more likely, I could use my lost dog as an excuse for disturbing the occupants. Scrunching though the deep gravel, I reached the polished oak and gleaming brass front door. Behind it was a porch roughly the same size as the lounge in my poor old flat. I caught a faint tang of metal polish as I reached out to press the glinting doorbell.

I waited. And waited, wondering if it had worked. Pressing again, I was on the point of giving up when Editorsaurus Rex appeared, dressed in jeans and a faded red sweatshirt. I'd never seen him casual before and the sight made me even more nervous than usual. A faint frown crossed his jowly face as, shuffling across the porch, he opened the front door. He was wearing fluffy white socks and sported a lurid mark on his neck, like a love-bite. I gulped, astonished my guesswork had paid off.

'Capstan?' his voice boomed. 'What the devil do you want? Have you been fighting? You're not getting your job back if that's what you think.'

It didn't seem worthwhile correcting him. 'Good Afternoon,' I said. 'I was … umm … wondering if you'd seen Inspector Hobbes today?'

Rex shook his head. 'Hobbes? I haven't seen him since you brought him along to my office. Damn it, Capstan, you should have learned to fight your own battles at your age. How old are you? Twenty-nine? Thirty?'

'Thirty-seven.'

He shook his head again. 'Is that it, then? And, please tell me, why you've got a dog chain in your hand?'

'I've lost a dog.'

'As well as Hobbes? It smacks of gross carelessness. Well, I'm sure when you find Hobbes he'll find your dog for you. Good Afternoon.' He closed the door in my face.

My mouth opened and closed, my hands fluttering stupidly. There'd been so much I'd wanted to ask, yet, as usual, he'd steamrollered me. Frustrated and angry, I started back down the drive, pausing by the garage, its doors gleaming with brass fittings set in varnished, panelled wood, below a row of glinting windows. Curiosity prompted a peek inside. To the left was a large silver car, a Daimler I think. Far more interesting to me was Hobbes's small car on the right.

I tried the garage doors. They were locked. I dithered, trying to think. Rex, it seemed, had lied and, unless he'd stolen the car, Hobbes must have been there, and, perhaps, still was. Maybe I'd been correct to think Rex was up to no good. My best course of action, I came to the conclusion, was to call the police and get professional help.

Jogging back along the drive, heading down the road to number 2, I presumed, in the circumstances, she'd allow me to use her phone. The net curtains moved as I trotted down the garden path by the side of a lawn, heavily decorated with gnomes. Though I rang the bell and waited, the door didn't open. Stepping back, I unleashed my most ingratiating smile on the window. The net curtains twitched again.

'Good afternoon. I wonder if I might … umm … use your phone? It's a sort of an emergency.'

Nothing happened. I rang the bell again and waited. A car, speeding up the road, stopped. A door slammed.

'Please can I come in? It's rather import … oof!'

A heavy hand, seizing my shoulder, turned me round. It belonged to a large, hard-faced, young policeman, though not one I recognised. For no reason, I felt guilty.

'Now, what d'you think you're up to, sir?' he said, politely enough but without removing his hand.

'I wanted to use the telephone.'

'There's a public call box opposite the village shop. Why don't you use that?'

'Because it's an emergency and I haven't got any money.'

'So you thought you'd get some here, did you?'

I was confident I could explain myself. 'No, I just wanted to use the phone. You see …'

The front door opening, the fat woman stood before me, red-faced, quivering with rage. 'Well done, officer,' she said. 'I've been watching him. He's been up and down the road, casing the joints. I'll bet he was the one who broke into poor Mr Roman's.'

'Look …'

'You can tell at a glance he's up to no good. What a scruffy, dirty, ugly, little man! He's obviously had a go at someone and been given a taste of his own medicine. What a brute! It wouldn't surprise me to learn he's a murderer, too. It's a good job I spotted him in time.'

'But …'

'And he's armed, just look at that vicious chain.'

'It's for …'

'Thank you, Madam.' The policeman, raising his hand to dam the torrent, looked me straight in the eye and smiled. 'Now, what have you got to say for yourself, sir?'

'I'm not a burglar. The chain's for my dog.'

'Oh really?' he said. 'I see no dog. Would you mind if I take a look in your bag, sir?'

I'd almost forgotten about it. 'It's not important,' I said.

'I'll be the judge of that, sir.' Taking it from me, he tipped it out.

A bundle wrapped in a blood-stained tea towel rolled down the path.

'Murder!' screamed the fat woman.

The policeman stepped back, a look of shock on his face. He poked the bundle with his foot and the meat jutted out.

'What is that?'

'It's a leg of lamb.'

'Why?'

'To feed a police inspector,' I said. I might have phrased it better.

'What?'

'It's for Inspector Hobbes, I'm looking for him.'

'Hobbes? Are you sure he's not looking for you, sir? In connection with the break-in down the road on the afternoon of the second of this month?'

'No, he's disappeared and I'm trying to find him.'

'I've heard no reports of the Inspector disappearing. He's not the sort.'

'This blackguard has probably murdered him,' said the woman, 'so he can escape justice. I bet he's the one who burgled Mr

Roman's.'

'Have you been in Mr Roman's house, sir?'

'No, well … umm … yes. I was with Hobbes at the time. It was after the break-in; it was part of his investigation.'

'I was there when the Inspector investigated and don't recall seeing you. You admit you were inside?' The policeman's expression turned as hard as his grip on my shoulder. 'I think, perhaps, you'd better come along to the station and answer a few questions.'

'No, I was there when he went back for another look. I need to find him, he may be in trouble.'

'I know Inspector Hobbes. He can look after himself, if anyone can. I'm afraid you're the one in trouble.' The policeman reached for his handcuffs.

In fact, the young policeman was the one in trouble, for at that moment the cavalry arrived. Or rather, Dregs did. Loping down the garden path with a deep woof, obviously believing I was in danger, he launched himself like a hairy black missile. The policeman, turning too late, Dregs thumped into his midriff with the pace and power of a punch. The poor man, doubling up, grunted, falling backwards into the house, banging his head on an occasional table as he rolled inside. The table collapsed under the impact and became a pile of occasional firewood. The woman screamed again – she was having a most exhilarating afternoon – and slammed the door.

Dregs bounced round me, butting and licking, as if he'd done something clever. I calculated that, though he had stopped me being arrested, he'd probably not improved my situation and I wasn't sure I'd now be able to convince the police to help me. In fact, the way things were going, I felt it more likely they'd arrest me for assaulting a policeman with an offensive weapon, namely a large, hairy dog and, if they banged me up in the cells, I'd have no chance of helping Hobbes. It appeared I was on my own, apart from Dregs, which was a dubious advantage.

I was about to flee the scene, when I remembered the leg of lamb. As I bent to pick it up, Dregs sniffed it and kicked soil over it in apparent disdain. Maybe he thought it would smell better after being buried for a few days. Still, he let me bag it and I scarpered, while he sat down, staring at the door, with his head on one side as if listening. I left him to it. He'd be able to find me if he wanted and I'd be better off without him.

I had to find out what was happening, though I had little idea how to go about it. Reason suggested that, if I sneaked into the Witcherleys' garden and kept out of sight, I'd at least have time to think. I darted up the road, taking some comfort no one else was about, concealing myself between the hedge and a bush. I seemed to be putting myself into, at best, an embarrassing situation and the pressure of thinking I ought to do something was crushing. My face grew hot and my stomach quivered at the thought of what would happen if I'd misread the situation. Yet, the longer I dithered the more I'd get the wind up. I had to be positive.

All the running and stress had left my mouth as dry as chalk, yet slaking my thirst was not my priority. Firstly, I had to relieve my bladder, a regular consequence of meeting Rex. Taking a quiet leak in the hedge, I began operations, deciding, as a start, to scout the garden, to get the lie of the land. Basing my movements on what I'd seen Red Indians do in old westerns, though I doubted they'd ever made so much noise, I stumbled, pushed and crawled through the undergrowth. In such situations, buckskins have distinct advantages over long overcoats. I kept kneeling on its edge or snagging it on branches and thorns, dampness spreading from the tweed knees of my trousers. When a trunk of a huge evergreen tree concealed me, I stood up, wiping the cobwebs from my face, a putrid stench making me retch. My hands were plastered in slimy, disgusting, sticky, brown gloop. I'd got it all over me, the pigeons flapping overhead suggesting the source. I wiped my hands down my trousers, which were already beyond hope, trying not to throw up. There was a downside to being a detective, yet I was not deterred.

I began my reconnaissance with a closer look at the house. The lowering sun, glinting off an array of windows on a single-storey modern extension, connecting the old part of the house to the garage, meant I was too dazzled to see much and my teeth chattered as, scurrying across the lawn, I pressed myself against the wall. Gulping like a goldfish, I peeped into the extension. It was the kitchen, though it looked more like a glossy advert, with lustrous blacks contrasting with creamy whites and the glitter of stainless steel. Although it looked impressive, almost like a work of art, I'd have taken Hobbes's homely kitchen any day, especially with Mrs Goodfellow's cooking.

My anger flared. How dare Rex pay me such a meagre wage when he could afford all this? The kitchen alone must have cost many times my annual salary and then they'd got the house and the cars and the holiday home and everything. It wasn't fair. Yet it was nothing compared to my rage at Rex's lie. How dare he lie to me? How dare he put me through all the crawling round in pigeon shit? How dare he put Mrs Goodfellow through all the worry? And how dare he do anything to Hobbes?

I stopped myself. He obviously dared a lot but what might he have done to Hobbes? How, in fact, could he have done anything? Even though the Editorsaurus was a big bloke, even heavier than Hobbes I guessed, he was fat and lumbering, whereas Hobbes was …Hobbes.

The door, leading into the kitchen, swinging open, I dropped to my knees in the rich loam of a border, flattening myself against the wall, praying nobody decided to venture out.

A whiny voice spoke. 'Shouldn't I at least give him a drink?' It was Tony Derrick.

'He's been in there for ages and …' he paused and muttered. 'OK. Keep your hair on. I was only asking.'

I could hear him moving about, splashing water, opening and shutting doors.

'Where d'you keep your coffee? Thanks … sugar? Milk? OK … cream it is then. Uh, which one's the fridge? I got it … single or double? Chocolate biscuits? Right … can I have one? I'm starving.'

The stream of questions continued for a minute or two and then there was silence. After a while, risking poking my head up, I satisfied myself the kitchen was empty again. Tony had spilt coffee by the sink and a couple of broken biscuits were valiantly attempting to soak up a dribble of cream splashed on the floor beneath the stainless steel door of what I took to be the fridge.

It meant there were at least two people inside, Editorsaurus Rex and Tony and, since Narcisa's car was parked outside, it was likely she was home, too. In which case, who was the 'he' Tony had mentioned? Hobbes? Or Phil?

A timid part of my brain suggested I was jumping to all the wrong conclusions. I tried to ignore it, because part of me was convinced Hobbes was inside and, since he'd been looking for Phil, he might also be there.

Keeping my head below the windows, I crept along the side of the wall like a commando, except commandos usually carry weapons they're trained to use and are not dressed in soggy tweed that's growing ever soggier. The shadows were lengthening and I guessed it had gone four o'clock. Though the huge, red sun was blinding, it wouldn't be long before it no longer peeped over the hedge.

On reaching the spot where the kitchen-extension met the old part of the house, I stood up straight, stretching cramped muscles, noticing a small, dilapidated shed in the far corner of the back lawn, somewhere I thought would make a brilliant hiding place. Scurrying behind it, I looked back, shocked to realise I'd been in full view of the upper windows of the house, but it seemed I'd got away with it. I resolved to be more vigilant, for a momentary carelessness might waste all my efforts and would lead, at best, to intense embarrassment.

Two fears were competing: first, if Hobbes and Phil were being held captive, I, too, soon might be; second, if, by chance or stupidity, I'd got everything wrong, Rex might simply spot me trespassing, call the police and I'd be a laughing stock again. My timid side just wouldn't shut up, urging me to run before I got into something I couldn't get out of. I forced myself to ignore what seemed only common sense, feeling I owed Hobbes something. Yet for a while, all I could do was lurk behind the shed, where the shadows concealed me.

Buttoning my coat, pulling up the collar, thrusting my hands into the pockets, I looked around in the half-light. To one side was a steaming compost heap, to the other, a heavy lawn roller, smothered under a blanket of enormous spiders' webs. Imagining the enormous spiders that had created it, I couldn't stop shuddering, so I forced myself to concentrate on my mission. I peeked round the side of the shed, observing the garden, bright and ruddy in the glow of the setting sun, encircled by a hedge, dotted here and there with tall trees. There was an ornamental pond, a covered swimming pool and a tennis court. A strange vision of Rex floundering about in white shorts, or diving into the water made me snigger, despite, or because of, my nerves. My imagination failed to conjure up an image of Narcisa doing anything similar.

A light coming on in one of house's upper windows, I jerked back behind the shed, very cautiously risking another look, hoping the dusk would conceal me. Narcisa, clad in a glossy blue gown, sat down in front of a dressing table by the window, dabbing something behind her ears, turning as if to speak to someone. Another figure moved into view and, though I could only see his back, his green Hawaiian shirt screamed it was Tony Derrick. He leaned on the window ledge, seemingly entirely at home in her bedroom. When she finished speaking he, nodded, kissing her on the lips and left.

I couldn't take that sort of thing standing up and had to sit on the roller, despite the spiders. Surely, Narcisa and Tony weren't lovers? What could she see in the weasely, whiney, grubby lowlife? If it came to that, what could he see in her? To be fair, she'd looked OK, elegant even, in the *Sorenchester Life* photo, if only because of the crust of makeup. Yet, perhaps neither was fussy. I couldn't understand how Rex fitted in and why he didn't just throw Tony out. I shook my head, glad I didn't live that way.

When I looked again, she'd removed her robe and was wearing only a flimsy, shimmering slip, held up by coat hanger shoulders. Her neck was scrawny, as if it had been stretched, and encircled by a triple string of pearls. As she ran a bony hand through her hair, I turned away, feeling like a peeping Tom. Yet, I had to take another look and this time, to my horror, she was quite bald, apart from a few fluffy, brittle tufts reminiscent of a lawn in a drought. Her sleek blonde hair was nowhere to be seen as she touched up her makeup. Then she stood, disappearing from view for a minute or so, returning in a loose, purple robe with a heavy gold chain around her neck. Bending, picking up her wig, she sat at the table to fit it, the sleeves of her robe slipping down revealing a bracelet. Even from such a distance I was sure it was the one stolen from the museum.

She walked away and the light went out.

17

As the last lingering tentacles of sunlight slithered below the hedge, I berated myself for failing to make real progress. I was convinced Narcisa had the dragon bracelet and reckoned it was a safe bet she'd stolen the other articles as well. So what? I didn't know why she'd taken them, or why Phil and Hobbes had vanished, or even if there was a genuine connection between the events. Of course, her ancestry might explain her interest in Romanian artefacts but why those particular ones? Surely, there were millions of old Romanian bits and pieces in the world? There had, in fact, been a fair number in Mr Barrington-Oddy's cabinet, yet only one had been taken. It dawned on me that asking unanswerable questions and beating myself up wasn't helping. I was prevaricating, yet I couldn't really blame myself, since I'd never done anything so frightening before. My nervous terrors were not at all alleviated by being alone in the dark.

A childhood memory returned, of an old book of fairy stories at Granny Caplet's, its grotesque illustrations scaring me silly. In particular, the skinny old witch in *Hansel and Gretel* had such a look of cruel wickedness she had haunted my dreams for months. I began to understand my unease, for the shed bore an uncomfortable resemblance to her tumbledown cottage, or it did in my imagination. I tried to laugh it off, for I was starting to believe Hobbes's tall tales. Even so, I couldn't stop myself patting the rotting wood, as if to reassure myself it was not built of gingerbread. He'd really had me going about that, and, despite everything, I smiled, coming to a decision.

'Right then, Andy,' I addressed myself, 'let's get out of here. It won't get any easier.' Forcing my mouth into a determined, devil-may care grin, I stood up, just as something rushed towards me, something too black to be mere shadow. I gasped as it sprang, knocking me onto my back.

It could have been worse, I thought, as Dregs's long, stinky tongue snaked over my face.

'Bloody dog,' I muttered, patting his hairy head.

I was all over dog drool and he was all over exuberance.

The back door of the house opened and Tony Derrick spoke. 'No, I'm not getting twitchy. I really heard something. I'm gonna take a look.'

A torch beam flashed across the lawn. Dregs, releasing me, loped towards it with a woof. Diving back behind the shed, I lay still, trembling.

Dregs growled the way he did when he wanted to play.

Tony screamed. 'Get it off!'

'Shut up,' said Narcisa, 'or the neighbours will be round complaining.'

A bright light flooding the garden, my hidey-hole was no longer dark.

'Get it off me!' Tony sounded as if he was going to cry.

'It's only a dog.'

'Get the bastard off!'

'Shut up, he's not hurting you.'

Something hissed and Dregs yelped.

'That's got rid of him,' said Narcisa.

'About bloody time. What is that stuff?'

'Pepper spray. It's not nice but he'll get over it, poor mutt.'

'Poor mutt?' Tony spluttered. 'It was Hobbes's bloody dog, you know? And Hobbes won't be too far away. You'd better hide the spray.'

She laughed. 'You're right, he isn't far away but, don't worry, he'll be no trouble.'

'What d'you mean?'

'You'll see,' she said. 'Now come along. There's still plenty to do.'

Their footsteps receded and a moment later the light went out. Dregs had come to my rescue again and I just hoped he wasn't going to suffer too much for it. Standing up, I brushed myself down.

Narcisa's assertion that Hobbes wasn't far away gave me reason to believe I was doing the right thing, yet her confidence that he'd be no trouble had me worried, even more worried than the prospect of running into her pepper spray.

Drawing a deep breath, I tiptoed across the darkened lawn, creeping around the outside of the house, peeping into every room. The furniture and carpets looked expensive and comfortable and nothing seemed out of place, except that I couldn't see anyone. As the upstairs lights were off, it was a puzzle, because, so far as I could tell, no one had left the house. I was baffled, though I was sure of one thing – I didn't want to be standing outside for too long. A brutal gust caught me in the back of the neck and goose pimples erupted over my skin.

'C'mon, you idiot,' I muttered, my breath steaming, 'you've got to do something.'

I stole round to the back door, which was locked. The kitchen behind it lay in darkness, though a small ventilation window above my head was open. Pulling myself up by the frame, kneeling on the narrow sill, I squeezed my head and shoulders through the window, standing up, carefully, wriggling and squirming. I'd got so far through that I was starting to worry about what I was going to land on, when something snagged. I couldn't slither forwards or push myself back and, losing my footing, ended up balanced on my ribs, a hard, pointy knob sticking into my solar plexus, despite the layers of clothes. An involuntary groan, partly pain, mostly despair, squeezed out and a new proverb came to mind: 'Don't try to squeeze through inadequate gaps in inappropriate clothing.' It wasn't snappy, yet I wished I'd thought of it beforehand. I writhed and wriggled and it made no difference.

Soft, heavy footsteps approached and there was nothing I could do except cringe and wait for whatever happened next.

'What's going on in here?' asked Editorsaurus Rex.

At such times it's impossible to be nonchalant, though I did my best, smiling, keeping my chin up, as the kitchen light flickered on.

I'd been discovered in a most embarrassing position. Slumping, dangling, I awaited my doom. A pair of fluffy white socks sailed into view across a sea of glossy black and white tiles and a soft, moist hand lifted my head.

'Capstan, what the Devil are you doing?' The Editorsaurus's voice sounded strange and there was curiosity instead of the fury I'd anticipated. My head dropped.

'Just hanging about,' I said, attempting an ingratiating grin.

'Oh, that's all right then. So long as you're not burgling.'

'Oh no, sir. I'd never do such a thing.'

'I'm very glad to hear it. Now, are you going to stay there all day, or are you coming in for a drinkie?'

I realised why he sounded so odd – he was dead drunk, though his speech was controlled and precise rather than slurred.

'I'd love a drink, sir, only I appear to be stuck.'

'I'm not surprised, it's far too small for you.' His voice grew angry. 'Not too small for Narcisa's rat-boy, though. Oh no, he squeezed himself in all right. Nasty, dirty, little sneak. Are you sure you're not burgling?'

'No, sir, I'm here for a drink. If you wouldn't mind giving me a hand?'

'Sorry Capstan. Of course, you are. It's very good of you to visit me on my birthday and I see you've brought a present. Thank you.' He took the plastic bag from me. It had been dangling from my arm for so long it was almost part of me.

The next few moments were painful and undignified. He lifted and shoved me, the window frame creaking, as if on the point of collapse. There was a tearing sound, a handful of buttons clattered across the tiles and I slithered backwards, feet scrabbling, landing heavily on my back in the garden. By the time I'd recovered my breath and got to my feet, Rex was lumbering away, swaying like an elephant, my bag twisting in his hand. I banged on the door but he was oblivious.

My skin, apart from the odd, additional scrape, had survived intact, yet most of the buttons from my coat, jacket and shirt were gone and my clothes were flapping in the breeze. After a few moments to recover, I had what I considered a great idea. Stripping my top half down to my vest, I made another attempt on the window. Though it was still a squeeze, after grunting and groaning and sweating like a wrestler, I began to slide through.

Then I stopped. The knob thing had snagged me again and my entire weight was suspended on my trouser waistband. I writhed and wriggled until, with a long, slow, zip-rending rip, I slid forwards, shedding my trousers as a snake sheds its skin. Gently, sedately even, I slithered onto the kitchen floor, looking back to where the tattered remnants of a once fine piece of tailoring fluttered in the breeze.

At such times it's important to count your blessings. I could count one: my underwear had survived. Apart from that, my situation was desperate. I glanced down at my muddy shoes, tartan socks and the long white underpants and realised I could count two blessings: they were clean on that morning. Still, if anyone caught me, how could I explain skulking in my ex-boss's house in my underwear? Besides, I still had to get home somehow. My face glowed as I imagined the photos in the *Bugle* and the sarcastic comments PC Wilkes would throw at me in the cell. Why did these things keep happening to me? All I'd ever wanted was a quiet life and I didn't deserve this. At least, though, I was in a place where I could wash my filthy hands and have a glass of water, both of which I did.

Then, with a lump of fear in my stomach and a cringe in my walk, I began to prowl through the house.

I found Rex in the next room, lying flat on his back on the deep, soft cream carpet, an empty gin bottle clutched to his heart, looking as peaceful as a sleeping baby, though no infant could fill the room with the noises he was producing. He snored, gurgling and farting like a flatulent hippopotamus and I doubted he'd regain consciousness for many hours. Retrieving my carrier bag, I left him to sleep it off, though, before going, I made free with his drinks cabinet. Opening a bottle of whisky, pouring a considerable measure into a crystal tumbler, I gulped it down. The liquid fire, searing its way towards my stomach, felt good.

I carried out a rapid search downstairs, where everything, apart from Rex, was quiet. Then, finding myself in the hall at the bottom of the stairs, I began to climb into the darkness, my footsteps muffled by the deep pale-yellow carpet, an admirable aid to sneaking, or so I thought until, reaching a landing where the stairs turned at a right angle, I glanced back. I'd left a muddy trail and there was nothing I could do about it, so wiping my feet, I carried on to the first floor, where a brass candelabra with three flickering candles rested on a small wooden table, providing the only illumination. I picked it up, surprised by its weight, and took it with me, since I feared turning on a light would draw attention to me. Candlelit exploration of an old unfamiliar house where I had no right to be was not a soothing occupation, every movement of the flickering shadows, every creak of a floorboard, making my heart race.

I looked into three empty bedrooms before finding the one in which I'd seen Narcisa and Tony. A flowery scent, overly sweet and cloying, seemed strongest by a small bottle on the dressing table. When I removed the stopper, I sneezed. It was a powerful scent, yet familiar. Averting my eyes from the crumpled white sheets on the four-poster bed, I noticed an ancient leather-bound book on a small table at its side. Putting down the candelabra, I opened it, a sheet of paper fluttering to the carpet.

It was a letter, written on Sorenchester Museum paper. Picking it up, I read:

Dear Mrs Witcherley,

I have acquired this volume, which I believe to be the one detailing the ritual in which you expressed an interest. My asking price for this exceedingly fine and rare copy is £10,000 in cash. In addition, I have knowledge of a fine bracelet with an established provenance to the Order of the Dragon. I am confident I can put it your way, for the right price. I must once again emphasise the importance of treating any such transactions in strict confidence.

Yours sincerely,

Ray Biggs, Curator.

Hobbes's suspicion about Mr Biggs appeared to have been justified. Replacing the letter, I examined the book. It was made of parchment or something, with heavy, black gothic printing and a smell of dust and age. On the first page was a woodcut of a castle, familiar to me from the label on the Romanian beer bottle and, a couple of pages further on, I came across an illustration of a dragon with its tail in its mouth. The text was incomprehensible, in a foreign language, yet, on seeing the word 'Dracul' several times, the hairs on the back of my neck rose and stiffened.

My worry and fear levels rising to critical, the animal part of my brain tried to convince me that Narcisa was a vampire and that I should run away. Though a more rational part tried to point out that vampires were fictional, I couldn't stop myself wondering if I'd ever seen her in full daylight. My teeth were chattering, my mouth was as dry as chalk and I was trembling all over. In fairness, I was in a weird Romanian woman's bedroom, lit only by flickering candlelight and I'd just discovered a book, apparently about vampires. Furthermore, convinced she was a thief, I hoped that was the worst of it, though I had a terrible fear she'd done something dreadful to Hobbes. Finally, I was dressed only in my underwear, which always puts one at a disadvantage.

In the circumstances, I think my nerves were entirely justified. Sitting down on the chair by the dressing table, I glanced in the mirror, shocked by how scared I looked, unable to suppress a paralysing horror that something was creeping up behind, yet, when

I forced myself to turn and face it, there was nothing.

I heard a click and a stair creaked. Someone was coming. Or was it something? Wanting to scream and run, I made do with diving under the bed and cowering like a coward.

'Where did you say you put it?' shouted Tony.

'On the table on the landing,' Narcisa replied from downstairs, 'and bring the book too – it's in the bedroom.'

'The candelabra's not here. Anyway, haven't we got enough already?'

'Don't be stupid. Just fetch it.'

'I'm not being stupid.' Cursing softly, he entered the bedroom and shouted, 'it was in your room all the time.'

His footsteps drawing close, I held my breath. When they moved away, the candlelight faded, leaving me in utter darkness and confusion. Tony had come from downstairs and Narcisa was downstairs, though I was certain only Rex had been down there. Where had they been hiding?

'There's mud on the stairs,' said Tony. 'Someone's in the house.'

My whole body going into an ecstasy of terror, I thought I was going to be sick. I wanted a wee; I wanted a crucifix; I wanted garlic; I wanted Buffy the Vampire slayer; most of all, I wanted to be out of there.

'It'll just be Fatso staggering around drunk,' said Narcisa. 'Now, hurry up. It's nearly time.'

I lay still until I regained control of my limbs. What was it nearly time for?

I crawled out, creeping towards the staircase, my legs wobbling as I stood up and tiptoed downstairs, which was now in darkness, apart from the glimmer of a distant street lamp lighting up the porch and hall. The mystery of Narcisa and Tony's whereabouts held no interest for me just then. I wanted out. Slipping into the porch, fumbling with the latch, almost sobbing with relief, I opened the front door, shivering as my body was exposed to the night air. I was about to run when, hearing muffled sounds from below, I realised they were coming from the cellars. I could have kicked myself; of course a house of this age would have cellars. I just hadn't seen the door.

The revelation didn't stop me fleeing. What did stop me was the chanting of deep male voices from below ground, making my legs all wobbly again. How many people were down there? Had I stumbled into some sort of Satanic Mass? Then, to my surprise, I chuckled, recognising the chanting as the same recording I'd heard the ghouls playing. Somehow, I found it soothing, because the ghouls, though terrifying, had as Hobbes pointed out, not been so bad. Not really. In fact, other than trying to bury me alive, they'd been pretty harmless. With any luck vampires, or Satanists, were similar.

Forcing myself back inside, fortifying my courage with another raid on the whisky bottle, I searched for the cellar door, finding it under the stairs, in plain view, if only I'd been looking.

As I put my ear against it to listen, it clicked open and I stumbled through onto a creaky wooden staircase, cool, damp air and an earthy odour surrounding me. There was light down there, candlelight, to judge from the flickering. I swallowed, tiptoeing down, as the chanting grew louder. A familiar scent struck me, the same cloying, flowery scent as in Narcisa's room, though heavier, if it were possible.

On reaching the bottom, I saw I'd entered a vaulted cellar, similar to, though even larger than Hobbes's. To start with, I was amazed at the quantity of wine down there. Hundreds, possibly thousands, of bottles were laid to rest in racks on the smooth limestone floor.

The light emanated from an archway at the far end. Creeping towards it, my footsteps echoing treacherously, I hoped the chanting would drown them out.

Flattening myself against the wall by the arch, taking a vast breath, I poked my head round the corner, jerking back, dazzled and shaking, as if I'd gone down with malaria. On the other side was a cavernous chamber packed with burning candles, where a forest of sturdy limestone buttresses supported a low ceiling. In the middle, in a space like a clearing, stood a stone altar. Next to it, on a wooden table, the Roman cup reflected red in the candlelight. What had scared me most, though, was the long, naked, glinting dagger, lying with its point to the cup. Though I'd not seen or heard Narcisa or Tony down there, in my imagination they were lurking in every shadow, waiting to do me harm. An incongruous thought occurred: I'd always enjoyed watching this sort of thing in films and on telly. It wasn't the same in real life.

Curiosity, wrestling with cowardice, got it, rather to my astonishment, in an arm-lock, yet without quite gaining total submission. The chanting rang even louder, muffling my clumsy footsteps, which was good, reducing my chances of hearing movement, which wasn't. As I slipped into the chamber and cringed behind the nearest pillar, I heard a cry of despair from a man, though not from Hobbes. It turned into a scream, taking all my strength, even as it blew the fog of trivia from my mind.

The cry echoed above the chanting. 'Water! Please! Oh Christ, it burns.'

Though pain and fear had distorted it, I knew the voice and any remaining animosity washed away in a flood of sympathy. It was Phil Waring and he was in big trouble. Fighting an impulse to rush blindly to the rescue, I told myself that getting both of us into a mess would not help. Despite my innate cowardice suggesting immediate flight, I steadied myself, acknowledging the importance of finding out precisely what I was up against, and where he was, since his cries, echoing round the smooth curved walls, confused my senses. As I became aware of other voices, quieter and indistinct, I wished I had Hobbes with me.

I sneaked a glance round the pillar, seeing no one, although a dark painting of a mediaeval king, hanging in an alcove behind the altar, made me start. Recalling Mrs Tomkins, the cook, telling Hobbes that Mr Roman had sold a creepy painting, I could easily believe it was this one, for there was nothing but malice in the King's eyes, nothing but threat in the way he held the long, naked, glinting dagger over a golden chalice. Dagger and chalice looked identical to the ones on the altar.

I shuddered as the chanting faded away. In the ensuing stillness, footsteps approached.

'Move!' yelled Tony.

My heart leapt and, for a moment, I thought I'd been discovered but he was shouting at Phil, whom he was goading into a stumbling walk with a spiked pole. His strange gait seemed to be more because he couldn't see than because of the chains weighing down his wrists and ankles. It was almost as strange to see him unshaven, tie-less and dirty, with sweat stains around his armpits, as to see him in a dungeon. He flinched as the chanting started again.

I shivered, wishing I'd been more careful with my clothes, that I'd had the sense to bring the whisky bottle, something far more useful than the leg of lamb I was still carting around like an idiot.

Tony, enveloped in a long, heavy, grey robe, with a deep hood, and only his beaky nose jutting out, reminded me of a vulture. Narcisa was close behind, wrapped in the deep folds of the purple gown I'd seen earlier, walking slowly, majestically, with bowed head, her arms folded across her chest, holding the book I'd seen in the bedroom.

Tony forced Phil to lie on the altar. Staying in the shadows, sneaking a little closer, praying they wouldn't see me, I slipped behind another pillar. When I risked a look, Phil was stretched on his back as Tony secured his chains. Narcisa stood over him, facing me. I jerked back, amazed she hadn't noticed me. Taking a moment for a better look around the chamber, I noted the small barred cell at the far end, presumably where they'd been holding Phil, but saw no sign of Hobbes. I couldn't grasp why they'd made Phil a prisoner, though it was not difficult to surmise that whatever they were planning would not be to his benefit. Only one person could put a stop to whatever was going to happen. Me.

I risked another glance. Narcisa was in the same position, Tony at her side. A few candles flickered close to where Phil was writhing uselessly against his chains yet, otherwise, the air was still. Narcisa raised her skinny arms, the heavy ring on her finger and the dragon bracelet on her wrist glinted; the chanting stopped.

She spoke into the sudden silence, reading from the book, her voice tremulous at first, as if she, too, was nervous. I couldn't understand the foreign words.

'What are you going to do?' Phil's voice cracked into a squeak.

She ignored him. Tony sniggered, glanced at her and went quiet.

'You can't do this.' Anger and fear competed in Phil's voice.

'Shut it,' said Tony.

Narcisa's incantation grew more confident, powerful, drowning out Phil's protestations, as I cursed myself, wishing I'd thought to pick up some sort of weapon in my search round the house. I didn't like the look of things one little bit, and the glittering dagger was never far from my mind. There was something in the way it sliced the light to suggest its blade was razor sharp: not something you'd choose for cleaning your nails but ideal for a human sacrifice.

'Hand me the sanguinary chalice,' said Narcisa.

'The what?' asked Tony from the darkness of his hood.

'The sanguinary chalice.'

'Uh ... you mean this old cup thing?'

'Just give me the bloody cup.'

'OK, keep your hair on.' He handed it to her.

'What do you mean by that?' Her voice was sharp.

'Nothing, just be cool. Can I open a bottle of plonk now?'

'If you must.' Narcisa, raising the cup in both hands, continued speaking in the strange, droning language. I saw she was wearing the gleaming dragon ring on her middle finger.

Holding my breath, I squeezed deeper into the shadows, as Tony walked past towards the wine cellar, returning with a bottle, opening it with the corkscrew on his penknife. She lowered the cup, placing it on the altar by Phil's head.

'Hand me the Dagger of Tepes,' she said.

'Uh ... the big knife?' asked Tony.

'Of course.'

Picking it up by the blade, presenting the hilt to her, he yelped as she grasped it.

'Ow! You nearly had my bloody finger off. You'd better be careful or you might really hurt someone.' He groped inside his robe and wrapped a handkerchief round his hand. The grubby cloth darkened.

'What are you doing?' Phil blinked at the dagger through red-rimmed eyes.

My eyes watered in sympathy.

'Shut up!' shouted Tony.

'It's all right,' said Narcisa. 'There's no reason why he shouldn't know. Not now. Mr Waring, I must apologise for detaining you like this, but you did poke your nose into my affairs at an awkward time. Yet, in its way, your arrival has proved most opportune. The ritual demands blood and your sacrifice will give me new life, so I must thank you.'

'Mrs Witcherley, what are you talking about?'

'Simply, you will die for me. Greater love has no man than to lay down his life.'

'You're going to murder me?' Unsurprisingly, Phil sounded terrified.

'No, not murder, sacrifice. Don't worry, the blade is razor sharp, as Igor has discovered to his cost. You'll not feel much and the expenditure of your blood will not be in vain. Think of it as an honour.'

Phil said nothing, shaking even more than I was.

'What d'you mean, calling me Igor?' asked Tony, whining. 'That's an insult that is. It's adding insult to injury. My finger's bloody sore.'

'Just a joke,' she said.

'But you're not really going to kill him are you? You're just going to frighten him? Make sure he shuts up?'

'Oh, wake up, you idiot. Do you really imagine I'd go to these lengths to frighten a journalist? If I'd only wanted to shut him up, I'd have got Rex to have a word with him. My husband is a fat old goat but he has his uses.'

'You told me no one was going to get hurt. You said red wine would do as well as blood.'

'You heard what you wanted to hear. Now, be quiet, I need to concentrate.' She resumed her chanting.

'No.' Tony faced up to her, pointing his finger. 'You called me an idiot and that's not nice. I thought we had something together, you and me.'

'Think what you want and be quiet.'

'I won't. You lied to me.'

'You were useful. That's enough.'

'You used me.'

'If I did, you had your fun and were handsomely paid. Rex's bank account is another of his good features.'

I wish I could claim I was planning a brave and intelligent intervention but, the truth is, I was cowering in the darkness, too terrified to move, yet holding a faint hope that Tony would somehow prevail.

'It's not right,' he whined. 'You said you loved me and that we were made for each other. It's why I helped you steal everything. It wasn't the money.'

Unable to believe his claim, to my horror, I snorted with disdain.

'What was that? I heard someone. Honest.'

'It doesn't matter,' said Narcisa. 'Just shut up and let me get on.'

'But someone's in here.'

I retreated deeper into the shadows, awaiting discovery and whatever came of it.

'It'll just be Hobbes,' she laughed.

'Hobbes? What d'you mean Hobbes?' Tony, pulling his hood back, stared around wildly.

'Mr Waring wasn't the only one snooping into my business. Hobbes turned up too, shortly after he'd let you go.'

'Where is he?'

'That's not your concern, he'll not interfere. Now shut up.'

So, Hobbes was down there and I couldn't guess what she might have done to him to be so confident. I stole towards the very back of the chamber, where there were no candles and the gloom became blackness. The heavy, almost narcotic, scent of flowers faded and I became aware, ever so faintly at first, of the feral odour I associated with Hobbes.

As Narcisa resumed her chanting, the strange words echoing hypnotically round the chamber, I hesitated, torn between trying to find Hobbes and trying to rescue Phil. The latter was in imminent peril, assuming Narcisa meant what she said, and I had no doubt she intended to kill, yet Hobbes would be able to stop her far better than I could. In all honesty, I'm not a fighter; I doubted I could overcome Tony and, as for Narcisa, something about her made me suspect she knew how to hurt a man. Besides, she'd got the pepper spray and the dagger. Again, I dithered, though I was starting to think that, if I couldn't find Hobbes very soon, I would have to do something.

Do or die – it wasn't a happy prospect.

'You're going too far,' yelled Tony, sounding angry and scared. 'Stop it now, or I'll stop you myself.'

Narcisa laughed. 'You're too late.'

Clasping the dagger with both hands, she raised it above her head. Phil screamed.

Tony, as fast as a weasel, caught her wrist, forcing her backwards. The hood of her gown fell back and for a moment her blonde wig clung to the top of her skull before sliding to the floor. Tony grunted, maintaining his grip, making her cry out, making her drop the dagger, barely managing to twist his foot out of the way as it stuck in the floor. His movement allowed her to break free, to pull something from her gown. Her back being towards me, I guessed she'd gone for her pepper spray.

Tony, his eyes bulging with fear, spun round and bolted. Narcisa turning after him, was not holding the spray but a small revolver. There were two explosions, shocking and painful in the confined space, sparks sprayed from the wall above Tony's head as he scurried through the arch, fleeing like a hunted rat. If she intended hitting him, and I'm sure she did, she was a rotten shot. I dropped to the floor like a pile of dirty washing.

It took a few moments to work out why I'd got a dead leg, and why a hole had appeared at the top of my left thigh, oozing blood and burning. A ricochet must have hit me, though it must have been nearly spent, because I could touch the bullet's distorted shape, slightly proud of my skin. It still felt red-hot. Licking my fingers, as you do when snuffing a candle, I tugged at it, almost fainting as it popped out with a sucking sound. Unable to suppress a groan, I lay, panting as the agony slowly subsided.

'Well, well,' said Narcisa looking down on me, her gun pointing at my face, 'fancy meeting you here, Mr Caplet. And dressed so formally, too.'

'The name's Capstan,' I said. 'I mean, no it isn't. It is Caplet.'

As she smiled, I stared at her teeth, trying to see if they were suspiciously sharp.

'Make up your mind. Rex said you were a ditherer. He still gave you many chances, the soft fool. I see you've been injured – a couple of inches over and you'd be a gelding. Well, never mind. Stand up.'

My wound throbbing, blood trickling down my leg, I pulled myself upright, leaning against a pillar for support. 'What are you going to do? Are you going to call the police?'

She laughed. 'Your reputation for stupidity doesn't do you justice. I'm going to have to shoot you. You've seen far too much.'

I rested my forehead on the pillar, its rough, cool solidity somehow soothing, though my heart was thumping, as if I'd run a marathon with Dregs. My breathing was fast and shallow and not enough and I could see Narcisa, as if at the end of a tunnel, raising her revolver, taking a step closer, taking aim. I thought she must really be a rotten shot to do that. But it put her within range. Swinging my arm, I watched the carrier bag, as if in slow motion, straining under the weight of the leg of lamb, describing a perfect arc straight into the side of her head. The revolver, flying from her hand, clattered on the stone floor as she went down like the great white hope.

18

A strange mix of elation and horror combined with sharp pain as I swayed over Narcisa.

'Who's stupid now?' I asked, silently thanking Mrs Goodfellow for my unlikely weapon.

Phil's voice brought me back to myself. 'What's happening? Andy, is it you? What are you doing here?'

Before I could respond, my leg buckling, I stumbled backwards into heavy, musty cloth, like a curtain, grabbing at it for balance. As it ripped away, I plunged into emptiness.

I dropped a long way before hitting something hard, if not as hard as I feared, and came to rest on a cold stone floor, lying flat on my back, stunned and winded. As breathing returned, I sucked in lungfuls of cool, fetid air, sitting up, still clutching a fragment of cloth, wondering what had happened, while my eyes adjusted to the faint light filtering in from somewhere above. I'd fallen into a pit, four or five metres deep at a guess, and, maybe three metres across. A pile of leaves in the corner had saved me from harm.

The leaves moved and an animal odour filled my nostrils. Something snarled and I leaped to my feet, despite the agony shooting through my leg, as an unkempt, ugly head emerged.

'Hobbes!' I gasped. 'Are you alright?'

Growling, he stood up, sniffing the air like a dog, staring without apparent recognition. It worried me. Even worse, he was looking at me the way a starving man looks at a steak dinner. Flattening myself against the wall, I edged away.

'It's me,' I said, 'you know … Andy.'

He was following my every movement, tense like a predator, licking his lips and swallowing.

'What's wrong? I'm sorry I fell on you … stay back!'

Blood, trickling into my sock, it felt as if I'd stepped into a warm, sticky puddle as I began to panic, fearing what the scent of blood might do to him. Then some words I'd heard a few hours earlier, when the world had been a friendlier place, came into my head, 'He'll be hungry and I ought to tell you, dear, he can get rather wild when he's hungry. You'd best take the leg of lamb.'

As I upended the bag, Hobbes pounced. I screamed as, with one hand, he tossed me over his shoulder into the leaves. Snarling, he turned his back on me, like a lion shielding a carcass from a jackal. Covering my ears to drown out the growls, the slurping, the tearing of flesh, the crunching of bone, I prayed the lamb wouldn't just be the appetiser. Nightmare minutes passed as the slobbering and cracking continued.

I had to get out of the pit or die, yet the walls were smooth and sheer, unclimbable except, maybe, to a gecko. I contemplated yelling for help, yet Phil was chained up, Tony had run away and Rex, even if my voice could reach him, was dead drunk. Accepting my fate with all the dignity I could muster, I began to cry like a snotty little kid. It wasn't fair after all I'd done.

That thought snapped me out of it. All my imagined brilliance in finding Hobbes and Phil, in knocking out Narcisa, came to nothing now I was stuck in that dismal hole. I hadn't actually rescued anyone, but at least I'd tried, which was no comfort whatsoever.

Hobbes stood up, loping towards me, still carrying a hefty chunk of bone. I shrank back.

'Thanks for that,' he said, 'I was rather peckish.'

'Hobbes?' I stared into his face. Bristles sprouted from his chin and flecks of raw meat were stuck to his lips and between his teeth as he smiled. By God, I had never been so pleased to see a smile in all my life!

'Yes. Sorry if I alarmed you.'

Getting to my feet, I damn near hugged the bastard. 'You scared the life out of me,' I said, damn near to kicking the bastard.

'Oops,' he said. 'We'd better get out of here, and quickly. Your leg needs treatment and Mrs Witcherley is waking up.'

'How can you possibly know that?'

'Trust me.'

'Umm … we can't get out of here.'

'We can try.'

'Haven't you tried already? You must've been down here for ages?'

He nodded. 'I did have a go, of course, but the rock's too hard and brittle.' He showed me his hands, his nails all torn and bloody. 'However, you may have provided a solution.'

Taking the bone, which he'd gnawed into a crude pick, he attacked the wall.

Stone chips flying in all directions, I hung back out of harm's way, sticking a finger into the hole in my leg to slow the oozing, though the sensation made my head float. I had to close my eyes until the nausea and faintness abated, yet it wasn't long before I could pay attention. He was not, as I'd supposed, making a mad assault on the wall. He was excavating ledges to serve as toe and finger holds.

'She's got Phil chained to an altar,' I said. 'She was going to kill us so I knocked her out.'

Hobbes, grunting, pulled himself up, wedging his feet into a small hole at waist-height. Bits of stone fell at my feet. 'I know,' he said. 'He's very frightened and she's regaining consciousness. I must work harder.'

I didn't bother asking how he knew. He was speeding up, despite having to hold on with one hand, the sinews on the back of his neck bulging with the effort. He still had a long way to go. Above us, Narcisa groaned and muttered.

Two thirds of the way up, he paused, gnawing at the bone's edge, sharpening it I guessed. As he examined it, he slipped, falling at my feet. Though he leaped back up in an instant, I'd seen the sweat streaming down his face and neck and heard how hard and fast he was breathing.

A light shone into the pit.

'Stop right there,' said Narcisa, standing above us, the revolver in one hand, a candelabra in the other.

Without thinking, I began hurling debris and, though I don't think I actually hit her, she obviously hadn't expected resistance and ducked back. Her head appeared twice more and volleys of rocks kept her at bay. Hobbes, ignoring her, was making astonishing progress. She didn't return again but once more, from a distance, I heard her intoning the strange words of her ritual.

'Hurry! She's going to kill him.' I nearly wept.

Stone chips flew as the incantation continued. I couldn't stop myself hopping in a frenzy of agonised helplessness, wishing I had some inkling what she was on about, wishing I could do something.

At last, Hobbes, stretching out a long arm, grabbed the edge of the pit, hanging for a moment by his fingertips. With a grunt, he swung up and onto the floor.

He beckoned. 'C'mon, Andy, and quickly.' Then he was gone.

My leg throbbed and spasmed as I began to climb, yet the holds were so far apart and so narrow, I only managed a couple before falling. Though pain made me cry out, I had another go and was balanced on a narrow ledge, stretching for a handhold when a shot rang out. The shock making me lose my grip, I slid down the wall, skinning my elbows and jarring my leg. I barely noticed the pain, as another shot echoed around, followed by a succession of shots.

'Hobbes!' I yelled and, forgetting impossibility, launched myself up the wall and over the edge. Narcisa screamed as I got to my feet. Hobbes had his back to me and he'd got her by the throat. She kicked and howled as he jerked her above his head, as if he meant to dash her brains out against the wall.

'No,' I said. 'Don't!'

He turned, staring at me for a long moment, as if puzzled, blood soaking his shirt front, dripping onto the stone floor. 'You're right,' he said. 'I should never hurt a lady. Thank you.'

He fell onto his face. She skidded across the floor like a stone, bouncing over a frozen pond until she came to rest against the altar and lay still. As still as Hobbes.

'Andy!' Phil cried, sounding desperate, 'get these bloody chains off me. Please.'

'Hold on,' I shouted, hurrying towards Hobbes. 'Are you alright?'

He wasn't. Kneeling, sweating with the strain, I rolled him onto his back. He didn't even twitch. Four neat round holes pierced his front and my hands were red and sticky with hot blood.

Putting my face in my hands, I groaned, knowing I'd failed. Yet Phil was sobbing and begging for release and, after what he'd been through, I couldn't blame him. My leg throbbed like a voodoo drum as, pulling myself together, I stumbled towards him. Hobbes, after all, had come here to rescue him, so it was the least I could do and the least seemed to be the most I would achieve.

Phil gasped as I reached him. 'Your face! What's wrong with your face?'

'There's nothing wrong with it,' I said, infuriated. I was trying to save his life and all he could do was insult me.

'It's covered in blood. Have you been shot?'

'Yes, in the leg.'

'But your face?'

'Oh ... umm ... it's Hobbes's mostly. He's hurt.'

Although I couldn't find the keys to the padlocks securing Phil's chains, I managed to unbolt the shackles that anchored them. He sat up, clanking and groaning like Marley's ghost, staring at me, looking puzzled.

'Andy,' he asked. 'Where are your trousers?'

'In the kitchen window.'

He nodded. 'Great. How did you get here? I thought I was going to die. It's been awful.'

As he sobbed, I wrapped an awkward arm around his shoulders, despite his stink.

'There, there,' I said, feeling useless and embarrassed, 'but I've got to help Hobbes now. She shot him.'

'Why? And why did she want to kill me? And why here? Like this? What's going on?'

Unable to give a satisfactory reply, I shrugged, hobbling back towards Hobbes, kneeling beside him, wishing I could remember what to do. The thing was, Rex, insisting that everyone working for the *Bugle* should know at least basic first aid, had made everyone take a course. Ingrid had been on mine, and having been far too interested in her short skirt to pay attention to anything else, the ABC of resuscitation was all that came to mind, the instructor having banged on about it for long enough. Unfortunately, unable to remember why, I could have kicked myself as the blood spread and steamed.

Phil knew what to do, of course. Clanking his chains, kneeling opposite me, pulling Hobbes's head back, he peered into his mouth. 'His airway's clear,' he said, 'and he's breathing, though not very well. I'll check his circulation.' He poked around Hobbes's neck. 'I can't find a pulse.'

My leg kept erupting into spasms of hurt and my body shook with cold and shock. The stink of hot, fresh blood and its tacky feel as it dried on my hands was getting to me, so, feeling my head floating, I closed my eyes and, had Phil not grunted unexpectedly, might have fainted. On opening my eyes, I found he'd beaten me to it, slumping across Hobbes like a wet blanket. I shook him. 'Wake up.' There was no response, except that he slipped to the floor, leaving it all up to me. I gritted my teeth.

At least I now knew the ABC stood for Airways, Breathing and Circulation and, though I couldn't find a pulse either, the blood still pumping from the holes suggested he was still alive and that I should plug the leaks. Without bandages or dressings, I had to improvise. Picking up the dagger, cutting strips from Phil's nice silk shirt, I removed my vest and, folding it into a pad, used the strips to bind it over Hobbes's wounds.

'Right,' I said out loud, though I doubted he could hear, 'that should staunch the bleeding while I go and phone for an ambulance. Don't worry.'

Pushing myself up, I staggered towards the arch, convinced

Hobbes was a goner.

'Stop right there,' said Narcisa.

Her makeup had run, she had a lump the size of a duck egg on her forehead, a purple bruise on the cheek where I'd hit her, and she'd put her wig on askew. Though she looked grotesque and battered, she was holding the revolver in a steady hand. I had a vision of myself standing before her, facing death, bloodied and shocked and surprisingly heroic. Strangely, I felt little fear.

'You couldn't hit a barn door at this distance.'

'You could be right,' she said grinning and her teeth looked uncannily white in the candlelight, 'so, you'd better come closer.'

'I'm not that stupid.'

She laughed and sneered, 'Oh, but you are. If you don't, I'll shoot him.' She pointed the gun at Phil's head.

Even she couldn't possibly miss at that range, so forced to comply, I limped towards her as slowly as possible, hoping for the best.

'Good boy,' she said. 'Now, if you don't mind, or, let's face it, even if you do, I want you to lift Mr Waring back onto the altar.'

'No,' I said.

'No is not the answer I expect when I've got a gun in my hand. Do you imagine you're being heroic? You ought to take a look in the mirror sometime. You're a mess. Now, move him before I get angry.'

'No.'

'There's no chivalry in young men these days. Are you sure you mean no?'

'No. I mean, yes, I'm sure I mean no.'

'Oh, well,' she said and raised the gun. 'Parting is such sweet sorrow.'

'And parkin is such sweet cake.' I couldn't help thinking that my attempt at a James Bond-style witty riposte hadn't quite reached the standard. They were hardly famous last words and I grimaced, though I didn't anticipate them being either famous or last.

She squeezed the trigger.

Nothing happened. She squeezed it again and again.

My mind was clear and any fear was minimal. I'd counted how many shots she'd fired. 'You're out of ammo,' I said.

Screaming, she hurled the revolver at me but it was a real girlie throw, one even I might have bettered. It clattered to the floor behind.

'Missed!' I glanced over my shoulder to see where it had landed and, in case she'd got more bullets, picked it up, finding it heavier than I'd imagined. Realising she was too dangerous to leave on her own, I knew she'd have to come with me while I phoned for help. I congratulated myself on forgetting nothing.

Except for one thing: the dagger. Terror chewed my guts, yet it was still lying beside Hobbes, out of her view. Unfortunately, it was not the only thing I'd forgotten.

She stuck the can of pepper spray in my face, squeezing the release, and it would have done for me, had the liquid burst out in a powerful jet instead of dribbling and dripping harmlessly to the ground.

'It's all gone,' I said, laughing, which was a mistake.

She leaped on me like an infuriated cat and, though I did my best against the clawing, spitting and biting, she'd taken me by surprise. A well-manicured talon, slashing at my eyes, I covered up as well as I could, feeling her sharp, varnished nails tearing my face. Squealing like a stuck pig, I shoved her down. She sprang back, this time more like an enraged leopard, and, my injured leg failing, I fell. She was all over me in an instant, hissing, screeching, gouging, biting. Her sharp teeth piercing my neck, I screamed, pushing and kicking her off, struggling to my feet, clutching the wound, sick and scared within. She'd bitten me and, as the realisation hit home, horror overwhelmed me. I feared I was doomed to become like her, one of the undead, her slave forever. I may not have been entirely rational.

'Help!' I cried.

Though she was sprawling on the ground at Hobbes's side, her teeth were still locked in my neck and, as I clawed at them, they dropped, clacking on the stone floor. I might have laughed if not for the pain and fear. False ones! Yet even as the relief hit me, she sprang up, wielding the dagger. Jumping backwards to avoid a slash, twisting to one side as she stabbed at me, I ducked and squirmed, fending her off with the brass candelabra. Too heavy and clumsy to be an effective weapon, it treacherously shed its load across the floor and, as I parried a lunge at my face, I stepped on a candle, skidding into a pillar. The candelabra clattered to the floor and, like a striking cobra, the dagger stabbed towards my throat. I took what I expected to be my last breath.

Fortunately, some things move even faster than cobras. The dagger, ceasing its attempt to skewer my larynx, flew upwards like a rocket, twisting through the air, sticking in the ceiling. A moment later, Narcisa, following a similar, if lower, trajectory, landed on her back in the middle of the altar, groaning. Her eyes opened with a look of puzzlement as if she was wondering how she'd got there and the Dagger of Tepes, falling loose in a shower of stone fragments, dropped towards her head. She screamed and was quiet.

'Hello, dear,' said Mrs Goodfellow.

'You?' I replied as intelligently as I could in the circumstances. 'How? You?'

'Well spotted, dear, it is me. Has she hurt you?'

'Yes, but Hobbes needs help.' I lurched towards him. 'She shot him.'

'Then I wish I'd hit her harder. Who's the attractive young man in the chains?'

'It's Phil – he was missing. We need to get Hobbes to hospital.'

'No.' I felt a faint rumble as if a heavy vehicle had passed on the edge of hearing. It came from Hobbes. 'No hospital.' The words emerged slowly. 'Fetch Rocky.'

'You have to go to hospital.'

'No. Rocky.'

'But …' I began.

Mrs Goodfellow shushed me. 'He's right, dear, we need Rocky.'

'But ...'

'The old fellow knows what he's saying. Hospitals can't help. He's different to you and me.'

I sort of understood what she meant and one look at her persuaded me there was no room for argument. 'What can Rocky do?'

'Same as last time. Patch him up and fix him.'

'He's not a doctor, he's a troll. And how do we get to him? Is he on the phone?'

'No. Can you drive, dear?'

'Umm ... no ... not really. I had a couple of lessons once. How about you?'

'I don't know, I've never tried.' She nibbled her lip, looking worried.

'Phil could drive when he comes round ... or there's the Editorsaurus.'

'Who, dear?'

'Upstairs. Her husband.'

'The fat, snoring one?'

'Yes.'

She shook her head. 'He's out for the count.'

'A taxi then?' I said.

'No, taxi drivers are reluctant to carry trolls, even civilised ones like Rocky and we need to hurry. You'll have to drive.'

'I can't ... I won't. It's out of the question.'

She gave me the look and knelt by Hobbes. Hobbling upstairs, finding the keys to the Volvo on a small table, I set off on my mission of mercy, no less scared than I'd been all evening.

To my amazement, the car started first time, though when I tried to turn on the lights, the windscreen wipers started instead. After a lot of stirring, I found a gear, stalling three times before getting going. My progress was reminiscent of a drunken kangaroo; I bounced, lurched and skidded down the drive. When I reached the end, I turned into Alexander Court, having first turned into the gatepost. The car rumbled and grumbled into the night and I allowed it to coast down the slope towards Fenderton Road until I had to brake.

Though I had to brake, I couldn't since my foot, hitting the accelerator instead, refused point blank to try another pedal. My hands locked onto the steering wheel and I wailed like a frightened baby as Fenderton Road came towards me at a surprising pace.

Headlights flashed as in desperation I turned the wheel, making the tyres squeal in agony. I thought the car was going to roll as it swung into the main road, just missing a van and a big green car, though not the tree.

There was a horrible crunch and the airbag pinned me to my seat, leaving me winded and shocked, yet unhurt, except for all the hurts I'd already got. My leg throbbed and oozed and the bite in my neck was stinging as if a giant wasp had scored a hit. I was light-headed, though glad to be alive, if only temporarily, for who knew whether false teeth could transmit the curse of vampirism?

The door of the Volvo opened with a crunch.

'Were you trying to kill yourself? Or are you just a bloody idiot?' A high-pitched voice berated me, though I couldn't see anyone.

I groaned, wondering if the first stage in being undead was not being able to see the living. Unbuckling my seat belt, I rolled out onto wet grass, icy cold on my exposed skin, making me leap up with a yell.

'Well you're alive and, bloody hell, you are bloody.'

I looked down into a small, worried face.

'Billy, thank God.'

'Are you alright? Did you find Hobbes?'

'He's been shot and I'm going for help, only I can't drive.'

He glanced at the wreck of the Volvo, his expression saying it all.

'I need to fetch a troll called Rocky who can save him, and you'll have to get me there before I change into a vampire, because I think I've been bitten by one. Don't look at me like that, it's true.'

'You'd better hop into the hearse,' said Billy with a look

suggesting he might be humouring me. Nevertheless, I noticed him finger the small silver cross round his neck. A minute later we were hurtling towards Sorenchester.

'Where am I going?' he asked.

'Left at the traffic lights and you'd better be quick. Hobbes is in a bad way.'

'OK then,' said Billy, calmly as if this sort of thing often happened on his nights out. 'Just one thing, though. Why are you running round in your underpants?'

'Because my trousers came off in the kitchen window, and would you mind turning the heating up? It's freezing.'

'Fair enough. Could happen I suppose.' Though he sounded sceptical, he did turn the heating up, as well as offering me a rug from the back.

We turned onto Green Way, flying past a long row of houses into the darkness of the countryside. He kept his foot down until we passed Brancastle, which lay in utter blackness apart from a lamp on the porch.

'Next turn on the left,' I said.

We swung onto the track towards the Olde Troll House.

I leaped from the car before it had even stopped, landing on my bad leg with a howling jolt, hobbling towards the front door, pounding on it like a Japanese drummer, ringing the doorbell frantically and then spotting the note pinned to the frame. It was too dark to read, so, tearing it down, I took it back to the hearse, which Billy had already swung round for the return journey.

'He's not answering,' I said, thrusting the note into Billy's hands. 'What's it say?'

Turning on the light, he screwed up his face. 'It says he's outstanding in his field.'

'Well I'm glad he's so modest,' I roared, 'but where is he?'

'Out in his field,' Billy replied, as if talking to an imbecile. 'He's standing in it. Actually, he might not be. Some big fellow's coming this way … doesn't look much like a troll to me.'

Rocky came striding towards us.

'Oo's tryin' to knock my front door down?' he asked in his guttural voice.

'It's me, Andy, I came here with Hobbes a couple of days ago.'

'Andy? 'ow the Devil are you?' A huge smile spread like a ravine across his face.

'I'm fine,' I lied, unable to spare any time for explanations of my state.

'You don't look fine, and I take it this is not a formal visit? You'll catch your death if you go running round dressed like that at this time of year. You'd best come in and bring your little friend. I'll put the kettle on.'

'Sorry, there's no time. It's Hobbes.'

''ow is the old boy?'

'He's been shot.'

'What? Again?' Rocky's smile snapped shut.

'Yes, he asked for you and he's in a bad way. Hurry … please!'

'Righto, lad. I'll get my things.' Running inside, he returned two interminable minutes later carrying a selection of small leather bags.

The hearse suited Rocky and appeared to amuse him. He lay down in the back. 'Most comfortable,' he said. 'Now, tell me what's 'appened.'

I told him as we sped back towards town. Billy nodded significantly when I mentioned Tony Derrick's involvement. Rocky was silent. The traffic lights onto Fenderton Road turning against us, we had to stop while a bulging, crop-headed youth in low-slung jeans swaggered unsteadily across in front of us just as the lights changed back to green.

'Shift your fat arse!' I yelled, furious at any delay.

Billy pumped the horn and the youth, turning, lurched towards us with an expression hinting at imminent drunken violence. It took him a couple of seconds to notice he was approaching a hearse. He hesitated, his glare fixed on Billy, propped up on a pile of cushions in the driving seat. His expression turned to puzzlement as he looked at me, covered in blood and half-naked. When Rocky sat up he fled. Billy flattened the accelerator.

'Fast as you can,' I said, 'and take a right into Alexander Court, just after the "Thank You for Driving Safely" sign.'

'Righto, Chief,' said Billy. 'Just past the broken Volvo, eh?'

I doubted I'd been away more than twenty minutes, yet I'd begrudged every second and, though Billy was by no means slow, I longed for the sort of speed Hobbes could squeeze from a vehicle. At last we turned into Alexander Court and into the Witcherleys' drive.

I leaped from the car, urging Rocky to move before Billy even had time to tug on the parking brake. 'C'mon,' I said over my shoulder, 'this way.'

Running into the house, I had to go back for the olde troll who was still sliding out, as slow as a slug. Despite my sore leg, I caught myself in a little jig of despair and frustration.

'Calm down, Laddie. I'm moving as fast as I can but there've been too many years and there's too much chalk in my joints.'

When, eventually, I reached Hobbes, his breathing was slow and ragged with bright blood bubbling round his mouth. Mrs Goodfellow had applied a new and improved dressing, discarding my blood soaked vest in a corner, placing a pillow behind his head, covering him in blankets. Narcisa was still sprawled on the altar where the Dagger of Tepes had ended her part in the story. I barely spared her a glance.

'How is he?' I asked.

'Not so good. So you found Rocky?'

''e did.' The olde troll creaked as, kneeling beside us with a cracking of knees like a ragged volley of shots, he began examining him.

It was too much for me, so I hobbled towards Phil, who, sitting against a pillar, his head in his hands, was groaning, his face as white as a vampire's, his eyes strawberry red, though I didn't think he'd been bitten. I wondered how long it would take me to turn evil.

'Someone had better fetch a stake,' I said, 'I'm going to need one soon.'

'Don't mention food,' said Phil. 'I'll be sick again.'

Billy joined us. 'Old Hobbesie doesn't look too good.' He wrinkled his nose. 'And someone doesn't smell too good.' He looked at Phil. 'I know you – you're the newspaper bloke who was hanging round with Tony Derrick. I told you he was a wrong 'un, didn't I?'

Phil nodded.

Billy returned to his hearse, coming back with a hacksaw that made short work of Phil's chains. Then he went upstairs, bringing us glasses of water, for which I was truly grateful, while Rocky set to work on Hobbes, the gleam of polished blades turning my stomach.

'What's been going on here?' asked Billy. 'This place is weird.'

'I don't really know,' said Phil, 'except Mrs Witcherley was trying to kill me, to use me as a sacrifice. She sounded insane. I'd been investigating her, not realising Tony was her stooge. I think he slipped something into my drink and next thing I knew I was stuck in the horrible cage. They got the Inspector too. He fell through the ceiling and I thought he must be dead. I don't know how long I was down here but she was just about to murder me when he reappeared like a demon from the black pit … and then Andy turned up.'

Though I wanted to play up my heroic part in the rescue, an urgent call made me jump to my feet.

'Come on, boys,' said Mrs Goodfellow, 'Rocky says the old fellow's got to be moved.'

Under Rocky's command, Billy unscrewed the cellar door, we loaded Hobbes onto it and carried him carefully upstairs. He was muscle-achingly heavy even for four of us – there were only four, because Billy couldn't reach. Lying Hobbes gently in the back of the hearse, his breathing sounding better, though his face was as pale as the moon, we piled into the front, a tight squeeze.

As we left I'd seen Rex, still snoring peacefully and felt strangely sorry for him: he'd have one hell of a headache in the morning.

We drove back to Blackdog Street at a funeral pace to avoid jarring Hobbes, who was limp when we carried him inside, placing him on the kitchen table like a huge turkey. Rocky, grim-faced and intense, assisted by Mrs Goodfellow, performed a variety of gruesome operations. I went to check on Phil, who having long since fled the gory scene, was slumped in the corner of the sitting room with Dregs, both looking mournful and blinking, presumably due to the effects of the pepper spray, but they appeared to be weeping. I returned to the kitchen where Billy busied himself with tidying up my bloody leg and applying stinging antiseptic to all my bumps and grazes. It was over an hour before Rocky finished, stitching Hobbes up with what appeared to be leather shoelaces, straightening up with a percussive rattle and, I hoped, a hint of a smile.

'Is he alright?'

The olde troll nodded.

19

'I reckon 'e should be just fine,' said Rocky, with a sudden grin that lent his time-smoothed face the illusion of softness, 'yet it was a close thing. You did well to get to me so quick, cos 'e wouldn't 'ave lasted much longer. And 'e was lucky she was a bad shot and ran out of ammo.'

'Wouldn't it have been better to get him to hospital?' asked Billy

'Not at all, young man,' said Rocky. 'They really wouldn't know 'ow to deal with 'is … Well, let's just say, 'obbes would be beyond their experience.'

'Umm … how did you know what to do?' I asked.

Under the table stood a bucket brimming with blood-sodden rags. Not so many days ago, it would have made me sick.

'Aye, well, I 'ad to patch 'im up last time 'e got a belly full o' lead – at Arras it was. The sawbones reckoned 'e was already a goner, cos 'e was so full of 'oles but 'e was one o' my lads, so I did what I could to 'elp and saw 'e wasn't like the rest of 'em. 'e pulled through then and 'e'll pull through now.'

A weight lifted from my soul and, though his big hand was covered in gore, I shook it.

'I'm only glad I could 'elp. 'e's a goodun. Now, I'll wash myself and we'll take 'im upstairs to bed. Then I must get back to my field, if your little friend wouldn't mind giving me a lift?'

Billy nodded.

'Thank you, young man. I'll stop round tomorrow and make sure all's well but 'obbes is as tough as old boots. 'e'll get better, though it'll take a few days.'

We carried Hobbes to his bed and Mrs Goodfellow tucked him in. Though he lay as still as a corpse, his face greenish, his soft, regular breathing was reassuring.

Rocky and Billy left together and Phil took himself straight to the police station to inform them he was no longer missing and explain why they should pay an immediate visit to the Witcherleys, leaving me alone with Hobbes and Mrs Goodfellow.

'Why does Rocky stand out in his field?' I asked, as she smoothed the sheets.

'It's just that his sort ...'

'Trolls?'

She shrugged, stroking Hobbes's brow. 'His sort enjoys communion with the earth. They say they like to stand and think, though mostly I reckon they just like to stand. They're good at it. Still, Rocky has a talent for patching up wounds and the old fellow reckons he was a damn fine sergeant in his day – excuse my language. Now, you'd best have a wash and get some sleep. You've had a rough day, too. I'll sit with him.'

'Thanks,' I said, for the church clock was striking two and I'd been stifling yawns for over an hour. As I started towards the bathroom, a thought stopped me in the doorway. 'D'you know, you're the only one who didn't ask why I wasn't wearing my trousers.'

'I expect you had your reasons. Now, hurry up, have a wash and turn in.' She smiled.

I followed her advice and very soon, and just in time, pulled myself into bed. Billy had been lavish with his first aid, covering me in a patchwork of plasters, bandages and antiseptic cream. Everywhere was sore and the bite in my neck throbbed even more than the wound in my leg. Despite this, I fell asleep in no time.

Something was tapping at my window. Getting up, drawing back the curtains, seeing Narcisa floating out there, her purple robe flapping like wings in the spangled sky, I shuddered and was trying to shut out the sight when her dead eyes met mine. She smiled, two rows of sharp wolf's teeth glinting in the starlight, pointing a blood red fingernail at the window. My neck burning, pleading with her to leave me in peace, I shook my head, yet had no power to resist as it opened. She glided in on a chilling breeze, clutching my hand, her grip so cold it burned, her glazed eyes staring into mine. I was paralysed as her thin lips, scarlet in a ghastly, white face, opened to speak and I knew, when they did, I would become like her. I heard words as if from a great distance …

'Wakey, wakey, dear. It's nearly eleven o'clock.'

I jerked into consciousness, my heart thumping. I was in bed.

'You were having a bad dream. Never mind, it's a fine bright day and your breakfast will be ready in ten minutes. Look sharp. I've laid out clean clothes for you.'

Narcisa wasn't there, just Mrs Goodfellow and Dregs, who'd been licking my hand. At least, I assumed it had been the dog. The curtains being drawn back, winter sunlight drenched me and I did not crumble into dust. My stomach grumbled to confirm I wasn't undead and, in the rush of relief, I whooped like an idiot before remembering Hobbes.

'How is he?'

'Not so bad now.'

She smiled and there was something strange, yet oddly familiar, about her. She had teeth in her mouth: the same ones I'd had stuck in my neck. I tried to ignore my horror.

'He had four mugs of tea,' she continued, 'and Sugar Puffs for his breakfast and now he's sleeping like a kitten. He said you saved him from the beast.'

'The beast? Narcisa?'

'I think he meant you saved him from himself. Now come on.'

She left, taking the dog, now, to my delight, fully recovered.

After washing and dressing, I limped down to the kitchen for a cooked breakfast as delicious and necessary as a breakfast could be. Finishing, I brushed the crumbs from my front as Mrs Goodfellow started on the dishes.

'I was really glad to see you last night,' I said. 'How did you find us?'

'Well, dear,' she said, picking up my plate, 'when you weren't back for your supper, I thought I'd better find you, so I called the station, who said someone answering to your description had run amuck in Fenderton with a dangerous dog, and I was just getting ready to leave when poor Dregs came home in a terrible state. I had to clean him up first. What happened?'

'Mrs Witcherley pepper sprayed him, which probably saved me, because she'd run out when it was my turn.'

Mrs Goodfellow nodded, tight-lipped, scrubbing the frying pan furiously. 'That new curate gave me a ride on his motorbike. He's got nice teeth – nearly as nice as yours, dear. He dropped me off in Fenderton and I was wondering what to do next when a ratty little fellow ran from the big house, screaming like his pants were on fire. I reckoned the old fellow sometimes has that effect on folk, so I took a look inside. The fat man was snoring his head off and I searched all through the house without finding anyone sensible. Someone had muddied up the stair carpet and I was looking at it when I heard noises from the cellar and went downstairs.'

'You got there just in time. The dagger was far too close.' I took a deep breath. 'I'll dry. Where's the tea towel?'

'Thank you, dear. There are clean ones in the drawer.'

Choosing one with a nice view of the Blacker Mountains, I began wiping a mug. 'Who'd have thought Narcisa would be killed by her own dagger?'

'She wasn't killed, dear.'

'But it stuck in her head, didn't it?' I hung the mug on the mug tree, where, clinking tunefully against another, it knocked off its handle. I pushed the evidence behind the packet of Sugar Puffs.

'No, only her ear. It pinned her to the table thing. She started moaning, trying to pull it out when you were away, so I had to give her a little tap to quiet her down. She's in hospital now, under police guard, more's the pity. After what she did to my boys, I'd like to have words with her.'

'She bit my neck and I was scared I'd become a vampire like her.' In fact, I was still nervous in case the change had merely been delayed.

Mrs Goodfellow, spitting out Narcisa's teeth into her hand, held them up to the light. 'With these? No, dear, she's no vampire. The real ones don't go in for all the Gothic nonsense, they don't need daggers or rituals and they always have lovely, gleaming, pearly whites. They shed the old worn out ones and new ones pop up, a bit like with sharks. I've got some in a jar – I'll show you later if you like.'

'Thanks.' I smiled, drying the last plate and stacking it on the dresser. 'Umm … is Sorenchester normal? I mean to say, is it worse than other places, you know, with all these ghouls and trolls and vampires and things?'

'I don't know quite what you mean. They're just folk, same as you and me, though a bit different, like the old fellow and Rocky. Most of 'em are no worse than anyone else and some are better. However, you're correct in thinking there are more round these parts than most places. That's because of the old fellow. He polices them fairly and they know there'll be no trouble unless they break the rules and, just as important, they know just what'll happen if they step too far out of line. He might appear soft-hearted to you, dear, but he can be quite strict when he has to be.

'Thank you for helping with the dishes. Now, I've got to take the dog for his walk and then I'd better get down to the shops.' She smiled. 'I'm right out of garlic.'

Life went on and I never developed a taste for blood.

Hobbes was very quiet and weak on the first day of his recovery, sleeping most of the time, waking to drink lashings of tea or Mrs Goodfellow's ginger beer. By the second day he was a little more alert, though his voice had diminished to a soft grumble I had to strain to hear. Not that he spoke much, relying on nods or shakes of his head to respond to questions. Now and again, furious growls, as if someone had kicked a wasps' nest, would explode from his room when Mrs Goodfellow gave him a bed-bath or fussed too much. I looked in from time to time, though it was clear he was only tolerating me. I think he was embarrassed at being seen in such a frail state.

Over the next few days, Mrs Goodfellow surpassed herself in preparing feasts fit for a king, though I can't imagine how she got her hands on swan and sturgeon. To start with, Hobbes ate comparatively little, so Dregs and I were well-stuffed with leftovers. Now and again, always after dark, Rocky turned up to check on progress, to eat crumpets and to express quiet pleasure at his patient's rate of recovery. His visits ceased after the fifth evening.

As my injuries healed, Dregs and I enjoyed long walks in Ride Park. One day, cashing in Rex's cheque, I paid off my debts. What little was left over, I offered to Mrs Goodfellow for my keep but she refused to take it. As a gesture of thanks, I tried to fix the loose floorboards in the loft and don't think I did too much damage.

One morning, from Tahiti, came a postcard, reeking of cigar smoke. I read it, though it wasn't for me.

Dearest Wife,

It's been nearly ten years since I went away to find myself. I now find myself in Tahiti where I have founded a naturist colony. So far I'm the only one. One day I hope you'll join me.

Your loving husband,

Robin.

The mystery of why he no longer required clothes was solved, though why they were such a good fit was still baffling. When I handed the card to the old girl she read it, chuckling.

'He's quite mad, you know? Still, I think he's happy.' She stuck it into a scrapbook with many others.

Hobbes began to sit up in bed with the aid of pillows, even getting up for short periods, though he was shaky and soon became grumpy. Still it was clear he was recovering at an astonishing speed – but, then, he was Hobbes.

On occasion, he received visitors. Though there weren't many, he seemed to appreciate them, especially a plump old guy called Sid who wore a black cape and had the whitest teeth I'd ever seen. Like Rocky, he only turned up at night. Superintendent Cooper paid a visit one afternoon. I'd expected someone fierce, whereas she was plump and motherly; she stayed with him for over an hour and he was thoughtful when she left.

One morning Phil came round, and it came as a jaw-dropping surprise when he introduced a tanned and fit-looking young man, who'd just returned from Hollywood, as Tom, his boyfriend, a nice enough chap – not my sort of course. I was happy for them. Admittedly, this was partly because it seemed to have removed one major barrier to Ingrid, or so I thought until Phil handed me an envelope. My delusion lasted until, opening it, I found an invitation to her wedding.

Phil, guessing the reason for my sudden dejection, pointed out that Ingrid had been engaged for a year and that I'd attended her engagement party. I could vaguely remember an evening at the Bear with a Sore Head when I hadn't had to pay for my lager, when some affable Scottish guy had been hanging around Ingrid, buying drinks for everybody. I'd not paid him much attention, being focussed, so far as I could focus, on preventing Phil getting too close. I could have wept, yet couldn't help feeling she'd found a far better man than me and, though I wished them both well, it felt like I'd been punched in the gut – except the ache lasted far longer.

Hobbes didn't speak about what had happened until, a day of winter sunshine cheering him up, he got out of bed, dressed in a shapeless brown dressing gown and strolled with me around the back garden. After a few minutes he sat on a bench, which was cunningly situated where it would capture any warmth from the pale sun. I sat beside him as he breathed deeply for a few moments.

'Well,' he said at last, 'I expect you'd like to know what

happened?'

'I would. The suspense has been killing me.'

He chuckled, deep and soft as distant thunder. 'I'll start from when I got back to the station. I had a short, if informative, chat with Tony before releasing him. I couldn't detain him any longer. After all, he had come in voluntarily.'

I said nothing.

A faint grin twitched on his lips. 'At the time, I entertained suspicions that Rex Witcherley had used the noisy party to cover the museum break-in and it hadn't occurred to me that Mrs Witcherley might be the villain. She seemed such a nice lady, though I'm no expert. I was planning to get my car and go straight round to see Mr Witcherley when I had a thought. Do you remember the scent of flowers on the glove fibres?'

I nodded.

'I knew I'd smelt it somewhere before and, finally, it came to me. It had been in Mr Witcherley's office and it was her perfume, only the cigarette smoke had masked it. I made sketches of Tony and Mrs Witcherley together and fell to speculating whether one of Mr Barrington-Oddy's assailants might have been a woman. His description of the taller one, vague though it was, fitted Mrs Witcherley and the other assailant could easily have been Tony.'

'Who you'd just released.'

He shrugged. 'I thought he might lead me to Mr Waring.'

'You were going to see Rex. How could he lead you if you weren't following him?'

He tapped the side of his nose. 'Tony's trail's is not difficult to pick up when you know where he started and I did go round to the Witcherley's eventually. Their house is smart, isn't it?'

I nodded. 'Too smart.'

'Mrs Witcherley came to the door and must have known why I was there, because she confused me by bursting into tears, confessing and begging for forgiveness. She said her husband had made her do it and offered to take me to see Mr Waring. Something about a woman in tears makes me soft-hearted, and it seems to have made me soft-headed as well. I believed her. She asked me to follow her to the garage, where she would show me something. She did.'

'What?'

'That I was a fool to trust her. Telling me to stand aside, she unlocked the garage doors and next thing I knew she'd squirted pepper spray into my face. I took a step back and I guess she must have opened a trap-door because I dropped through into the pit.'

'Why would she have a pit?'

'It was an ice store. There used to be a millpond in Lower Fenderton, down by the river, from where they'd cut ice blocks in winter, storing them underground to keep things cool before we had fridges. She must have adapted it. I don't know why, though I'm certain it wasn't done for my benefit. Anyway, it was a long drop and, though some old leaves broke my fall, it knocked me out, I think.'

'Phil said you'd dropped in.'

'Yes, and I felt he was there, though he wasn't making much sense. They'd doped him and, when he came to and complained, she sprayed him.'

I grimaced in sympathy.

Hobbes continued. 'Being stuck in the pit with no way out, unable to get a signal on my mobile, all I could do was wait and see what she had in store for me. At least it gave me time to listen, to think and to piece together the story. It was clear she was the villain and Mr Witcherley was not involved at all. I grew hungry, thirsty, furious and desperate until you dropped in with the leg of lamb, which was most welcome. How did you do get there?'

I related my own sorry exploits and, despite skipping the most embarrassing bits, still felt like a bumbling incompetent. He didn't see it that way.

'You did well,' he said.

Though I don't know if he meant it, it cheered me up.

'You know,' I said, 'I really thought you were going to attack me when I fell in.'

'Well,' he said, 'I didn't.'

Something in his eyes stopped any further questioning along that line.

'Thank you,' I said. 'So, what was Narcisa trying to achieve?'

'Ah, now that is interesting. You know her family comes from Romania? Well, she seems to have got it into her head that she was descended from Vlad Tepes ...'

'It was his dagger?'

'Possibly. It certainly looks like the one in his portrait. You saw it?'

I nodded.

'Vlad's father, being a member of the Order of the Dragon, Vlad was known as Dracula, which translates as "son of the dragon".'

'What's that got to do with Narcisa?'

'I'm afraid Mrs Witcherley, driven mad by increasing signs of her own mortality, became convinced a blood ritual would help her regain her youth.'

'Why Phil's blood?'

'His investigations were becoming a danger to her and his blood was as good as anyone's.'

'Tony thought they were only going to frighten him,' I said, 'and tried to stop her.'

Hobbes nodded. 'I'm not surprised. Though he is nasty, vindictive and greedy, he's not a killer.

'From what I heard, Mrs Witcherley had an old book detailing a blood-ritual, which seems to have put the idea into her head and began collecting specific artefacts that were, on the face of it, connected with Vlad Tepes. They were certainly Romanian and date from roughly the right period and, although it's anyone's guess how authentic they are, they undeniably match items shown in the portrait, which Mr Roman had sold her. I believe he elevated the value of his dagger by modifying the painting – he was good at copying and pastiche.'

'I saw the book,' I said. 'Biggs from the museum sold it to her and offered her the bracelet.'

'So the superintendent informed me,' said Hobbes. 'Mr Biggs and Mr Roman were in cahoots but failed to realise how dangerous she was. Anyway, as you know, Mrs Witcherley eventually got her hands on the Roman Cup, the ring and the bracelet. She picked up the altar at a church jumble, though it wasn't for sale.'

'What about Jimmy? Who killed him? And buried him? And then dug him up?' I shook my head, still baffled.

'I never believed Mr Roman's account of the break-in,' said Hobbes, 'and we proved he'd lied when we found the violin in his car boot. As I see it, Mr Roman refused to listen to Jimmy when he demanded money and threatened to call the police. Jimmy left in a fury, ending up getting drunk at the Feathers, where he had the misfortune to fall in with Tony, who'd been working for Mrs Witcherley since she caught him breaking into their house.

'Jimmy made some wild threats about what he'd like to do with Mr Roman's dagger, though I doubt he meant them, and let slip that he knew the combination to Mr Roman's safe. Tony told Mrs Witcherley, who was desperate to get hold of the dagger and promised Jimmy money to steal it, which must have sounded like the answer to his problems. For her, it was considerably cheaper than paying what Mr Roman was demanding. Sadly, he caught Jimmy in the act and there was a struggle. I suspect the fatal injury occurred on the lawn outside the French windows. Do you remember I draw your attention to that soggy patch?'

'Yes,' I nodded. 'Oh, I get it! It was soggy because Roman had swilled all the blood away.'

'I fear so, and I believe he did it immediately after killing Jimmy.'

'With the Dagger of Tepes?'

'Indeed.' Hobbes looked grave. 'Poor, silly Jimmy.'

'And poor Anna.' I still felt sorry for the sweet-faced little woman.

A thin film of cloud dimming the sun, I shivered. A murder story is no longer a mere shock-horror entertainment when you know someone involved in it.

Hobbes sighed. 'Mr Roman, panicking, buried the body in the grave, which I suspect he'd previously used as a hiding place for smuggled antiques. He was not as respectable as he made out.'

'But why that particular grave?'

'Simply, it was hidden from the road, yet Mondragon is a Romanian name and there may have been a deeper reason. The secret probably died with Mr Roman. Tony, who had been keeping an eye on things, witnessed the killing and the disposal of the body and tried to blackmail him into handing over the dagger.'

'Which was still in Jimmy's back.'

'Right.' Hobbes nodded. 'Tony didn't know that at first. He had, however made a note of the safe's combination and broke in himself when Mr Roman refused to hand it over.'

'Ah,' I said, 'so, there were two break-ins and Tony was the one who left the piece of paper behind. It was clever to spot the clue on the back.'

'Thank you.' He looked pleased. 'Carelessness has always been Tony's downfall. Anyway, Mr Roman must have felt the pressure building, what with the killing and the blackmail and a second break-in. It was the final straw when the violin section came to his house and called the police.

'It was obvious where the dagger was hidden, so Tony dug it up – on the very night we happened to be in the same graveyard.'

'That was a lucky break,' I said.

'Lucky?' He winked and his smile broadened. 'Yes, it could have been luck.'

The cloud passing, a haze of gnats took the opportunity to dance in the sun's spotlight and, for some obscure doggy reason, Dregs began digging a patch of garden, a cone of mud balanced on his nose. Mrs Goodfellow called us for lunch and, since she regarded Hobbes as an invalid, fed us the world's tastiest, creamiest, chicken soup. Speaking was out of the question, for it demanded total dedication. Dregs was far too muddy to be allowed inside and his dismal howls were the only sounds, apart from those of eating. He howled even more when Mrs Goodfellow pounced, hauling him upstairs for a bath. By then, he'd learned the futility of trying to escape.

On ending our meal, we adjourned to the sofa, where Hobbes continued his summing up.

'We come now,' he said, 'to the museum break-in.'

'It still seems ludicrous,' I said, 'to go to all that trouble for one bracelet.'

'But not to Mrs Witcherley who had lost all sense of proportion. In fact, it was only after learning about the Order of the Dragon that I began to get an inkling of what was really going on and felt old Romanian superstitions might be at the bottom of it.'

'Why did Biggs tell us the bracelet was from the Order of St George? Didn't he know?'

'Of course he knew. He was trying to mislead me. He'd learned of Mrs Witcherley's obsession from Mr Roman, acquired the bracelet with museum funds and was attempting to sell it to her. He was too greedy, so she stole it, which explains why he knew only one particular article out of all the thousands in the boxes had been stolen. Knowing he'd lose his position and reputation if the truth came out, he tried to throw me off the scent.'

'Where is he now?'

'Lying low and hoping everything will blow over. He'll have some awkward questions to answer when he returns.'

Mrs Goodfellow brought us tea. Hobbes's injuries had scared her and she was still subdued, which, at least, meant she didn't keep materialising by my ear with a shrill, 'Hello, dear.' I was grateful.

Hobbes, thanking her, took a huge swig and sighed. 'The lass makes superb tea. I really missed it when I was down the hole.'

I nodded and took a sip. 'What about the Roman cup?'

'That puzzled me,' he said, 'until Augustus explained its origins. I came across an old tale about Vlad Tepes ordering a gold cup to be left next to a fountain in his kingdom. Anyone was free to use it, but anyone foolish enough to steal it would be impaled, which must have been an excellent deterrent. In addition, there were rumours that Vlad drank the blood of his enemies to keep young. The cup vanished after his death and Mrs Witcherley got it into her head that the Roman cup and Vlad's cup were one and the same. I wouldn't be at all surprised if Mr Roman had led her to the conclusion.

'Next came the attack on Mr Barrington-Oddy and the theft of the dragon ring, which was when I began to pick up the chain that led, link by link, to Mrs Witcherley.'

'And Phil?'

'Well, Andy,' he said with a ferocious frown, 'if you hadn't been stealing his business cards to further your nefarious schemes, you might have seen his note on the computer, suggesting he was investigating Mrs Witcherley.'

I hung my head. 'I'm really sorry.'

Laughing, he patted me on the back. I could tell he was still weak because I stayed on the sofa. 'Only joking. No harm came of it and you learned something about yourself. No one's perfect, we're all a mess of contradictions and impulses and yet we can train ourselves to rise above them. At least, for most of the time.

'Mr Waring, who was trying to work out precisely what Mrs Witcherley was up to, unfortunately, trusted Tony, who was apparently a valuable source of information, for the right price. Tony played along, taking his money, remaining loyal to Mrs Witcherley. He doped Mr Waring, and the rest you know.'

I nodded. 'Tony claimed he wasn't doing it for the money and thought she loved him. I think he changed his mind when she started shooting.'

Hobbes chuckled. 'Well, perhaps he does have a better side. Let's hope he chooses his next lady more wisely.'

'Where is he now?'

'Gone,' said Hobbes. 'The superintendent said he'd packed his bags and fled. He'll be back. He always comes back.'

'What'll happen to Narcisa? Will she go to prison?'

He shrugged. 'Maybe, though she'll have good lawyers and the most likely verdict is "not guilty by reason of insanity", or whatever they say these days. That's assuming she's in a fit condition to stand trial.'

'There's one other thing,' I said. 'Would the blood ritual have actually achieved anything?'

'Yes, it would have killed Mr Waring.'

'No, what I mean is, if she had drunk his blood would it have given her youth back?'

'I doubt it. Leastways, I've never known that sort of thing to work. Drinking a goblet of warm blood is enough to make most people sick, which is why they normally swap it for red wine, though Ribena will do at a pinch.'

'Oh. Umm … there's one more other thing.'

'Make it the last then,' he said, 'I'm going for a lie-down.'

'OK. What was she going to do with you?'

'I don't know.' He yawned. 'Happily, thanks to you, I never found out.'

'It was nothing,' I said. 'And I'd have been killed if it hadn't have been for Mrs Goodfellow. She deserves the credit.'

He stood up. 'What you did was a great deal more than nothing. The lass did well, but Philip Waring and I would have been dead without you. I told him what you'd done.'

He turned away, walking slowly upstairs, leaving me in silence, partly basking in the praise, partly embarrassed, finding it hard to cope with praise after a lifetime of criticism. I was overwhelmed by a strange emotion that felt like happiness and lasted far longer than on the previous occasion.

Next morning when I went down, Hobbes was dressed in his work clothes, as if nothing had happened. Mrs Goodfellow, materialising under my ear with a joyful, 'Good morning, dear,' cackled at my jump.

I enjoyed breakfast, though not as much as Hobbes, who wolfed down three full plates of bacon and eggs and several mugs of scalding tea. Afterwards, I walked with him into town and, though icy rain was blowing into my face, I was smiling, feeling like a hero.

We stopped off at the *Bugle*, where I congratulated Ingrid. She smiled, blushing, and it hurt, though I was, genuinely, happy for her and only a little jealous of the lucky Scottish guy. She told us Rex wasn't in because he was looking after Narcisa, who'd had a breakdown. Phil caught my eye and grinned. I grinned back, happy to see him alive and well, wondering what I'd ever had against him.

As we were leaving, Ingrid stopped me. 'Andy,' she said, 'I'm sorry I got so upset with you the last time. Phil told me that you helped rescue him and Mr Hobbes. Thank you.' She kissed me on the cheek.

I walked away in a daze. I wished her well, I really did, yet there was an aching emptiness inside where something was missing. For the first time I could see her for what she was: small, dumpy and worth a million times more than my idealised portrait.

'Never mind,' said Hobbes as we stepped out into the street, ''tis better to have loved and lost than to have been shot by a crazy woman.'

Though I smiled, my mind turned back to dark places. 'Umm ... there's a question I must ask. It's really been bugging me.'

'Fire away.'

'Could you tell me what's behind the door in the cellar?'

'Of course I could.'

We walked in silence for a few moments.

'Umm ... will you tell me?'

'I will ... probably.'

In the distance, somebody shouted and glass shattered.

'When?'

'At the appropriate time. However, right now there's constabulary duty to be done.' As he loped away, he was grinning.

Acknowledgements

I would like to thank the past and present members of Catchword for their support, guidance, and encouragement: Geoffrey Adams, Gill Boyd, Liz Carew, Jean Dickenson, Rachel Fixsen, Susan Gibbs, Richard Hensley, Rhiannon Hopkins, Nick John, Sarah King, Dr Anne Lauppe-Dunbar, Dr Rona Laycock, Peter Maguire and Jan Petrie.

I would like to thank Jan Henley for reviewing an early manuscript, Natasha Wagner for proofreading and Mark Ecob of Mecob for the series covers. Thanks go to all at Impress Prize for New Writers for shortlisting this novel – a very welcome vote of confidence.

Writers in the Brewery and the members of Gloucestershire Writers Network have also provided much appreciated support.

Finally, a huge thank you to my family, to Julia, and to The Witcherley Book Company.

Also available

Inspector Hobbes and the Curse
unhuman II

Wilkie Martin

Again set in the Cotswolds, this is the second instalment in the adventures of Inspector Hobbes, Mrs Goodfellow and Dregs, as narrated by the still disaster-prone Andy Caplet. It is a rip roaring, funny and moving tale of Andy's infatuation with a dangerously beautiful woman, starting off during investigations into sheep deaths and the mysterious disappearance of pheasants. These incidents appear to be connected to a rash of big cat sightings, and something horrible seems to be lurking in the woods.

Is Andy cursed to be always unsuccessful in love, or is the curse something much darker, something that will arouse his primeval terrors?

The Witcherley Book Company
ISBN 9780957635128 (paperback)
ISBN 9780957635135 (ebook)
ISBN 9780957635173 (ebook)

Scan QR code to view book sample
(www.book2look.co.uk/vBook.aspx?id=NqlwpcMhNm)

WILKIE MARTIN

Wilkie Martin's novel *Inspector Hobbes and the Blood,* was shortlisted for the Impress Prize for New Writers in 2012 under its original title: *Inspector Hobbes.* As well as novels, Wilkie writes short stories and silly poems, some of which are on YouTube. Like his characters, he relishes a good curry, which he enjoys cooking. In his spare time, he is a qualified scuba-diving instructor, and a guitar twanger who should be stopped.

Born in Nottingham, he went to school in Sutton Coldfield, studied at the University of Leeds, worked in Cheltenham for 25 years, and now lives in the Cotswolds with Julia, his partner of 30 years.

www.wilkiemartin.com   Wilkie Martin Author Page facebook

A Note From The Author

I want to thank you for reading my book. As a new author, one of my biggest challenges is getting known and finding readers. I'm thrilled you have read it and hope you enjoyed it; if you did I would really appreciate you letting your friends and family know. Even a quick Google+ or Facebook status update or a tweet really can make a difference, or if you want to write a review then that would be fantastic. I'd also love to hear from you, so send me a message and let me know what you thought of the book. Thank you for your time.

Wilkie

September 2014

Scan QR code for some sharable links to this book

(www.book2look.co.uk/vBook.aspx?id=ZrFHGPVxgR)

Made in the USA
Monee, IL
28 March 2020